LETTERS FROM SWEETWATER

DR. DALE GARLAND

To my wife, Mackie Garland, my sister, Mae Hensley, and my editor, Jan Trost. Constant has been their support by encouraging, suggesting, sometimes prodding, and always inspiring. Without them, this book would be nothing.

CHAPTER 1

Time, in paradise, has neither a beginning nor an end; nevertheless, it possesses all the fullness of the eternal now. Mortal time is different, however, and it is in that realm where once occurred an event so far-reaching and profound that its effect resounds even yet throughout all of creation. Known as the original sin, it became the genesis of a universal war involving the forces of good and evil. And although caught in the no man's land in between, humankind cannot assume a neutral role in the conflict, for what is at stake there is the fate of every soul.

With horrifying suddenness, the evacuation had begun, turning his existence into a living nightmare. Yet there was no way to escape, not while he must keep moving. Oh sure, there was the promise of a new a beginning, brighter tomorrows, and unlimited adventure, but all of that was well beyond his ken.

Then he heard them, almost indiscernible at first, a cacophony of voices with one sounding so familiar, it caused his heart to skip a beat. Could there be life beyond this valley of the shadow, could hope live again? Unfortunately, it was at that exact moment when great hands, groping fingers of steel, clamped onto his throat and across his head. His world began to spin, and the gray-gloom deepened to pitch-black darkness. And that's when, emanating from some source unknown, a tiny pinhole of intense brightness penetrated his enlarged pupils to ignite something deep within. Starting as a thin pencil of light, it quickly expanded into a vast tunnel of swirling radiance, beckoning him forward. Meanwhile, a loud swooshing sound ushered in something quite extraordinary; time and space inexplicably became as one, setting him free from whatever had tethered him to the old domain. Yet the light continued to draw him toward its brightness, as a moth to a flame. His real destiny now lay immediately ahead, away from the darkness and in the sunshine of a new day dawning.

Jubilant at his arrival open arms, both warm and tender, engulfed him to welcome him home. Wet with tears and sweat and, yes, a little blood, he lay exhausted on his mother's breast. Jesse Gernon had survived a near-death experience to find himself face to face with reality; he had just been born, and all was well with his soul!

A full moon, bloated and ostentatious, seemed too bright, too resplendent, even for a midsummer's night. That, however, could be nothing more than an illusion caused by brushing up too close to old High Top, Sweetwater Valley's most prominent peak.

The inauspicious birth of August 2, 1936 occurred exactly one hour and seven minutes prior to Jesse's arrival. Sunday mornings on the head of Sweetwater, usually come as quietly as the soft fall of dew. This, of course, was no usual Sunday morning; Maude Jordan, mid-wife to most of Graham County, had just seen to that.

"Whew!" she puffed while reaching toward Dave. "Now, Son, let's see that bottle again." Maude knew exactly what it would take to help her unwind. "You sure got yourself a dandy."

"They my gosh, woman, what did you expect, he's a Gernon, ain't he?" The new grandfather had gone to fetch Maude when it became evident that the hour of delivery was nigh. On the way it hit him; a big celebration was in the making, so a quick side trip to Charlie Ammons' place seemed obvious. Charlie, Dave's brother-in-law, claimed to make his moonshine for "just a select few." "Yes," many would agree, "for those few sober enough to find their way there."

Wasting no time, Maude packed a few things in a paper bag, and then climbed aboard his waiting Model-T. Before leaving, however, Dave insisted that she have a "little taste." At first, she refused, but after some urging and with the counsel that it would help "steady up her nerves," the dedicated mid-wife took a generous turn. Dedicated to her calling she had resisted all further offers until now.

Maude detected a change in attitude, however, the warm glow that earlier had brightened his social side was beginning to wane. "Hum-m-hh," he growled, reaching for the hip pocket of his overalls. With a begrudging glare, he offered the flask, but on second thought reclaimed it long enough to take a deep three-swallowed snort of his own. Now, with less than one-third remaining, he handed it over.

"They, for Pete's sake," he roared after she took a swig, "save me a little bit!"

Ignoring his remonstrations as she would a feist dog nipping at her heels, Maude again lifted high the crystal drippings. This time she left just enough to cover the bottom. It brought her obvious pleasure to watch Dave's ruddy complexion turn a rich purple.

"That's going to put you on your butt, Maude, and you'll deliver no more babies this night. You just mark my word on that!"

"They Lord have mercy, Dave," she countered. "You know as well as I do, Charlie Ammons' waters his stuff down 'til it's weaker than cat pee. Why, I could drink a quart of it and never feel a thing."

"I've got news for you, little lady, Doc Cranford's getting ready to put you out of business."

"Yeah, well if he does you'll wind up paying him a whole lot more than just sip of whiskey. You wait and see! Besides, I come up here to help Wade and Edith out, not you. Why, I wouldn't pull that sorry hide of yours out of the fire, if you fell in."

A quiet snicker from a corner in the room, silent until now, put an end to the banter. Sitting there astride a nail keg and finding obvious amusement with the conversation was the good wife of Dave, Mary Gernon. The real source of her joy, however, came from now having a grandchild.

Dave immediately seized the opportunity to deliver what he hoped would be a knockout punch. He roared in with an uppercut. "Look at Mary over there; why, she's been around whiskey all her life and you don't find her drinking like a sailor. Heck, they ain't nothing as sickening as seeing some half-drunk old hussy out crying and puking all over the place."

Unscathed, Maude brushed off the blow with a smile, and then counter-punched.

"Yeah, unless it's some big sot a laying flat on his back and begging God for mercy after pitching a month's drunk... Son, I remember what shape you'as in three months ago!"

Using evasive action, a tactic that always worked well in the past, the heavyweight slugger switched fighting styles. "Heck, I ain't going sit here and listen to this; I'm going in there and take another look at my grandson. After all, he *is* a spitting image of me." A Cheshire cat grin had replaced the one of rancor only moments before.

For the first time Mary spoke up, "You'd better keep that nose out of there! Edith ain't going to put up with you. So why don't you take Maude on home;

you can see little Jesse in the morning… after you've sobered up." This act of assertion was such a departure from her usual meekness that it caused Dave to consider the advice.

It was as if on cue that Wade, the proud new father, stepped through the door, grinning from ear-to-ear. "By golly, he's a dandy, ain't he? The little fella just dropped off to sleep. You know he looks just like me; Edith even agrees with me on that."

"Well, he must do it then, 'cause that's the first time I've heard of her agreeing with anybody," Mary mewed.

Unperturbed, Wade gushed on; "I don't know what we'd have done without you, Maude. We were getting awful worried by the time I heard that old Ford of Pop's a rattling up the hill. Here's that five dollars I promised you... now is that going to be enough?" The amount tendered had been the going rate for years.

Maude began collecting her things, cramming them into a paper bag. "Lord, Wade, I hate to take your money, Son," she said while reaching for the wrinkled bills. "But, I sure do appreciate it though; it's all I've got to live on. The only thing I ask is that you not go looking for that sorry Doc Cranford, if you and Edith ever take a notion to have another'un."

"They, my goodness no!" he seemed surprised. A look of consternation crossed his face, deepening the long vertical crease in his right cheek. It imparted a look of distinction.

Knowing that Charlie Ammons remained ever diligent to his calling and with an eye on Maude's money, Dave chimed back in. "Time to go, woman! If we're going to get you home by daylight you'd better jump in the car!"

Maude, after playing such a leading role in the opening scenes of Jesse's life, left the stage not to reappear again until his first grade of school. Very well, he knew of her, however, because each year on his birthday Dave, with renewed enthusiasm, recounted the story. He loved to relate how he had prevented certain disaster by getting Maude there "just in the nick of time." Each year the stories got better and better as his memory improved with age. Both Dave and Mary took great pleasure in the fact that Jesse was born in their house, a little four-room chestnut log structure with mud for the chinking. For a few more months, until Wade and Edith could afford a place of their own, it remained home to two families. The depression years had a way of keeping families together.

Dave proved to be a true prophet. Doctor Cranford indeed did dislodge Maude and became the "baby doctor" for Graham County. Within a matter of two short years, a dramatic change in her duties occurred when she became an assistant janitor at the Robbinsville Grammar School. Loving every child she saw, she worked there until her seventy-seventh year and then suffered a near fatal stroke while on duty. Maude Jordan died three months later, with many hundreds attending the funeral.

One of the most awesome responsibilities ever entrusted to humankind is that of parenting. As inexplicable as it may seem, an all-wise Creator somehow sees fit to entrust the fate of little infants into the hands of two inexperienced young lovers. He knows exactly what He is doing, however, for by some manner still unknown, He guides them in their on-the-job training to do a good work. They, if obedient to their calling, learn to nurture, shelter, protect, defend, correct, guide, and school their baby, all because they love it. From some deep, innate source they seem to know that life must have balance, be enjoyed, shared, dedicated and, above all, be experienced. In the ideal, as they grow with the child, they come to know that the greater purpose of life is but to prepare for the next one. From deep within, whether it is accepted or not, there is a vague awareness that this life is but a sojourn. One that in due course leads to a new beginning, just as the former did from ovum to fetus in getting here.

Wade and Edith, it seems, did not sense the gravity of all this at the time, and to their credit merely reveled in the joy of the moment. With great tenderness, Edith re-positioned the tiny pale-blue blanket around Jesse for about the tenth time within an hour. Upon awakening, there was no crying. He had been asleep, not in a crib or cradle, but snuggled up close in the soft curve of her body. It was a warm nest where he could be lulled by the same heartbeat rhythm that from early on had set the tempo to his soul. Jesse drowsed, sleeping a dream wonderfulness that only a newborn can know.

Opening his eyes again, he saw the moon through an open window; great bundles of silvered beams streamed across his tiny face. Wade noticed the mesmerizing effect first, and whispered to Edith, "Little fella can't take his little eyes off the moon. You reckon what he's thinking about?"

"Wade," she softly crooned, "Jesse ain't thinking about nothing. Babies just like bright shiny things and, besides, it's the way he's a laying."

"They my gosh, Edith, how come you can't see nothing but what's right in front of you? Why, I'd bet a dollar bill he's thinking about how pretty it is."

"Oh, for crying out loud, you're more moon-struck than he is. Jesse don't know nothing about how pretty anything is. It's a way too early for him to do that."

"You always find something wrong with what I say," he replied in resignation. "I reckon according to you I don't know nothing about nothing, but someday I hope you'll finally be able to see my side of things, once in awhile."

"Well I ain't going to say no more about it," she said. This while wiping away drops of moisture from her eyes. *He can be so hateful,* she thought.

Meanwhile, Jesse continued to stare out the window, drinking in the glory round about him. Unseen to all but to his tender eyes was a light far more brilliant than that given off by the moon. The fact is that while newborns find it difficult to focus they, at the same time, are sensitive to portions of the light spectrum not accessible to adults. Jesse used this special ability to watch a visitor hovering just outside and craning to get a better peep of her new charge. Had he been able to express himself, he would have told of her beauty and splendor. However, the sparkling of her tiara was what captivated his attention the most.

From the earliest awareness of himself, Jesse somehow felt he was a little different. After much introspection at a later stage in life, he came to the realization that he had the nature of a poet.

The artist, merely by applying paint to the canvas, creates an illusion larger than life. The poet, however, dwells in that greater dimension. A musician is able to weave masterpieces out of nothing more than vibrations of air. Yet words from the poet, when added to the melody, can set a heart on fire. Many, when seeing things the way they are, may question why. The philosopher says, "I dream of things that have never been and ask, *why not*." A poet, in turn, supplies the inspiration to make it happen. Jesse, of course, agrees with Kilmer when he wrote.

"Poems are made by fools like me,
But only God can make a tree."

Nevertheless, he would add:

"Yet, a poem may sometimes bring,
Thoughts so dear the angels sing."

Possessing neither compass nor map, Jesse had made it to Sweetwater. He now faced two roads, both with the same destination; which would he choose? As a poet, would it be the one less traveled?

CHAPTER 2

It is in the rich soil of childhood where the most tender and choicest memories are wont to grow. Such vintage produce yields succulent flavors that tends to linger long, even unto the after-years of an extended life. Interestingly enough, this selfsame fruit may taste even sweeter then, than at first it did.

Jesse sowed the seeds for an abundant harvest for it was during his early years that planet Earth began to encounter some of its greatest challenges. His generation, their feet planted deep in a world that had known little change for most of recorded history, now found itself facing an uncertain future. Many old and accepted customs no longer seemed relevant, to be likened, perhaps, unto over-ripe grapes ready to fall from the vine. He, coming along at a time near the end of the Great Depression and just prior to World War II, realized a season ideal for a crop of robust recollections.

The good people of Sweetwater cherished one another, treating neighbors and friends the same as family. They liked to do their visiting on Sunday afternoons, and one such occasion provides the backdrop for Jesse's earliest memory. He was just under the age of two and living in Harwood Cove when he and his parents paid a call on Dave and Mary. Imprinted on his mind is a scene of three beautiful girls dancing and swirling about him. They, clad in bright dresses, had him at the center of their frivolity, all were laughing and in high good cheer. The memory persisted as a happy one, despite learning later that he stood before them stark naked.

His next set of moments, frozen in time, came some four months later during the Christmas season. They lived now in a brand new home, a tiny two-room bungalow that Wade had built with the help of his brother Ray. Set at the upper end of Dave's cornfield, the dwelling was about a mile from the place of Jesse's birth, yet several hundred feet higher up on the mountain. The only way to reach this alpine aerie was by way of a dirt path, and everything and everybody that made it there did so, either by walking, riding on horseback, or using a sled. Edith named the place "Hoot Owl Holler."

At this elevation, mountain breezes kept the summers cool. A spring gushed just outside their door, providing both ice-cold water and the means to preserve milk and butter. This, by the clever use of a small wooden box set partially immersed in the branch. Fuel for heating and cooking came from the surrounding woodland, and their vegetables from a tiny garden. In addition, they supplemented their diet by picking wild blackberries, strawberries, and raspberries. Dun was their source of milk, she being the first cow that Wade and Edith owned. If ever there proved to be one thing the two could agree on, it was that in buying her they had made a wise investment, indeed. Never did they want for eggs since Grandma Gernon, Dave's mother, had given them a large brood of Rhode Island Red chicks for a wedding present. Progeny from this thoughtful gift lasted until Jesse reached his teen years, despite regular and frequent harvesting for "fryers and stewers." A couple of "fattening hogs" penned up at the edge of the cornfield, along with a plentiful wild game supply, kept their larder well stocked. Wade either carried on his back or sledded in the other staples as needed. Jesse had ample reason to appreciate living in the love, warmth, and security of this home.

When the Gernons moved in they had not one, but two children, for it seems that some eighteen months after Jesse came along, a beautiful daughter named Mae also joined the family. From the start, Jesse loved Mae and wanted to welcome her into his private world, but soon a competitive spirit developed between the two. He treasured his seniority and harbored no plans to relinquish its benefits; meanwhile, she grew ever more impatient to enjoy equal status.

That year winter came early to the higher elevations and by mid-December a snowstorm swept through, leaving over eight inches on the ground. Hoot Owl Holler, being nestled amid the northern slopes, sequestered away enough of it beneath the tall evergreens, for them to have a white Christmas. Edith prodded Wade into taking a small cedar from one of the nearby ridge tops. He complied, but only after raising a mild protest. "Why they ain't a bit a need in it Edith, them young'ins are a way too little to want one, and I don't see no sense in it neither. I never had one growing up."

"Well, my young'ins are going to have one, they need to start learning right now how people away from here do things. Besides, I can't help it if you'as raised like a heathen."

Wade placed the tree right next to the little battery set radio that provided them with near static-free music the entire Yuletide. The tree, covered in icicles and adorned with homemade red and white decorations, had the magic to turn silver into gold when struck by the glow of a kerosene lamp. Christmas morning came as a happy surprise to Jesse after he found a present under the tree. He just could not believe it, this despite being told for weeks that Santa was coming. He became ecstatic to learn that the little blue truck with a red bed and yellow wheels belonged to him, and after pushing it across the floor toward her, wanted Mae see it. Delighted at his attitude, Edith readily obliged by holding her down to his level where Jesse pushed his truck toward her face. "See!" He exclaimed. However, the word had hardly left his lips before the toy belonged to Mae. Her hand, faster than a cat's paw, had claimed a prize.

Jesse screamed! Being stuck in the eye with a needle would have been less painful.

Wade joined the fray, "My gosh, Edith, what's wrong with that young'in, anyway?" Jesse continued to bellow at the top of his lungs while Edith focused on trying to wrest the vehicle from Mae's iron-like grip. At last, with Jesse back in possession of his truck, she handed the troubled tyke another reason to cry; a few sharp smacks to his rear.

"Edith, for Pete sakes this is Christmas morning! You ought to be ashamed of yourself... Whupping the little feller like that."

"Christmas ain't got nothing to do with it! These young'ins need to learn they're going to mind me, and besides, Jesse is getting to be a way too stingy with Mae. I don't blame her one bit for what she did; after all she's just a baby."

Wade spoke again, but this time in a more conciliatory tone. "Son, go back over there and try to make up with your little sister." The twice-wounded truck driver, now distrustful, seemed more than a mite hesitant to obey. Snubbing, he edged forward, but not before he dropped his shiny new toy on the floor out of Mae's reach. Both parents beamed satisfaction when he lowered his head to lay it gently against Mae. Big brown curls pressed against her tummy at about the same instant that hands, lightning fast, shot forward again to capture another prize. This time she got hair, fists full of it.

Jesse never forgot that it is possible for blue eyes to flash fire and never would he trust a platinum blonde again. His last memory of that long ago Christmas morning was one of looking through tears and seeing Mae, on all fours, scampering across the plank floor toward his abandoned toy.

Winds, hatched south of the Great Plains, left their home to find wings in the Mid-West before soaring high above Cheoah's tallest peaks. From there they drifted down to the waiting valleys below, laying great splotches of green on all the fields and woodlands. Springtime brought a healing balm to the winter-ravaged land of Sweetwater in March 1939. Jesse looked with great favor upon the earth as she returned to her former glory. Across the wind-swept slopes, he watched the mountainside slowly turn from drab-gray to verdant green, and he was pleased.

Early in June, Jesse's uncle Keith came for a few days visit. Born in the mountains, he had moved to the piedmont as a teenager and now worked there in a cotton mill. It was important for Keith to take some time off and get to know his new niece and nephew. He felt close to Edith, they being the two youngest in a family of seven. Keith loved song, not millwork, because his heart was an instrument tuned for music. With the features of a handsome Scot Highlander, he had coal-black hair and fair skin. Jesse and Keith played together for hours on end under the shade of tall, age-old walnut trees. Sometimes early in the morning they could hear the far-away sounds of a steam engine as it sent its plaintive cry deep into the hills.

Jesse incessantly begged Keith to tell him about the great trains he had seen in wondrous and far away places. Keith played the harmonica, and occasionally would break into song with a voice that rang pure and clear across the glen. Jesse never forgot how this brought tears to his eyes, but even so, he would plea, repeatedly, to have him to do it again. With a twinkle in his brown eyes, Keith would tease Jesse for a while before giving his rendition of something like the *Wabash Cannon Ball.* Still, it was never enough to satisfy Jesse. The visit ended much too soon when Keith suddenly left for Gastonia, the cotton mill was calling him back.

Later that month a new tradition developed in Hoot Owl Holler; one destined to bring heartache. As so often is the case, it started innocently enough with Wade bringing home candy to Jesse and Mae. Initially, he would do so only if he happened to pass Stumpy Adams' store on the way home. Before long, however, he found himself going further and further out of his way just to make "the little fellas" happy. Jesse learned to wait in the evenings and exult at the sight of his sweat-grimed daddy drawing into view. Unfortunately, it was not daddy, but a tiny brown paper bag filled with candy kisses he longed to see. Edith saw trouble brewing and spoke her piece about it; "Wade, you're petting them young'ins to death and you know good and well it's not right to do that."

Her good husband responded with skepticism. "They, Lord have mercy Woman, you're wrong about this. Why, it's a sight just to watch the little fella start grinning the minute he sees me a coming up the hill. I swear they ain't nothing I like better, than to bring 'em some candy."

She tried talking to Jesse too, cautioning him against the very real possibility of disappointment. Like father, like son, however, her advice went unheeded; obviously, they both were thriving on a full diet of misconceptions. Wade loved the attention and Jesse loved his candy. Thus, as the days of summer waxed long Wade found that his hours of work did also. One particular afternoon Jesse left the house with a pipe-dream that his daddy might make it home a little earlier than usual; he wanted to be there, just in case. He went straight to his favorite spot, and climbed to the top rail of the fence. From there he could see all the way down to the curve's far bend. Predictably, however, it took only a few minutes before he got bored and that sent him in search of something to do. First, he piled up rocks to throw at birds when they came within range. However, before long he tired of this too, so it was in sheer desperation that he turned to eating a few blackberries from briars recently picked-over by his mother. Since it was chocolate and not blackberries he craved, this project, too, was doomed to failure. That is when he spotted a sassafras bush to climb. It was just about the right height, but when its limbs kept breaking off he finally grew disgusted and quit.

There was only one thing left to do and that was return to the fence to wait, and wait he did until a tired old sun finally looked poised to drop beyond the far horizon. It was then that he finally spotted the stooped figure of his daddy plodding up the hill. Nearly exhausted, Wade was walking slower than usual; it had been scorching hot all day, and the work unusually brutal. At quitting time, he found himself over a mile from the store and that meant having to walk the distance twice, only to get a five-cent bag of candy. Truly, the trip was not worth it and common sense dictated that he go on home. Nevertheless, Jesse was straining his eyes in the gathering dusk, hoping just to catch a glimpse of the precious cargo. Yet, he could not see it! With all his might he yelled, "Daddy, where's my candy at?" Clear as a bell, the voice of desperation rang through Hoot Owl Holler.

"Son," exasperation called back. "I didn't get you none this time. I was just too tard to make 'er by the store—but I'll do it tomorrow." His weakened voice searched for a little understanding. It would not come from Jesse, however, not after such a long afternoon of waiting... So, was this to be his reward, then?

Well, that was just asking too much... and tomorrow. He may as well forget that, tomorrow was completely out of the question. Disgusted, he reached for the pile of rocks and began to express his extreme displeasure at a most insensitive parent.

Remarkably, even after a week had passed he still carried the faint red marks on his legs and back, left there by a sassafras branch Wade found handy to reach. Edith could never relate the story without spilling tears, ones of laughter, that is; but Wade and Jesse both failed to see the humor in it.

In the endless chasms of eternity when our finite understanding expands enough to search out the deeper meanings of life, perhaps then God will impart to us a more complete appreciation of the material existences. Why, for instance, was it more expedient to halt the entire solar system for a day than to have Joshua wait overnight, and then finish his battle with the Amorites? This question, or one like it, regarding the iron-will of a man, was what Edith wondered about with Wade when it came to moving off the mountain. They argued about it for months, indeed many years, even after it had become a moot point between them.

Edith had grown tired of living like a hermit, "These young'ins are going to grow up scared to death of strangers. And every once in awhile I'd like to look around and see somebody else's face besides yours," she said.

"Why, there's everything you need right here, Edith!" he replied. "And besides, you've got the best-looking man in Graham County, so what more could you want?" Turning serious, he then seemed willing to make a concession. "Tell you what, one of these Sunday mornings we'll all get dressed up and head out to church, and then, by Ned, you'll see some other people."

That this did not come even close to meeting her demands makes it quite clear why she never let up. "I'm giving you fair warning, Wade Gernon, either you find us a place down on the creek, or I'm leaving, and I'll take the young'ins with me, too! I'm tired of being camped out up here on the edge of Dave's cornfield. For goodness sakes, can't you see there's more to life than having a roosting place in Hoot Owl Holler?"

Wade could not see it and never could, but after three months of solid bickering, he was ready to look for a house. Remarkably, one right there on the head of Sweetwater was available. Terms were good, like paying rent, yet not all the news was to Edith's liking. Now they would be living less than a half-mile from her in-laws and it was a much easier walk than before.

Still and all, she was glad to be moving, so on the last day of October they loaded up the sled with their belongings, and headed for the new place. Pulled by a team of enormous horses, Jesse rode along listening to the runners whisper their sad goodbyes to him.

No other place would ever come close to being so exclusively his, yet as it faded from view, it was gone forever. Soon, they tore the house down, and Hoot Owl Holler existed no longer, except in memory.

CHAPTER 3

The whole of Creation in its listless journey away from the ramparts of Eden has ever been on a mission for the restoration of all that was lost there. In a microcosm then, this same quest still occurs in the life of every individual.

Jesse and his family were a part of this greater migration as they too, pursued their destiny. Doing so, however, with very little hope that the move would somehow make all their dreams come true. Surprisingly, Jesse suddenly saw his world expand exponentially in both size and opportunity. No one could have been more delighted than he at finding that a better way of life waited for him in a place later called "the house beside of the road." Ecstatically, he ran from room to room and all over the yard, exploring their new home. It was love at first sight. As an older structure, its allure, over the years, had enticed many a family to live there. Wallpaper and having two bedrooms were a new to him. He and Wade would share one room while Edith and Mae would sleep in the other. The front porch and a narrow strip of fenced in yard would make great places to play.

Out back, a small gray and weatherworn barn sat near the center of a three-acre pasture that Dun took to immediately. A lean-to chicken shed, and a brand-new outhouse completed the ensemble. There was a lot more than that to like, however! A tiny brook bubbled and babbled all the latest secrets to a huddled copse of willow bushes found stooping low, they not wishing to miss a single whispered word. Scattered cattails, tall and aloof, stood ramrod straight showing they were far too pious to entertain such trashy and low-down gossip. In truth, a portion of the pasture was a marshy bog and home to some very strange creatures, indeed. Above all this stood High Top's brooding presence, as it did most of Sweetwater Valley.

Edith was a new person. She had grown up in more urban surroundings than Wade did, spending her childhood, first in Bryson City and then later in Kannapolis. It pleased her to be among people again, but even greater was the joy she felt at seeing her children so happy. She found it hard not to laugh when they came running in from outside shouting: "They's another'n a coming and boys it's just a flying, too!." Such excitement arose from the occasional car or truck seen plying past their house. Invariably, red was their favorite color, with blue, and then green ones making a close second and third.

Edith drew consolation from the fact that they finally had cut the ties, and was not having to live with, or on the land of, her in-laws. Being fiercely independent, she considered this as a victory. Interestingly, Wade blossomed, too. He, being naturally gregarious, found it stimulating to be near the epicenter of a world that made him flower. Edith, now more than ever, wondered why he had put up so much resistance against moving from Hoot Owl Holler. The more that folks came to visit, the happier he seemed, and after awhile found that a day without company was a day to be grouchy. At first, Edith resented this, but soon came to realize that just as independence was fundamental to her survival, being with people was to his.

The house beside of the road continued to work its magic and, although they were in love, Wade and Edith began to truly live the love they felt. They drew closer during this time than at any other period of their long marriage. It was then they came to know, but could not share with Jesse or Mae, that a beautiful life was just beginning. Such must wait for the coming of spring and for April to manifest. They were about to learn that one of life's greatest gifts is having more family to love.

Wade and Edith grew up under very different circumstances. To her the contemporary life was a goal, but to him it was an enigma. Although born in 1913, he truly was a product of the nineteenth century. Raised mostly by grandparents, they taught him that one must cling tenaciously to the old ways, so he cherished the mountains and the seclusion they offered. Being of British stock, going up the tree of life as far as either ancestral side dared climb; he was true to his heritage with its devotion to both land and horses. A man of the soil, his idea of heaven as hitching up a team of fine dapple-grays to pull a number 10 turning plow to rip up great furrows of rich mountain loam, and doing it on a warm April morning amid flurries of sweetly perfumed apple blossoms swirling all about him. Wade would have felt just as much at home in the fields of Devonshire as he did those of Sweetwater. He truly believed that God created man to cultivate the earth and that he must earn a living by the sweat of his brow.

Before moving from Hoot Owl Holler, he had found new employment, working for the WPA. This New Deal program was a godsend to many struggling families at the time. Like most of those on Sweetwater, the Gernons did not think of themselves as poor, all they asked for was a chance to work. To them, the American dream was just that, a dream, but a job was hope. Wade and Edith thrived in the optimism they found by having steady employment, and for the first time were able to make a few plans for the future.

Wishing to keep it a secret from Jessie and Mae, Edith slipped a Montgomery Ward catalog out from under the bed and began to think about Christmas. She had stashed it there just for dreaming, until "things started looking up."

Wade worked outdoors six days a week, ten to twelve hours each day, and did so with great high spirits. He never grumbled about this, except when the weather kept him home. However, Jesse and Mae liked the rain and snow, for then his sack lunch often became their impromptu picnic. In it, they would usually find biscuits of ham, or jelly and butter, and occasionally even a store-bought cake. It was on such a day of inclemency, about a month after moving from Hoot Owl Holler that Dave came in unannounced.

"By golly, folks," he announced, "I just got us signed up for the commodities. Roosevelt's going to help us put a little meat on the table for a change!" His enthusiasm, obviously given extra spirit by another trip to Beech Creek, met Wade's wonder.

"Do what?" he asked with evident concern. "Why, my goodness, Pop, we don't need that, I've got steady work now and, besides, commodities are for folks on the welfare."

"They, heck no," Dave chuckled. "Anybody can get commodities. Why, Son, it's just surplus stuff that if it ain't used they'll burn. You get more groceries than probably we'll ever use, and even some of them old Arish potaters, but we can throw them things out." Pausing to grimace, he let out a loud, empty belch. "Soured stomach!" he complained before burping two more times. He was now ready to take his big cut at the despicable vegetable. "The things ain't fit for nobody to eat."

Jesse had moved up to stand beside his grandpa. "Old Jamup here, he'll be getting a big bag of raisins. Son, you just wait and see," he assured. "Now listen to me folks, what you need to remember is that we ain't out from under that Hoover Depression yet. But, this is just exactly what it'll take to get us back on our feet again."

Wade looked over at Edith, wondering about her reaction; it amazed him that she actually seemed to concur. "What do you think, Edith?" He asked cautiously.

"Well, they ain't no doubt about it, Wade; a little help right now could make a big difference in us getting through Christmas." Such a matter-of-fact response reflected her practical side. "Once we get straightened out, though, we probably can make it pretty well on our own then," she added thoughtfully.

"By Ned, that settles 'er then!" Dave gloated. Never shy about claiming victory, he was eager to get on with trying to educate a pair that obviously was too naïve. "Yeah, I've got us all signed up and by next Thursday morning you'll see me riding up Sweetwater in Hoyt Millwright's delivery truck. Look, just about every family on the creek's been getting commodities for over a year now and it's time we started, too." Jesse, open-mouthed as ever around his grandfather, was even more agog this time. Dave reached down to tousle his hair. "Roosevelt's going to see that you get a lot of them good raisins, Jamup, and, why, I bet you could get your mother over there to cook us up a big rice pudding, what do you think?" Dave early on had captioned him Jamup, a moniker that stuck until Jesse was well into adulthood.

When Thursday rolled around so did the commodity truck, rumbling its way up Sweetwater with Dave, indeed, sitting bedside the driver. Jesse arose early, big things were in store, and he wanted to be a part of it. Edith noticed right away his angst, and it concerned her. The incessant fidgeting was bad enough, but it was his constant asking as to when they would get there that really got on her nerves. Finally, in exasperation, she responded with a few questions of her own, "Jesse, what in the world are you expecting, anyway? Do you think they're bringing you some candy?"

Jesse quickly perked up at this. "Candy?" his face beamed a ray of hope.

"No! ... They, Lord have mercy, no!" she shot back. "I've been wondering though, what's causing you to act this way? Don't let Dave make you think you're getting something you ain't, 'cause we've already been down that road before."

Finally, it arrived, pulling up in front of the house with Jesse waiting in the yard. With mouth agape, he watched Dave jump out and start moving boxes onto the porch. Jesse actually showed very little interest in this activity. However, when it became clear that nothing else was to be unloaded, he began to fret. Dave took notice and asked him, "What's the matter, Son? I figured you'd be tearing into them raisins by now."

"I didn't get to see him," he mumbled.

"Get to see who?" Dave pealed low thunder.

"Him!" a finger pointed at the driver.

"Well, by Ned, I can fix that." Dave liked nothing better than solving easy problems..

"Come out here a minute," he yelled while beckoning spiritedly. "I've got somebody who wants to see you, so get your butt out of that truck, and say howdy to Jamup here."

It astounded Jesse to hear Dave speaking like this, especially to such an important person! Here Dave was talking to him, just as he would to anybody else. Jesse had heard of him all his life, often spoken of in near reverential tones, with Dave usually the one most passionate about it. This, indeed, was an enigma.

When the door opened a portly middle-aged man, wearing a pearl-gray fedora, stepped to the ground. "Well, perhaps for just a minute, but I do have other stops, you know." That he was smiling showed the flattery he felt; at least somebody recognized the importance of his work.

Jesse reacted by running up for a closer look, and after a long moment of close inspection exclaimed, "It is! Well, I can't believe it, Dave told the truth, it's Roosevelt!"

Trying to remain somber, Mr. Millwright squatted down to place his hand on Jesse's shoulder. "Son, I'm not Mr. Roosevelt, but the next time I'm in Washington I'll be sure to tell him about you. He'll be glad to know, and I'm certain of it, that there's such a fine little fellow like you getting these commodities. I hate to disappoint you, but my job ain't quite as big as that of President. Shake my hand, though, Buddy, and I'll be looking forward to seeing you every time I make a trip up here." Mr. Millwright grinned at Dave and winked as the two new pals clasped hands.

Jesse, for a long while, had trouble believing otherwise than that; he had been in the presence of greatness. In any event, the new relationship only deepened during the next eight months while the Gernon household got commodities. Of more value than any goods received, however, was the lesson that Edith learned. She now knew, whether for good or bad, that one must never underestimate the influence a grandfather may have on his grandson.

Christmas, not mentioned for months, had all but been forgotten in the mayhem of moving. It was only after making out an order to "Wards" that the good parents decided it was time to let Jesse and Mae tell Santa what they wanted.

Opening the wish book was not unlike that of taking a trip to the North Pole; for in both places one could find all the elves' treasure on display. The two quickly entered into a spirit of the season, doing so by sweetly sharing the magic pages with one another. Unfortunately, this blessed time of sitting together, head to head, and picking out presents did not last. Before long the toys came between them, for after making a choice, the selected item immediately became off-limits to the other. This created many hours of bickering and fighting that ultimately led to Edith taking the book away. She did so, however, with great reluctance even though it was now in shreds.

Christmas, 1939, brought Clark and Lorraine in from Gastonia. Wade had five brothers, but Clark was the one most like him. Both were fair-skinned, had jet-black hair and brown-hazel eyes. Their personalities attracted others to them almost instantly.

Lorraine, Clark's young, pretty wife usually wore her honey-colored hair in an upsweep.

The visiting couple had married in July. He, at the time, was twenty-two and she had just turned fifteen. After a blissful honeymoon in Myrtle Beach, they moved into a small apartment next door to her parents. Since the nuptials, many hours had gone into trying to teach her a few basics about homemaking. Clark's efforts had met with some success in all areas except those of the culinary arts. There, about all he could claim for his patience was that she could now open cans and heat their contents on the gas range. A willing learner, Lorraine worked hard at not burning everything she put to the flame. Even the simple task of brewing a drinkable cup of coffee was still beyond her grasp. Clark arrived with the secret hope that Edith might somehow help him transform this beautiful child-bride into a reasonably good cook. Unfortunately, Edith never learned of his plan, that because all her efforts centered on trying to keep Lorraine from crying her eyes out.

Lorraine had never seen mountains before and since they arrived after dark, her first impression was not a pretty one. It was just at dawn when she stepped out onto the porch and lifted up her eyes unto the hills. That is when she met High Top face to face. Her shriek was so panther-like and ear splitting that it literally set every dog in the neighborhood to howling. Yet even in this moment of extreme anxiety she still managed to babble out; "Oh, look at that big ugly thing! ... Dear God, please help me! I feel dizzy, like I'm about to fall off of it!"

Her scream brought Clark running at top speed, dressed only in boxer shorts and a sleeveless tee shirt, his feet barely touching the floor. Normally of pale complexion, he now was chalky white. "Oh my Lord, Sweetheart, what happened? What's the matter, Honey? Tell old Clark what's wrong."

Lorraine could not talk for sobbing. She looked and sounded so pathetic that Clark quickly lifted her into his arms. Such, for him, was an effortless task although she was far from being a child. A story that lingered around Sweetwater for years was that at the age of 16, he walked home from Robbinsville carrying a hundred pound bag of cow-feed under each arm. Supposedly, he made the nearly six-mile trip without stopping once for rest. Lorraine weighed about a hundred and ten pounds, but he found her far easier and much more pleasant to lift than a bag of feed. After about five minutes of bawling she finally wailed out, "That big old ugly thing...when I look up at it, I get car-sick. So Honey, if you love me, if you *really* do, take me home right now!"

By then, Wade was at their side and eager to help. "Lorraine, baby, you'll get over this in just a little bit. Go in there now and let Edith fix you up a big breakfast. That'll do the trick!" While a bright grin, a quick twist of the head, and an exaggerated wink, added much emphasis to his words, her crying went on unabated.

The sobbing went on and on; in fact, it did not stop the entire time they were there, except for two occasions: The first occurred when they opened their presents, and the second was when they departed for home.

Considering such a flawed beginning, one might think the Yuletide was doomed to failure. Nothing, though, could be further from the truth. Actually, everything went along pretty much as expected throughout the season. Now that is not to say Lorraine did not get sympathy or attention, she did. Once the family realized that she was inconsolable, however, they just accepted it as a fact.

Actually, Christmas had started just a few days after the last one, but Jesse and Mae were completely oblivious to it. Wade was in Andrews a few days after the first of the year and by some good fortune happened to be in Nichols Department Store. The owner, a kindly person, was taking down holiday decorations with the idea of buying new for the next year. Seeing Wade, and perhaps under the influence of inspiration, offered to let him have the old stuff free. Edith was beside herself when she saw what they had. To her, this beautiful trove was a treasure she could use for many years to come. Truly, it is, as exemplified by this generosity, more blessed to give than to receive.

Gestures of good, often perceived by the giver to be quite insignificant at the time, may ultimately be recorded in the album of life because of their impact on the lives of others. Thence, at the proper time, be borne on wings of seraphim to some far and distant shore, where those involved will celebrate these "little deeds of kindness" throughout the endless ages of eternity.

On the eighth day before Christmas, Edith sent forth her husband to ask of some tree in the forest to make the supreme sacrifice. Wade, having learned his lesson the year before, assented to her request and did so with lithesome heart. Lifting a double-bit axe to his shoulder, he stepped forward to seek out the innocent, that it might exchange a lifetime of anonymity for one splendid hour of glory. Unable to find a suitable fir of proper size and shape, he elected to chop down a stately holly bush. Although quite festive looking and covered with red berries, Edith could not contain herself at the sight of it. "Wade, what in the name of goodness do you mean, anyway? Nobody's ever used holly to make a Christmas tree out of."

"Listen," he said. "I've tromped all over that mountainside above Grandma's place and this is the only thing I found that might half-way work. They ain't no pines or cedars up there, not with any shape to 'em... And I ain't going on nobody else's land a looking for one, neither." It was true; he had searched over the entire three hundred acres that Grandma owned, without success. Grandma Gernon, grand-matriarch of Sweetwater, was most circumspect about any intrusion on her land by anyone, except family. Such an attitude existed with her neighbors, also. They might very well offer you the shirt off their backs, but respecting property lines was something else.

"Wade, half the time I don't know whether to hug your neck or kick your hind-end. But, I guess I'll just have to learn sometime or other, if you're born a mountain-hooger, you'll die one. Although still skeptical, she looked at the tree with an eye toward its possibilities. Not willing to appear too easily persuaded, she took her time. "Well, it'll probably be better than me decorating one of these fence posts out here in the yard," she scowled. "But I swear, Wade, if I didn't watch you; you'd do away with the whole idea of Christmas. Just give the young'ins their things, and then let 'em grow up without ever knowing there was such a thing as a Santa Claus."

Indeed, with the high tide of her objections slowly ebbing away, he now felt it safe enough to step a little deeper into troubled waters..."Sugar, that's kinda the way I've been thinking too. Don't you reckon when the packages come we ought to just go ahead and let the little fellas have their things? They don't understand about Santa Claus, anyway, and it'd be awful to keep their toys from 'em, especially if something bad was to happen."

Suddenly they realized that Jesse and Mae had not missed a word of it.

"Wade, for crying out loud, would you listen to yourself! Where's your mind at, anyway?" Edith's frustration had just hit a new high. Scanning the two upturned faces, she wondered if the big secret was now history. "Be quiet!" She mouthed, using the opportunity to display her anger. However, almost immediately felt bad about it and softened. "The mail-boy brought a package today and I reckon we got everything," she whispered."

"Got what?" Jesse asked expectantly. Mae, by his side looked up with eyes big as saucers; she, too, wanted to know what.

Abruptly, a sudden December wind knifed its way to the bone. Quickly she hustled the two inside and away from the chill.

On the way, Jesse repeated his question, but Wade waited until they were indoors before attempting an answer. "Why, Son, yesterday I run up with one of old Santa's workers and he handed me something for you and Mae.

Meanwhile, Edith had slipped quietly into the bedroom to reappear moments later with a small book in hand. Sitting down, she drew Jesse's chair up close and lifted Mae onto her lap, then started reading from the title page. Yet before she could utter the words "Puss and Boots" Mae began squealing in laughter. The source of her delight came not from the book, although its cover displayed a brightly clad feline with broadsword, hip-high riding boots, and a feathered cavalier hat. No, that wasn't it at all, Mae was having a fit over her mother's tummy; it seemed to be getting bigger every day

That evening, with the holly nailed to the floor, Jesse and Mae drank hot cocoa and watched their mother wash carefully each shiny leaf. Next, she delicately rubbed wax onto the green foliage, creating an illusion of raindrops and ice. After that, strand-by-strand, piece-by-piece, she put on the decorations until the most beautiful and shining object Jesse had ever seen, came into being. He could not take his eyes off what surely must have made the angels a little homesick, so great was its glory.

Edith was not happy though, even with enough decorations to fill several boxes, they still had no star for the top. Wade and Mae were thrilled too, almost as much as Jesse, but not so Edith.

After Lorraine arrived, one of the first things she did was offer a tearful observation, "That tree needs a star!"

Although Edith felt vindicated, she was quick to address what she deemed to be an impropriety, "Well we can't put something up we ain't got, now can we?" Although the retort had a sharper edge to it than intended, she made no effort to rectify the misconception. Lorraine seemed surprised, but after a few moments of awkward silence, left to look for her black coat hanging in the bedroom. Attached to its lapel was a new brooch that Clark had given her just before they left Gastonia. The triangular shaped silver angel was about five inches long and three inches wide at its base. The shiny bauble, spangled with white rhinestones, was quite striking. After unfastening it and with Edith's help she placed it atop the tree. The two stood back smiling, Lorraine cried softly as everybody admired her contribution. It was the only tree the Gernon Clan would lay claim to that year and it now looked perfect!

Saint Nicolas came at exactly one minute past midnight, bringing all the things that Jesse and Mae had picked out. They awoke at dawn to find the handiwork of a jolly old elf, whose magic had turned pictures into toys! Jesse quickly located his red tricycle and a pearl handled cap-buster, both positioned near the tree. Strapping on his six-shooter he jumped astride the three-wheeler and began to alert everybody that Santa had come. Mae's scream had already done that, however; being loud enough hear out in the road. When she found a doll sleeping beside her in bed, it took several minutes to get her calmed down. Amazed by the magnitude of this reaction, the astonished parents finally got her to look under the tree where she found her tea set. Jesse and Mae shared many a Christmas after that, but none ever contained the magic this one did. Never again would Santa Claus seem quite so real.

Indeed, while brightness certainly did prevail in the Gernon household that Nativity Season, an even greater glory awaited them outside. During the night, a sharp drop in temperature caused all the fog on the mountaintops to freeze. It had drizzled rain for over a week with no evident change in sight at bedtime, but when the sun arose to a clear sky, what a change it found! The azure vault, illuminated to exquisite brilliance, imparted its shimmering luster to a seemingly endless range of blue-glistening mountains. The frosted ice shimmered like silvered crystal in the morning radiance. Transformed too, were the dowdy and weather beaten old woodlands; they, into a majestic playground of incredible white that now was a place fit for the elves to vacation in. After all, they had just earned the right to enjoy one.

CHAPTER 4

Jesse, happy as he was, still had one wish unfulfilled and that was to ride in Clark's car. Ever since they drove up in their black '37 Ford, he had been hoping for an opportunity. He had begged his mother to ask about it, but she was quick to discourage such an idea. After much pestering without success, he decided it was time to do it himself.

Pedaling the new tricycle, he went straight for an answer. "Uh Clark," he said in a voice barely discernable above the squeak of his vehicle.

Clark, working hard at not losing too much face to his straight razor, did not respond right away. Not taken aback by the non-reply, Jesse dismounted and quickly climbed up on the bedside chair, to stand at his uncle's elbow. This time he roared out in a manner reminiscent of Dave. "Hey Clark! Son, Look at me?"

This time Clark noticed. His lathered face exploded with laughter. "Hey! By golly," he whooped. "Well Jesse, I see old Santa found you after all."

The night before had been spent teasing Jesse and Mae that since they did not have a chimney, Santa might pass them by. Turning to the bed, he playfully smacked Lorraine's bottom, then after a low whistle sat down on the edge. "When we get us a boy, Honey, I want one just like old Jamup here. What do you say?"

Lorraine sniffed a few times before mumbling an unenthusiastic response, "I don't know, Darling, let's wait 'til we get back home. Maybe we can talk about it then."

Chuckling, the good-natured uncle looked again at his nephew. "What's up, Rooster?"

Jesse finally had his chance. "Clark? Uh, Clark, you reckon I could get you to take me for a ride after while?" The request, barely a mumble near the end, was hard to understand. However, Clark caught the drift, "Why, you betcha Jamup! I'd be tickled to. We need to wait 'til after breakfast though; ...okay?"

Jesse's assent was a happy but tacit nod.

"Okay then, you run in there and get you some clothes on and tell Daddy what we're up to," he instructed.

The tricycle sprouted wings; it was the best news possible. Wade joined in to make it official. "By Ned, we'll both go and watch that big V8 high-gear the mountain!"

High gearing the mountain was a test many of the men of Graham County often put to their machines, mostly because it gave them a chance to earn bragging rights. Reckoning was that any vehicle capable of pulling the mountain in high gear was very special, indeed. Ford and Chevrolet drivers alike, when able to do it, boasted unendingly about their superior make. On occasion, the more vocal owners came to blows over some outlandish claim.

To Jesse's chagrin, breakfast was slow in coming and they finished late, but, after all, it was Christmas morning. Nevertheless, it still left him feeling a little chafed. Finally, a few minutes past ten, Clark went outside to warm up the motor. Jesse watched from the front room as white smoke slowly engulfed the car, before drifting skyward. Much of the heavy frost had melted from the windshield by the time Edith dragged him from the window. He needed proper attire for such weather and that meant wearing the blue snowsuit Alice had sent him a few days earlier. She was Edith's older sister who, although having been married twice, had no "young'ins" of her own. Determined to share in the joys of children, Alice doted on her nieces and nephews. Her package, one of several mailed each year, had been opened immediately upon arrival.

When Jesse saw Mae wearing a snowsuit too, it made him a mite edgy. *Now what does she think she is doing,* he wondered? The answer was not long in coming. Wade whisked her up while reaching down a big rough hand for Jesse. "Come on, Son," he called as they swept through the door and headed for the car.

"How come she's a going?" Jesse grumped, while making a face at her.

The car felt toasty-warm as he found a seat between the two adults. Wade held Mae on his lap, thus giving her the best place for looking out. Clark was quick to notice the inequity and offered a solution. "Hey, Jamup, slide on over here and stand next to me. Just hold onto my shoulder. Fella like you needs to see out too, don't he?" Clark's understanding helped to offset Mae's impertinent grin.

"Okay, Buddy, goose it a little bit to get your speed up before we hit the mountain." Wade was full of optimism. "We need to show them old Shivalay drivers what a Ford can do. By Ned, if we don't top out in high gear at over thirty miles an hour, I'll eat this old hat of mine."

Clark grinned confidently, nodded, and then calmly shifted from second into high. They traveled about a hundred yards before reaching the steeper incline. By then the car had accelerated to about forty and was beginning to negotiate the first of many winding curves. "Wade, I believe it's going to tear this mountain all to pieces, I can't feel it straining one bit. In fact I may have to let off a little before the next turn."

"Son, you've got yourself a real winner in this 'un," Wade jubilated. The proud brother could not have been happier, had he been talking about a prize racehorse.

"Yeah it's an even better automobile than I thought; you know I nearly let 'em sell me a '38 Chevrolet at the same price, but I'm glad now I didn't." Clark looked over and winked at Jesse. "What do you think, Jamup?

Jesse's excitement matched that of his father, but for reasons that were entirely different. He loved riding, yet he had the car radio on his mind; he could not imagine such a thing. "Can I turn it on?" he asked.

Wade was quick to refuse the request, "Not yet, Son, let's see what this big V-8 can do first." To see Jesse cower before such a mild rebuke puzzled Mae.

"Wade's attention never left the driver. "Listen to me, Buddy; you're a lot better off with this Ford, for what you paid for it, than if they'd just give you that Shivalay. Heck, a car like that ain't nothing but trouble. Why it'd break up a rich man trying to keep it going and I swear you couldn't law one off on me." Wade was never reticent about speaking his mind.

The car continued to move smoothly up the mountain, taking each curve with ease, until they approached the most precipitous stretch. Well known were the hazards of this place, not only for the steep grade, but also for a stiff switchback turn. Being the test's most demanding section, it was a given that all ascending vehicles would lose much of their momentum there. The goal, therefore, was to head into it with as much speed as possible, and then exit without having to downshift.

Under the expert guidance of his older brother, Clark entered at optimum speed, then proceeded forward, all according to plan. Wade felt comfortable enough to fire up a Lucky Strike. However, that is when their strategy began to collapse, for that is when they met an oncoming Chevrolet. The highway, officially designated as a two-way thoroughfare, was, in fact, only a single-lane road. In most places, it was just wide-and smooth-enough for one vehicle to proceed at a time. Common sense dictated that as drivers chanced to meet, both should slow down and move to the right while passing. Occasional, however, some dolt would be unwilling to abide by the rules and insist on taking their half in the middle. Unfortunately, this exact occurrence was now in process, making it a test of the mettle and metal for both man and machine alike. Clark quickly realized he would have to pull sharply to the right and almost stop, if he wished to avoid an accident. Under normal circumstances, he would have slipped the car into a lower gear and then crept forward without mishap. Such, however, was not an option this time, so he left it in high gear. Immediately their speed dropped to about ten miles an hour, with stalling of the motor now a very real possibility. In the meantime, Wade had rolled his window down to unleash a tirade of expletives at the other vehicle.

With similar greetings emanating from the other car, a war of words quickly escalated into a battle of brandished fists. Then all at once, it became evident that something quite extraordinary was in process. Incredibly, the black coupe' was still inching along, and, as of yet, the motor had neither trembled nor faltered. Not picking up speed, not losing speed, it moved inexorably along while passing through the steepest part of the mountain. Wade, silent and transfixed, sat staring at the speedometer, its needle just hovering barely above the peg. With every nerve strained, it was as if they, by will power alone, could keep it going. "Tell you what, Son," Wade instructed. "Let back on the pedal just a *leeetle* bit, we don't want to smother 'er right now."

Clark swallowed hard, and then nodded nervously. Wade's cigarette, almost forgotten, seared his lips. Disgusted, he snuffed it out in the ashtray. The car continued to roll with the throb of its motor matching exactly the heartbeat of its driver. Both men knew the engine could die at any moment, yet they were riding a thoroughbred, one that would carry them either to victory or to months of ridicule and derision. Wade, well acquainted with the Chevrolet driver they just passed, knew that he was fully aware of their situation. An eternity seemed to fit nicely into a ninety-second slot, but then, slowly at first, the Ford began to breathe easier.

At that instant, with their mouths dry and every muscle strained, the wailing sounds of fiddle music suddenly broke the spell. Unnoticed, and at an opportune moment, Mae had switched the radio on, thinking it might perk-up the mood.

Reaction was immediate and incredible. Wade let out a war-hoop that brought even a somber Jesse to tears of laughter. Mountain hoedown added even more to the celebration. From there on up to the Stecoah Gap, they rode without slowing down and "topped-out" at just over thirty-five miles an hour. They had, indeed, high-geared the mountain!

Clark parked in the gap, at a spot where they could look down on the community of Stecoah. The little village, sister to Sweetwater, looked toy-like and serene from so high above. Wade jumped out, cupped a hand around his face, and let out a shout that even Tarzan would have envied. Keeping it at full volume, he yelled out the conquest two more times, just for good measure. Obviously feeling much better now, he strode back to the car wearing a huge Cheshire-cat grin. The smile showed no signs of abating as he zipped open a new pack of Lucky's. It was time to celebrate. Offering one to Clark, they lit up and simultaneously exhaled into a moment of special silence.

"By golly, old Buddy," he said, "that's the best Christmas present I could ever get!"

Felt rather than said was the sentiment that the greatest thrill of victory often comes, not from winning, but by beating the odds to do it.

Clark turned to gaze westward across and beyond the mountains of Sweetwater. After a long moment to think, he looked back at Wade and spoke. "Look down there across the Oakfield Ridge; can you see that little basin? That's where we all used to play; running up and down those ridges like a pack of foxhounds. Yeah, when you work in a cotton mill 60 or 70 hours a week, and breathing in all that lint, you get to thinking about times like that. Oh, we had to work awful hard back then just to get by, but it never seemed to hurt us like millwork does. And do you remember that place over there in the Hogue Cove where we used to go camping out?... prettiest spot in the world. But them days are all over with," he sighed. "I accept it though, my Lord, after all, I'm a grown man. But what really hurts is to know that I won't ever be able to live here again. Anyhow, even if I could, Lorraine wouldn't. She just hates the mountains; ...says it's too lonesome here."

Clenching his teeth, the muscles bulged enough to look like twin agates instead of mandibles. Clark took in a slow, deep breath and then exhaled. The soft sound of resignation was palpable. "But that ain't what I wanted to say, Son, there's something else we need to talk about. First though, you've got to promise you won't tell this to nobody, and certainly not Lorraine." His eyes pleaded even more earnestly than did his voice.

If he did not have it before, he certainly had it now: Wade's full attention.

"Why, Son, I don't understand this, you know you can trust me and always could... but what are you getting at, anyway? Is there something wrong? Something I can you help out with?" The urgency of his questioning demanded an immediate answer and nothing short of that would do.

"Oh, I've wished a million times now that I'd never got married, yet nobody knows how much I love that little girl. Lorraine means more to me than anything in this world and it's just I can't stand the thoughts of ever having to leave her; or, for that matter, her being hurt."

Impatience forced Wade to break back in. "My goodness, Son, you'uns just got married! Can't the two of you work it out? I'll talk to Lorraine and Edith can, too, then once we get her over being so scared of the mountains, she'll like it here. By Ned, I wish you'd said something earlier, why I can get you a good job working with me on the WPA." His demeanor abruptly turned philosophical, "E*verybody* knows you have a lot of problems when you first get married. I'll guarantee you this though; she'll learn how to cook one of these days. Take me and Edith, why we didn't always get along good, like we do now. Just give it a little more time and watch, she'll move up here with you, and then you'll see that your old brother was right." At this, he reached over to lay an arm across Clark's shoulder, shaking him several times in the process. Two hearty slaps between the shoulder blades made his point.

Quick laughter by both dispelled much of the tension and allowed Wade a moment to breathe easier. However, when Clark resumed speaking his words took back their ominous tone. "No, I wish to God that was it, Wade, but, Son, it ain't. You remember back last spring when I wrote Mom and Pop about being in the hospital with a high fever and sore throat. Well, I thought I'd got over it. Yeah, I was weak for a while, but figured anybody would be, so we decided we'd go ahead and get married. It never crossed my mind that anything serious might be going on, since most of the time I felt pretty good. I did notice, though, that while we were at Myrtle Beach my feet started swelling. So after we got back I went to the doctor and he said it was just little kidney infection, and gave me some pills. I took every one of 'em, but it seemed like I just kept getting worse. The swelling didn't go down and my back started hurting. Well, anyway, last week he sent me to a specialist over in Charlotte where they gave me good examination. My doctor there said the throat infection I had back in the spring had damaged my kidneys. He thinks I probably have Bright's disease."

"Wade looked bewildered, he was utterly dumbfounded. "My goodness,

Son, what's Bright's disease, anyway? I've never heard of that before. Sounds bad though, just how bad sick are you anyhow?"

"It can be pretty bad. It's where your kidneys get scarred until they can't take the poison out of your blood anymore. Sometimes the germs from strep throat will cause it, and they say that TB can, too. From what I was told, once your kidneys are damaged like that, they'll never be healthy again. And if the disease continues, they finally get so bad that most people die. Right now, they don't have a cure for it, but some of the doctors at Bowman Gray are working on one. I don't think my kidneys are all that bad yet, but if this keeps on, somewhere along the line they will be."

Wades' shoulders began to shudder as the awful hand of sorrow pummeled him unmercifully. Twisting toward the window, he knew he could not speak. Jesse looked away embarrassed; he had never seen his daddy cry. Mae, however, pressed tightly up against him, close enough to push his hat sideways. She felt no such shame and put her hand on his face, touching the tears in an attempt to wipe them away.

Clark tried to console his brother. He spoke in a soft, calm voice, "I'm not done fighting yet, Son. And, why you ought to know me better than that! Us Gernons don't give up without a good scrap and, besides, this disease may have already run its course. I'll just take good care of myself and try to keep from getting another infection. Besides, who knows, they've got good doctors down there at Bowman Gray and they might come up with a cure yet. But even if they don't, you know I ain't afraid. I would hate it though; hate it awful bad for Lorraine… her along with Mom and Pop. And, of course, the rest of you, too, but you've got your own lives to live. Lately, I come to realize that I've not always lived the way a fella ought to. I was just thirteen when I got saved, but really I don't think I knew what I was doing. Anyway, I never went much to church, even after that. I've been thinking, though, that when we get back home me and Lorraine might join that little church there, where she was baptized."

Wade forced himself to look at his brother. He expected to see a face dark and sad, but instead he beheld a countenance that was almost angelic in its brightness.

The two sat in silence while, remarkably, even Jesse and Mae kept quiet. A gift perhaps from providence, that gave them time to prepare for what was about to happen. Indeed, something quite unexpected did follow when a spiritual synapse occurred. Simultaneously they accepted the fact that all things of earth must ultimately return to the earth. Everything, that is, except the fully surrendered soul; it and it alone will slip these terrestrial bonds and survive. A deep peace slowly swept over them both.

An unknown quantity of time drifted by in silence before Clark rolled down his window, but immediately the gust of an arctic wind nearly swept his breath away. "I hated having to tell you this, Brother, but you know as well as I do it had to be done."

Wade groped for just the right words, something he was unaccustomed to doing, "Clark, I ain't just saying this to make you feel good, but you look the picture of health, Son. And, by golly, it's been several months now since you first got sick. So, I've got a feeling you're going to beat this thing. Truth is though; we've all got to put our trust in the Man upstairs …don't we?"

The look that flashed between them confirmed what they had just experienced. Neither could know that ten years must yet pass and a world war be fought before it all would come to be.

A loud cracking sound made by the breaking of frozen timber reminded them that they were still in the here and now. That, and with Mae squirming around like a wiggle-worm in hot ashes, gave them reasons enough to head home.

Coasting down proved to be a far easier thing to do, than making the trip up, and once back they found the rest of the family there waiting for them. For Wade this was an excellent opportunity to share the victory, and that is what he did, over and over. "By Ned you ought to have seen that big Ford a high-gearing the mountain," he gloated. "Why, dad-gum, I'm ready to trade old Edith in on one, just as soon as I find somebody who'll swap with me."

Half in anger, half in fun, she was quick to retort. "They ain't no doubt about it, he'd do it, too! But then where would he find anybody to do all this cooking and cleaning for him?"

"My Lord, Edith, wise up! With a good Ford I'd have a string of women running after me."

"Oh, they'd run *after* you alright, they'd run *after* they saw what they had; and they'd run like a scalded dog, too! Why, if I had a lick of sense I'd be running right now."

In spite of the banter, an air of gaiety prevailed. They celebrated with fireworks, gifts, and lots of food. Edith had prepared a baked hen with gravy and dressing along with hot biscuits, mashed potatoes, and canned cream corn. To round it off Effie brought a huge platter of sliced ham with two bowls of potato salad, enough food that the table could hardly hold it all. For several days, the wood stove had been turning out cookies, cakes, and pies. This had been a happy time for Jesse and Mae; they loved banqueting on all the delicious aromas. Grandma Gernon also sent one of her special fruitcakes. It, long a Sweetwater tradition, had been prepared from a recipe that dated back many generations, perhaps even for hundreds of years. Typically, they consisted of twelve thin layers of spiced sweetbread, each covered with a coat of rich homemade apple butter. The cake then aged for a week or longer, before serving.

The day ended, as do most Christmas Days, filled with warm feelings of nostalgia, yet overlaid with an aura of unfulfilled desires. The next morning Clark and Lorraine loaded up their car for the long trip home. Lorraine could smile now; her teardrops had dried. Many hugs and kisses accompanied the send-off as they pulled away. Waving goodbye, Lorraine cheerily called back: "We had the best time in the world and I can't wait to see you again!... I love you all!"

CHAPTER 5

In the twilight of reality, the struggle is to distinguish shadow from substance. Yet, it is in this realm of dusk, lit by the flickering fire of human faith, where angels are wont to dwell.

Although the pale sunlight added little warmth to the February morning, Dave's four-day-old growth of beard owed its luster to the brightness. Yet it was heat, not light, that he craved most as seen by the coarse trembling of his hands. So far, every effort he made in trying to hold steady the mug Edith handed him had proven futile. Finally, by mustering all his concentration on clasping both hands around it, he was able to transfer a little of the coffee to his lips. Even at that, however, much of the liquid sloshed down his chin and onto his overalls. No wonder he shook, he had just spent the night, in zero weather, perched atop High Top. He had kept from freezing to death, but barely, by remaining in the glow of a small campfire and a pint of Beech Creek's finest.

Dave Gernon was a foxhunter and the last of a vanishing breed, but his brand of the blood sport was completely different from that of the English nobleman or early Virginia planter. While they rode in equestrian pursuit to the hounds, he by no means wanted any part of such a "crappy sport"; it definitely was not his cup of tea. No, enjoyment of the Appalachian style hunt comes from the baying sound of Walker dogs while they pursue their amazingly resilient quarry. Mountainous terrain offers an arena especially well adapted to the needs of a motivated spectator. For after an initial climb to some suitable spot, the sportsman may then direct his full attention to the sound of proceedings from ridge top to valley, hill to dell, all without expending any further effort, right up to the end of the chase. Here again is noted a difference in the two styles of hunt. The highlander aficionado desires not to see an end his adversary, but rather prefers running the fox to ground and thus preserving it for another day.

"Could I get you to twist me up a Prince Albert?" he pleaded. "These old hands are shaking so bad I just can't do it." This request for a roll-your-own cigarette required both dexterity and practice, and Edith was uncertain whether she possessed either. After several attempts, however, a reasonable facsimile soon had blue halos encircling Dave's wide brimmed hat.

To the extreme, Jesse's grandfather was an avid follower of three great passions in life. In order of preference, they were foxhunting, prizefighting, and politics. Little else mattered to him and once he chose a principal in each field, all the others became mere and insignificant. In addition, he was an incorrigible prankster with the uncanny ability to pull the same joke, repeatedly, on friends and family alike. Once he uncorked a trick, the sound of his laughter could reach up to a quarter mile away. However, the poor victim had better not try repaying the favor, lest they risk unleashing the fury of hell. He possessed what might be termed a one-way sense of humor, yet being a great conversationalist, he was able to spellbind listeners with stories from a seemingly endless supply of anecdotes. Those foolish enough to challenge his word on any subject stood in awe at the zeal of his convictions. Religion held very little interest for him, causing many to think he was an atheist. When asked by local ministers about his soul and salvation, he blustered back, "Why, shoot, I'm a Roman Catholic and have been ever since I learned they weren't no other Christian church but them for over fifteen hundred years. The way I see it, all the rest of you ain't nothing but a bunch of renegades. No sir, I couldn't, in good conscious, be anything but a Catholic." He felt to be on solid ground here since the nearest diocese was at least fifty miles away.

This morning, however, there were more serious matters on his mind than church; Dugan was missing. Dugan, his most prized foxhound, had, along with two other dogs, "burned a fox's tail" for over five hours before running him to ground. It was soon thereafter that two of the three were back at the campfire, but not Dugan. Two hours of tooting on the horn proved futile, leaving the impassioned owner only more to worry about. Usually such trumpeted sounds from his specially made instrument would summon back even the tardiest pack member.

"Right now, Edith, I'm just plumb wore out. Think I'll go on home and get myself a little sleep and if he ain't home by the time I get up, I'll head back out to find him. Could be he's trapped in a hole somewhere; you know Dugan's bad to go right in after a fox, and that can be dangerous."

Edith knew well her father-in-law's disposition and felt concerned enough to wish him encouragement, "Why, yes, he'll probably show up after while, so if I'as you I'd go on home and get myself a little rest. Anyhow, they's been many a time when he was a lot later than this, getting in."

"Yeah, that's right," he sighed in agreement. "But I just can't help worrying about him."

"I'd be glad to fix you a little bite to eat, if you'll let me."

The depressed hunter remained adamant; "No, I reckon not, guess I'd better get on home." Grimacing noticeably, he then grunted loudly, the arthritis was acting up again and this time it coursed down his back and legs. Carefully, he raised himself from the chair by pressing against its seat and arm; "Curse this old rheumatism anyhow, it's just about got me eat up." The two hacking coughs that followed were now a permanent part of his chain-smoking habit.

Jesse had been closely following the conversation, and now saw that it was time to make his move. "Dave, I think I'll go with you," he stated matter-of-factly.

"Why shore Jamup," Dave brightened. "Run get your things and we'll go."

That Jesse's mother had other plans quickly became apparent, but soon relented after listening to a heart-rending plea. Mae, too, was raring to go, but she, not being nearly as adept at gaining sympathy, failed miserably with the mad fit she pitched. With a wink and toss of his head, Dave whisked Jesse away before Edith changed her mind about him as well.

The two loved conversing with one another and early on had agreed to dispense with such terms as Papaw or Grandpa in favor of using their given names. It made Jesse feel grownup to do it that way.

Dave set the pace, walking in front as they crossed a badly tilted foot-log. As always, it was in much need of repair. "They, hell-fire!" Dave hollered while trying to maintain his balance. "What's it going to take to get Jim to fix this stupid thing… somebody to fall and break a hip? He's so cock-eyed sorry I don't want people to know we're brothers." Jim still lived in the house with their mother, Grandma Gernon.

With the creek behind them, Jesse raced up the slope to a spot known as the "milking gap." There, they decided to pause until Dave caught his breath, but it didn't take long before Jesse found himself fully engrossed in a tale taken from the long ago. Listening to the saga proved so engaging, he missed the warning signs of danger that lay lurking for him in the nearby shadows. Unfortunately, they had encroached on the territory claimed by Sweetwater's most feared denizen.. It was a well-known fact that from this site many a terrorizing attack had occurred against a host of women and children alike. Jesse and Dave, indeed, were tarrying near the lair of the infamous Nasty-Bill, a huge gander owned by Grandma Gernon. He had a wicked beak that could pinch large, nasty looking blood blisters on the toughest hide. Pinpoint and deadly accurate, Bill usually got what he aimed for, and few be there were who did not howl in agony after falling victim to his fury. Not only did this over-sized feathered fiend make life miserable for intruding humans, but pets and domestic livestock also, suffered under his bullying tactics. Eventually, they all learned to avoid any confrontation with this mean-natured rowdy.

Jesse had often heard of Nasty-Bill and dreaded the day they might meet up, but in the planning of this trip, he had completely forgotten about him. When he looked up to see the great intimidator making straight for him, he was horrified. Actually, all he saw was a set of gigantic wings, a long serpentine neck, and a head making vile hissing sounds. Jesse suddenly realized he was staring directly into the flickering, wicked eyes of Nasty-Bill.

While still some six or seven feet away, the evil gander became air-born; the obvious intent being to bring poor Jesse down. Bill, though, did not reckon on Dave Gernon and that was his mistake. For suddenly a very bellicose grandfather whisked his stupefied grandson off the ground to a level just above that of flight. He accomplished this like a matador rotating his cape before the charge of a bull. Bill never knew what hit him, but he certainly felt the full impact of a big hob-nailed boot that sent him sailing some ten feet beyond where he had planned on landing. He never looked back while squawking loudly and running toward the branch.

Jesse would never forget the encounter, it, and the sudden appearance of black-watery droppings that stained Bill's otherwise snow-white tail-feathers. It took several months for the big gander to return to his dastardly ways. However, being ever true to a nature that was both incorrigible and nasty, this tough old bird ultimately made it back to the barnyard where he lived out a long life.

Climbing through the fence, adjacent to where Grandma Gernon milked the cows, Dave stopped to stare wistfully up the hill at her house. An inexplicable rift existed between the two that Jesse was oblivious to at the time. Later, he watched it deny them much of the joy that otherwise might have been theirs. At times, on special occasions, they were able to set aside their differences for a while. Invariably, however, something happened to bring back the old dispute and alienation once again took over.

Nearing Dave's house they stepped off the frozen roadway to avoid a patch of hard ice and that is when a big white-tailed bunny scampered furtively away. "Hey, did you see that, Jamup?" Dave feigned alarm. "Son, you could've got yourself bit there, so let's try to be a little more careful! Besides," he said, "we may have disturbed her nest. You know there ain't nothing any better than a good rabbit egg?"

Jesse quickly followed Dave's example by cautiously poking through the weeds. "Look they's a chicken in there!" He exclaimed excitedly.

Dave motioned that he be quiet, as the spot was marked where one of Grandma's big Dominecker's sat motionless. Easing back, Dave whispered his plan. "Son, let's go on to the house and I'll have Ray come back later. I've got an idea that old hen is just a setting there trying to keep warm, but if we disturb her now she's liable to jump up and break every egg in the nest."

This seemed to suit Jesse just fine. "Do you reckon we could get Mom to fix me one?" He asked, knowing his grandmother preferred this appellation.

"Yeah …I guess, but I didn't think you liked eggs."

"Not hen eggs, I don't, but I want to try a rabbit egg and see what they're like."

From there into the yard took them only a matter of moments, they then climbed the steps onto the porch. Unfortunately, Dave had let the flickering light of hope brighten his outlook. "Maybe old Dugan's made 'er back, he declared optimistically." However, wishing would not make it happen and once they entered the house, the darker angels of his nature took back over.

"Run to the spring and get me a bucket of fresh water!" he ordered gruffly. Angrily, he slid a chair closer to the stove and began forcing off his boots. Then with both feet extended toward the fire, he watched twin spirals of steam slowly eke their way out of his socks. Several moments passed before he spoke again, but when he did his voice sounded bitter, "Didn't get a wink of sleep last night, not with Dugan lost." The house was bereft of all sound, except for those he made. "Mary, how about you getting in there and fixing me up a bite to eat before I lay down! I need to get a little rest before heading back out again."

Twisting around in the chair, he saw faces staring at him from the front bedroom. He spoke again, "Now where's that fresh water I asked for?" Dave's wrath was a fire that could spark remarkable performance; so it was as a single movement that Edward and Frank vied for the bucket. Suddenly, their sole purpose in life was to quench their father's thirst. Frank was eight, while Edward had just turned eleven.

Leaving together, they returned in time to hear Dave telling Ray about the rabbit's nest. Ray smiled broadly, his amber eyes twinkled with glee; the nest would soon yield her harvest. Dave turned to his breakfast in silence, but would not touch the coffee since it still might prove to be more than he could handle. Being ever in search of peace, Mary did not ask questions; experience had taught her that discretion, more often than not, was the better part of wisdom.

Dave flung his fully clad body across the bed in the front room and immediately the house became quiet as a tomb. No noise, not a sound would be tolerated while the lord of residence was sleeping. Any cough or sneeze could easily set off such a slate of expletives that the guilty party might very well find themselves suddenly bereft of a hind-end. Fortunately, it was only a matter of moments before his snoring reached such decibels that it seemed safe to risk some movement. With a finger to his lips, Frank motioned for Jesse to follow him quietly to the bedroom. He wanted to show his nephew some of the treasure he had accumulated over the years. To Jesse, Frank actually seemed more like a big brother than an uncle. He had a congenital ocular condition that, when excited, made his eyes dance. When Frank pulled a shoebox from beneath his bed, Jesse watched the mysterious rhythm begin. Its hypnotic affect only added magic to the moment.

Neither seemed to realize just how cold it was in the unheated room; however, Jesse was fascinated by the numerous items he saw. He went from one to another, breathlessly examining each piece. There was a white-handled hunting knife, dozens of flint arrowheads, a compass, an Indian head penny, an old pocket watch with just one hand, buckeyes, a genuine toy police badge, some colored ribbon, yards of fishing line with sinkers and hooks. Tossing aside a roll of tinfoil the size of a softball, he chose instead several pieces of broken colored glass, while avidly fingering a whole cluster of other unclassified objects.

The day quickly became one for Jesse to learn from Frank's imagination. His stories ranged well beyond merely recounting the history of artifacts, for what he whispered caused the object's intrinsic value to increase exponentially. For instance, one of the arrowheads had once belonged to a famous Indian Chief, his name now long forgotten. He discovered it in the Mountain Field, near mysterious place some said was a staircase to heaven.

The knife was also of historical interest since it once may have belonged to Daniel Boone. Oliver, another of Jesse's uncles, had found it lying beside an old trail near Sevierville, Tennessee. Speculation was that perhaps the great hunter had lost it there while on expedition in the area. Although no evidence existed to support such a claim, there was none to the contrary either, so why be skeptical?

Seemingly, they had hardly scratched the surface of Frank's archeological dig when Dave was heard grumbling around in the front room. He had slept for over two hours and it was now past one-thirty. His stated wish was to be on his way before the weather turned cold again. Without prompting, Mary handed him a fresh pair of socks and Jesse watched as he laced up his boots using strands of yellow rawhide.

"Jamup, did you get yourself some of them rabbit eggs yet?" he asked, now sounding a little more approachable than before.

"Not yet," Mary answered. "We've been a waiting on you to get up before I fixed anything."

"We got fourteen," Ray proudly stated, lifting high a bowl filled to the brim. Across his forehead, a shock of wavy-black hair rendered the misleading look of innocence to his face

"Well, by golly, get in there and fry us up a mess then, I could eat half a dozen myself." To this, he winked and added, "And be careful, Old Woman, don't mix 'em up with hen eggs, 'cause if you do, Jamup here won't eat a bite. The one that laid these snapped at him, and Nasty-Bill tried to get him too, but I kicked that sorry gander's tail into the creek. He won't be bothering us for a while, will he, Son?"

Soon, Mom had the eggs fried, fixed the bacon, and warmed-up the remaining breakfast biscuits. Jesse would have eaten even more than the four placed before him, had they been offered. They were, by far, the best he had ever tasted. Still savoring their flavor, he smacked his lips and vowed never again to touch anything laid by a chicken.

The sun had played hide and seek with a flock of high-flying snow clouds all day, making Dave wax uneasy. He knew if the weather turned bad, Dugan was doomed. Deep facial lines told of the stress he felt while reaching for a small mattock; it was a handy tool to have if what he feared proved true. His heart ached at the thought of digging in the frozen ground after a trapped dog. Just as he started for the door, they heard a knock that rattled the windows. Startled looks passed from face to face, for rarely did anyone knock at their door and certainly not with this audacity. Dave appeared uneasy as he lifted the latch-bar and found himself staring into the bluest eyes he had ever seen. Before him on the porch was a giant of a man. One who must have stood at least six feet five and looked to weigh in excess of two hundred and fifty pounds. The bushy, red-haired stranger resembled a big grizzly bear, and his full beard only added to the affect. However, a friendly smiling face and a Walker foxhound cuddled up in his great arms, spelled all the difference.

"Hi," a gruff voice boomed. "I'm Michael Goodman, but everybody calls me Mike. I've got something here I think might be yours."

Dave prided himself at being courteous to visitors; this time, though, he just stood there looking dumbfounded. It took a full minute to get his voice back, and when he did, he asked the man in.

"No thanks," Michael laughed, "I don't have time right now. I found this dog lying next to the road down there at the mouth of Sheehan Cove and somebody said it might belong to you. He is barely able to walk, so I carried him all the way up. I don't think he's hurt bad, though, since there's no bleeding and none of his bones appear to be broken. I'd say he's just bruised up a bit, probably been bumped by a car… But you'll be all right in a few days, won't you, Boy?" Dugan perked up noticeably, he liked the man.

Meanwhile, Dave's face had gone from ashen-gray to purple. "Well, I know just exactly who did it! You wait right here and I'll get my gun, then we'll go down there and I'll fix him!"

That Michael considered this outburst to be utterly absurd and childish became obvious by the deep scowl seen crossing his face. Once the tirade finally hushed, Michael asked Dave to step outside where they might have a word in private.

Feeling obligated by getting Dugan back, Dave made no protest as together they moved down the steps and out beyond hearing range of the house. Those left inside could do noting but wonder as they peered around the curtains, trying to watch the proceedings. Michael placed his left hand on Dave's shoulder, and then with his right lifted heavenward, began to deliver what appeared to be a lecture. They remained thus for about five minutes with Dave never once opening his mouth. Only an occasional nod marked the extent of his participation. When at last it was over, they shook hands and Michael spun on his heels to be quickly gone.

"Smartest man I ever met," Dave said, sounding almost humble. Later, they all agreed that Michael's appearance and disappearance had a definite mysterious quality about it, but even more noteworthy was the remarkable impact it had on Dave's subsequent behavior.

CHAPTER 6

Ray brought Jesse home where they heard the good news; Keith was coming in for another visit.

"I'll bet you anything he's got something big to tell us," Edith said, displaying the letter.

The blank look on their faces indicated the need for her to elaborate.

"Well, according to this he'll be on the bus Monday, so we can ask him then. But I think I already know; that boy's got marrying on his mind. Yes, that is exactly what it is and I can only hope he knows what he's doing. Lately, I've had this awful feeling about Keith, had it ever since my bad nightmare the other night. I saw him and some other feller trapped in a dark hole with grapevines growing all through it. No matter what they did or how hard they struggled, they just couldn't get out." Edith was not ready to share the full extent of her forebodings; not yet, it was just too depressing to talk about. *Some sorry hussy is fixing to ruin Keith's life for him,* she reasoned.

Two days later a dapper young man in a Panama hat stepped from a taxi to sprint jauntily toward the porch. He carried by the handle an imitation leather brown valise. Jesse stood with his mouth agape watching. After tapping him on the forehead, Keith cheerfully quipped; "Hold on there a minute, here's a bad 'un; and I know one when I see it… this is a rotten egg." Keith's brown and white alligator oxfords matched perfectly the tan slacks and green Argyle pullover that he wore. Amid such buoyancy, it took a sister's love to see in him a sport and not a smart aleck.

"When's the big date?" she asked with a knowing smile. "I figured it out the minute I got your letter." Acting positive was a hard thing to do when she felt so uneasy.

The wry smile that twisted Keith's lips seemed to be all that he was willing to share for the moment, however. Forced to be patient for a while longer, Edith admitted to herself that, at least, he *appeared* to be happy, and that was worth something. *Besides*, she conjectured, *all this worry may be for nothing, anyhow.*

Opening up the bag, he removed a gray-striped railroad cap and tossed it at Jesse. However, with Mae, he just seemed to ignore her while she waited and waited and waited; was Keith testing her patience? It seemed that way right up to the point of an explosion; but just when the meter hand reached the red zone, he tied a big blue and white scarf over her head. Edith and Keith watched the two as they laughed and played with their presents; in turn, the youngsters were amazed at Keith. They loved to watch him prepare to smoke. With practiced precision he would deftly shake a cigarette from its package, thump it exactly three times on his thumbnail while reversing ends on each excursion before lighting up. The task was performed with such style and élan that they ran to watch each time he did it. Keith and his modern ways were a marvel.

Taking a seat he patted himself on the stomach; "Everything's still okay, ain't it?" Once reassured that indeed it was, he smiled at Jesse while removing from his wallet a snapshot. Starring longingly at the tiny photograph his mind suddenly returned to an event experienced earlier in the day:

"Nothing like these layovers, huh?" The big man flashed a friendly smile.

"Oh I've come to expect it," Keith laughed. "And it seems like every time I get to Asheville it happens."

"Yeah, me too, I think it's now just a fact of life... want some coffee? The café here makes a pretty good cup and it'll help to pass the time."

Keith followed the tall, redheaded stranger past several rows of waiting room seats into the tiny eatery. The constant sound of bus arrival and departure announcements accompanied them to a booth where moments later a server appeared to take their order.

"It's a busy station," Keith observed.

"Yeah, and getting busier all the time; did you notice they had two Greyhounds and five Trailways parked back there?" Keith's companion was now watching his every move.

Feeling a little uncomfortable, Keith began wondering if it had been unwise to place himself at the disposal of such a powerfully built man. "I think they just called mine," he lied.

"No, Keith, yours won't be leaving for over an hour yet, so relax and enjoy the coffee!"

"How do you know that?" he asked nervously. "And I don't remember giving you my name... Hey, what's going on here?"

"Settle down, Son, there's no magic to this. Remember I was standing right behind you when you asked about the bus. And as far as your name, I saw that on your valise tag, so you see it's all really quite simple."

Keith looked sheepish. "I'm sorry, guess I've been reading too many detective magazines lately; they make me jumpy."

"No, I think it's the detective *work* you've been doing with Earl. That and this other thing," he said knowingly.

Keith suddenly felt skewered. "Well, we all have our problems," he blustered.

Lifting his cup, the stranger's eyes never wavered from Keith's until he finished relating a situation he seemingly knew all about, even down to the minutest detail.

Keith was aghast. "You're a Federal Agent with the Revenue Department, ain't you? But even so, how could you possibly know all this?" The stranger's eyes, lilac-blue and shining with kindness, seemed to reach deep into his soul.

"No, I'm not a Federal Agent," he chuckled. "And don't worry; your secrets are safe with me. Actually, that is why I am here. I am on a mission to advise you against discussing this with anyone, and that includes Edith. I know it's something you'd like to do, but there's a potential here to do a lot of needless harm. Remember, once word gets out it takes on a life of its own, and can never be recalled. I strongly encourage you, Keith, take a step back, and let the dust settle. Trust the Lord to take care of matters and ultimately all will be well." Here, let me give you this, read it carefully and then pray for strength. Someday its full meaning will be made clear." With that, a piece of paper exchanged hands

Suddenly, a loud crash of falling dishes caused everyone in the diner to look toward the kitchen, but when Keith turned back around the mysterious stranger had vanished.

"Well, are you going to let me look at it, or not?" Edith demanded, referring to the photograph.

"Oh, I'm sorry," he apologized, "my mind must have wandered off. Here, here this is my honey; her name's Kathleen Akers, and we're just about ready tie the knot. She works the first shift and I'm on the second, but after next week we'll both be on the first!"

The relief that Edith breathed was more than just a little obvious, as she gazed at the image of a beautiful blond girl, one perhaps in her late teens. Although entirely different from what she imagined there were many questions yet that needed answers. Such a sentiment pervaded her next comment. "Well, she *is* pretty, I'll say that, but you don't know very much about her, do you Keith? Now this may sound little of me, but is that a recent picture or is it something she had made years ago! …Another thing too, has she ever been married before? You know, Son, you have to be awful careful about these things."

Keith did not blink an eye, but calmly took on the task of providing his sister with assurance. "I made it with my own Kodak last Christmas at Lucinda's house. That's her mother's name, and no, she's never been married before, never. But, why don't you write and ask Alice about her? If you think you're worried, you ought to have heard her before they met. With those big black eyes a boring holes straight through me she said, 'Now, Keith, you know we're not common here and I won't have you go dragging some little tramp in on us.' But do you know what, once she met Kathleen, butter wouldn't melt in her mouth. Goes around telling everybody what a doll she is. There's something else, too, you might like to know: Ida Sluder is her aunt." Ida was the wife of Robbinsville's Mayor, Bruce Sluder, who, in turn, was a close relative of the Rose family.

"Well, if Alice thinks so much of her, why hasn't she written me about her? No, I'll see this thing through for myself. I don't mind telling you, Keith, I don't feel real good about this. Right now, though, I've got to be thinking about supper, Wade'll be here pretty soon, and you know how grouchy he gets when it comes to eating late."

Seeing the need for wood to stoke her range, she asked that he bring in an armload from the porch. Quick to oblige, Keith was still filling the bin when he asked a puzzling question. "How long have you had that big red dog out there?"

"What dog?" She asked quizzically. "We don't have a dog and as far as I'm concerned we ain't getting one, neither. Dogs have just about taken over Sweetwater the way it is, so why don't you go out there and run him off."

"No," Jesse hollered, "I need me a good dog; where is he, Keith." Curiosity compelled that they all go to the porch and have a look for themselves. There they found the biggest, friendliest hound dog Jesse had ever seen. He had light amber-colored eyes, a short, reddish coat, and a thick tail that looked half the diameter of a man's arm. In dimmer light, the huge canine could possibly have been mistaken for a panther. Plainly visible were long striate marks on his hip that extended, first to the abdomen and from there to the top of his head. The Scars that told a gruesome tale of some long ago bear fight, were marked deep enough to last a lifetime.

The dog appeared embarrassed by all their attention and responded by thumping his tail over the floor. To Jesse it sounded just like Jim's stallion, Fred, kicking impatiently at the stall boards when it was feeding time. Turning from his side, he crawled forward, as an overgrown puppy would while looking straight up and at the woman of the house. She found him to be irresistible. "What a nice dog," Edith crooned while rubbing his head. "What's your name, pretty dog?" she asked using baby talk to offer several. Jesse joined the guessing game and tried Dugan, but that was to no avail. Keith too suggested a few, but none earned even a passing glance. Mae was dead certain that "doggie" worked and would try nothing else. It was only by a stroke of good fortune that Jesse called him "Mike," doing so in deference to the man who had saved Dugan. At this, the big red-beast jumped up and began barking right in his face.

So, Mike it was and that settled the issue, but now he not only had a name, he also had a home. Their new pet was the first one to greet Wade when he got in from work. "What's that big old ugly dog doing out there?" he asked grumpily. Pushing back the front door again, he spoke directly to Mike. "I'll swear to God, I'm plumb wore out tonight and don't need somebody's old bear dog a laying around the house like this. Edith I believe the big red devil just growled at me."

"He just got here, Wade," Edith defended. "Besides, the young'ins like him and I do, too. Now I doubt Mike growled at you, but the way you're acting, maybe he should have. You know, it wouldn't hurt a bit for us to keep a big dog around the place. They's all kinds of men who walk by here everyday, going back and forth to town, and you never can tell when something might happen. Times ain't like they used to be; a person just can't be too careful anymore."

The sudden realization that they had a guest instantly made a new man of Wade. "Well, by Ned, would you look a here?" He then began an exaggerated search by peering around as if looking for something. "Where are they, Son?" he asked. "That wife and them young'ins of hers? I know they're bound to be here somewhere. Edith got your letter Saturday, and by golly, she's already got 'er all figured out. She's got you married up to some old hag about twice your age, with at least a half a dozen snotty-nosed young'ins to raise."

Edith was quick with an answer. "Well, I ain't ashamed to say it: I was afraid some old hussy might be trying to make a fool out of him. I know this though, some men's candle don't burn too bright when it comes to bad women." With that she cast a disparagingly look at Wade, and then added, "Even if it was lit at both ends."

Keith saw a need to lighten up the conversation. "Well, I'll tell you what, you give me about ten more years, and I'll have that old woman with about half a dozen young'ins. Then you'll be right after all."

Not wishing to sound impolite, Wade waited for the right moment to ask his next question. "What brings you up here this time of year, Son? Usually we'd expect to see you around the Fourth."

Suddenly Keith's demeanor turned somber. "Well, you know Mommy and how she gets when a baby on the way. She couldn't come right now, so I told her I would. She'll be here this spring, though… Then, of course, there's what me and Kathleen have cooking… And obviously, that changes everything," he added with a grin.

Keith chose his next set of words with care, while a thoughtful look crossed his face. "There *was* one other thing, but after what happened in Asheville today, we won't go into that, except to say that something has come up. Something I had hoped we might talk about, since it involves the family, and, of course, it's not something I can discuss with just anybody. Then too, I could be jumping the gun here, anyway, and I really don't want to do that. I believe, though, once I tell you about today, you'll agree that the best thing I can do is just keep my mouth shut, at least for the time being."

Finally, Jesse got what he had been waiting for, Keith going through the ritual of lighting up again. Wade, however, was not impressed; he could have had one half-smoked by that time. Meanwhile, Keith related what had occurred during his two-hour layover in Asheville, taking care not to divulge too much.

"Oh, baloney, Keith… who and what was he talking about anyway?" Edith asked incredulously.

"Well, of course, that's what has to be kept secret!" Keith responded with a chuckle. "Actually, it's a serious situation which could cause a scandal by my talking, and none of us want that. Keep in mind now, I'd never seen this fellow before today, yet he knew everything about me. I'm fully convinced that he was somebody special, maybe an angel; so you can see, can't you, why I'm not at liberty to say more?"

If Keith thought such a decision would bring a round of approval he was in for a huge disappointment.

Edith looked stymied. "Well, how in this world could he know anything? And as far as him being an angel, well that's just nonsense! Why, my goodness, Son, somebody's played a trick on you and I wouldn't pay one bit of attention to it. No, you go right ahead and spill the beans. Sounds to me like he was crazy, either that or on dope or something. Why, you never can tell… he could have even been one of them old homeos, for all we know." The longer she talked the more convinced she became that Keith should share his information.

Wade joined in to soundly denounce the stranger too; "Son, I've heard tell of fairies hanging around bus-stations, but never an angel; so I'm like Edith, I'd speak my mind and let the chips fall where they may."

Keith remained adamant, however. "No, I'd be afraid to... Really, I shouldn't have said anything. The only reason I did, though, was that I thought you'd understand. He told me some other things, too, but I certainly don't feel comfortable talking about that, either. Not now!"

"Tell you what, Keith, you go ahead and tell it, and then together we'll decide what to do. After all, if this really concerns the family, then I have a perfect right to know." A moment of silence slowly festered before she continued. "Now, we're not talking about Matt Rose here, are we?" Such a reference was to their father who had absented himself several years earlier to start a new family in Georgia.

"They, Lord, would you listen to that!" Keith laughed derisively. "What I think of Matt Rose shouldn't be said in mixed company. This thing has nothing to do with anything like that; it's stuff I hope turns out to be nothing more than a tempest in a teapot. Who knows, it may turn out to be so trivial that before long I'll be hard put to remember any of it. I say it's time we changed the subject, though, so let me tell you what we've planned for the wedding."

Edith rose from her chair in a dither; she was in no mood to accept this rebuff gracefully and certainly didn't want hear about a wedding. Testily, she announced that supper needed her attention and abruptly left the room. Flustered too, Wade repeatedly ran thick fingers through a shock of black hair, forcing it straight back. He started to say something twice, but wisely chose just to hold his peace. Keith, feeling a little uncomfortable, slipped a harmonica from his shirt pocket and after rapping it several times across the palm of his hand, sent a strain from "The Great Speckled Bird" wafting softly through the evening air. An entranced nephew drew close while Mae climbed aboard his lap to curl up, purring like a kitten. This was the Keith of old, and it was good to have him back.

Wade, not one to hold a grudge began to soften noticeably. "When will you be going back, Son? He asked.

"Well, the powers-that-be are expecting me there on Wednesday, so I'll be riding that two o'clock bus out of here tomorrow."

Wade scowled. "Boys, you Roses sure like to keep the road hot, don't you?"

Keith acknowledged his tight schedule and they talked on until supper. Edith, in less than an hour, managed to make salmon patties, mash potatoes, fix pickled beans and corn, bake biscuits, and perk the coffee, all without uttering a word to Keith. Appetites were so good that not a crumb remained for Mike to eat, leaving him to howl in protest. Wade, unlike Dave, had very little sympathy for big-mouthed canines. Edith, on the other hand, felt delighted at the opportunity to please him. Meat scraps from the night before, combined with a half-dodger of day-old corn bread, made a veritable feast for him. Within seconds, it was all gone, vanished before a hungry maw that operated much on the same principal as that of a powerful vacuum cleaner. After carefully checking for any loose crumbs, he then resumed his self-assigned sentry post at the door.

Later, pale lamplight peeped at Jesse from beneath the door while he lay in bed listening to a drone of voices drifting in from the adjoining room. The hypnotic effect was so overpowering that the next thing he knew it was time to get up. Wandering into the kitchen, he was still drowsy, but could tell that things were just too quiet around the breakfast table. Keith seemed unperturbed, however, helping to pick up the dishes and he even offered to dry as she washed. Edith was cool yet polite with her refusal. "No, thank you, Keith, I wouldn't dream of it. You're liable to tell me some big secret and everybody knows what a blabber mouth I am."

He chuckled while lifting Mae up to his shoulders; she squealed in delight leaving little doubt as to whom her favorite uncle was. "Edith, I wish to goodness I could tell you, but you know in your heart I can't. That fellow in Asheville put the fear of the Lord in me, and I'll bet you anything it would have you, too. I'll tell you what, though, within a month from today, unless something happens, I'll send you a letter explaining everything."

Immediately a cooled relationship began to warm up and within minutes, the two were chatting amiably again; talking about family and others, just as they did when he first arrived.

Soon, too soon, it came time for him to leave and the morning sun hid its face. Drizzling rain created a somber mood that caused the mountains to loom darkly in their faces, appearing too tall, too dark, and too close. Rising a thousand feet above the valley floor, they gave the illusion that Sweetwater was some great hall built solely for the gods, and any mortal found loitering there was definitely most unwelcome. Even High Top, still garbed in the blue-gray of winter, looked cold and unfriendly. Keith was the only one who seemed happy as he stood in the front room next to his valise. Jesse and Mae drew close and listened as he agreed to write, at least once a week, until the wedding. "No promises after that," he feigned despondency. "Who knows, I may not be my own man then," he said with a big grin.

Edith did not take the remark to be very funny and was quick to tell him so. "Well, Son, you'd just better watch where you're stepping, because sometimes crap don't stink until it gets stirred up."

Keith rubbed his chin, "Oh, by the way," he said. "There is something I can share with you!"

She perked up noticeably. "Why, Son, I knowed you'd come to your senses. It's a lot better not to keep things bottled up, especially when you know good and well I can be trusted."

"No! No," he countered, "not that, and besides you heard what I said. No, here's what I was talking about." He then produced a small folded piece of paper taken from his wallet. "Right before he left, that feller handed this to me. Keith then read very carefully, taking time to search each word as if it alone held the key to a deeper message.

Thou must go to the valley
And walk the dark glen
Seek ye the Light
To be found therein."

"Sounds like a riddle to me and a little bit scary, what do you think? She asked.

"Scares me a little, too, but I don't know. The man said that someday its meaning would be made clear."

"Well, I still say he's crazy. Anyhow, be careful and write to me next week, like you said… Be sure to tell everybody hello and to come when they can. Looks like the rain is about to slack, so I guess you'd better leave."

"Yeah," he agreed, "I'll start out walking and if nobody picks me up before then, I'll catch a ride at Stumpy's. From town I can get a taxi over to Topton; may have to wait a little while there, though, before the bus gets in."

"Better early than late," Edith responded.

"I ought to be home by around nine tonight," he said. "Not having to be at work until the second shift tomorrow gives me a little extra time to rest up," he added. Kissing each one goodbye, he then left with the same jaunty step that brought him there the day before.

Mike remained in the yard until Keith was well past the bridge, some fifty yards away. Jesse, Mae, and Edith stayed on the porch where they could watch him a little further. He seemed to grow smaller with each step, and with each one, a word from the twenty-third Psalm chimed through Edith's mind.

'Yea, though I walk through the valley of the shadow of death, I will fear no evil.'

Two weeks later they admitted Keith to the Gaston Memorial Hospital in critical condition, he had bacterial encephalitis. Commonly called at the time, "brain fever," the condition was so serious there was little expectation for him to live. In an era before effective antibiotic therapy, sulfa drugs offered little hope for complicated cases such as this. Keith sustained an uncontrollable fever, running one hundred and five and up to one hundred and six degrees for more than a week.

Standing at her scrub board, Edith at first did not notice that a bright red Ford coupe had pulled up to the front yard. It stopped, started to move away, then found a parking place beside the road. Its driver stayed put for a long five minutes before she fetched her message to the door. By then Edith had prepared herself for the inevitable knock. Wiping dry her nervous hands, she invited the stranger to come in. However, once she recognized what was happening, her eyes never left the yellow envelope.

"Are you Missus Wade Gernon?" the woman asked coolly.

"Yes, I am," Edith, responded. "You ain't got bad news there, have you?"

"Well, Ma'am, I do have a telegram for you, but I need your signature first." She then produced a pad that was lined for such and once it was duly signed the message changed hands. Stunned by the tersely worded communiqué; Edith saw that it was from Willard, her oldest brother.

"Keith bad sick… Stop... In hospital… Stop… Come now… Stop"

Blood rushed from the expectant mother's head causing her legs to wobble.

"Let me sit down," she mumbled while reaching for the back of a straight chair.

"Here, I'll help you, let me hold that, I'm sorry about this, you know I always hate it when I have to deliver bad news."

"No, I'll be alright in a minute, I just felt weak and swimmy-headed there for a second or two. I'll swear, but he was just here a few days ago and looked healthy as a horse. I just can't understand it." Edith sounded almost apologetic.

"Lord, how I dread these things," the woman reiterated with compassion. "Is there anything I can do to help, anything at all? It's your brother, ain't it?"

Nodding sadly, Edith suddenly caught sight of Mae standing over the washtub in a chair, perilously balanced, but tilting toward the wash water. Unclear was it, as to whether Jesse was trying to hold her back or shove her in. Edith did not wait to find out as she moved with the speed of a cheetah to scoop up a straying hind. "My Lord, you can't turn your back here for a minute!" Several loud smacks to the bottoms and legs of the two young laundry aides sent them on their way to look for a new vocation.

That the visitor could expose her sense of humor with an uncontrollable snicker had a remarkable effect on easing the tension.

"I appreciate your help, but I reckon I'll have to find me somebody to come in and take care of Wade and these young'ins, so I can go to see about him. I just hope the little feller can make it." Tears filled her eyes as another wave of reality hit again. With so much unknown, her fears knew no bounds. Was he still alive, and how did he get sick in the first place? Forced to think ahead, she had everything worked out by the time Wade got in from work.

"You and the young'ins will have to stay at Grandma's while I'm gone," she said. This while handing him the wire; it was best that he read it for himself.

Wade too was shocked, but quickly turned empathetic as he helped facilitate her plans. Grandma seemed pleased at the chance to keep Jesse and Mae, so the next day found Edith on the same two o'clock bus that Keith had taken just two weeks earlier. All the way to Gastonia, the dream she had had about him earlier kept coming to mind. Met at the station by a darkly countenanced Alice, Edith's first words were to inquire about his condition.

"Barely hanging on, and he's in a coma with his brain inflamed. Been running a high fever of over one hundred and five now for nearly a week and I don't know how much longer he can last. But the doctors all say that even if he does makes it, this temperature has probably ruined his mind."

Edith stayed for a week and during that time, the fever broke, but he remained critical. They finally learned that most likely he would survive since the temperature was now under control. However, no one could know when or indeed if he would ever awaken. Considering the delicacy of her condition, the family all insisted that she go back home. Therefore, a very sad and exhausted sister returned to the mountains, back to her husband and back to her children.

Almost daily the mail brought word, yet very little of it contained new information. Finally, at the end of another long week, she got Ma's anguished letter. "Keith has come out of it, but right now he doesn't know any of us and he can't even remember his name. He's awful pitiful. All we can do now is keep praying that the Good Lord will give him his mind back." Edith cried all evening, sitting with her handkerchief and unconsciously accepting the solace that Mike offered. *Was this,* she wondered, *what the stranger meant when he wrote, 'Thou must go to the valley and walk the dark glen'*?

In that darkened room with only the sound of her thoughts to listen to, the words of the twenty-third Psalm again coursed through her mind. "*Yea, though I walk through the valley of the shadow of death, I will fear no evil,"* and then, "*For Thou art with me... For thou art with me..."* The additional words became her mantra of hope, a ray of sunshine to pierce the darkness.

At bedtime, Wade tried to cheer her up. "Sugar, I believe before too much longer old Keith will be back on his feet again!"

"I hope so," she said, "but the way things are looking right now, I just don't know… Do you remember that bad dream I had before he got sick?"

"Ah Lord, Hon, you have so many, which one are you talking about?"

"Oh, for heavens sakes, the one where Keith and some other feller were trapped in a hole full of grapevines, I told you about it!"

"Oh, yeah…" he answered unenthusiastically.

"Well, when I think about it, I get to feeling that something else bad is about to happen. You don't reckon it will do you?"

The answer to her question was already on its way.

CHAPTER 7

Little of import changed in the days that followed except for Edith's better acceptance of Keith's condition. That perhaps, but never the limits it might impose. Indeed, her nature was to deny all suggestions that the damage to his brain was anything except temporary. Jesse and Mae, in a rare departure from their usual demeanor, became cooperative, such to the point of causing extra worry. By being just "too good," the fear was that this could be an omen that something bad might happen to one of them. However, in the end the parents surmised that they, too, felt the gravity of Keith's condition and merely wanted to show how much they cared.

Near the end of February, a definite feeling had developed that things slowly were returning to normal. Normalcy is one of life's great blessings and Edith was truly looking forward to it happening.

The hope of an early spring lifted all spirits enough to inspire a spate of outdoor activity. Mike was pleased with the company, but spent most of his time just sniffing out old boundary markers and establishing new ones.

The morning sun felt warm on his back as he cocked an ear, listening to the whine of a now familiar truck motor. It was an easy sound to distinguish from the usual background dissonance of mooing, barking, hammering, and other noises generally heard in a rural neighborhood. On Tuesdays, the raucous prattle of Sweetwater's gathered denizen was also a part of the morning hubbub. Invariably they clustered at Orr Branch Road, waiting there on the rolling-store. Phelps' vehicle usually arrived around ten o'clock, but many of the customers got there earlier, hoping to be among the first in line. Not only did this assure them a better choice of merchandise, it, more importantly, allowed a little extra time for gossip.

With this, the first sign of Phelps' truck, Jesse began begging for candy. As always, Mae did her part too. Edith, remembering their recent good behavior, turned a sympathetic ear and quickly gathered up a few eggs for barter. She knew that the driver, Art Cochran, never refused to trade; after all, it meant double the profit.

Rolling-stores were essential to this mountain community. They brought in staples that otherwise would have been difficult to obtain. Without personal transportation, the task of getting in supplies posed a definite challenge for most families. Not only was buying important, but also there was the need to barter since they had eggs, chickens, animal pelts, ginseng, and other produce to trade. The rolling-stores stocked most food staples along with cow, hog and chicken feed, lamp oil, patent medicine, tobacco, and special order sundries. Slung beneath the truck carriage was a cage for hauling chickens. It was their squawking that most distinguished the sound of a rolling-store from other vehicles. Moreover, it was music to the ears of those waiting to do business.

With Mike leading the way, they quickly joined the gathered throng to await their turn. Jesse, good at throwing rocks, busied himself targeting a road sign some twenty feet away. Mike kept a close watch on Edith and Mae. Actually, his eye was on two men standing near the mailbox, ostensibly there to catch a ride into town. One looked to be about forty, was black-headed, and had eyes that followed every move Edith made. His companion looked to be about ten years younger than he was and had dirty blond-colored hair. It would be hard to determine the object of his attention since he was extremely cross-eyed. On his arm was a beautiful gold watch that glistened brightly in the morning sun. Mike was determined to stay in concert with the older man, crouching every time he made a step in their direction. With the bristles of a wild boar, he feigned movements while emitting a low growl. That was the only sound he made, but his ivory-colored fangs looked to be well over an inch long. He was ready for a fight and waiting only for the word, but Edith scolded him instead. However, her rebuke was so mild that no one thought it to be sincere. Nevertheless, the warning was sufficient; the stranger had seen enough. Some five minutes later, when the mail car coasted to a stop, Ed Jennings took on two additional passengers.

Jesse and Mae thought their turn would never come; getting there late meant everybody else was ahead of them. To make matters worse, each customer seemed determined to bring Art up to date on all their family's doings. Art, himself given to the gift of gab, appeared to be in no hurry either. Their time finally came, however, and at first, it appeared that there now was very little from which to choose. Cochran, though, was a magician and pulled selections out of his hat that were not readily apparent. While doing so he made the off-handed remark that their dog looked very familiar. "Well, I hope not," Edith hedged, "because me and the young'ins have got awful used to Mike and we'd sure hate to lose him. He showed up on our porch a little over a month ago and ever since then it seems like he's been a part of the family."

Art smiled broadly. "Oh, I doubt he's the same one, but I do know a feller by the name of Vincent Sharpe over on Mountain Creek who had a dog like him. It's been missing now for quite awhile though, and chances are a big bear got his'n." Art chuckled over his ability to dispense wisdom. Secretly he gloated over the power that was his by being able to hear dirt on half the people in the county. Edith left the rolling-store feeling sick at her stomach. Meanwhile Jesse and Mae celebrated their good fortune; each had a bag of orange-slice candy of their own.

She worried that night about Mike, but Wade let it have little effect on him. Ahh, Lord Honey, you can't never tell about a dog like that and I wouldn't pay no attention to Art Cochran, everybody knows what a big blow he is. I've been sick today, and lately my stomach ain't acted just right either. You know I keep this old headache so I think maybe I'll just clean up and go on to bed early. Try to get me a good night's sleep for a change."

She began to hope that somebody, almost anybody but Dave or Jim, would drop by for a visit. Company always perked him up and she needed that right now, but it did not happen. However, when morning came she awoke with a much brighter outlook. "Why, Art sees all kinds of dogs," she reasoned, "and I doubt seriously he ever saw Mike before. No, I think Art is bad mistaken here and besides he probably forgot all about it five minutes later. What do you think, Wade?"

Finishing a plate of biscuits and gravy, two eggs, lots of butter and a thick slice of pork shoulder, he was set for another day of work. Jesse loved getting up early to drink a little coffee in his milk and sit at the table with his daddy. It was fun to hear them argue, they had mastered the art of keeping two different conversations going at the same time. This, while constantly injecting new subjects into the mix.

"I guess so, Edith, but you know my stomach still ain't just right and I'll bet you a quarter this old headache is back, before dark. Have you noticed too, my face has this pale-reddish flush to it? Looking in the mirror this morning, you could see it real good then."

"No, you look just like you always do, but if you didn't I'd never say so, 'cause it'd probably put you in the hospital. To hear you tell it, you're always pale or your face looks flushed, one or the other. I think it's all depends on what light you're using. Now this may not be to your liking, but to me you look as healthy as a horse. Getting back to Mike for a minute, though, do you know a Vincent Sharpe who lives on Mountain Creek?"

"No, Edith, I don't, but I've heard of him and they say he's a pretty mean fella. I don't know him myself, though... I'll swear to God, Woman, I can't get one bit of sympathy out of you. One of these days, after I'm dead, you'll wish you'd been better to me."

"Wade, you'll be around to pee on my grave long after I've been gone for years. If you ever do really get sick though, I'll be the first in line to give you sympathy, but not one minute before. But back to the matter at hand, I don't care how mean that feller is, he ain't getting my dog! Not unless he's got a lot of proof that Mike belongs to him."

A light tap at the front door signaled that Bill Morrow was there and was ready to leave for work. More than merely a co-worker to Wade, Bill was a cherished friend. Being several years older, he, over the years had become a trusted confidant and advisor to Wade. Grace, Bill's first wife, died with the flu soon after he returned home from France. He'd served there as a doughboy during the Great War. When he remarried, it was to the former Maye Edmonds, Wade's second cousin. Tragedy seemed to dog his every step with the loss of their firstborn, a son. Ultimately, however, they had three beautiful daughters to bless their home. Bill loved to visit with Wade and Edith, but the real object of his attention was Mae. Often he would revel; "I'll swear to God if she ain't the spitting image of Grace." He would roar in laughter at her every outburst and then exclaim, "Now if that ain't just like her! Look at them blue eyes, why don't you know they're just full of fire!" Edith and Wade never felt comfortable at delighting over such tantrums. Yet from early on, they learned not to attempt remedial measures in his presence, lest being chastised. A logging accident, several years earlier, had left his leg seriously damaged with a residual limp that made him easily identifiable, even at great distances.

He stood at the door waiting while Wade got his coat and lunch pail. Reaching into a shirt pocket Bill handed Edith a small brown paper bag. "Give this to Mae," he whispered, "and let Jesse have a piece too. A stick of candy is good for them now and then, don't you know." Jesse smiled his appreciation; Bill Morrow was a big man.

Immediately after they left a drowsy hush settled over the house that lasted until well past daylight. Meanwhile, Edith hummed to herself and washed the breakfast dishes. She then used the pale light of a kerosene lamp to comb her hair and freshen up a bit. At about ten o'clock, while sweeping the floor, she looked out to see Mike acting strangely. He was pacing like a caged tiger, walking from one end of the porch to the other. Despite the chilly air, still frosty from the night before, he was panting. She opened the door expecting, as usual, that he would be right in her face, demanding attention. Instead, he all but ignored her. Now, he seemed single-minded in purpose; one of trying to see the unseen. Not only was Mike edgy, he was so much so that he could hardly hold still.

"What's the matter, Boy?" she cajoled. "I've never seen you this way. Has Dave's old fox hounds got you upset?" Her father-in-law had left the night before on another hunt and she wondered if the baying hounds had set him off. Patting his head seemed to have little effect on the huge animal; he barely acknowledged her presence. A low-pitched, half whine, half growl, was the only answer he gave. Turning back to the house Edith softly admonished him. "Settle down, Son, it'll be all right, I won't let anything happen to you."

Indeed, things did seem to go better for a while, but abruptly it all ended with the sharp, angry sounds of loud barking. Edith rushed to the window to see the same two men he had taken issue with previously. They were standing in the road gawking at the house. Suddenly, waves of fear surged down her spine, causing events to take on an eerie, unreal quality. Then she saw it, the yellow handle of what looked like a switchblade knife protruding from the older man's hip pocket! A quick survey of the situation made it patently obvious they were up to no good. Spellbound, she watched the two exchange nods; perhaps this was a signal to move in. Convinced now that evil was upon her, Edith recognized at once the need to take defensive action; but what could she do.

Feelings of helplessness attended the drama set before her. It was like watching a slow-motion movie. However, Mike's disposition was not nearly so passive. Crouching low, he moved into action and began to stalk the stalkers. He made not a sound, and the only way one would have known that he threatened was by the sight of bared teeth and a row of high standing bristle. Obviously, these signs were not lost on the strangers, for they immediately began to pull back. They moved quickly, stepping some ten paces up the road and away from the house. However, Edith instantly recognized this to be a matter of tactics, and not retreat. Both defenders were in full accord here, neither would have accepted for a moment that any real lessening of danger had occurred. Acting accordingly, Mike began a howling-growl that sounded more akin to the roar of a lion, than something a dog might make. At the same time, he started to patrol the front perimeter; his sleek muscled body rippled in the morning sun. Remarkably, the big canine seemed eager to take on the strangers; not a hint of fear showed in his bold prance.

Meanwhile, Edith too, moved into action by swooshing Jesse and Mae into the tiny back bedroom just off the kitchen. Its side-door opened onto a narrow strip of yard some three feet below; without steps, the exit typically saw very little use. She asked Jesse if he knew how to operate the latch. Grim faced and pale, he tried to smile before demonstrating that he did. Next, Edith calmly instructed that should they hear her scream, they were to slip out the door and run hard toward a willow thicket located near the bridge. From there, they were to follow the creek up to the foot-log and then go to Grandma's, where she would get help.

Sobbing softly they started to fret by realizing that so much might depend on them. Loving arms became wings to enfold them as a mother hen does her brood. Angels cannot be mothers, but mothers sometimes are angels, and this one was prepared to give her life. Hushing them with words of assurance, she then headed for the kitchen. For a moment, her eyes flashed blue fire as she reached into a drawer and pulled out a large butcher knife.

At the window again, it startled her to see how much closer the younger man was to the house, but where was the other one? Although beyond her field of view, he still was very much under the watchful eye of Mike. The dog had not stopped moving, yet his boundaries now were much smaller than before. His mouth, white-lathered in froth, was a terrible sight to see. Edith quickly stacked several empty canning jars up against both the front and back doors, thinking they might provide her with a few precious extra seconds of warning.

She watched the stranger again nod his head, and then start forward. Edith knew they meant business this time. Immediately, Mike went for him, he had been watching for such a move and this was it. Edith nearly fainted. She feared that at least one of the men might make it through. Suddenly, a loud scream erupted when Mike brought his man down. Fangs tore deep into an arm and were going for the throat, when another player suddenly stepped center stage.

It seemed from out of nowhere Dave had appeared and now was standing there with a gun hanging loose in the crook of his arm. "MIKE," he hollered. Then in a more commanding voice, he yelled even louder, "GET OFF OF HIM!"

That is when Dave spotted the other man, "They hellfire what's going on here, anyway! Wait a minute, just hold it right there!" A cocked rifle instantly leapt to his shoulder. As an expert shooter, he could hit tiny objects when tossed into the air, and have very few misses. His marksmanship was legendary and perhaps this had preceded him, because neither man slowed down until they were well past the bridge, racing toward Robbinsville.

Moments later Dave sat perched at the porch's edge with his feet planted flat on the ground. A cigarette, stuck at the corner of his mouth, belched smoke blue enough to match that of the morning sky. Jesse moved in to sit by his side while Mae slid in on the other. They watched as he shook his head in slow wonder. "I'll swear, ever time I try to do better something like this happens. I promised Mike, you remember that feller don't you Jamup? Well I promised him I'd try to stop this old cussing. But, you know, when you get mad they ain't a thing else that'll do, it just ain't natural not to." Turning then to Edith he asked, "What do you reckon them two were up to, anyway? It looks to me like they'as a trying to break in on you. Old Mike there would have killed that yeller-headed feller if I hadn't stopped him. I kinda hated to do it, though, because I never did like to hurt a good dog's feelings."

Edith, still shaken, was in no mood to disagree, "I'm satisfied you and Mike just saved our lives. He held them off 'til you got here. I feared, though, that one might make it through." Mike got up and moved over next to Mae before plopping down again; she looked dwarfed beside him with his huge head resting in her lap.

"I doubt they'll be back, but I'd better hang around for a little while, just in case." Obviously, in good-humor, Dave took the opportunity to say why. "Boys, we had us a good race last night. Run old Adolph all over the head of Pin Hook and Mountain Creek, too, with Dugan a nipping at his butt all night long." Customarily, Dave gave foxes from the different neighborhoods names that were currently held in low-esteem..

Still clutching the butcher knife Edith left the porch without a word only to reappear moments later with a huge pork bone in hand. It still had lots of meat still clinging to it. Earlier, she had planned to use it to season a pot of pinto beans, but now she had something better in mind. Mike was ecstatic with his reward.

Visibly upset when told of the day's events, Wade tried for weeks to find out just who and where the culprits were, but all such efforts ultimately proved futile. Leaving word at Stumpy's store, along with several other places in town, he vowed the search would go on until he settled the score.

After two days of nervous watching, Edith began to feel a little better, her courage now bolstered by the presence of a .38 special. Edith's brother Arnold had left it with her the day following the incident. He had stopped by on his way back home to Gastonia. Along with the weapon, he also brought late news of Keith, but obviously was quite unsuspecting about what had happened.

His habit was to make several trips each year to Graham County, with most of those being impromptu. This time he had come to spend a few days fishing with his uncle Granville, who lived on the banks of the Little Tennessee River. Keith's illness made it mandatory that he also visit Sweetwater, but the truth of the matter was he never really needed an excuse to travel. Arnold just loved to be on the road. This propensity Wade saw as a family trait and one to exploit. Of his in-laws, he often remarked, "Them Roses are a different breed and none of 'em can sit still for more than five minutes at a time. Why, by Ned, I think they're all just a bunch of gypsies."

"Keith would've been a lot better off if he'd just died," Arnold opined while fingering his lips and chin. He gazed at Edith through eyes that reflected brown pools of deep sadness. "I'm not sure he even knows what his name is, and he don't act one bit like he used to. Poor little feller's a stranger to me and I can't stand to be around him. Why it's the pitifullest thing you ever saw."

Astute as ever, Edith discerned the real reason for his trip was the fact that in times of crisis, Arnold simply could not abide being around those he cared for. "Well, he's got to be some better, because for a long time there he was completely out of it. According to what Alice wrote, he couldn't even get up to eat or use the toilet by his-self. I realize, though, and I think we all do, he'll probably never be out and on his own again."

Nothing but small talk ensued until she felt comfortable enough to tell him about the previous day. During her recount of events, Arnold's gaze shifted to somewhere beyond the ceiling; he seemed fixed on a notion. When finally she stopped, he pulled back one side of his leather jacket to reveal a pearl handled revolver. A few moments later, after making certain she knew how to fire it, he placed an even dozen shells along side of it on the table.

Before Edith would allow him to leave, she asked if he knew anything about a family secret that Keith might have mentioned. His puzzled look was not exactly what she was looking for, that and the big belly laugh, which accompanied his resounding "No."

"You're not talking about the little scrap he got his-self into, are you?"

She felt chagrined for even bringing up the subject. "I have no idea what you're talking about?"

Sensing frustration, Arnold offered a little more. "Oh it was nothing; Keith got his-self into a fight with somebody there at work. They said it happened maybe a few days before he got sick. Not much to it I don't reckon. But that brings something else up, though. What do you think about the Earl Akers' case?"

"I don't know a thing in the world about that either," she said without enthusiasm.

Well, it's getting to be a big thing down there. If you think for a minute or two you'll remember it. They found Kathleen's brother murdered about a week after Keith got sick; probably about the time you arrived. I never met the man myself, but Keith talked about him all the time." Arnold spun his story while spinning the empty cylinder-chamber of the weapon. "Recently, they let it out that Earl was actually an undercover agent for the Revenue Department, trying break up a bootlegging ring. Unfortunately, nobody's been arrested yet for the killing." Suddenly, his wrist snapped the pistol shut; it, too, could speak the words of death. "I talked to Willard the other day and he said Hester was sick over it. Earl, you see, was her preacher."

Edith bit her lower lip, while moving her head slowly back and forth. She still looked mystified. "Oh, I think maybe I heard something about it before I left. At the time, though, with Keith so bad off, and not knowing anything about him, I guess it just didn't sink in." *Hmm-m, So, I'll bet he was the other feller in the dream, then.* She reasoned. *The grapevines, though...I wonder now what role they play in all this.*

Five days later, the sound of a truck obviously attempting to park in front of the house interrupted supper. Wade, never one given to wondering, left the table immediately to investigate. Moments later muffled voices from outside were heard drifting back. Jesse quickly decided he too should make a presence, but first glanced at his mother for approval. It scared him to see how pale she looked. "Go see who it is, and then hurry back," she whispered huskily.

CHAPTER 8

A tall, angular man, probably in his fifties, with gray-brown hair and a prominent facial scar stood talking with Wade. He had one foot planted squarely on the porch, with his knee bent just right to provide a prop for his elbow to rest on. The two were so engaged in conversation, that they hardly noticed Jesse when he joined them. The talk sounded serious, yet both remained respectfully amiable. However, Jesse soon detected that something was terribly amiss and did not like what he heard. Mike was not in the picture; in fact, had not been since the stranger arrived. Perhaps most perplexing of all, though, was the sound of whimpering that came from beneath the porch.

"Edith!" Wade yelled. "Come out here, I want you to meet Mister Sharpe, he says he owns this dog."

When Edith stepped to the door, it was with a look similar to that demonstrated when she picked up the butcher knife. Sharpe never met her gaze, preferring rather to mouth his amenities to the ground. "Pleased to meet you Mrs. Gernon, I sure do hate bothering you folks like this, but Art Cochran said y'all might have my dog."

"Vincent here knows Mike," Wade explained affably. "Described him down to a tee, even told me how he got them big scars. Said he is probably the best bear dog in western North Carolina and that he got him as a pup. "

"Yes, Ma'am, more than once I've been offered a hundred dollars for that dog, but as bad as I need the money, it wouldn't touch him," Vincent sounded like a braggart, and Edith hated that in anybody. "Yeah, I raised old Red from a pup and thought I'd lost him after that big bear fight. Got ripped wide open, so we left him out in the mountains for dead, but you know about two weeks later that, the pitiful Son-of-gun come a dragging in. Down to nothing but skin and bones, he was. Yes sir, by Gravy, he'd pulled through on his own!" At this, Mr. Sharpe looked under the floor and tsked his tongue several times, "Come on out of there you red devil! Come on, Boy, let's go home!" Mike's answer was a low growl. Cracks in the porch floor allowed only dim filtered light, yet it was enough for Jesse to see a flash of ivory fangs. "You'd better come on, or I'll get my rope and drag you out!" Vincent said, on his way to the truck.

Once he was out of earshot, Edith turned to Wade; "I ought to get my pistol and put this low-life on his way," she breathed hatred. "You know as well as I do, Mike don't want to go and I've always heard that possession of anything is nine-tenths of the law."

"My Lord, Edith, I hate to say this but that dog is his'n, and you can't shoot a man for claiming what he owns. Just watch the way Mike acts, he knows him. Heck, you've treated Mike so good that he don't know who he belongs to. So let's just settle down now and don't start something over this."

First Jesse, and then his mother began coaxing Mike to come out on his own. They didn't want to see him dragged out, so by the time Mr. Sharpe returned the dog was in hand. However, Mike did not greet Vincent with enthusiasm. In fact, his tail stayed tucked and he gave another low growl when the leash changed hands. "Hush up, Red! Or I'll fix you good when we get home… Now be quiet!"

For the first time Edith spoke directly to Vincent. "He likes to be called Mike, not Red, because that's his name. Now you may own him, Mr. Sharpe, but he really belongs to me. Even if you kept him a hundred years, he'd still be mine." With that, she reached down to pet Mike for the last time. Her tears rained down on the dog's head, causing him to look up with eyes that seemed to say, "Don't worry, I'll be back." Unable to watch him go, she turned toward the house as they drove away.

Later that evening, husband and wife lay side-by-side and talked late into the night. "I just can't understand it, Wade, he was so happy here. Why do you reckon the good Lord let that old Vincent Sharpe find him, anyway? You know as well as I do, he won't be good to him. I just keep thinking that if we'd only stayed away from the rolling store, or if Art Cochran had kept his big mouth shut, then none of this would've happened."

"Ah Lord, Edith, I don't know why things happen the way they do. Maybe its like Pop says; the devil takes care of his own while the Lord just ignores His."

Well, I'm beginning to believe that every time something good happens, you can expect something bad to be right behind it."

"Honey, if you keep talking like that it's going to make us both blue, so let's just change the subject to something better. You know we need to be awful grateful for what we have; like them little young'ins in there. We ought to be thankful for one another, too. Let me tell you how pretty you are!"

"Hmmph," she snorted. "Wade Gernon, I know exactly what subject you want to change this to, and you ain't near as smart as you think you are, Buster!"

Two days later, it was early in the morning when a familiar bark sounded from the front porch. Mae screamed at the sight of him; he stood grinning at the door when Edith rushed to open it. Mike looked gaunt, yet his eyes were brightly beaming. A short piece of chain still clung to his collar that obviously had snapped during the escape. They all knew the visit would be a short one, but decided to make the most of it anyway. They dedicated the entire day to Mike and he enjoyed every minute of it, by romping, and playing with Jesse, tumbling Mae all over the yard and just adoring Edith. Sure enough, at sunset Vincent Sharpe's truck pulled up in front of the house again. This time Mike went away for good. The last word they got of him came several months later in November. Even Wade seemed distressed at the story, "Don't mention a word of this to Jesse and Mae," he whispered, "but Mike got killed last week. A big bear cornered him up against a cliff and he died in the fight. Made me sick to hear how Vincent Sharpe bragged that at least he got his-self another bear. I couldn't help remembering how lucky it was that Mike just happened to be here when you needed him."

Edith's soulful response was bitter; "Wade, he didn't just happen to be here and luck had nothing to do with it! You know as well as I do that Mike was here for a purpose. He was the only dog I ever had and there'll never be another'n like him."

One of the immutable laws of Mother Nature is that she does not long abide a vacuum. Thus, only a few days after Mr. Sharpe took Mike away the second time, Jesse found himself another dog to play with. Buck actually belonged to Jim and he, too, had survived many a bear fight. A huge black and tan, he had sired most of the younger mongrels that roamed Sweetwater, a feat that endeared him to nobody. Jesse, however, liked him and he liked Jesse. The two became inseparable during the early days of spring that year.

The experiential process of buying space with the currency of time turns out to be not so much a transaction as it is a journey. Of the many pleasures to be realized, on this the grand tour, are those unanticipated vistas that invariably pop up along the way. Adding luster and color to the landscape, they also engender enough wonder about what lies over the hilltop or around the next curve, to make life truly worth the living. One never knows what a new day may bring, a lesson well learned by Jesse on the morning of April 15, 1940. Awakening somewhat later than usual, he crawled out of bed in a bad mood. He felt he had a perfect right to be cross, considering that his daddy had never made it to bed the night before. Slipping on a pair of overalls, he stormed out of the bedroom determined to have it out, once and for all. However, two surprises awaited him in the front room; one was to find a bed there with his mother in it. Wade rushed forward to announce the other, "Jamup, I want you to meet Max, your new brother. Last night old Doc Cranford brought us a big baby boy; said we could keep him too, by golly!"

It would be no exaggeration to claim that the backwash from a hummingbird could easily have blown Jesse over. Edith smiled sweetly, and then pulled the cover back enough to reveal a tiny, squirming bundle of red arms and legs. Jesse edged closer to peer down; it was as if he expected an alligator to jump out at him. Though still feeling a little sore headed, he was willing to gaze for a moment at this object that suddenly had become the center of everybody's attention. Admittedly, he lacked experience in judging babies, yet he failed to see anything remarkable here. He saw nothing remarkable that is, until the baby opened his eyes and looked deep into Jesse's soul. From that instant forward he became remarkable. Jesse loved his brother immediately and it seemed as if he always had, after that, he could never imagine what life was like without him.

Late that evening another unexpected vista hove into view when Winnie Shelton showed up. This blond and buxom eighteen-year-old would be a live-in, hired to do the housework while Edith recuperated. At the time, ten days of bed rest were mandatory for all mothers following childbirth, and it was a custom rigidly kept. In a matter of hours, Winnie had a little lamb and everywhere that Winnie went, Jesse was sure to go. He followed her around all day, and was her little man. Jesse was in love. No chore was too menial or too ignoble to dissuade him. The one thing he liked doing best was to help her hang the diapers. Watching them flutter on the line reminded him of snow-white angels spreading their wings in the wind.

Jesse was not the only one to be surprised that day in mid April. Yet, unlike him, when Mae drifted in, she at once accepted the fact of having a new brother. His sudden and mysterious appearing seemed to her just another thing to happen. Rushing over to the bed, she jerked back the cover and began cooing at this marvel of love. In a moment of curiosity, she touched his face and giggled. The sight of his dimpled chin set her off. "Here, let me have him," she demanded.

Edith carefully re-arranged the newborn by pulling him a little closer. Her hand shook from exhaustion, yet it was tender as she stroked Mae's hair. "Honey, Max is too little right now to be handled, but when he gets bigger you'll be able to help out a lot then." This did not satisfy Mae, however, for the moment she was content just to gaze and wonder at the face of a miracle. Surely, he must have fallen right out of the sky.

Wade scrambled eggs and fried wheat flitters for breakfast, but this caused quite a stir. The house, already in a dither, now took on an air of frivolity. Jesse could not get over seeing his daddy scurry around the kitchen, trying hard not to burn everything. Mae enthusiastically joined her mother in jocularity by calling him "Miss Gernon, their maid." The teasing continued until "Miss Gernon" gruffly put an end to it. "Now wait just a dad-burn minute here, by Ned, this thing's getting out of hand. I try to help out a little bit and this is the thanks I get, being made fun of."

"Young'ins," Edith chided. "Your daddy's been awful good to us this morning, it ain't easy on him trying to fix breakfast and act like a two-year-old at the same time."

Winnie took exemplary care of the Gernons, but the days seemed to fly by in a twinkle. One morning Jesse caught her packing to go home. His love for Winnie had grown deeply during the ten days, and she had grown fond of him too. Obviously, he resented the fact of her leaving. Edith had mixed feelings; she saw the humor in her son suffering from his first case of puppy love. Yet she also felt a little jealous at watching him draw close to another "mother." Her dilemma did not last very long, however, for Jesse's world came to a sudden and catastrophic end. It happened at the hour of her departure when he discovered that Winnie had a husband. To make matters even worse, he also learned that they, too, were expecting a baby. Doctor Cranford would bring it in just a few months. That did it! Edith watched as he, now disillusioned and bitter, tore around the house before slamming the door on his way outside. She bit back laughter at seeing a lot of Wade and Dave in him. *Maybe it's best I just* let *him blow off a little steam, he'll settle down.* Meantime, an awful storm began to rage in the backyard; the sky darkened, loud cursing and banging sounds all contributed to the din. *Surely, this is about over with,* she winced, but in fact it was not. That is when she heard a loud, hurt-filled yelp. Looking out the window, she saw Buck running for his life amid a hail of rocks. He seemed frantic to get away as he headed for home. The dog had made the mistake of trying to reach out to a friend, but his reward was a blow to the backside by a three-foot piece of two by four. Amazingly, within seconds after getting a taste of the hickory tea Edith served him, the storm abated.

Later that day, he learned the good news; Ma was coming to stay for a few months. Ma was Edith's mother, Ella, who liked to spend time each year with as many of her children as she could. Because of Jesse's impatience, Edith had resisted sharing this with him until now. Her belief that it might help him get over Winnie proved to be correct, for a broken heart needs more than time to heal, it also needs love and understanding. Jesse's grandmother had lots of both.

She came in on the afternoon mail, arriving three weeks and two days after Max was born, with here suitcase strapped to the top of Ed Jennings' car. He had placed it there so that the trunk would be available for extra seating space. His '37 Chevrolet not only delivered the mail, but it also provided taxi service. "Ellie, I'm really glad to see you back," he said. The permanent flush of his face matched well a head of sandy-red hair that was just beginning to thin.

"I told Edith, the Lord's willing and if nothing happened, I'd be here right after the baby came. I guess you heard about Keith, didn't you?"

"I did, Ellie, and felt awful sorry about it too, but I've got to hurry now, have to be in Stecoah by five o'clock and I'm already running late. Maybe you can tell me about him the next time."

Once she saw him, Ma was captivated with Max, and quietly set about tending to needs that really required little or no attention. Holding him close, she silently sent up a prayer of dedication. Fascinated, Jesse looked at her face and that of his little brother in the afternoon sun; they seemed to glow in the glory of the moment.

When it was time to unpack, she handed out the presents; to Jesse she gave a cowboy shirt with pants and boots to match. He thought it was Christmas again. However, when Ma presented Mae with a pair of white lace-up shoes and a blue print dress, she was not quite so impressed. Mae let Ma know right away her displeasure by refusing the gifts.

"Now what about a young'in like that," Ma shook her head in disbelief. "If she could ever learn to appreciate things the way little Jesse does, I'd be able to treat her better. You know Edith, Mae won't let you be good to her. Now I aimed on buying her a pair of boots too, but they did not have any her size. She is awful rebellious, and you'd better try to get a handle on her and the sooner the better!"

Meanwhile, Ma unconsciously reached down to draw Jesse a little closer to her side.

At suppertime Ma flew in to help, she prepared a pan of candid sweet potatoes, and then set the table. Edith, meantime, patted out the dumplings to go with the chicken, now cooked to near doneness. A pan of large brown biscuits all but floated out of the oven to make room for the peach cobbler.

Ma finished chopping up a head of cabbage, using it to make her specialty: a tangy, sweet, and salty vinegar slaw.

Wade did not care much for that, but lived for the chicken and dumplings. Stepping through the door, he made straight for Max and woke him up; this after Ma had just gotten him to sleep. Looking sheepish, he turned around to greet his mother-in-law and subject her to a little kidding. "By golly, Ellie, I'm glad to see you made 'er in! Still wearing that same old apron, I see... You will, I reckon, right up to the Pearly Gates."

Edith had heard enough. "Well, at least she'll be welcome there! But if you ever come in here waking up that youngun again, you're liable to end up at the other place, before your time."

With chicken for supper, it would take a lot more than talk like that to discourage Wade. Once finished, the beautiful spring evening with it soft warm breezes filled him with wanderlust, so he abruptly decided to go pay Grandma Gernon a visit. Edith thought it was a good idea, and suggested that he take Jesse and Mae along, too. She had questions to ask and privacy would certainly insure a better discussion.

They were barely alone before Edith began. "Arnold tells me that Keith ain't a bit better off now than he was, and that he'll never get over it. Another thing, too, what ever happened to Kathleen Akers? It seems to me she's just dropped off the face of the earth. You know I only met her the one time there at the hospital, and I guess that was either right before, or right after her brother was murdered."

Ma looked bewildered, not knowing where to start, "Well, you know how Arnold is! Why he ain't been to see Keith but once, and I'm not sure he even went into the room then. Oh, he's definitely give up on Keith alright; he did that right away, so don't pay no attention to him... And as far as Kathleen, well she had been just about living at he hospital until Earl was murdered, but I reckon after that she just couldn't take it any longer. So, if you met her, it had to have been right before he died, she didn't come back after that. Losing him and you may just as well say Keith, too, was probably more than she could stand."

Edith nodded sympathetically. "I hate now I felt the way I did about her, but I was afraid Keith was about to make a bad mistake."

"We all were, but that's a thing of the past. ... Oh, you asked about where she was; well I really don't know, but Hester says she went off somewhere to live with her folks. I guess it was just too hard on her to stay there in Gastonia. "

"Well, what about the murder case? I've never heard the beat, and it worries me too, it being this close to the family and all. Keith knew something and I figure it must have involved what Earl was investigating." Edith said.

Ma seemed puzzled, but showed no interest in pursuing it. "For the longest time there, with us not knowing whether Keith would make it or not, nobody would mention Earl's death around him. They were such good friends," she added, shaking her head. Earl was two years older than Kathleen, and could really preach a good sermon. He'd become a pretty big evangelist and I'd listened to him a lot on the radio, especially after Hester made her change. He and that Preacher Claude Conway had been running a tent revival together. They were both awful good looking and about the same age. You may know of Claude, he grew up over on Painter Creek, but since he's been preaching there around Gastonia for several years, probably not."

"No, I've never heard of him, neither one as far as I know. At least, not before this happened."

"Well, they say he was murdered sometime around midnight and was left to lay there with his throat cut until the law found him. They'd been tipped off to watch for a load of whiskey to come in later that night, otherwise he wouldn't have been found until daylight or later. Whoever did it, though, took what little money he had on him along with a gold wristwatch. It was a brand new Bulova, he'd bought just a few days before. From what I hear, the law still has no idea who did it, but common sense tells you it had to be them old bootleggers."

"Why, of course it was, that just stands to reason. But you say they still have no suspects, huh?"

"From what we hear they don't, but really I don't know that much about it... Hester keeps up with it a lot more that I do. She was at the meeting that night, but she left early. This thing has just about got her killed. Why, she looks like somebody whose been hit by a freight train. She thought Earl was a saint and Claude, too. Why, she hardly ever missed a night going to the meetings and she's convinced that it's because of her conversion, that the Lord is giving her this baby. She's already had it dedicated to the Lord."

"Well, I know very little about such as that, especially before one's even born," Edith sounded skeptical. "But I'd been meaning to talk to you about her. I've never been able to get along much with Hester and I really don't know why. It just seems like there's always been this thing between us… and it bothers me. With the baby due in August, I just hope she ain't somehow got herself messed up in a murder case. This has got to be worrying Willard to death, ain't it?"

"If so, you'd never know it, not by the way he acts anyway. She said she left there early that night and that's about all she's ever told me. She won't talk much about the baby either, at least not to me. But I'm hoping for boy. You know, sometimes I think I may be partial toward the little fellers. I fear that nothing will ever be good enough for it though, not with them a wanting one for so long."

The conversation suddenly lost its steam allowing time for them to finish the dishes, wipe up the table, and toss out the dishwater. Edith then launched into what she considered was the main reason for their conversation. There's something I need to ask you about, but first let me tell you this." Briefly, she out-lined Keith's experience with the mysterious stranger in Asheville, and his subsequent refusal to share any of the secret with her. "He never mentioned anything like this to you, did he?"

Ma's look of perplexity led Edith to delve further into the details. This time she added the part about the poem with its prophetic overtones. And even though Ma had already heard it, she repeated the episode about the break-in attempt. "Something just now occurred to me," Edith scowled. "I might be crazy here, but you don't reckon all this is somehow tied in together do you? If so, then we've not seen the end of it yet, not by a long shot!"

"You never can tell, Edith, we just have to put everything in the hands of the good Lord. But as to what Keith knew, that sleeps in a mind that may never wake up. Along about the time he got sick, all he wanted to do was talk about Kathleen. I never saw a person so foolish over anybody in my life. That's a thing of the past, though, and he'll never get married." Ma lifted her apron to wipe carefully the lens of her glasses that suddenly had fogged up. "I've been grieving over something, Edith, something I need to say. You know we ain't supposed to worship anybody but God, and it worries me that Keith might have made an idol out of her. He could be eternally lost!"

"Oh, I don't believe that for a minute!" Edith shot back. Keith was just like anybody else in love. Why, what you're saying would mean he's being punished for using his free will, something we all do. And why would the Lord take his mind away for doing that? With it gone, how could he repent? No, it sounds to me like you're blaming God, and I thought that went against everything you believed in."

Ma looked hurt, "No, Edith, I don't blame God. I could never do that. And down deep I don't believe that about Keith, either, but as a mother I'm worried. I just pray that you never have to go through anything like this with one of yours. You know I place my trust in God. I believe that whatever may befall us, He's right there with us and in the end, He'll be fully justified. The book of Job says, 'Yea though ye slay me, still I will trust in thee.' In another place, it's written that 'man who is born of woman is of few days and full of trouble.' Someday He'll bring good out of all this, I just know He will!"

As with most conversations, the longer they persist the more apt they are to turn into gossip sessions. These two escaped such a fate when the wandering trio returned home earlier than expected.

"What's wrong?" Edith asked, seeing Mae in Wade's arms.

"Ah Lord, Edith," he defended, "they've been working in them old bees again. Jim had about a dozen swarms today and Mae got stung. Her little eye is swole shut, but Grandma put some Bruton's snuff on it. She's about quit crying now. I'll swear to God, though, I can't stand to see her hurt like this. But you know she hardly made a whimper. Mae's just like me Edith, tough'ern a pine knot, that poor little thing is. I just wish it had been me instead of her." Planting a big kiss on his daughter's forehead, he handed her over to the mother.

Carefully, Edith inspected the swelling. "Well, for crying out loud I ought to have known better than to let you two go together. If anybody's going to get stung around here it's bound to be Mae." Turning to Ma, she continued to scold. "I'll bet you anything she's stuck her head right down in one of them bee-hives and Wade let her do it, too. He don't know a thing about raising young'ins."

Tilting back her head to take advantage of the bifocal, Ma peered at her granddaughter; one brilliant blue eye, now magnified, glared back at her. "Why, Edith it ain't Wade's fault and they ain't one bit of need in blaming him over it. Now let's just be thankful that little Jesse here didn't get stung, too. I'll go get my snuff and put a pinch of that on her; Old Dominion is a lot stronger than Bruton's."

Once satisfied that things were under control, Wade felt comfortable enough to wonder about the leftover chicken. "You don't reckon there might be a bite of that and some of the dumplings still here, do you?"

Next morning early found Ma tending to Max. He smiled and she saw heaven open up, he cried, but when she held him close, he stopped and the hand of God touched her heart. Ma loved "little Ikie;" as she called him; this after his great-grandfather Isaac Rose, and anytime she sat in the rocker without him, Jesse and Mae were there vying for her lap and begging for Bible stories. Their favorite was David and Goliath with the one about Noah's ark a close second. However, when she told them about Jesus she always cried. Not wishing to see her sad, they did not ask to have those repeated. This caused Ma to misunderstand their motive and it worried her to no end, thinking that she might have failed in her attempt to portray Him properly. Truly, the great Desire of her soul was the "Desire of all nations."

When the last Saturday in May rolled around, it proved to be a high time for the family because Wade had the day off. By ten o'clock, everybody had made it outside; Ma, on the front porch rocking Max; Wade and Edith tilling the garden, while Jesse and Mae ran amok in the yard. As the temperature rose, so did their spirits and Edith did not seem to mind it too much, as long as they stayed put. Sunlight gilded the firmament, the air was laden with song from a hundred bluebirds, and the heady scent of lilac accompanied their every lilting note. Sweetwater was aglow and Heaven must have looked on with envy. Such, perhaps, until Jesse and Mae decided that playing in the garden would be a lot more fun than the yard. They had trampled over only a few hills of beans before Edith put an end to the magic of this incredible morning.

"If I catch you two back in here again I'll bust them butts, now you get back in the yard, and stay there."

'My Lord, Edith, you're being a way too hard on 'em again, they just wanted to help. Besides, have you forgotten how much you liked to play when you'as a little girl?"

That started it off and before long husband and wife were not speaking, Mae was wearing Jesse's cowboy boots, Jesse sent Buck, who had wandered by, on his way home under a hail of rocks, and Max now had the colic.

Tranquility finally returned, however, this time but for a season.

Jesse was in the backyard when he heard it, an awful grinding sound he would never forget. Instantly, he realized that something terrible was happening, and yet he felt too afraid to move. In a trice, he came to realize the existence of death without understanding its meaning. Adding to this dismay was the blare of a car horn that sounded precisely like the prelude to a never-ending opus. By then, however, he had made it to the front, where he saw that his daddy was already there. Wade had jumped a four-foot high fence and was now nearing the front of a big green car parked sideways in the road. A still smoking, but motionless brand new Oldsmobile sat turned and pointed straight at the house. Beneath its front bumper, looking surreal and out of place, lay a head of platinum-blond hair.

CHAPTER 9

The driver, Mr. Walt DeHan, slowly opened his door; however, just one-step was all he could take before collapsing. Wade, now at Mae's side, had been far from silent in getting there. Screaming her name, he was at once both praying to God for mercy and cursing himself for being such a negligent parent. Later he would come to realize there is a Power that is always in control, One who hears, understands, and forgives, for He also knows what it means to lose a child. At this time, however, Mae was Wade's only thought, and she greeted him spitting like a cat. It seems the car had bumped with just enough force to topple her over, yet leaving not a single mark on her. Edith quickly satisfied herself that Mae was all right, while remaining completely oblivious to the sight of Wade emptying out his stomach into the ditch line. Meanwhile, Mr. DeHan, now deathly pale, had made it back to his feet and was wobbling toward the house.

They all moved to the porch where they could recount the moment of horror, over and again, to one another. Mae had dashed out of the yard and into the road, running directly into the path of Mr. DeHan's automobile. He had been out enjoying the morning too, taking a ride in his new Olds and was traveling about 35 miles an hour when it happened. All he could clearly recall was seeing a tiny slip of humanity streak across his view. Obviously, he had reacted to such an exigency in the same manner that any septuagenarian would have, but not today, however. He had no explanation for it, but he had responded to the emergency in a manner that reached well beyond his normal abilities. Here he was, one moment coasting along without a care in the world, and the next finding himself parked sideways in the road.

Jesse and Ma headed for the spring to get a bucket of water and that is when they realized Mae was missing, and immediately perceived it to be cause for concern. Edith feared that she could have sustained emotional harm, so once again they felt s dark tide sweeping them along. Jesse quickly ran to the backyard where he checked both the toilet and barn. Several uneasy minutes must yet pass before finally, and on her on, Mae emerged from the car. Mad as fire over the fuss, she merely saw the big Olds as an opportunity to climb inside and pretend that she could drive. Once matters had settled down again, however, she wanted to know where the pretty girl was, the one who had shoved her out of the way. Not having the foggiest idea what she was talking about, they reasoned that the scare probably had somehow befuddled her thinking.

Ma stayed through the Fourth of July when Alice, Edith's sister, and her husband Nathan Pinkerton, came in for the holiday. They drove up in their year old Chevrolet. This handsome, but narcissistic couple made quite a pair; both were spiffy dressers that demanded the full circle of spotlight on whatever stage they graced. Alice brought mixed news about Keith; he was now out of the hospital, yet the doctors said he would always require close supervision. He had, as termed by the neurologists, permanent amnesia. Only a limited amount of memory reconstruction would occur and that to be over a period of years. Yet, they warned the family, he probably would never be able to recall certain details about his past life. They were not to press him to do so, either. From that time forward, the family would always refer to his illness as, "Keith's amnesia."

Nate and Alice stayed just one night and that was more than enough for Wade. Edith loved her sister dearly, that being with good cause for, although Alice truly doted on all her family, Edith was her favorite. They being the same size, Alice brought boxes of clothes along. She had worn many of the dresses only once or not at all. The two giggled like teenagers while Edith tried them on, prancing around and pretending to be a model at a style show. After listening to about an hour of it, Wade decided to display some style of his own by giving them a good look at his grumpy side.

"Can't a man get just a little rest around here? And Edith, I'd like to know where in the devil you think you can wear clothes like that to, here on the head of Sweetwater?"

"You keep acting the way you are, Buster, and I'll wear this black 'un to your funeral." She threatened.

Wade was not so much perturbed over their antics, as he was at having to put up with Nate. He had never liked this brother-in-law anyway, but now that he owned a new Chevrolet, all pretenses were off. He was not rude to his guest, but he was not slapping any backs either. Edith, early on noticed the coolness, "I'd be ashamed, if I'as you, acting this way around my people. After all, they just come in once in a while."

"Edith I don't mind Ellie being here, not one bit in the world or Alice either, for that matter. But that old Shivalay driver in there, I can't stand the looks of him. I'll put up with your people anytime they want to come, and you know it's the truth. After awhile, though, by Ned it's like the old song says, 'Just one Rose will do.'"

Pointedly, he then nodded in her direction; "And a rose by any other name still smells like a rose."

"Yeah, and a Gernon by any other name still smells like a fart-blossom, too!" she added without missing a beat.

After Ma left with the Pinkertons, Edith did not hear from her again until she wrote announcing the birth of Willard and Hester's baby. Claude Earl was a big red headed boy. He weighed nearly eight pounds and was so large that it nearly killed Hester to have him. Being in labor for over forty-eight hours, she had to remain hospitalized for seventeen days. However, the new mother was undaunted. She claimed that the Lord had performed yet another miracle by bringing a new soldier into the world that was already battle hardened. Much care, she averred, had gone into the selection of his name by remembering the two preachers that made it all possible. She also was quick to remind those who would listen that Claude Earl was an anointed child; this while likening herself unto Hannah, the mother of Samuel in the Bible. True to Ma's prediction, soon after his birth Willard and Hester vowed that nothing would ever be too good for Claude Earl.

As the year, 1940, wore on, Jesse, Mae, and Max all grew, both in stature and in favor with their parents. Christmas came with three stockings on the wall, and as usual were hung there with great care. Thus, it would be until the time was long past when none would be there at all. Again, Wade knew better than to protest bringing in a tree. Actually, it seems that both the tradition and spirit of the season had finally won him over. Unlike the year before, they spent Christmas Eve without company, except for a very brief visit from Santa.

Naturally, he left a few toys under the tree, but mostly he fetched them some much-needed clothing. Edith, having already been well taken care of by Alice, got very little extra; Wade, however, fared quite nicely, receiving new slippers, a shirt, pants, and a heavy dress coat; all good enough for church wear. The children each got two complete outfits and a new pair of shoes.

Christmas Day dawned cold and sunny, despite the fact that earlier in the week three inches of snow had fallen. However, the winter weather had departed with such alacrity that now only a few scattered patches of white still remained. After donning their new clothes and enjoying a sumptuous repast, they all seemed eager to go out visiting.

Grandma stood waiting at her front door to greet them; she had spotted them coming up the hill. Grabbing Max, she pulled him up close while railing against Jim for not having a bigger fire going in the fireplace. Jim detested chopping firewood almost as much as he did repairing footbridges and normally would keep no more than a few sticks on hand at a time. Wade, though, loved to cut wood and immediately set about enlarging the pile.

After an hour of making the chips fly, he had racked up several days worth, then wasted no time in getting a big fire roaring. "Wade is so much like his granddaddy!" Grandma exulted, knowing this was exactly what he wanted to hear. However, she was prepared to show her gratitude in a more tangible way and did so by inviting them back to the dining room. There a tall walnut cupboard, known by generations to be the ultimate treasure trove of spicy and delectable morsels, held her delicious stacked fruitcake. At once, she proceeded to slice them off several generous servings.

Since daylight hours in winter are short, an early end to their visit was inevitable. Grandma bid a reluctant farewell, and then watched from her porch as they made their way slowly back down the hill and out of sight. The sun was just about to set, but not without leaving a few warm reminders behind, spots that clung to its dying rays. It was near the milk gap, in one such place, where the little family paused.

Jesse looked up to gaze at the huge tawny, bronze colored thunderheads that hovered low on the horizon. He turned then to see his parents move silently together and embrace. Just a simple expression of love between husband and wife, between a man and a woman, yet it preceded a remarkable event. For it was then, at the end of a day set apart to celebrate the Nativity, that Heaven chose to give earth another gift. Unseen but felt, celestial agencies watched Wade lift Mae astride his shoulders and pull Jesse closer to his side, Edith held Max snug up against her breast. In the flickering wink of a star, an eternity passed and the world stood still. Suddenly the sky became a shining jewel, a ruby that slowly transformed, kaleidoscope-like, into a soft mother-of-pearl hue. When Providence smiles all of creation is set aglow, this time in flaming colors of pink and magenta.

Mortals are made of perishable material and cannot long stand at the portals of eternity. On occasion, however, Omnipotence shields them long enough to get a glimpse of the Promised Land. Such happened to the family of Wade and Edith on Christmas Day, 1940; and it may well be they gazed upon that selfsame paradise which beckons to us all. Incredibly, they knew not what had happened; they only felt their love deepen for one another. This had been a good day in the life of a happy family.

Another New Year lay just ahead, one that would see an end to the old order and the beginning of America at war. Had they known what awaited them they might well have trembled at the prospect, but then perhaps not, for could it be they knew that angels were watching over them?

***

We are passengers on the river and the river is unfathomable, never stopping it moves with relentless speed. At once both dark and vexing yet majestically awesome, it is a gift from God. We are bound to the river, going where it goes and we can never turn back or move forward faster than the river flows. All else is altered, but the river never changes. Passengers come and go and someday we, too, must leave the river, yet it will go on; for time is the river and it goes on forever.

Kyle Reece was born a year and five months before Jesse, yet he seemed much older. While this was apparent to others, it was even more evident to Jesse, for Kyle was bigger and wiser than he with sparkling brown eyes that looked as old as time itself. Kyle and Jesse thrived on each other, playing all day long without a word of dissent. When outdoors together, they roamed the fields and hillsides for hours, never letting the cold of rain or fog spoil their walk. The hauntingly beautiful pictures that Kyle painted for Jesse about his sister Bonnie stayed in the minds of them both. She was about twenty months older than Kyle was, but died with rheumatic fever at the age of five. He told how, before getting sick, she would climb the apple tree in their backyard at twilight and talk to the stars about their mother, who had died just a year before. There, with her arms stretched toward heaven, Bonnie would beg to be with her, and so, it happened.

The first time Jesse ever saw Kyle was just after Clark and Lorraine's visit to Sweetwater. He lived with his father Joe and four older sisters Marie, Arlene,

Selma, and Anita in their house at the head of the creek. Built on Cherokee land, it was the last one up before reaching Stecoah Gap. Kyle was the apple of his daddy's eye and frequently accompanied him on neighborhood jaunts, as well as trips into town. It was a Saturday afternoon, late in January and around three o'clock when the pair showed up at the Gernon's front door. They were on their way home from Robbinsville, having just walked the two miles from Stumpy's store where their ride had terminated. Since it was such a cold and blustery day, a few minutes before the fire would feel good. Joe was Edith's first cousin and they enjoyed visiting with one another anytime it was possible. Kyle had a full box of Moon Pies and after only a few minutes together, was willing to share one with his newly discovered cousin. While the two had liked each other instantly, after this magnanimous gesture their friendship was sealed. Sitting in Jesse's bedroom, they told each other wonderful stories. Kyle, it turned out, was a great hunter and angler, while Jesse claimed to be a master at riding the tricycle. Soon, however, Jesse found himself completely enthralled by his adventuresome new pal and his bear hunting exploits.

A few months later Joe and Kyle came by on their way to Dave's house; it was after a little persuasion that Edith let Jesse go along, too. While eager to encourage the boys' friendship, the potential for misadventure by their elders was a legitimate worry to have. Joe and Dave, lifelong friends, always enjoyed having a few good nips anytime they got together. The rub came, however, in getting them to leave it at just a few.

The day got off to a great start when Mom treated both boys to a biscuit with jelly and butter. After that, Frank got the ball to rolling by naming several games they might play. Jean wanted to be included too, and since it was warm and sunny their horizons knew no bounds. After about an hour of follow-the-leader, hide-and-seek, and softball, their enthusiasm was beginning wane until Frank suggested a horse biscuit fight. Immediately, that became the game of choice for everybody, but Jean. Her attitude bewildered them when she declined to participate, claiming that slinging manure at one another did not sound much like fun. Such a view confirmed their perspective that girls were not much fun either. However, even this sport soon lost its glamour once the combatants ran out of dry ammunition. Forced now to hurl freshly dropped rounds at each other, a once classy adventure suddenly turned into dirty warfare.

Mary was appalled at what she saw and banned the trio from her house until they scrubbed up. She pointed to the spring branch, and then handed each a bar of lye soap. Ice water, they quickly learned, is hard to bathe in without freezing to death. Next, she gave them some of Frank's old clothes, then they stood, blue and shivering, behind the kitchen stove trying to warm up. It felt luxurious there, almost hypnotic, enough to make them drowsy. To stay awake, they helped her "look" the pinto beans in preparation for cooking. For more than one reason they felt lucky that she had built a big fire to put them on.

Meanwhile, Dave and Joe had found their way up to Charlie's, but were back now and enjoying another drop of his finest. "By dog, Joe," Dave laughed, "these boys still smell like horse crap to me. Don't you think we ought to put their clothes out there in the garden? They'd make dandy fertilize?"

"Well, that'd do a whole lot more good than this crap you're spreading." Joe said. The laconic answer came as a surprise to his drinking partner.

"What the heck you talking about, Joe… Hah! I know," He laughed. "You're just mad 'cause I said Billy Conn is going to whup old Joe Lewis' tail for him. He'll do 'er, too, and I'd put money on it. You just come back down here and listen to it with me on that little Philco over there." Dave pointed toward his battery set next to the window. Attached to it was a one hundred foot aerial that gave the radio excellent reception.

"Foot, I ain't got no money to bet with, and you ain't neither. But you're wrong this time David, Billy Conn is good as whupped. The minute he steps in the ring with the Brown Bomber it's all over with. You saw what he did to Max Schmelling… knocked him out in the first round; now, Son, reach me that bottle over here again." Joe was proud that he and the world's heavyweight champion shared Native American blood. However, the name Schmelling he spat out as if it left a bad taste in his mouth. A veteran of the Great War, it was his way of expressing contempt for the "Bosch," who had mustard gassed him in the Argonne. It left his lungs damaged beyond repair.

Matters quickly returned to joviality as the two old friends sought more common ground to plow; this time, however, in fields less rocky. Frank and Kyle played together making bows and arrows from willow branches and last years weed patch. Jesse preferred playing with Jean in her playhouse, where she had some old pots and pans, and of course a toy tea set. They played and fantasized quietly beneath the bowers of a sassafras grove with branches that swayed gently in the spring breeze. Had they listened, they might have heard a few of the secrets told by the Druids of old, and still trilled in the lyrics of every songbird.

"The friends of my childhood again are before me.
Each step wakes a memory as freely I roam.
With soft whispers laden, its leaves rustle o'er me.
The ash grove, the ash grove, alone is my home."

Jesse would never hear this traditional Welch melody without feeling some of the music that lilted his heart on that bewitching day so long ago.

The afternoon passed on the wings of a zephyr, bringing in its wake a rapidly approaching weather front that drove them inside. There they found Dave and Joe had finally achieved their ultimate goal of getting dog drunk. In fact, they had passed out, irking Kyle to no end. He tried first one and then the other to awake them from their stupor, yet without success. Jesse's final memory of that day was one of seeing Kyle sitting astride Joe, patting his face, and trying to arouse him. Frank got Jesse home just before dark and barely in time to save an angry mother from "coming to get him."

The next morning dawned blustery and overcast with Edith being surprised at seeing Joe and Kyle out so early. They wanted to stop by for just a moment on their way home, but neither looked very happy. The father had a bad headache, could not hear out of his left ear, and felt dizzy. The son had nothing to say and in general, acted sore headed. Interestingly, Edith learned that neither Joe nor Dave could hear out of their left ear; both seemed to be suffering with many of the same symptoms.

"That ought to be a lesson to you for messing with that old stuff, why it's going to kill you both. I hear tell lots of folks are sick from drinking bad whiskey that's coming in here from somewhere. You don't reckon you got a hold of some of that, do you?"

"No, I don't drink anything but the best; what Charlie Ammons makes is all I'll ever touch." Joe hoped to head off another lecture; he just wished whiskey came at the same price as advice. "It feels like a big plug of wax is stuck in my ear making it hurt like heck. Mary heated up some salt water to use. It seemed like it helped right after we put a few drops in, so the minute we get home I'll do it again."

Edith watched the two make their way up the mountain; she was worried they would not get home before the weather turned worse. Nothing further was heard until the next morning when Ray came in, saying that Dave had suffered the whole night through with a bad earache; that, despite having using heat and frequent applications of warm salt water. He still was no better and needed to borrow some aspirin, along with a little whiskey, if Wade had any. Edith readily supplied the aspirin, but knew nothing about having alcohol. Later that day Joe's daughters, Marie and Arlene, came to the door with much the same story. They all were beginning to get worried.

"If I was you, I'd get Doctor Cranford to take a look at him; this thing seems awful strange to me. He and Dave both got this way right after drinking that old whiskey. They said it come from off of Beach Creek, but they ain't no telling what was in it," she admonished.

CHAPTER 10

Another day came and went without either showing any improvement, in fact the dizziness waxed worse after they spiked a fever. When vomiting ensued, both families realized it was time to act. Together, they hired Nathan Gernon to take them to Doctor Cranford's office, but once there both men needed help in getting to the second floor suite. The doctor was just beginning to see his first slate of afternoon patients, so they had to wait for over an hour before he could get to them. Doctor Cranford was in the early stages of Parkinson's, an affliction that eventually caused him severe symptoms. Even now, it was beginning to limit his ability to work through patients swiftly.

"My gosh, what've you got in there?" he bellowed, while extracting a chunk of evil looking matter from Dave's ear.

"I don't know, Doc, but I sure feel's a lot better now that it's out."

He repeated the procedure for Joe, giving him the same quick relief, but it left both men looking at each other mystified. Then the good doctor did an analysis.

"Well I'll be, would you look at that," he laughed unceremoniously. "Somebody's planted pinto beans in your ears and they swelled up, looks like they've even tried to sprout. Tell you what; if there was anything in there besides muddy water, they'd a grown, too."

Much talk and conjecture accompanied the trip home, but no real answer was immediately forthcoming. Both felt victimized, yet really did not know where to turn. Mary reminded Dave that she had fixed pintos the day before his troubles began; only Jesse remembered seeing Kyle positioned over their heads, and he was not talking.

For two years, Jesse and Kyle walked together before their paths led them in different directions. Kyle was a born leader. Cherokee blood and its deep spiritual roots had bonded with a Scottish nature to create within him the gift of extraordinary insight. This he displayed many times over as the two would peradventure upon animal habitats, fishing holes, old trails and other facets of existing as well as past life. Jesse admired this ability in Kyle, such that he never once felt jealous about it.

Kyle had a brown leather aviator cap, the type popular right after Pearl Harbor. It closely replicated the original with a chinstrap and goggles. However, this item of dress almost cost them their friendship, for it was one thing they never shared. Jesse once asked Kyle to let him wear it; but in the face of an abrupt refusal, he never brought the subject up again. From that time forward, the easy camaraderie they once shared no longer existed. The two remained close, yet it was not the same. Jesse took from the experience, never to trade a priceless gift for a trifle of material wealth. He feared, upon reflection, that perhaps earlier he had unwittingly committed a similar offense and this was mere repayment for an act of his own insensitivity.

When Joe Reece died, it left Kyle orphaned at an early and tender age. Subsequently, he moved to Cherokee to live. After that, his trips back to Sweetwater were limited to only an occasional brief visit. And most of those occurred during their early teenage years with their old friendship never rekindling. The next time they had a real encounter was on the gridiron field. In high school, Kyle became an outstanding quarterback for Cherokee. Standing over six feet two and tipping the scales at nearly two hundred pounds, he was the star of the team.

Jesse, much smaller in size, had not yet made first string, but looked forward to playing against his illustrious cousin. Soon after the game began, things were looking bad for the home team of Robbinsville. Kyle, almost single-handedly, was winning the contest by rushing over top of and past players of inferior ability. He scored one touchdown and was well on his way to another, when the right tackle on the defending team left the field injured. In desperation, Robbinsville's coach looked around for another victim. He had already lost several of his best and now must seek talent from the ranks of the untried. Jesse could hardly believe his good fortune when the finger pointed directly at him. "Son, get in there and plug up that hole; their big quarterback is making us look like a bunch of first graders"

This little pep talk was all Jesse needed, his head felt light, but he was not certain whether that came from excitement or fear. The next play came straight at him and he threw all all 150 pounds he carried right at his cousin to bring him down at the line of scrimmage. The finding that Kyle, too, was but mortal surprised no one more than it did Jesse. Ultimately, the contest ended with Cherokee taking it, 7 to 0. Jesse stopped Kyle every time by repeating the same performance, over and again.

After the game, an ecstatic coaching staff met Jesse on the field, telling him he had just made first team. He played against many clubs after that, but not one, in his estimation, had a player with the star quality of Kyle. With very little help from his teammates, he had beaten Robbinsville on their home court. There was one thing, however, that bothered Jesse, and it did so for many years. After the first two or three tackles, he looked into those familiar brown eyes and said, "Hey, Kyle, I'm Jesse your cousin!" In response, not a flicker of recognition occurred and this hurt Jesse far more than any head-on collision they had during that night of play.

Only in maturity could Jesse come to understand just how much Kyle had been forced to give up during those short few years. In dealing with such severe losses he, no doubt, had blocked out certain, nonessential, memories. Obviously, he could not allow himself to reflect on events taken from this extremely painful era of his life. They never saw each other again, but Jesse always asked about him when he talked to family members or with mutual friends. Kyle passed away while only in his early sixties, and after Jesse learned of it, he espoused a hope. Perhaps they, on another and better journey, might get together and ride part way again on the river, as once they did before.

***

The weather turned unusually warm for January and remained that way until the last week of the month. Jesse overheard his daddy talking with Dave after supper one night, "Pop, what did the weatherman say?"

"A cold front is passing through the mid-West and they expect temperatures here to drop down to around zero tomorrow night. It'll stay cold then for several days, so I think maybe in the morning would to be a good time."

Wade needed only a second to decide. "That settles 'er then, by Ned, I'll take tomorrow off and we'll butcher him."

Such news did not set well with Jesse. He had watched their Yorkshire grow from a tiny piglet into a huge porker that now weighed in excess of 300 pounds.

Meanwhile, he had become more and more attached to the animal. One great pleasure he had was to slop the hog. Jesse enjoyed listening to Ben slurp his way down to the bottom of the trough, eating to his heart's content. Neither he nor Ben seemed to realize that this was all according to plan and the quickest route to an early demise.

Next morning, before daylight, Dave arrived with his .22 rifle. It was much against Edith's advice that Jesse accompanied the men out into the frosty dawn. Wade, though, felt it would be good for him. "Let him grow up a little, Edith, he has to learn sooner or later."

However, it troubled Jesse to know the answer even before he asked; "Dave are you going to shoot Ben?"

"Yeah, Son, I am, but just think about all that good meat we're going to get. I bet a dollar you'll eat your weight in them good backbones and ribs before it gets dark tonight. You remember that big mess of tenderloin I brought down here last fall, don't you. Well, we'll have ourselves a lot more of that after while." None of this helped to ease Jesse's apprehension, yet the bitter cold now seemed hardly noticeable. When the dreaded crack of the rifle sounded, he nearly died along with Ben. Listening to hooves beat against the sty planking, trying to recapture a life now fleeting away left him feeling weak and shaken. However, his reaction to all this was far milder than the one exhibited by Max a few years later. At that hog killing, he pitched such a fit that they were still talking about it fifty years later. From the moment he learned what was up, Max began to protest. Had he been able to get a gun, a slaughter would have taken place all right, but not the hog's. That time when the rifle sounded, they heard him scream all the way to Grandma's, a good quarter mile away. After that, the practice of butchering would never be the same, or be considered as just another part of farm life by the Gernon family.

This day, however, the ugly business of meat production ran according to protocol. Once bled, they cleaned carcass of hair by pouring near boiling water through burlap sacks onto the hide. This combination of heat and water loosened up the bristle so that the smelly job of scraping could begin. With that accomplished, a gambrel stick helped to hoist the hog upside down for intestine and organ removal. Meanwhile, Grandma Gernon, cane in hand, had made her way to the backyard where she was warmly greeted by everyone except Dave. Having participated in many hundreds of hog killings, her help was essential. When it came to processing meat, Grandma knew exactly how and what to do. Trimming the fat from entrails for lard rendering, mixing herbs, and spices for sausage, preparing the head for souse meat, on, and on, leaving very little for waste.

Jesse and Mae got the bladder after she cleaned and washed it thoroughly. Then in a manner dating back to time immemorial, she used a hollow reed to fill the structure with air. After two days of drying, they would have themselves a large balloon to play with. Her presence made all the difference in helping Jesse feel a little better about losing Ben. Yet, no one would ever know how it took the shadows to hide his tears at feeding time that night.

Following a very long and bitterly fought battle, spring finally emerged as the clear victor over winter. Mountain laurel was quick to celebrate the peace by bursting into bloom on every hilltop and ridge. Willard, Hester, and Claude Earl were fortunate, indeed, that their trip coincided with such a splendid show. They arrived late Friday evening, driving up in a new Dodge. Mae, riding Jesse's tricycle across the porch, was the first to spot their car as it pulled into the yard. Several days earlier Hester had written to expect them, but the news received mixed feelings; while Edith looked forward to Willard's visit, she dreaded even the thought of Hester. Of course, the opportunity to see Claude Earl excited her. Sentiments, however, ran almost counter for Wade, he loved to flirt with Hester, but Willard's tendency to boast always intimidated him. He would reserve judgment about Claude Earl until he saw him.

Three long honks on the horn gave official notice that they had arrived. Before the sound died, however, Mae was already at the car. Willard looked so much like Keith that she greeted him like a long lost friend. This pleased him so much that instantly she became a favorite, but Hester was not nearly so impressed. Extracting herself from the back, she carefully helped the ten-month-old out of a seat they had shared for nearly two hundred miles. Mae reached for Claude Earl, demanding to get a better look. "Here, let me take him," she insisted.

"Let's get a few things straight right now, Young Lady, you're to keep your hands off this baby. He ain't used to being around young'ins, and I don't want him catching something either."

Willard did not like what he heard. "Hester, the child just wants to see her new cousin, and as far as I know she ain't got nothing to catch; unlike some others I know of."

"Are you throwing off on my family? If you are, then we'll just turn right back around and go home. I don't intend to be run over here just because you happen to be with Edith and think she'll take your side."

Edith and Jesse were right behind Mae in getting there, but not in time to hear the exchange.

Without bothering to ask, Hester quickly laid claim to Jesse's bedroom, proceeding then to instruct Willard exactly where she wanted the baby bed placed. On her way in she glared at Max, now just past his first birthday, to whisper another word of warning. He, too, was to keep his distance from her precious prodigy. Fortunately, Edith remained oblivious to all this; else the visit would have been a short one indeed. "Little fellow's awful sensitive to everything," Hester yelled over his wailing. "Just knowing he was headed for the sticks, got his little bowels to acting up. You know don't you Edith, it's a miracle that we've got him."

Edith stretched high on tiptoe in an attempt to get a glimpse of a face that now looked about as red as his flaming hair. "I can't tell who he favors," she confessed.

"Well, of course he looks just like his daddy, who else would he favor?" Such a hateful reply caught Edith by surprise, but she quickly recovered.

"Hester, I know this may sound awfully strange, but I never noticed Willard's red hair before. The ice in her voice chilled the air.

Hester immediately changed her tune. "Oh, I'm sorry, Edith; I really didn't mean to give you a short answer. It's just that this little fellow has got me worried to death with his diarrhea. That beautiful red hair comes from my side. You know, not all us Carters are black headed. Take my sister Marilyn, her hair's the color as corn syrup. If you look close at Claude Earl, though, you'll see he's the spitting image of his daddy. Oh, I'm so proud of him." Smoke brown eyes swept over her son in a gentle caress; a doting mother cherishing her beloved's tiny frame. "You wouldn't happen to have a few extra diapers would you? We've used up most of his getting here."

Having spent much the afternoon preparing for the visit, Edith had supper just about ready to serve. The night before Wade had caught a fryer and cooped it up behind the back steps so that it would be handy when needed. Jesse and Mae had watched anxiously as Edith placed the pullet's neck on a chopping block where, with one smooth swing of the axe, she put an end to the squawking. They wondered how anything could still move and flop around like that after its head was gone. Interestingly, for the time being at least, they both lost all taste for chicken. Wade, however, was ready to eat the moment he stepped through the door, but his first comment was to pay homage to a new car. "I see some folks have moved up in the world. A big new Dodge, well they're a whale of lot better automobile than them old Shivalays, I'll say that."

Willard beamed with pride. "Well, I'm not one to brag here, but, yeah, I got promoted to first shift supervisor two months ago and you know Hester there, she talked me into it. By George, though, it does make going to work in the mornings a lot easier. We're thinking now about a new house, too, just as soon as we find one big enough. But boys, I'll tell you what, them fellas there at Firestone are eat up with jealously. By the way, I'm looking for a few good hands; I couldn't talk you into going to work for me, could I?" Suddenly, Wade looked like somebody who had just let one the table. Grinning broadly, Willard acted as if he knew exactly who it was.

The main entrée was so good that not a single piece of chicken remained. Even Jesse and Mae forgot about the great sacrifice made on their behalf. Edith's biscuits and gravy were the crowning touch, until her blackberry cobbler arrived. After liberally sprinkling the dough with sugar and lacing it with copious amounts of butter, the oven had brought it to a toasty brown. Hester's eyes looked big as saucers when she sweetly purred at Wade: "Honey, would you puh-leese pass me some of that goo-od looking cobba-lah over heah?" Edith nearly gagged. So exaggerated was this southern drawl. She not only lost her taste for pie, but her sentiments toward the whole Confederate cause also suffered.

Wade, still a little edgy over his conversation with Willard, suddenly perked up. "By golly now you're talking, Scarlet, but cobbler ain't the only good looking thing around here. A pretty little belle like you could make the South rise again!"

"Puddin," Edith mewed softly, with a touch of the old south clinging like Spanish moss to her syrupy-sweet voice. "Now, don't you pay no mind to Rhett heah. Yes, he's all heart, but it's harder than a rat turd and just as black." She sounded so pleasant that no one noticed her shoe deftly removing two inches of hide from Wade's shinbone, doing it with the same smooth motion she used to decapitate the meal's main entree.

Hester received a polite refusal after offering to help with the dishes. Pleased to be off the hook, she left quickly to be with Claude Earl. Meanwhile, Wade and Willard moved outside to look at the car with Jesse tagging along. "Tomorrow, we'll give her a try at high-gearing the mountain, if you think she's up to it," Wade challenged.

"Oh, this Dodge will flatten that mountain, Son, they ain't no doubt about it. Yeah, I've got to go to Tuskegee tomorrow evening, but we'll take her up to gap in the morning." He spoke with a lot more confidence than Wade wanted to hear.

Back in the house, it did not take long before the conversation turned to Keith.

"Ella still has to take care of him like a baby." Hester offered.

"Yeah, but he's lot better now than he was this time last year," Willard added.

Edith felt somewhat uncertain as to how best to bring up the subject of Keith's secret, so she moved warily up to the water's edge before tossing out a line. "Before he got sick Keith was troubled over something, but I guess now we'll never know what it was."

Willard's eyes darted for Hester only to find hers waiting on him. Edith missed nothing. It was just a nibble, yet an expert angler knows that it takes a lot of patience to make a catch.

Reeling back in, she cast further out into the deep by asking about Kathleen. She hoped her lure would not drift too far into the shallow waters of gossip. Hester, however, had very little news to share. Wade then asked about Earl, wanting to know about any progress in the case.

"Well, they have two suspects. A pair that Hester knows, and I may have seen 'em too, but just don't remember it. According to what everybody says, they come by the hospital while Keith was there."

The daggers that Hester shot caused Willard to grimace noticeably. "Oh Lord," she moaned, "I hate to talk about this stuff; it gives me a sick-headache every time I do. But yes, I am acquainted with Lance Boyle and Guy Fowler both...not too well, though. They worked for the evangelistic team, off and on for years, however, that was from behind the scenes. Actually, I guess you could say they were part-time employees. Now, while I don't have much use for either one, I still find it hard to believe they did it."

"I don't see why!" Willard exclaimed. "I wouldn't be protecting a bunch of bootleggers, if it were me."

"Well, you're not me, so let's just leave it at that," she replied softly.

"Tell Wade and Edith your part," he nodded deliberately.

Slowly and gingerly, she lifted from her bodice a lacy handkerchief to blot away the tears that suddenly had welled up in both eyes. Seconds passed while she stared at the ceiling, then compressing her lips she blinked twice more before speaking. "Well, on the night it happened I left the meeting early. Actually, it was just as soon as the preaching was over, and that was probably around ten past nine.

Usually I hung around for a while, but since I hadn't feel well that day I decided to go on home. The only reason I'd gone in the first place was because they'd planned on having a special prayer for Keith, and I didn't want to miss that. I'd been on the bus for just a few minutes when I noticed that it had started to drizzle rain. It had looked like it would all afternoon so naturally, I'd taken my umbrella along, but when I reached for it, it wasn't there. I realized then that I'd probably left it at the meeting, so at the next stop I exchanged buses and headed back.

"In hindsight now I realize that the extra hour this took was probably not worth it and that I should've just let it go, but I didn't. See, the umbrella was a special Christmas present from Willard and I was afraid if I didn't go back, it might be gone for good. Well, anyway, when I got there most everybody had left. I did notice, though, Lance's car and Earl's too; both were sorta up and back behind the tent. So, I went on into the main auditorium, but liked to have never found my umbrella since all the lights were off.

"I could hear somebody talking, but at first I couldn't understand a word they said. I could tell, though, it came from back behind the podium, that place I call the Holy of Holies. So by moving up and listening closely, it was obvious they were working on something, and by then I had figured it out; Guy and Lance were cutting canvas to make signs for the upcoming meetings. I could hear Earl talking, too, but not wanting to bother anybody I just turned around and left without letting them know I was there.

"I figured on catching the next bus out and since I had been there only a few minutes I knew it would be by at 10:40. I'd barely made it down to the stop, however, before Claude drove up. Said he'd just dropped a member off and would take me home too; it was on his way. He allowed that Earl and the others were about done and would be leaving pretty soon, so he'd probably just get in the way."

Edith looked thoughtful. "I hate to stop you, but I need to know what those two look like?"

"Who? ...Oh you mean Guy and Lance. Well, Guy Fowler is blond-headed with an eye that turns in. I guess you could say he's probably about thirty. Lance Boyle is a little older than that, maybe ten years; he's black headed and has buckteeth with several missing."

"Well, I may just know who they are then," Edith said. "I wonder if they've tried to break in on anybody else besides me," she added caustically.

"Do what?" Wade looked shocked.

"Just something I figure," Edith replied. "But we'll talk about that later."

Willard was following things closely, but felt it was time to get matters back on track. "Hester, I remember you telling about going back to the tent, but this is the first I've heard about anybody still being there. Who knows, it could be something the law needs to hear about, too." Turning then to his hosts, he continued; "Oh, by the way, they've never found the murder weapon yet, but think maybe it's one of them big switchblades. They even had the Boy Scouts out combing through the weeds, but so far nothing has turned up."

"What about the wristwatch, any leads there?" While Wade directed his question toward Willard, his eyes never left Hester.

Willard nodded grimly. "Yeah, that watch is what they picked them fellers up on. According to the papers, they caught Guy Fowler wearing it around. He claims to have bought it from Earl a day or two before the murder. Several witnesses, though, have come forward to say that Earl had it on the night he preached his last sermon. They had to let 'em go though, with no more than that they didn't have a case. Until a weapon is found and they can tie it to one of them; that or other evidence comes forward, they can't be brought to trial. From what I hear, though, there may be enough that Earl collected on 'em to file bootlegging charges; them and another feller or two.

"The meetings had been used as a cover, and when you stop to think about it that made a perfect set-up. Then having those two working there as odd jobbers was just icing on the cake. Somebody or other tipped off the Feds, and that's when they got Earl involved. It's a good thing they got him and not the other feller though; Claude Conway, in my opinion, is just another crook. But you'd never convince Hester of that. Actually, I wouldn't be a bit surprised to find out that he was one of the bootleggers, too. There ain't nothing that man is past doing, even up to the point of taking Earl out."

"They, Willard Rose! You know better than that!" Hester aimed her finger at his face.

"Well, have it your way then, he sighed. But, from what we hear they've probably got the goods on those two for bootlegging. No doubt, they would have had more if Earl had lived. As I understand it, several people may have died from drinking the stuff they peddled. Earl gave his life trying to nail that bunch and I just hate to think they might get away with it."

"I guess it's alright now to tell this, don't you?" He asked, looking with an uncertain eye toward Hester. "I only learned about this myself, not long ago. But

Hester here, helped Earl with the investigation. If I'd known what was going on though, you'd better believe I'd have raised Cain over it."

"Now you're stepping over the line again, and that's going to get both of us in trouble!" Hester slowly shook her head back and forth before directing her next words toward the ceiling. "The man never knows when to stop running that mouth."

Turning back to Willard, she continued. "You know you shouldn't be talking about this, but now that you have, I need to explain it. Look, the main reason I waited to mention this to anybody was because I've been scared to death. It makes sense that whoever murdered Earl, wouldn't think twice about coming after me too. Especially, if they thought I'd helped him with the investigation. Why, I lived in fear for several months after it happened, and it was only here lately that I got nerve up enough to tell Willard about it. I figure now, though, they must realize that if I knew anything it would've already come out. But I still worry and will until this thing is finally settled."

"You were involved in this deeper than I thought," Willard peered at her suspiciously.

"Well, actually, I really didn't do that much. After Earl took me into his confidence, all he asked of me was to watch for anything that looked suspicious, but with two hundred or more people showing up every night I soon saw I was over my head. Of course, at the time, I had no idea that Guy and Lance were involved; I only learned that later. After about a month, he called it off, saying things were getting just too dangerous and that he wanted me to stop. Oh dear Lord what a tragedy, I just wish he'd got out of it too!"

Glistening great pearls of perspiration suddenly appeared on Hester's brow, perfectly accenting the ivory color she had just turned. "Excuse me," she uttered, and then dashed from the room. Willard was right behind her all the way into the yard, there to support her forehead while dry-heaves wracked her convulsing torso.

CHAPTER 11

Dawn broke, revealing a bloated band of dark-countenanced clouds that behaved like a bunch of leaky old men dribbling their way across the Appalachians. After a big breakfast, Wade was eager to put the Dodge to its test, but not Willard. This apparent lack of enthusiasm was a fact not lost on Wade. "I doubt she can do 'er, Son. Now don't take me wrong, you've got yourself a pretty car that's probably fine for the kind of driving you do around Gastonia, but here in the mountains it takes a V-8 like Ford makes."

"Ford's a cheap automobile, Wade; not in the class of a Dodge. No, I ain't one bit worried about it high-gearing the mountain."

"Well, by Ned, let's give 'er a try then. I figure it'll do just about as good as a Shivalay. Why, ever once in a while one of them can do it, too." Since the car was a sedan, Jesse and Mae found good seats in the back and after a few minutes of warm-up, Willard was ready. Hester and Edith stood watching from the porch as they sped by. For a change the two had something to agree on; the utter nonsense of it all. To them it was ridiculous, and who but a man would care whether an old car could somehow manage to wheeze and rattle its way to the top in a gear that was inappropriate, to start with. They found it absurd.

Still pale from the night before, Hester turned to her host with a question: "Besides high gearing the mountain, Edith, what else do the people here on Sweetwater do?"

"Ah-h Lord, it seems like a lot of our time is spent trying to teach folks from Gastonia a few manners," she answered matter-of-factly.

"I don't know for the life of me what to do, Edith! I try my best to get close, but you just won't let me. I get along fine with all my other sister-in-laws, but not you, so what's the matter?"

"It's hard to let a person get close when you expect them to stick a knife in your back, but it's like I always said if you want to have a friend, you've got to be one."

Claude Earl let out a loud wail, letting them know he needed a change. Later, without prompting, Hester brought up the subject of Keith. "Willard's still trying to find out who jumped on him… You know all about that don't you?"

"Are you talking about what happened before he got sick? All I heard was what Arnold told me, and he said that Keith had been in a 'little scrap,' but made it sound like there wasn't all that much to it."

"Well, Willard and Arnold decided to ask around about it, and what they learned was that a few days before Keith got sick, he took a beating. It happened there at the mill, back behind the building in that little alleyway. There were two of them, and they had his mouth and nose bleeding. Fortunately, a co-worker happened to come along about that time; otherwise, they might have killed him. The co-worker said they took something out of Keith's shirt pocket before taking off. Keith wouldn't talk about it, though, not to anybody."

"Oh my Lord, poor Keith, but who do you reckon it was? I guess nobody calld the law, did they? Assault and battery, not to mention robbery, is a serious matter."

"There's not a thing the law would do; they're all too crooked. Willard and Arnold both say they'll take care of it themselves. In my opinion, if anybody knows anything they're afraid to talk. I had Willard ask the doctors whether they thought this sort of thing might have caused Keith to get sick. One said he didn't think so; that was Doctor Blair, our regular doctor. But when the brain specialist heard about it he said, 'Why yes, definitely that kind of injury could very well have caused it.' Of course, that's all beside the point now, anyway. Keith will never get his mind back, and we all need to accept it."

Seething, it was all Edith could do to keep from slapping her. *Why you little snip! You could care less about Keith, and you know a lot more about all this than you're telling. But it will all come out in the end, you just wait and see!* She nodded silently.

Edith tried once again to talk about Keith's so-called secret.

"I have no idea what you're talking about!" Hester snapped, sounding indignant.

Uh-huh, Edith thought. *Touched a nerve didn't we?*

The crunch of gravel out front was the first indication that the car crew was back. The lack of celebration seemed somehow foreboding as they paraded single file through the front room. Disappointment hung so heavy that Hester rushed up to Willard and made a big fuss over putting her arms around him. "No, no, I don't need that," he brushed her off.

Edith was more direct at addressing the situation. "What's the matter, Wade, you look like somebody who just inhaled a fly," she laughed.

Mae gave the news. "Boys, you should have seen us a high gearing the mountain! Uncle Willard hollered just like Daddy does and he looked so funny!"

Edith shot a look at her husband, now seen moving quickly through the kitchen. "Where are you headed, Wade... you're not trying to *dodge* us, are you?"

"No, Edith, I've got chickens to feed, somebody around here has to do a little work once in a while." Jesse and Mae followed behind, finding that he had a lot more to do than anybody might have suspected. Enough that it kept him busy until Willard and Hester started loading up their car. Wade came around the side of the house to wish them well as they prepared to leave. It was the first time they spoke since reaching the gap. The visit had been an interesting one, indeed for just as their coming had stirred up mixed feelings, so, too, did the leaving. Wade seemed to be the one most affected, standing there looking long-faced as they drove away.

"Cheer-up, Rhett," Edith encouraged. "Just remember that tomorrow, after all, *is* another day."

***

Events of Sweetwater continued as much they had for most of Jesse's life until one Sunday in late August. Waking up earlier than usual, his thoughts returned immediately to the night before when he fell asleep still wondering why his daddy had not made it home. Such behavior was unlike him and as the evening waxed long, even Edith began to worry. In an effort to hide her concern, she made a pan of fudge while teasing Jesse about being so glum. She allowed him to stay up and listen to Amos and Andy on the radio. Laughing at Kingfish and his conniving antics helped to dispel some of the anxiety, yet he still felt uneasy at bedtime. Thinking back, he could vaguely recall a big commotion during the night, when a litany of accusatory questions and equally querulous replies cut through his fog of sleep. However, the mist had quickly thickened up again, leaving him stranded somewhere deep in the nether regions of unconsciousness. Later, the call of nature sent him hopping out of bed and toward the toilet. Since it was not quite daylight yet, he yielded to the temptation and just peed off the front porch. That is when a large dark object slowly began to take shape in the twilight gloom. Rubbing his eyes, he half expected to see it disappear, but when it did not, he made a beeline for the car. Wade had talked about one ever since Willard and Hester's visit, yet had received absolutely no support from the family. Derided and even called a dreamer, he eventually quit talking about it. This, however, was no dream staring back at Jesse; it was a Model-A Ford.

They had to pry Jesse loose from the steering wheel when it came time for breakfast and Wade just could not keep from bragging about the deal. "That old Ben Rogers," he exulted, "you've seen him Edith, a little wormy looking fella. Well, he eased up beside me and I could tell he was up to something by the way he kept blinking them eyes. You know how does when he gets nervous. Anyway, he finally got around to it, 'Wade,' he said, 'what would you give me for a good car? Times have been hard on me lately and I could make you a real deal.' Well knowing it was a good 'un, I just let him talk for awhile, acting like I really wasn't that interested. But when he got to squirming around and was about to leave, I ask him. 'Ben,' I said, 'what kind of money are we talking about here?' Well, he was ready for that and said that since it was a '31 model, he'd have to have a hundred and fifty. But I told him that was a way too much, that I could maybe see a hundred and ten. Now that got us started and after a good hour we finally settled on a hundred and thirty cash, but it all has to be paid within a week; cash on the barrel head."

Wade went on to explain that he subsequently took the afternoon off to make a trip to the bank. They, he quickly learned, would finance up to a hundred dollars, *if* he could get two co-signers. Bill Morrow immediately volunteered and today they would make a trip to Stecoah, where he would ask Lloyd Christy too, for help. Not only was Lloyd Wade's uncle by marriage, he, also, was his hero.

Edith was not so much concerned about getting co-signers as she was in meeting fifteen-dollar payments each month. Wade begged to differ. "My goodness, Sugar, we're already paying out half that much right now by having to hire us a way everywhere we go. Talk is that the TVA is getting ready to build a big dam over at Fontana. Now they pay you good money, and from what I hear, they're ready to take on just about anybody wanting a job. But by golly I'll tell you what; you just let old Wade worry about making the payments."

That is what she did, and from the moment he put pen to paper the fretting began. Edith refused to give him comfort, not from a mean spirit, but merely being firm and resolute. Fact was, he paid off the loan two months early and never once was late at meeting his obligations.

This day, however, continued to be one for the books, not only did the Model-A high gear the mountain, "It pulled 'er humming like a sewing machine right through the gap," Wade bragged. They arrived at the Christy's about two o'clock that afternoon. Wade had wanted to leave earlier and get some of his aunt Lydia's cooking, but Edith wouldn't hear of it. "Wade,' she said, "we ain't barging in on them like that! They're cultured folks and we can't go in there acting like a bunch of heathens."

Lydia's cooking skills were legendary, matched only by the elegance of her table. She scolded them soundly for not being there earlier. "My land," the velvety-soft voice of a lady exclaimed, "I told Lloyd at dinner today I had fixed all this food, hoping somebody would come home with us from church. But, you know, not a single soul did. Of course, it was just us then. Now, you say you've already eat! Well, the next time I expect you to come and eat with us!" Her snow-white hair, a beautiful living cameo, nodded in unison to each word.

To Jesse their house was a mansion. Lloyd was a master carpenter and had built this impressive two-story structure with his own hands. Six bedrooms, hardwood flooring, French doors, and an elegant curved staircase, however, the building's most salient feature was a massive stone fireplace with its walnut mantle piece. It held a huge clock with Roman numerals that announced the time around the world by chiming every half hour. Such affluence caused Jesse to spend most of his time wondering how anybody could be so rich. Lloyd too, made a great impression on Jesse. As the archetype of a Scottish chieftain, his fierce piercing eyes peered out from beneath a heavy set of brushy brows. No one ever stood in the presence of Lloyd Christy without recognizing that here was a man of bearing. Nor was it possible to doubt, after speaking with him, that he was not a man of his word. Lloyd served with valor in the Great War, bringing home many memories of incredible experiences, yet rarely would he share these with anyone until World War II started. After that, it was only in the hope his experiences might somehow benefit another comrade-in-arms.

Getting his signature was but a matter for the asking. The balance of the afternoon slowly evolved into a time of pleasant conversation. Lydia, always the consummate homemaker, considered baking to be her forte. Possessing an artistic flair, she was in constant demand for weddings and other special occasions. Her greatest delight, however, was sharing this talent with family and friends. Evidence of this was the delicious dessert she served her guests before they left for home, and except for Jesse, they were happily content crossing back over the mountain. Unfortunately, he felt a little sick, and yet was afraid to let on. *I hope,* he thought, while struggling with his conscience; *this ain't God punishing me for sneaking another piece of that coconut cake. Them other two were awful small.*

Wade and Edith sat quietly enjoying the ride while listening to the motor purr. They had no way of knowing what pivotal role the car was about to play in their marriage.

The next Sunday morning found them all at church. Heretofore, both the distance and the weather had made such trips so difficult, they were limited to just a few each year. Wade sported a new Stetson and looked sharp in the dress pants and shirt he got for Christmas. Mae and Max looked like twins, dressed in their color coordinated blue and white summer outfits. Edith was stunning in a print dress Alice had picked out with her in mind. Only Jesse felt self-conscious about his apparel, but that was because he had trouble keeping his pants up. With hips virtually non-existent, trying to support trousers designed for wearing without a belt, proved a most daunting task. This became especially difficult after both buttons pulled loose from their shirt attachment. He wondered what people thought, seeing him walk around with the front of his britches all wadded up. Turning loose, however, was not an option, so he kept a tight grip on things. Fortunately, Edith finally noticed his dilemma and tried to help by pinning his pants to the shirt. She only had one large safety pin, however, and while that helped to keep the front up, it still did not prevent the back from sagging. He resorted to bunching up one side and holding on there, but kept bumping into people with his elbow. One kindly person inquired about appendicitis, prompting Jesse to switch sides, but by the time Sunday school was over his spasm-wracked hand hurt like the toothache. When at last the final "Amen" sounded, he beat everybody out the door to go racing for the car.

Not everyone experienced such a bad time, however. After church, Wade and Edith paired up with Jack and Fannie Woodcock. This couple, a little older than the Gernons, was friendly and seemed delighted at the chance to have new blood circulating through the church-body. While the two men were somewhat acquainted, neither Wade nor Edith had met Fannie before. She came from Hanging Dog, a community near Murphy. The Woodcocks' two daughters, Ann and Mary, were both in early adolescence, while Carl, their only son, was about Jesse's age. Jack was self-employed and in the past had worked mostly out of town. Lately, however, he was spending more and more of his time at home. They lived in a nice house on Pin Hook, some four miles distant from the Gernons. However, by using an old mountain trail that passed just above Orr Branch road it was possible to take a short cut. The walk was easy to make and usually took about thirty minutes.

Standing around, the new friends talked for what seemed like hours to Jesse, with everybody but him having a big time. Mae and Carl showed out by running circles around the car, squealing, and laughing. It was enough to make one sick. He thought the nonsense would never end, but mercifully, it finally did. Unfortunately, for the rest of the day all he heard about was the Woodcocks, and to make matters worse his parents were the greatest offenders of all.

"You know," Wade chortled, "I like that old Jack, he's a real Ford man and did you hear the way Fannie bragged about our car? By golly, we might just have us some good friends here."

"Yes," Edith readily agreed, "they ain't no better place than church to meet people, and I hope you noticed how well behaved Carl was. Why, Mae and Max both just loved that boy to death, but not Jesse though, he acted like a sick cat or something. Sometimes I just don't understand that young'in."

O dear mortal must thou so soon forget
The many brave struggles others have met.
Grace with courage, unmarked, unknown
Pray then their fate be not thine own.

Church fellowship soon evolved into such close friendship between the couples that they began planning much of their lives around each other. So enthralled was Wade with the Woodcocks that he failed to notice it, when Edith slowly began to back away from the relationship. Indeed, a definite cooling on her part occurred immediately subsequent to two remarkable events. The first was when Addie Gernon, good wife to Dave's brother Charlie, took Edith aside. "How well do you and Wade know the Woodcocks?" She asked, not wasting words on customary greetings.

"Well, mostly just seeing them here at church, that and the few times we've had meals together. But why do you ask, is there something I ought to know?"

Addie let the question dangle in the warm autumn air long enough to look around to see if anybody else might be listening. Once satisfied they were alone, she continued. "Edith, you know I've never been one to pry or tell others what to do. However, Charlie and I have been watching you and Wade with those people and we decided to warn you about their reputation. They always seem to get very friendly with new members, visiting back and forth and making all kinds of to do over them. Then before you know it, that family breaks up. Now, I don't personally know that much about Fannie, some folks, though, say she's man-crazy. And there's a lot of talk that Jack makes moonshine whiskey; is a bootlegger and that he's in some kind of trouble with the law."

Edith was aghast. "Why, Addie, they've always acted like perfect Christians around us. Of all the time we've spent together I've never seen or heard a thing that's out of the way. But I'll tell you what; me and Wade will be watching things from here on; you can count on that!."

Addie smiled paternalistically, "I firmly believe in the Golden Rule, Edith, and can only hope that you might treat me the same way I have you. The Lord only knows our families needs all the help they can get, so keep in mind what I just told you. A word to the wise is sufficient and I felt it was my Christian duty to tell you."

The next incident followed close on the heels of the first, with events taking place much like those of a two-act play. Edith did not have long to wait before the second curtain slowly began to rise.

CHAPTER 12

All through the sermon, Edith's mind raced in review, yet she found nothing to support Addie's allegations. *Charlie and Addie are probably wrong about this,* she decided. *Why yes, I've seen Fannie, a time or two, studying Wade awful close, but that's just the way some women are. And,* she further conjectured, *as far as the other couples go, I'll bet anything their marriages were already on the brink. No,* she decided, *I need to see a lot more than this before I go around passing judgment on people.*

Right after church the usual crowd gathered in the parking lot to chat. Wade, ever the brilliant conversationalist, took the lead and soon had everybody's attention; everybody's that is except Edith's. Seeing others there, including the Woodcock's, she took Max and went on to the car. After that she had the task of herding Jesse and Mae into their seats. That's when Jack, quite unobtrusively, moved away from the group, and ambled up to where she stood. With his back to the crowd, an exaggerated grin widened his face when he asked; "What are we going to do with that Wade, anyhow? I'll bet he keeps you entertained all the time, don't he?" By the use of a much-practiced uplift to his brow, Jack's eyes suddenly blared and brightened. For the first time Edith noticed a lacy fine scar that tracked unevenly across most of his chin.

"That's only when he's got an audience," Edith sighed. "But yes, Wade *can* be a show-off… I reckon it could be worse though," she chuckled.

"My goodness, if I had me a woman like you I'd keep her entertained all the time... know what I mean?" With that, he reached over and used his forefinger to trace the letter "J" on her arm. To Edith the long, thick nail looked exactly like an eagle's talon.

A sudden chill swept through her body as she drew away from his reach. "No! –No! Don't you ever do that!" She shook her head angrily.

"Oh, no I'm sorry! They, Lord have mercy, Edith, I didn't mean a thing by that. There ain't nobody, and I mean nobody who I think more highly of than you and Wade. My goodness, I guess I thought we were all so close now that we could kid each other a little bit. You're not going to be mad at me are you? I swear to you I'm sorry about this, and it won't happen again… I promise you that. We can still be friends, can't we?"

Flustered and still angry she stammered, "I can take a joke as good as anybody, but make no mistake about it; I don't put up with funny business."

"Well, we're still good friends then," he laughed good-naturedly. "Tell you what; I'm planning on being home this next week, so I may just cut across the mountain and come by to see you folks one evening. I think we need to get together, more than just here at church, don't you? That way you don't leave the door open for misunderstandings. Yeah, I'll be over, so how about us looking forward to that?" His eyes blared again to brighten up what Edith would later refer to as a "crap-eating grin."

She pondered all the way home whether or not to mention the incident to Wade; that and Addie's admonition, but decided on both counts that keeping quiet made more sense. *Probably,* she thought. *I'm making a way too much over this. Why, I doubt I would have thought that much about it if Addie hadn't said what she did. No, I still need more proof than this before saying anything. Besides,* she mused. *Wade really likes Jack and Fannie.*

By Tuesday, she was feeling completely at ease with her decision. Meanwhile she had learned from Wade that Fannie was making them a quilt and wanted it to be a surprise Christmas present. However, Fannie's neighbor, Lexie Lane, had let the cat out of the bag. Wade swore to Lexie not to mention it to anybody, lest word get back to Fannie and ruin a good friendship.

October; a month designed, to give us a little glimpse for heaven, yet it has a mundane side also. Jesse loved watching long chorus lines of leaves go tripping along in the breezes, foolishly dancing to their own swansong. Edith saw it as an opportunity to dig potatoes and "holing them up" for winter.

Donning a hat after getting Max settled down for his nap, Edith assigned Jesse and Mae the job of keeping an eye on him while she went outside to work in the garden. Things went smoothly for over an hour until she oddly "felt" someone watching her. Looking up, she wiped her brow while her gaze drifted from the house to the road. That's when she saw Jack Woodcock standing there snickering.

"I wondered how long it'd take for you to notice," he said. Stepping over the low fence between them, he was still chuckling when he reached for her hoe. "Here," he said. "Let me help you with that. You know I just love digging taters, especially big old spuds like these. What kind of seed did you folks plant, anyhow? My goodness, I've never seen the beat!"

"Yeah, they're a sight all right; we plant half our crop in Sequoias and the other in Green Mountains. Wade claims it don't matter to him one way or the other, since he don't plan on eating none. That's the way the Gernons are, though; they all say that, but I'll tell you what, I've never seen one yet who couldn't put a peck away when they're put before 'em."

Edith rubbed the back of her neck, exhibiting a worried look. Known for not beating around the bush, her question went straight for mark. "But what are you doing here, anyhow? I thought you said you'd be coming over some evening. Wade won't be getting in much before dark, so you'd better leave and come back then."

"To tell you the truth, Honey, I'm glad he ain't here," Jack suggestively lifted his brow to blare his eyes. The habit was beginning to get on her nerves. Again, she noticed the scar on his chin; it now looked pink and raw. "You know," he continued, "ever since Sunday I ain't been able to sleep a wink. I can't get you off my mind. Why, just touching your arm was like a bolt of electricity running right through me. I figure you felt it, too, so I wanted to get over here and let us talk about it." At this, he gave a long, highly suggestive wink.

Without saying a word, Edith reached for her hoe back. "When I touch you up beside the head with this hoe handle, it may feel like a bolt of electricity, too, but I doubt you'll be going around talking about it. Bud, you've stepped over the line this time and I'm giving you exactly ten seconds to be on your way. When Wade Gernon hears about this; you won't have no trouble at all keeping me off your mind then, I can guarantee you that! Why, you ought to be ashamed of yourself; you've got a wife and them three little young'ins, and here you are acting like some peach-orchard boar." With that, she took a hard swing at him, but being quite nimble, Jack moved easily out of range.

Standing in the road, he felt safe enough there to smirk; "I wouldn't say nothing about this if I was you. They ain't nobody going to believe it, and you could just make Wade suspicious. He'll get to thinking that maybe you've been running around on him and that'll put an end to your marriage. I've seen it happen before!"

"I'll just bet you have, you sorry devil! Stay right where you are and I'll fix you!" Quickly, she disappeared into the house, where seconds later a .38 special flew from its roost atop the dish cabinet, to land squarely in her hands. It was to no avail; however, Jack was no longer around. To say that she was in a state of near hysteria would be putting it mildly; nervous laughter, mixed with tears, accompanied the gun's return to its nest. Overwhelmed and overwrought, Edith threw herself across the bed where she wept bitterly for nearly an hour. Not only did she feel betrayed, but now, more than ever, she felt conflicted; should she tell Wade or not? What Jack had suggested could very well come about. Perhaps it would be best, after all, just to remain quiet and hope to steer Wade away from this unfortunate relationship. Deep within she feared the day he found out. However, when and under what circumstances would that be? The answer to both questions would come a lot sooner than she expected.

Wade hardly had time to hang up his hat and jacket before Jesse ran to him with the day's most salient event. "Daddy, Jack was here and when he left, Mother cried." He liked being the first to deliver news.

"They, do what?" Wade asked, sounding a lot more than merely interested. He turned to Edith with a look that demanded an immediate answer.

"Why, Jesse, that's not what happened!" she said, smiling innocently. "Oh, I was out digging potaters when Jack stopped to talk for a minute. I reckon he stayed home this week and was over here for some reason or other. We talked there in the garden for a few minutes. But you know, right after that I got the awfulliest headache. I think maybe, it was from being out in the sun too long. I did cry a little bit after laying down, but directly got to feeling good enough to cook supper, so I'm all right now."

A look of relief accompanied Wade's next remark. "Well, I hate I missed old Jack, boy, he's a dandy!" Caution and doubt had just purchased a few days of peace; unfortunately, it would prove to be at the expense of their trust and relationship.

CHAPTER 13

"Looks like the Woodcocks are going to be eating high on the hog." Wade observed cheerfully. The sound of his high good humor was deceiving, however. He was dealing with guilt after purchasing an Orange Crush for himself. *That nickel could have bought the young'ins a bag of candy,* he thought.

"Would be if Stumpy here didn't charge so much," Fannie complained. "I really don't know what people are going to do if these prices keep going up. They're sky-high already and every time I come in here, he's gone up again. Why, these four little bags of groceries are going to cost me well over three dollars," she scowled, shaking her head sadly. Meanwhile, the storeowner had finished totaling up the cost.

"That'll be exactly three dollars and sixty-five cents, Mrs. Woodcock," he announced pleasantly.

"I'll need to have you add that to my bill, Mr. Adams; we'll try to put something on it by the first of the month." The tone of her voice matched exactly that of the merchant's.

"Yes, Ma'am," Stumpy replied, sounding flat, all the buoyancy of his former enthusiasm had fizzled out.

"Have you got you a way home with that?" Wade asked, sounding concerned.

"No, but Lord, I'm used to it. Why, many is the time I've walked that two miles up to the head of Pin Hook with a twenty-five pound bag of flour slung over my hip. You know, having Jack work away so much, I've learned how to be pretty shifty. You've got to be, if you're going to make it."

"Well, by Ned, let's just load up that old Ford out there and I'll have you there in ten minutes. We can all use a little help now and then."

The Model-A, created for roads like that of Pin Hook, rattled smoothly along the two miles of dirt track to get Fannie home in short order. She, however, appeared to be in no hurry to get out.

"Wade," she said, giving him her best Mona Lisa smile, "I feel like a princess, the way you treat me. I don't think I can remember anybody who's ever been quite this sweet to me before."

Laughing, he replied; "Why, my goodness, Fannie, this ain't nothing. There ain't a thing in this world I like doing better than to help somebody. I told Edith just the other day I'd give folks a ride anytime they needed one. I've seen a lot of times when I could have used one myself."

Fannie turned her next comment toward Edith. "I have often wondered if your wife really appreciates what she's got. It's a shame, but some women just can't see the forest for the trees and I've noticed she gets awful short with you at times."

Uh huh, Wade thought, *by golly other people have noticed it too, I've been right all along!* Although he felt affirmed, sharing such thoughts never entered his mind. "Well, Edith's a fine woman, Fannie, and a good mother, but like all couples we do see things a little different at times. I reckon, though, a fella ought to be thankful for what he's got."

"Now, ain't that the truth. You're a smart man, Wade Gernon, and I just sit in Sunday school sometimes, admiring the way you say things. I guess what with Edith growing up down there in Kannapolis, she just don't see things the way we do here. Yeah, I reckon it's the truth, us mountain folks *are* a little different."

"Yeah, we are," he agreed, "They's a whole lot of things I could tell you, but I don't like talking about a person behind their back. No, it's always best not to say too much."

"You're about the finest feller I know of, always thinking of others," she said, reaching over to rub his upper arm. "My goodness, what hard muscles," she admired. "Well, I've got to get in there now and cook up some supper for them lazy young'ins. You know, if Sonny would ever help out just a little bit when he's home, I could learn them girls how to cook and do some house work."

"Sonny? ...Who's Sonny?" Wade looked puzzled.

"Oh," she laughed, "that's Jack, it's what his family all call him; I'm sorry."

"Nah-h, that's okay, it's just I'd never heard him called that before. He grew up down around Lincolnton, didn't he?"

"Well, yes, but he was born right here in Graham County. Getting back to them no-good young'ins of mine though, ever bit of their raising is laid on me. I'll swear, Wade, he ain't worth killing half the time. Well, thank you for the ride and you'll never know how much this has meant to me. I really needed somebody I could just sit and talk to for a minute." With that, leaned over and pecked him on the cheek.

All the way home Fannie's words kept echoing through his mind. *She's right, by Ned; Edith does get awful smart with me at times. And I guess it is the truth, too, me and Edith are a lot different from one another. Thing is, and I'll never understand why, she just don't see my side of things the way Fannie does.*

Minutes later, he was home, but not in a mood to listen when Edith started giving him a rundown of the day's events. Almost immediately, however, she perceived his frame of mind and stopped talking. *He's tired,* she decided, *and that always makes him grouchy, so I'll just hush.*

Sunday morning found them back in church with Edith doing all she could to keep her family away from the Woodcocks. With Jack, it was easy, since they both knew the score and he kept his distance. Wade and Fannie, however, started chatting like two Magpies the instant they saw each other. Edith felt her hackles rise. *Watch him,* she thought, *always too tired to talk to me. Now though, you'd think he'd just run across a long-lost buddy, the way he's acting. But it'll just pay for me to keep my mouth shut, and maybe pretty soon he'll get the message.*

Confident her plan would work; she had no way of knowing that even then events were gaining the momentum to come roaring through their lives like a runaway train. Wade and Fannie were spending more and more time together and before long, he was at her house nearly every afternoon. Meantime, his and Edith's relationship continued to deteriorate. Nothing she did or said seemed to please him, and he could have cared less about the things she insisted on telling him every night. Paradoxically, the more she tried the more distant he became, making her try all the harder. Edith was in denial and at first merely ignored the storm warnings, but the waves kept washing higher and higher, while the skies continued to darken. Thus, when the first gale struck, it did so with fury.

On the Sunday morning following Thanksgiving, events were set into motion by Lexie Lane's whispered comment across the pew. "I hope you're keeping an eye on Fannie, Edith."

"No, I ain't, but why should I?"

"I really ought to keep my mouth shut here, but Wade's been spending an awful lot of time over there."

"Edith's face suddenly became a mirror that reflected anguish. "Say what? Oh that!" she laughed, surprised at her ability to act rational. "Just remember, Lexie, what they say about a wife being the last to know. But you need not worry there, Wade could beat that." Unfortunately, her words rang with a hollow sound.

"I hope one day I'll learn not to blab everything I know, but his car *has* been over there an awful lot lately. Let me ask you something, though, did he say anything about her making you a quilt?"

"Well yes, yes he did," Edith demurred, "but I've not mentioned it to anybody"

"Well, I was just thinking, maybe that's it, he's been over there helping her get it finished," she lied.

"Wade's has always been a way too good hearted for his own good. Every time I turn around, he's off helping somebody." The smile Edith flashed, said nothing about the way she felt.

Since it was between services, Wade was part of the great exodus that went outside for a smoke. When he returned to his seat beside her, Edith barely grunted at him. He mumbled something back, but it was unintelligible. She was glad not to talk right now anyway, not with such dire thoughts whirling like an eggbeater inside her head.

The next three days came and went without her addressing him directly, even once. Meanwhile, an enormous volcano was building pressure, making it evident that an eruption was imminent. Wade felt the tremors, yet he hoped the danger somehow would dissipate before an explosion occurred. Each morning he awoke hoping that he had his wife back again, warm and conversant, like before. Invariably, however, he found her belligerently silent and scowling. Finally, on Wednesday evening, right after getting in from work, he dealt with the problem directly and demanded to have some answers. "Edith, I want to know what the heck you've got your dander up about, anyway. You ain't spoke two civil words to me since Sunday and I'm getting tired of it."

The buildup of tension was so evident that Jesse, Mae, and Max all had sensed it, too. Now, they suddenly felt the shock waves of an explosion.

"You don't deserve two civil words, and you'll be lucky if I don't kick that sorry hind-end of yours off of Sweetwater!" With her chin thrust forward, Wade saw hell staring at him through two narrow slits that once were eyes. *My gosh, she looks just like Matt Rose standing there!* Many people considered Matt to be one of the meanest men ever raised in Graham County.

Max rushed to grab his mother's leg and started bawling like a calf; Jesse sobbed uncontrollably while Mae stood in the middle of the floor screaming. To their credit, the parents immediately realized what havoc they were wreaking and quickly agreed to settle things later. Implicit to this hastily called truce was a tacit understanding that neither party was giving way to the other.

Virtually thrown together, supper was a complete failure, serving only to complete the evening ritual and help propel events forward toward bedtime. They all retired early, but it was to no avail. The children fought the good fight, each believing that peace ultimately rested on their ability to stay awake. Fortunately, or perhaps unfortunately, the forces of sleep finally prevailed and sometime around midnight, their part of the battle was over. Such marked an end to the armistice, allowing then for the real war to begin. Two well-prepared antagonists quickly picked up their arms with the intention of really having a go at it.

Like goose down at feather-plucking time, accusations and denials quickly filled the air. At first, neither party heard much of what the other said, so intent were they at getting their point across. Moments later, however, they got down to the sober business of arguing. That level of disagreement, unfortunately, soon deteriorated to one of name-calling before the quality of conflict dropped yet another notch. This time they settled on merely yelling insults at each other. Remarkably and inexplicably for a few blessed moments an interlude of quiet seemed to settle over the zone of conflict. Hope desperately wanted to breathe a sigh of relief, but, alas, it was not to be.

"Just explain to me what you've been doing over at her house every evening. You ain't got no business being there! One or two trips might have been all right, but the way Lexie tells it, you've been hanging around there like an old dog does when there's a dog in heat. I wish to God I'd put my foot down when you brought that car in here! I had a feeling then we'd made a bad mistake. But no, you thought you 'as crap on a stick, didn't you? Well, let me tell you, Mister, all you need is a wooden leg!"

"My gosh, Edith, what are you talking about? That car ain't got a thing in this world to do with it! And you're wrong about Fannie, too! She's had an awful time of it, trying to keep her family going, what with Jack gone so much. She ain't got nobody else to talk to and all I ever wanted to do was just be a friend. If you hadn't been so standoffish and cold lately, she wouldn't have needed me to be there in the first place! I just plain don't understand you, Woman; why, you ought to be ashamed of yourself, treating her like that!"

"I'll tell you right now it ain't your place to take care of her, she's got neighbors. Here's something else too! I've got a good reason to keep my distance from that family. And you know as well as I do they ain't a thing wrong with me; that's just your way of shifting the blame!" Edith was yelling again. "You're the one who needs to be ashamed here; fooling around with an old rip that everybody knows is a hussy! Now, I didn't want to have to say this, hoping to spare you, but it's about that sorry husband of hers. He came by here that day I was out digging potaters, grinning like a possum, and trying to get something started. I put that sorry whore-hopper on his way; would have shot him, too, if he'd just a waited!" Her rage, now boiling, sent a torrent of tears cascading down her face.

Wade laughed mockingly, "Well, hello, Fuzzy! So, now we're finally getting down to the real story, are we? I thought they'as more to this, than you let on! Old Jesse said you cried when he left, and you didn't even try to deny it, did you? Just passed it off as if it was nothing, but, by Ned, the truth will finally come out, won't it? And here you are a blaming me, now ain't *that* something?" The sound of a word can be far more damaging, than the actual meaning, it conveys.

Mae, the first to reach the scene, immediately let out an unworldly wail. Quickly, Jesse and Max joined in loud enough to make the rafters ring. Edith, by this time, had pulled an old cardboard suitcase out from under the bed and was beginning to pack her things.

"I'm leaving you, Wade Gernon! You know good and well I've always been faithful and this is just an excuse to hide your guilt! You're a liar and you know it, too! Who could ever trust you again after this; why, I'd be a fool... No, just as soon as it gets daylight, I'll get Nathan to take me to Topton to catch the bus... And I'll be gone for good."

To see his mother packing to leave cut Jesse so deeply he could never quite get over it. Wade, on the other hand, seemed quite untouched.

"Go head and leave, I don't care! In fact, I'll be glad to see you go! But you don't have to, because me and the young'ins here are moving up to Mom and Pop's."

By then, the bawling had reached such a crescendo; it effectively put an end the fight. Words were useless when hurled against such a formidable wall; it took over an hour to get the house settled down again. Besides that, neither party seemed to have much of a stomach to continue. All hope for sleep now was gone, leaving them just to lie in bed and lick their wounds. Neither could know that the other was praying, not only for the night to end, but also for strength to make it through.

Joy, they say, cometh in the morning, but only to the heart ready to receive it. Edith and Wade met the day with no such attitude; they both were still in a state of near shock. Red, sensitive eyes find it hard to focus in the sunlight, making reality easier to discern by beholding the shadows. Edith found this to be so in the twilight of emotion while sitting on the edge of her bed weeping. Now suspended somewhere between anger and fear, she ignored the half-packed suitcase lying next to her that had become a symbol of their marriage. Two halves split asunder, yet still attached with its contents, dirty laundry and all, exposed for the whole world to see.

Wade wasted no time in gathering up the children to move out. Edith, however, just sat there in a near catatonic state. Meanwhile, Dave and Mary found themselves the instant custodians of three bewildered children. Wade's only explanation was, "I put up with that bull-crap just as long as I could, so, by Ned, me and the young'ins have left her."

Mary acted surprised without being too quick to make a remark. She welcomed the grandchildren, yet realized that at best the arrangement would be a short one indeed. Dave, on the other hand, was not surprised; he had seen trouble brewing for days, he was, however, overwhelmed. He loved children for visits, but did not want them around constantly. Inevitably, he knew, they would end up receiving attention that rightly belonged to him.

The three immediately made themselves at home, prowling around like three chipmunks at acorn time.

That evening Wade had barely begun to give his side of the argument when the front door sprang open. "I'm here to get my young'ins," she stated unequivocally, leaving no room for debate. Perhaps the fiercest anger in all of nature is that of a mother bear protecting her young. Wade saw this in Edith as she gathered up her "cubs." He knew better than to get in the way, knowing either her life or his would be at stake. Many years later when recounting the story to Becky, Jesse's youngest daughter, Edith ended it with a post-script. "When I finally come to my senses, I decided that no one was ever going to take my young'ins away from me. Wade knew better than to try and stop me, too!"

"No, Pawpaw would know better than that." Becky agreed. W*hy, Nanny is just as mad right now, as she was fifty years ago!*

It was several days after that when Wade moved back home, making it a time for much soul-searching. Though fiercely drawn to the children he loved, he missed Edith, too. As much as he wanted to deny it, memories of how things had been before, haunted him. She, however, felt little sympathy for Wade. She believed he had made a bad situation even worse by his accusations. Finally, like a balm for the heart, time inexorably began to heal.

The chilly winds of fall inevitably fetch a change in the weather, but when they arrived this year, they also brought along a kind of reconciliation. The pair began to discern just how perilously close they'd come to losing it all. Vowing together, they agreed never to venture this near the edge again. While such was commendable and perhaps even wise, it kept them from ever truly addressing the many underlying factors involved. Thus shackled, they shared a lifetime of hurt and distrust, never quite able to forgive, never willing to forget, yet determined to go on. Without access to, or even the knowledge of some wise and impartial counselor, they had no one to turn to. The best they could do was to depend on the love that brought them together in the first place. Now, however, it must also be strong enough to withstand the winds of doubt.

Not surprisingly, the Woodcocks no longer occupied such a hallowed spot in the Gernons' heart. Indeed, from that time forward it was only by happenstance when their paths did occasionally cross. At first, Wade refused to attend church anymore. He was so discouraged that it would take several years before he was willing to darken the door of another. Rather, he much preferred to take the family and spend Sunday afternoons in Stecoah with Lloyd and Lydia. It was following one such a visit, late in February of the next year, when quite an intriguing mystery emerged.

Early in January Edith's mother, Ma, along with Keith came to Sweetwater with plans for staying awhile. It shocked Jesse and Mae to see how haggard Keith looked, his sunken eyes and a blank stare made a stranger of him. Of course, they knew about his illness, but until now had no idea what the actual cost had been. No longer did they have an uncle who could turn every train whistle into the fabulous "Wabash Cannonball." Another change in Keith was his deepened faith in God. Prior to this he had been a nominal Christian, but now he approached being fanatical. Virtually every time a church door opened, he was there and such was the case this particular Sunday. He and Ma attended services together, and then following lunch, she left him home to go for an afternoon's visit with Grandma Gernon. Obviously, Wade and family were in Stecoah, where they stayed until nearly dark.

Immediately, after they got home the mystery began to unfold. Keith ran up to the car in an agitated state. His vocabulary, already severely compromised, waxed even worse under the excitement. Wade could hardly make out a word he said. It took all of Edith's perceptiveness to learn that something dreadful had happened to their little chicks. A few weeks earlier, Wade had purchased fifty white leghorn hatchlings by mail order and they were just beginning to show their wing feathers. Keith led the way, taking them first through the back yard then past the barn and from there on to the privy. A three-quarter moon allowed just enough light for Edith to see the puzzled look on her husband's face. It belied any faith that he otherwise might have had about his brother-in-law's ability. Wade simply could not figure out what Keith was agitated about. Then they heard the peeping. At first it sounded faint and far away, yet somehow right beneath their feet. Keith pointed to the toilet seat where, incredibly, a chorus of desperate little voices rose in lament. Wade rushed over, cocked his head sideways, and then motioned for quiet. It took only a moment to figure it out; "By Jacks, this toilet hole is full of baby chickens!" This amazing statement seemed to hang on its own petard.

Edith was quick to make the essential enquiry. "But how in the world could that be? You don't reckon ... do you? Keith, you didn't put 'em in there did you?" Patently obvious was it that she cared more about Keith's culpability, than she did the poor little chicks.

Keith reacted immediately; he was not about to take the blame for this. Shaking his head angrily, he appeared deeply offended by the question. Then stabbing at the air with his forefinger, he pointed toward the Orr Branch Road and Pin Hook Mountain. "A man from there," he sputtered. "Him, it was him who put the little biddies in the hole."

Wade was more interested in how to get them out, than he was in how they got there. Rushing to the house he quickly brought back a kerosene lantern to hold above the seat opening; sadly, he could not see a thing. Next, he loosened the seat from its mooring and eased it back away from the structure. Unfortunately, this uncorked a plethora of appalling odors that handicapped their efforts even more. Despite such deplorable conditions, however, he could now peer deep into the shaft to see a mass of tiny yellow feathers milling about.

"Edith, run and get me the hoe," he yelled, now with a plan in mind. Moments later, she handed him the implement and watched as he stretched to reach the bottom by holding onto just the tip-end of its handle. No matter how he manipulated it, however, not a single chick made it out. For one thing, the rescuer could not see what he was doing, while the poor victims had no idea of what was happening. "Let me think a minute," he said while nervously plowing thick fingers through his hair. That is when an ingenious idea suddenly blossomed; why not tie the lantern onto the hoe handle? This would provide better lighting, so that both he and the chicks could see what they were doing. It may seem farfetched, but it worked! Doing so, far better than anyone could have expected. Each time he lowered the contraption, they would, one by one, hop up and stand on the back of the hoe. By repeating the process fifty times, Wade was able to save the entire brood.

The mystery remains, even unto this day. Who did it and for what purpose was such a lowdown trick pulled? Latter-day discussions between Jesse and Mae led to the conjecture that perhaps Jack Woodcock was the culprit. If so, then what was his motive; could it have been revenge? Cruelty to animals is well-established criteria in identifying the sociopath personality. If, indeed, Jack was to blame, then that might very well help explain certain other events, especially those surrounding the murder of Earl Akers. Interestingly, not long after this happened Jack surrendered to the authorities in Gaston County on charges of the manufacture, transport, and sale of illegal whiskey. Subsequently, he made a deal by turning states evidence on the others, getting off, himself, with a slap on the wrist.

With the matter at hand, however, no proof exists that he played any role in it at all. Alas, it seems now that this enigma must forever remain exactly what it is: an unsolved mystery.

CHAPTER 14

Despite the many thousands of miles separating them, the bombs that fell on Pearl Harbor also shook Sweetwater. Indeed, the "Day of Infamy" was still in the making when Dave, nearly out of breath, rushed in shouting. "By golly, we're in for it now; the Japs have just bumbed Pearl Harbor!"

Wade, busy trimming redundant leather away from the work shoe he had just half-soled, looked up in dismay. "Huh… do what, Pop? Where the devil is Pearl Harbor"

"It's in the Hi-wahuan islands where we've got a big Navy base! I just heard it on the radio and they don't know yet, but think the Japs are fixing to invade." Jesse had never seen his grandfather so worried, deep wrinkles enfolded his nearly bald pate. Wade switched on the set and suddenly the room went silent to the sound of an announcer's voice repeating the grave story. Thus began a four-year nightmare; one filled with goose-stepping Nazis, samurai swords, swastikas and rising-suns. Neither Sweetwater nor the world would ever be the same.

A patriotic fervor quickly swept the land, one that would remain unparalleled for the remainder of the twentieth century. It was a time unique in America's history with scrap metal drives, ration stamps, people in uniform everywhere, war bond sales, speeches, sermons, flags, banners, and tears enough to christen a nation for war. Rightly perceived as an all-out struggle for survival, it was enough to inspire the people to greatness through a unity of purpose.

Jesse worked hard, joining with others to gather up scrap metal for the effort. He was both surprised and amazed at their success. Near the railroad tracks at Robbinsville, he saw great piles of iron, steel, aluminum, tin and other metals grow until they stretched for several blocks along Depot Street.

At school, he proudly carried a picture of General Douglas Macarthur on the cover of his writing tablet. The full-face profile of this great American included the familiar corncob pipe perched cockily beneath his gold-braided visor. However, what Jesse liked most in the photograph was his magnificent eagle-like gaze that saw victory just beyond the horizon?

War's grubby finger touched the heart of the Gernon family, too. Oliver was already in the Army and later, when he was old enough, Ray joined the Navy. Clark's efforts to volunteer proved futile, however, because of "health reasons." This became cause for concern by the family, however, Clark was quick to disallow it, saying that he just had a "little kidney infection" and would try again later. Wade had a defense job and three dependant children, therefore, had a low-priority rating with the draft board. Later, when called up near the end of the war, he too was "turned down," because of his high blood pressure.

Having entered the service several months before Pearl Harbor, Oliver served in the infantry. Six weeks following D-Day, badly wounded he almost died on the field of battle near Mortain, France.

Ray became a Navy frogman, and served in the Pacific theatre where oftentimes he found himself in enemy waters with only a knife clenched between his teeth for protection.

When war ended, both Oliver and Ray returned home hoping to re-establish a life for themselves. Oliver quickly married and moved to Robbinsville, while Ray suddenly found himself the undisputed champion of upper Sweetwater's young people. He truly enjoyed planning hikes, picnics, camping out, wooden-wagon races, fishing trips, and many dozens of other activities. Although still in school, Frank acted as his unofficial assistant and together they were always dreaming up something to do.

Jesse liked hiking the Appalachian Trail, especially those times they went to the cliffs. This steep outcropping of granite formed the upper face of the mountains directly across the valley from High Top. From there lay Robbinsville to the southwest, while to the north Fontana Lake glistened blue and bright in the distance.

Balanced near the rim of a three hundred foot drop-off was an immense boulder that young men, from generations past, had tried to dislodge. Mercifully, however, all such efforts had failed. What an unappreciated blessing it is that the feckless ambitions of youth mostly go unfulfilled! If they had succeeded, much of the upper portion of Sweetwater might very well have ceased to exist.

Jesse, not unlike his forebears, felt inclined to try; he genuinely believed that he was the one destined to make it happen. At the age of ten, the thought that actions have consequences never entered his mind. What did, however, was what a sight it would make, that, and the avalanche of accolades from peers he, no doubt, would enjoy.

It was a warm Sunday morning late in March when Jesse, Frank and their cousin Walt Hyder, set out with a plan designed to put them in the history books. Walt, somehow, had obtained several sticks of dynamite, thus giving them a reason to feel optimistic. Unaware of such, Ray gave the trio a lift up to the Stecoah gap and thus unwittingly became partner to this ill-conceived scheme.

By following the Appalachian Trail, they hiked along the mountain crest for most of the two-mile journey. Considering it took nearly three hours to make the trip, they quickly agreed to eat lunch before tackling the project. Jesse was all for it, since it was his backpack that carried the explosives. The last part of the trek had been a near vertical ascent, causing him to slip and fall several times. Walt, the one who procured it, smiled coyly, and then made a confession; "Yes, they had plenty of dynamite, alright, but not any percussion caps. What we have to do is try and figure out some other way to set the stuff off," he explained.

However, everything they tried failed; even a cherry bomb would not do it. Smashing it with a huge rock produced nothing, as did hurling rolls of it at the boulder. Finally, in desperation, they used a high-powered rifle to shoot it, but still nothing happened

Could it be that from behind the scenes some Infinite Wisdom was hard at work trying to save them from themselves? Meanwhile, they incorrectly reasoned that the substance was just too old to "blow up." Little could these neophytes know that nitroglycerine, with the passage of time, tends to settle out of suspension; thus making it even more explosive. Highly trained experts in the field of detonation are wont always to use extreme caution when handling such material.

The year 1942 found America mobilizing for war. Government plans, made initially in an era of relative peace, were either scrapped or received priority attention, all according to the needs of national defense. Such was the case for building Fontana Dam. This immense TVA project had originally been conceptualized as a flood-control measure, that, and to awaken the huge quantities of hydroelectric power, known sleep in the beautiful Little Tennessee River. With construction originally slated to begin January 1, 1942, this date became inviolable. However, at the special behest of a President who saw the need to have additional power available for an ultra-secret program already underway at nearby Oak Ridge, they advanced the day for completion significantly.

Wasting no time, Wade applied for a job there, getting one by the end of February. Now, for a change, he would be able to work hard and realize a decent wage for his efforts. To be paid time and a half for all hours worked over forty and double time for weekends and holidays far exceeded his wildest dreams. He was like a hungry child who had never had quite enough to eat before, suddenly finding a feast set before it. He could not get enough, fast enough. Since Fontana was over forty miles away, he planned to come home only on weekends. However, that would be every other weekend and then for just a one-night stay. So excited was he, that the prospects of such a grueling schedule did nothing to hamper his spirits. Edith, however, believed it would not last. “Why, Wade, you’ve hardly ever been off the head of Sweetwater before. You’ll be home again within a week, just mark my word on it.”

“Edith, that just goes to show you, Woman, you don’t know old Wade Gernon here. By Ned, I’m a lot better man then that, you just stand back and watch the money come rolling in.”

“Time will tell,” she nodded knowingly. “Oh, I got a letter from Hester today… Willard finally made her go to the sheriff with what she’d overheard there at the tent that night. She said they finally had arrested Lance Boyle and Guy Fowler for bootlegging. Listen to this, though; Willard somehow found out they’re the same ones who jumped Keith, and he’s as mad as fire over it. But this is what will really get you; Jack *Woodcock* was the ringleader of that whole bootlegging mess! Of course, they charged him for that, but they also nailed him for moonshining. With all three out now on bail, though, nobody’s safe.”

“Say what? They, Lord have mercy,” Wade whistled, taking a long second to think. “Well, I’m not too surprised, knowing what I do about that fella. I’ll bet you a quarter, he’s the one who killed Earl Akers, not the other two... Oh, my gosh, Edith! Just think what could have happened to you and the young’ins.” Suddenly, a veritable avalanche of feelings crashed down around him.

“It scares me to think about it,” Edith smiled wryly. Seconds later, she continued from the letter; “Well, Hester complains that the law was not very nice to her. She figures it was because of her waiting so long before going in. Said her and Claude Conway both are now under investigation and that the whole thing has become a nightmare.”

“Why, all that pretty little thing has to do is roll them big eyes and she’ll have half the deputies eating out of her hand, like a bunch of little pups," he offered brightly.

"Yeah, well you ought to know," Edith sighed. "She's had your tongue a hanging out long enough."

Jesse would look back on this as a time when he struggled mightily with his feelings. Since Wade's trips home from Fontana were infrequent, Jesse came to appreciate the few hours they had together. By their very nature, each visit became a special event for celebration. Invariably, Wade came home just brimming over with good humor and bringing lots of candy and other presents. Nevertheless, Jesse missed his daddy, especially at night. At eventide, when shadows walked the dark hallways of his mind, he feared that some steel-helmeted storm trooper might come to get him.

Construction work was new to Wade, yet he caught on quickly and soon had earned the respect of both fellow workers and supervisors alike. It was only natural that when a better position opened up, he was the one to get it. That's how he got the job to work on one of the two main cranes at the construction site. As he would later say, there was not a lot of hard work to it. About all he had to do was walk just a few hundred feet twice daily to lubricate parts of the giant machine that would keep it operating. Usually, this took only about an hour to complete, but the walk was what made it all so fantastic! With the top of the dam at four hundred and eighty feet above the riverbed, Fontana was destined to become the tallest dam east of the Mississippi. The crane rose an additional one hundred feet above that. His task was to tread an eight-inch-wide beam for nearly one hundred and fifty feet, apply the lubricant and then return.

Strolling among the clouds could make almost any heart grow feint, but not his. He never once lost his nerve or his balance; yet as is so often the case, it was another and totally unrelated circumstance that nearly cost him his life.

CHAPTER 15

Monday mornings, for Wade, usually made him blue. Not this time, however, he had been able to stop the alarm clock one precious second before it went off. Others still sleep now would remain undisturbed. He and two more workers shared space with Effie and Howard, Wade's sister and brother-in-law. Their tent was located in a temporary housing section some three-quarters of a mile from the dam site. So far, everything had worked out beautifully, even though they all had different shifts. No, it was not home but matters could have been a lot worse, and Effie was without peer when it came to cooking. He moved stealthily between the cots, using the five-thirty twilight for guidance; soft snoring on every side reminded him to tread lightly. When Effie nudged his shoulder, he quickly realized that she had already begun her workday. Without speaking, she beamed a big honest smile and nodded; it was her signature greeting and one that always made him feel about ten feet tall.

"Here's you two biscuits with ham," she whispered, "and I fixed an extra one with egg; you'll need that after getting on the job." Along with the breakfast, she also handed him a brown paper bag that bulged with lunch. After finding a seat at the small folding table near the door, he began to make loud slurping sounds with his coffee, trying not to scald his tongue. Suddenly, the realization of what he was doing caused him to stoop forward in an embarrassed snicker. By pouring the hot liquid back and forth between cup and saucer, he found a much quieter way to solve the dilemma.

On their way to work, it had become customary for most to take a shortcut through the blasting zone. The practice, although frowned on by administration, was not expressly against TVA policy since procedures were in place to give adequate warning if danger was imminent. Normal operating procedure called for giving three separate siren blasts: one at fifteen-minutes, a second at the ten-minutes, and then two short alerts one minute prior to the detonation. However, on this drizzled and fog-shrouded morning of early August things did not work out quite that way. It seems someone new had just started the job, but, unfortunately, doing so without much training. On his own recognizance, he made a key decision. One, he thought would save the company both time and money. He simply would cut all those redundant signals down to just two, with the final one to occur exactly five minutes before the scheduled event. This, he concluded, would provide more than adequate time for anyone to take cover. A major problem with this reasoning, of course, was the fact that no one besides himself knew of the rule change. Thus, there was no way of knowing that the first warning a person got would also be their last.

Entering the zone Wade heard what he thought was the fifteen-minute warning. Confident there was still plenty of time, he did not hurry knowing he would exit the area in less than ten minutes. Strangely, all seemed eerily quiet with not even birdsong to cheer the morning. Later, he also recalled how the atmosphere felt much like it does before a bad storm hits.

The explosion nearly knocked him off his feet, so powerful was it. Although obviously surprised, he felt no immediate fear. The mountains seemed to teeter before his eyes. *Oh my gosh,* he thought. *I may not make'er out of here.* Looking toward the sky, he saw it filled with specks that would rapidly turn into a deluge of falling rocks. His first impulse was to run, but in that moment of uncertainty, he noticed a stranger standing by his side. The abrupt realization that someone else was in this nightmare, too, brought little comfort to him. Remarkably, an abiding sense of peace suddenly filled his breast.

"Don't move, Wade!" the big man boomed. "Just stay right where you are, and you'll be all right!" Immediately, the impact of falling stones sounded all around them, some the size of watermelons, and although hitting right at their feet, not a pebble touched either one. Finally, when the heavy thudding stopped, Wade, for some reason, looked up the slope to a sight that caused his knees to buckle. For bound straight for them was a monstrous boulder. Evidently, the initial shock had loosened it enough to create another equally deadly threat. It looked to be on track to land right where they stood. Remarkably, even in the midst of all this, Wade noticed that the stranger had the bluest eyes he'd ever seen. "Just stay right where you are," a calm voice said. This time Wade felt better about listening. Together they watched certain death loom larger with each ground-shaking bounce. It seemed never to deviate an inch from a direct path that led straight toward them. When it smashed the ground for what surely would be the last time before landing squarely on them, was when another miracle occurred. Amazingly, the big rock careened off to the left and missed them both by a good six feet. Together, they broke into uncontrollable laughter, hugging, and slapping each other on the back like two long-separated brothers at a family reunion. Wade was surprised that the stranger knew his name, but who was he? Feeling no compunction against asking, he turned to the man for an answer.

"Why, among other things I've been called Mike," he chuckled. The good-natured laughter that followed all but shut out any further enquiry for the moment.

Wade felt lost without his hat, he then recalled losing it to the initial shock wave. Looking around, he soon located it half-hidden beneath a piece of rock the size of a dishpan. That brief instant, with his back turned, was all the time it took for Mike to be gone. After scouring the landscape and finding it empty, Wade was bewildered. Without a place to hide, where in the world was he? Indeed, not a soul could be seen anywhere.

"Where the heck did he go?" Wade asked, once out of the valley of death.

His boss looked puzzled. "Son, what are you talking about? Then without waiting for an answer, he continued: "Buddy, we ought to be just about now picking you up in pieces. That charge was a sucker punch, and when I saw what had happened, I said to myself, some poor devil is going to get it. I tell you if I hadn't seen it for myself, I never would have believed it. You did the right thing, though, kept your head, and stood dead still both times. I reckon the good Lord took care of the rest of it for you. But I'll tell you what, Pal, and they ain't no doubt about it, you live a charmed life."

"Are you sure a big red-headed scutter didn't come by here? Wade asked... Said his name was Mike something or other. He knew exactly who I was, but I can honestly say I never laid eyes on him before."

"No, Wade, they ain't nobody but you come out of there. I think maybe this thing's got you messed up in the head, Son. They say sometimes it'll do that when you come that close to getting killed. Did your life seem to flash before your eyes?"

"No!" Wade said, looking irritated. They ain't nothing wrong with me."

"Listen here now; I guess if that had been me I'd still be scared. But no, the only thing I saw come out of there, besides you, was a big old yeller dog, and boys was he a high-tailing 'er, too!"

When Jesse first learned of the incident, he was approaching manhood, yet even then, it sent chills up his spine. Wade never backed away from his claim that another man, indeed, did stand by his side the day terror rained from the skies.

As incredible it may sound, on this very selfsame and fateful day another momentous incident occurred, one destined to leave an indelible mark on Jesse. The first day of school proved to be, singularly, his most traumatic event yet experienced in life.

Soon after she started the first grade, Jean began to share with Jesse some of her classroom occurrences. Being less than three years older than he, Jean always seemed more like an older sister than she did an aunt. Since she made school sound so interesting, he could hardly wait to get started himself. With two years to go before he was eligible, his impatience grew thin and before long, he was making life miserable for everybody. Continuously he pestered her to play school with him; he wanted her to be the teacher and show him how to read and write. Merely thinking about the classroom was so wonderful that it got him up early every morning just to see her off.

She brought home many books and he loved looking at the pictures while she read to him. Most of the stories had long, hard-to-say words with some he had never heard of. His favorite was one about a duck named Henry who was afraid of water. One day it rained so hard, his trailer flooded; forced then to either sink or swim the big-footed amphibian quickly mastered his fears. Jesse loved the story so much that he insisted on hearing it everyday.

He turned six on the day that school started; legally, he could have waited another year, yet in the face of such eagerness who could have denied him? For nearly two weeks, he had been counting the days. Each morning became a time to exult, seeing that he now was one day closer to the goal. At night, he could not sleep, but that did not matter, it merely gave him more time to think about the new adventure ahead. For years, he had stood with the neighborhood students as they gathered to wait on the bus. His heart ached to be a part of the crowd when they laughed and chided each other. He would have given the world to be aboard that big yellow bus when it pulled away. Perhaps one day should he live so long, it might happen, but most times, he doubted it.

Finally, it did, though, and of course, Jesse and his mother were the first in line to get a good seat. Once at school, things looked to be getting off to a good star, especially after he learned that Miss Walker would be his teacher. He felt he already knew this wonderful person, since Jean had told him so many good things about her. Just to sit at her feet would answer all his prayers. Kindergarten, at the time, was essentially unknown in this part of the world, yet he had managed to learn the alphabet and could even read a few words. Feeling he could keep Miss Walker busy pasting gold stars by his name, Jesse secretly hoped the others would not be too envious of his advanced standing.

Edith accompanied him to the room and even helped the young scholar find a suitable seat at a table near the front. After that, he was eager for her to leave. And once she was gone he stood up and looked around trying to find a familiar face or two, but not a single soul did he recognize. About half the class milled about, probably having a good time. They acted as if they already knew each other, which in fact was the case. This group lived in town and had played with each other for years. The other half, however, was either crying or looked as if they might start at any minute. After observing them, Jesse began to feel his first pangs of uneasiness. Never had he seen so many unhappy faces in one place at one time. It was at this most inopportune moment, with Jesse standing there open-mouthed and gawking, that Miss Walker chose to make an example of him. "Jesse Gernon," her voice rang loudly. "You've been assigned a seat, now go find it! I want you to know that you're not out on some mountaintop foxhunting with your grandfather, this is a classroom, so try to remember that. The room went deadly silent for a second before an outburst of loud guffaws erupted from the town crowd. Several of the boys pointed fingers at him while snickering. His mind continued to echo these derisive acts long after his face stopped burning. In fact, they would never quite fade away.

Occasionally it is possible to point to a single event and say that it changed the course of one's life, either for good or for bad. Such, however, is not the case here. No, while Jesse had never been so humiliated, enough that death would have been a welcomed reprieve, he, nevertheless, survived. No single episode could possibly have that much impact, hardly so. Unfortunately, though, it did set a precedent and put into motion a pattern that persisted throughout the year. For a teacher to take out her dislike of a student's grandfather on the grandson was unconscionable.

Jesse suddenly developed a deep hatred for school. His natural desire for learning, just beginning to flower, was nipped in the bud by the killing frost of cold insensitivity. He did not feel accepted by the other students and, what's more, he did not care. Besides, he could not read either, not that he wanted to now.

Arithmetic made no sense at all and recess was awful, especially those silly games they played. What he hated most, however, were the rules that regulated bathroom use. At home, he had always gone to the toilet as nature dictated, but not here. Sometimes at recess or lunch, he would forget to go and that got him into a lot of trouble. Most of the time he could hold it, but once in a while he could not and that proved disastrous. Afraid, no terrified is the better way to state it, of asking Miss Walker for bathroom privileges; he knew that if he did, she, invariable, would announce it to the entire class, while citing the need to be more diligent about such. He, therefore, usually chose to just sit silently and suffer while petitioning heaven for strength. School prayer was never an issue for Jesse.

During the first few weeks of school about all he did was wander through the halls and hang around the playground. Everybody and everything seemed somehow unreal and dreamlike, much as if he was in a daze. He could hardly wait for the final bell to sound and head home. He missed being with his mother; he missed Max and even missed Mae. Every afternoon he would walk through the door, pitch his lunch-pail onto the table, and declare with absolute resolve, "I quit and ain't never going back, neither. I've learned all I want to, I don't like school, and I don't like Miss Walker."

"Why, Jesse," Edith tried not to sound ridiculing, "you don't want to grow up and be an ignorant old man who can't read or write, do you?"

With this and a little tough love, she usually persuaded him to be back on the bus the next school day. Yet, as the year progressed, he came to think of it as by divine providence that multiple episodes of tonsillitis kept him home. Therefore, it came as no surprise when he failed the first grade. Few doubted, however, that this was due more to attitude than to sickness.

And those lingering sounds of derision? Well they, these vignettes of the sub-conscious, came back, time after time, to haunt him, right up to and through his doctorate level of education. Never, it seems, could he put behind him that first year of school.

***

None, save One, was there a soul that breathed
Who lived a life, not self-deceived.
And none, save One, was there of woman born
Whose face of calm didn't mask a storm.

For all that's called love, save the love of One,
Brings more hurt than hate has ever done.

Shortly after Willard and Hester's experience at the sheriff's office, they had another equally salient event to occur. Willard, angry over Keith's treatment and Hester's involvement with Claude Conway, decided it was time to pay a visit. The more he thought about it the more he liked the idea, especially now that he had so many new and troubling questions to deal with.

"I don't think talking to them would be a good idea," Hester argued. "Reverend Conway is a busy man and I doubt he has time to talk to just anybody. Besides, I don't want you messing with them other two... that *could* get you hurt!"

"Well, I don't consider myself 'just anybody' and don't worry about me; I can handle myself. If we don't start now, we'll never get to the bottom of this, and you know me, I don't like loose ends. Another thing, too, the way that detective kept pairing you up with Conway bothers me a lot."

They had no further discussion about it for several days until one night in early April when he brought the subject up again. Hester remained adamant, saying she did not want to hear another word about it. Thinking matters settled, she relaxed into a routine that lasted until the following Monday afternoon when Willard returned home from work. That is when she learned he was on his way to confront Claude and the others, on their own turf. Surmising that there was no way to reason with him, she snatched Claude Earl up from his nap and climbed aboard the car with him. Not a word passed between them on the way to the little town of Lowell, where the revival tent was now located. Upon arrival, however, she began to plead once again that he not do it. "It's too dangerous," she said, "taking on three men, or maybe more, ain't a smart idea, not by yourself, anyway. You need to get somebody to help, maybe Arnold; at least he's got a gun." Willard made no response. Normally, this transplanted highlander was putty in her hands, but not this time. Now a solid rock of determination, he sat pale and tight-lipped; a thin moustache of tiny dew-like droplets glistened brightly in the afternoon sun.

"Willard, just look at all these cars, can't you see that Reverend Conway is busy? I'd say he's probably ministering to somebody right now, so why don't you leave him alone? You know good and well we ought not to be here doing this."

"Yeah, well I've put this off just as long as I aim to; I need to have a talk with this bunch, for I plan on getting to the bottom of a few things. Besides, I owe this to Keith, so just hush.

Claude Earl was acting too cranky to walk, so she hoisted him onto her hip and began matching steps with her husband. As they moved along her voice crackled like fire. "Now, just what are you talking about?" she demanded to know.

Not bothering to respond, he merely stepped up the pace and continued onward toward the big canvas shelter. Heat from earlier in the day had accumulated in the soggy flaps to create an atmosphere of dank, musty air. Remarkably, the heavy smothering effect acted to sedate Claude Earl enough to keep him quiet the entire time they were there. Their eyes needed a moment to adjust, once they stepped into the tent's dim, but empty interior. However, they immediately detected Muffled voices coming from the area designated by Hester as the Holy of Holies. Willard suddenly and unexpectedly seemed uncertain as to what to do.

The little group moved up to the front row of seats where they now were in a much better position to listen than before. Hester quickly identified the voices of Claude Conway, Lance Boyle, and Guy Fowler. "I think it's all three of 'em," she whispered, sounding scared. When it became evident that the talk was trivial, Willard stood up ready to break into the conversation. That is when Conway's strident laughter abruptly broke through; just the tone of his voice grated Willard enough to make him bristle.

"Women? Let me tell you about women! Why, half the ones in my congregation have got the hots for me. The trick, though, is just to keep 'em at arm's length."

Fowler sneered. "Yeah, like you did Hester Rose! Huh. Is that how she got pregnant?"

"Hey, that's a low-blow!" Conway complained.

That did it; wearing a face reflecting the paleness of death, Willard pushed back the flap and entered.

"You sorry, low-life bastards! We've go score to settle here, and it'll be done too… just make no mistake about it!"

CHAPTER 16

Had a tornado roared through the tent, Claude Conway could not have been more shocked. For once in his life, he was at a loss for words. He opened his mouth to speak but only dry gasping sounds escaped through his thin, worm-like lips. Looking furtively around, he spotted Hester and that gave him steam enough to wheeze out a question. "What's he doing here? I thought I told you to keep that slug away from me. You want him to know everything, do you?" With his composure now partially regained, he looked directly at Willard. "So you're going to give me the pleasure of beating you, huh? Well, by golly, sir, you've come to the right place." Still breathing hard, he looked over at Hester and smirked. "You'd better get out of here, little Lady, 'cause this ain't going to be very pretty."

"Get him!" Guy Fowler urged. "He's got no business being here." One eye glared at Willard while the other pointed directly at his nose. "Let me have him when you're finished, I want to slice one of them ears off and make me a watch fob." Unmistakably, the click of a switchblade sounded, it was not unlike that of a coffin lid latching shut.

Lance, too, was itching for action. "You've got two witnesses here," he yelled, "so go get him!" At this, he shoved Willard toward the center of their circle.

Willard was off-balance when Conway charged him like a bull. Emitting a wild guttural roar, he covered the six feet at full-tilt to bury his shoulder into Willard's stomach, driving him straight back. Somehow, Willard managed to keep his feet until the rush lost its momentum, and then by clasping both hands above his head, he slammed Claude hard between the shoulder blades. The blow severed all contact between the two, leaving them to stare wildly at each other. Loud, labored breathing was the only indicator that any action had taken place.

Claude started for Willard again, but this time he was ready. Claude had no way of knowing that his opponent had once been a reasonably good Golden Gloves boxer. He had fought as a welterweight and although the finer points of pugilism now eluded him, his muscles still remembered. It was as if he had been in the ring just the day before. Immediately upon assuming a fighting crouch, two sharp left jabs flickered like the tongue of a copperhead; one slammed Conway's right eye while the other drew blood from his nose. Willard back-pedaled then stepped sharply to his left as Claude, now out of control, lunged forward again; this time walking straight into a hard right cross that drove him to his knees.

"Give me that knife," he shrieked at Fowler, "I'm going to cut his guts out; this ain't no fair fight!" Instantly, the weapon appeared in the hand of the one called Reverend, and he was ready to wield it. Pointing the six-inch blade directly at Willard's face, Conway led the two in a slow circling dance of death. With eyes locked, they moved in silent unison, the stalked, and the stalker; then Conway, ever the aggressor, moved in for the kill. Willard was partially able to parry a slashing thrust aimed at his throat, but paid the price with his left forearm. Immediately, a searing wave of pain surged to his shoulder. Unfortunately, the preacher maneuvered Willard into a corner and began to take advantage of the situation. It now appeared that only a few seconds remained before the inevitable happened. Yet one must never discount the element of human courage, for sometimes it is this quality, so illusive and so unpredictable, which has the ability to tilt the scales of fate.

Claude made another pass, cutting Willard across the right elbow; however, this time it was not as severe as before. Yet the sight of so much blood triggered some primitive instinct within him to make his move for the kill. Thinking he had his man, a loud, weird laugh rippled from a throat that only recently had proclaimed the joys of brotherly love. Before this ungodly sound died away, however, Willard somehow managed to grab the wrist that held the dagger.

The fight quickly intensified to its highest level, yet as the two struggled back and forth, Willard was finally able to drive his knee deep into Claude's groin. It was enough to loosen the preacher's grip, and in a fresh burst of adrenaline, the weapon changed hands. Willard now was the one on the offensive. Drawing from a heritage that had survived for a thousand years by the blade of a dirk, his Scottish nature now roiled with fury. Wielding the blade, he felt it strike his adversary's abdomen before he gave one awful tug to the handle. Actually, Conway's broad leather belt took most of the damage, with the tip taking only a small portion of adipose tissue. The preacher staggered and then fell backwards, exposing a throat that was ready for the slicing. Quick as a cat Willard was upon him, but that is when Hester's scream broke the spell.

"No! No! For goodness sakes, Willard, don't do it! Claude Earl needs his daddy!"

Probably no other single set of words could have affected Willard so dramatically, stopping him dead in his tracks, although the knife remained poised to do what he might ask of it. "What? What did you say, Woman?"

Feeling that she had stayed the action, Hester bit back the tears while reaching over to lay her hand on his bleeding right arm. "Why, Honey, I couldn't just stand by and let you do that; it could get you hung for murder. This bunch would claim that you came in here and started a fight; so what chance would you have? Me and little Claude Earl need you! Now, put that thing down and let's get to a doctor; you're bleeding to death!."

Claude squealed like a stuck pig once he saw his own blood. Guy Fowler cautiously moved in to take a closer look: "You ain't cut that bad," he muttered, "it'll take a couple of stitches, and you'll need a new belt, that's all."

Willard dropped the switchblade onto the sawdust as they exited the tent. This to the sound of Conway's threats; "Rose," he screamed, "I'll fix you, by heavens; I'm swearing out a warrant on that sorry butt of yours!"

Hester attempted to wrap his left arm with one of Claude Earl's clean diapers, but Willard would have no part of it.

"Keep that thing off of me," he snarled while shifting gears. "I ain't hurt that bad, not where it shows, anyway." Willard had always held Hester in highest esteem and secretly felt he was much more in love with her than she was with him. She had always possessed his heart, at least up until today.

Hester, however, would not to be rebuffed; "We're going to the hospital and get you bandaged up; why, you're bleeding all over the place. Here, give me your arm," she said, sounding determined. Heretofore, she loved him even though for years they had been drifting apart. Suddenly now, however, all that had changed; he had fought for her and was ready to die for her. What a man he was! For the first time in a long time, there were real feelings behind her words. That they had been so long in coming meant nothing, not if he would only but give her a chance.

Against his continued remonstrations, she was able to fashion bandages around both arms. Yet when they turned bright red almost instantly, it was enough to stay any further arguments about the matter. It took thirty-two stitches to sew up his left arm and eighteen for the right. The attending physician reluctantly agreed to let him leave without hospitalization; meanwhile, Hester felt vindicated by the lecture he gave Willard over trying to avoid treatment after sustaining such injuries.

Contrary to his threats, Reverend Conway never invoked the powers of the state against Willard. However, Willard's opportunity to avenge Keith had come and gone. It was only a few weeks later that Fowler and Boyle's case came before the federal court to receive sentences of five years each at hard labor.

The mystery surrounding the murder of Earl Akers continued to bedevil authorities since very little evidence had been unearthed to work with. Unfortunately, this continued to be true even after three years of investigation, but suddenly and from a source completely unexpected, they got a break.

Two young men were tossing football in the empty lot behind their house when the older one spotted something on the ground. Glinting in the afternoon sun, the object seemed to beg for closer inspection. Stooping to pick up what he thought was a piece of scrap chrome; the young athlete was surprised at finding a long-bladed knife. He had seen switchblades before, but this was the first time he had ever held one. Clearly visible on one side of the yellow handles were the carved initials "LB." Testing the button, he found that even with a rusted spring it still worked. He tried it several times, first by forcing the blade closed and then allowing it to swing back open. The movement was slow at first, but became easier with each effort. He continued working the mechanism until it demonstrated a noticeable click. A portion of the blade was stained brown with rusty red material filling the crevices around the spring. After warning his brother to keep quiet about it, the matter may well have remained in anonymity, had fate not intervened.

Outside the purview of their parents, the two continued to admire their treasure for several days. However, as with anything new, the glamour soon wore off and when the older of the youths left it inadvertently in his pocket, the secret was out. In checking the clothes for laundry, their mother came across something that was both evil looking and unknown to her. The father, however, was not so much in the dark. "My Lord," he yelled, "that thing's illegal! What's it doing here, anyway?" With a little detective work, they soon had the answer and by living as close as they did to the murder scene, the next question was obvious. Could this be the missing weapon?

Merely say that the sheriff's office was pleased would be a gross understatement. It was precisely what they had been hoping to get! Well-known was it that they had two prime suspects, yet did not have enough evidence for a conviction. While Lance Boyle and Guy Fowler had been seen leaving the murder site at approximately the time of the slaying, it was all circumstantial. Authorities needed something more tangible to tie them to the case, and now they had it. Jack Woodcock had secretly made a deal with the authorities in order to get a lighter sentence for his part in the manufacture, transporting, and selling of illegal whiskey. By getting immunity, along with five years probation, he stood ready to testify how he saw Lance throw what looked like a knife into the weed patch, after rubbing it against his pants leg. Without the weapon, however, it was merely his word against theirs and since all three were convicted criminals, his testimony would essentially be worthless. Now, though, it would appear Jack's account was true, saying he had been there watching them from the shadows. This development, along with the finding of Earl's watch on Guy Fowler, gave the state a strong case and now they could move forward.

Already incarcerated for bootlegging, the two were easy to locate. The next day Lance Boyle and Guy Fowler were again charged; this time, however, for the first-degree murder of Earl Akers. Remarkably, when their handcuffs snapped into place, the clicking sound heard was not unlike that made by a switchblade.

Immediately, and from many different sources, a plethora of questions emerged. How do you tie a weapon without fingerprints to the suspects? What other evidence, if any, did they have against them? Were there others involved, also? On and on it went. Meanwhile, the Rose family had questions too. What, if anything, did Keith know about it? Moreover, to what extent was Hester involved. The justice system would deal with the public's concern, but only time and good detective work would find answers to the other.

CHAPTER 17

Jim Gernon began showing up nearly every weekend Wade made it home from Fontana. They would sit and talk for hours and at first, Jesse thought nothing of it; after all, having neighbors and family in was only to be expected. Soon, however, Jesse correctly surmised that something, this time, was different. For one thing, Jim and Wade kept making trips up the road to look at a big old ugly house that was haunted. He and Frank had once ventured up to the front door, where weird, awful moaning sounds sent them speeding on their way.

The house was one that Jesse's great-great-grandfather had built when he first moved to Sweetwater. Soon after his passing was when it all began, people seeing his spirit wandering around, that and other scary manifestations. Many a truthful person swore to it and Grady Gernon, brother to Dave and Jim, often stated that there was not enough money to get him to spend another night in the place. Fact was he had tried it once and once was enough. It seems that sometime between the bewitching hours of two and three a.m., he woke to the clanking sound of a chain dragging across the floor. Next, large balls of fire came rolling through the house, moving from room to room, terrorizing him. Somehow, he knew that should one touch him, it might prove fatal. Not wishing to test the theory, he made his escape between emanations, and, once outside, immediately vowed never to return to the abominable place. Anyone who knew Grady would tell you he was a man of his word.

Jesse still loved the house they lived in, but one day in early November, he learned that once again they would be moving. It chagrined him to see just how ebullient his daddy had become. "Honey," Wade spoke to Edith, "we're finally getting us a place with enough room for these young'ins to grow up in. And, by golly, I've always wanted that little farm; it belonged to my great-granddaddy

Charles. Why, everybody knows it's the best piece of ground on Sweetwater and they's land enough there to grow anything we want to. I'll bet you a dollar bill it's got at least thirty good fruit trees on it, too. Yes sir, little Lady, I'll tear out them old bedrooms next to the road and build us a big front porch there. Then when we add those three rooms back on, we'll put 'em where they are supposed to be, on the other side of the house." After erecting the original structure, a new road, for many years, had caused it to face in the wrong direction.

Jesse did not have the heart to look back as he rode the last sled load that moved their things to the new home. With great fondness, he would always remember living in "the house beside of the road," for it was there he learned that love can bring hurt as well as joy, but it was nearly always worth the risk.

Although only about two tenths of a mile separated the two residences, the distance actually reached from Jesse's childhood into his youth. Edith and Wade spent many hard hours trying to prepare the new nest for their fledglings. Unfortunately, however, they heard not one peep of approval from them. Jesse was constantly grumpy and complaining, saying he could not find his things and that the house was too cold, this despite a roaring fireplace that Wade kept going full-time. Mae ran around entering blocked off bedrooms, areas of possible danger. She made a habit of facing off with her mother over every issue. Max, normally content just to putter around, now was irritable and edgy. Definitely, there was a haunted-house feel to the place, with the resident spirits there showing no evidence they would willingly share their domain with anyone. After all, they had had the place to themselves for years, maintaining the status quo by an occasional exhibition of horror. Usually, a few groans or a fireball or two was all it took, now, however, it appeared that greater works than these were needed if they hoped to gain back their cherished oasis of rest.

Hence, it was shortly thereafter that Edith started hearing the midnight horse. It would come galloping up at full speed into the yard, stomp and snort, rear up, and then tear around to circle the house. After making several laps, the mysterious steed would then leave just as suddenly as it appeared. Next morning a close examination of the grounds invariably revealed nothing, no tracks, or other evidence to support her story. However, Edith was not alone in hearing this equestrian apparition, for Mae swore to it as well. At first, it manifested almost every night, but since the desired effect of creating a vacancy never occurred, the frequency of appearance dropped off significantly after a few weeks. Remarkably, the midnight horse never quite left for good, for upon a rare occasion, even unto this day, an encore presentation is given.

Gradually, and almost against his will, Jesse found himself liking their new home. By that time, however, the winds of winter had been howling through the ancient apple trees for weeks. Wade kept them warm, actually near the point of overheating from a huge supply of firewood he kept on hand. On warmer days, Edith dug potatoes out of the frozen ground from a crop that Jim had planted but never harvested. Earlier in the season with prospects of selling the house, and being lazy, he had decided to let the new owners have the pleasure. They loved roasting potatoes in the fireplace beneath a layer of hot ashes. Usually it took about thirty minutes to get the spuds just right. Buttered and sprinkled with salt, they then made a delicious snack. Another treat, they also discovered, was to pour sorghum syrup over cornbread, especially onto the crust.

One night in late January, lying in bed, Jesse and his daddy had a long conversation. With part of the house partitioned off, they found it necessary to sleep in the living room. Jesse liked it; to him being able to drift off while watching the red glow of embers in the fireplace slowly fade, was a luxury. This night, however, the usual hypnotic effect of flickering coals seemed to have little effect on either of them.

"Daddy," Jesse asked after watching his father flip restlessly in bed.

"What, Son, what is it? Can't you go to sleep neither? I thought you'd dropped off a long time ago."

"No, Daddy, I was just wondering, though, when will you be quitting over at Fontana and be home like you used to?"

"Well, Son, I guess sometime after the first of March I'll be home most nights then, but I'll still keep my job there. It's just that I'll have a way back and forth after that; several of us men will be riding together. Why? Are you afraid when I'm not here?"

"No! No!" Jesse lied, "I ain't afraid of these old haints, not a bit. It just gets lonesome when you're gone, and, besides, I thought you said we'd be doing some farming next year."

"That's right, Jesse, we will be, and that's one reason I can't sleep. It keeps running through my mind how me and you can clear some of that land up there above the road, and put it into corn. You know, our grandparents made a real garden spot out of this place and, by Ned, we can do it, too!"

Father and son talked deeper into the night about buying a horse, fixing up the barn and corncrib, building new pigpens, a chicken house, those and many other projects. Jesse's interest was peaked most, however, by the thought of finding a pair of young oxen to buy. He could already see himself in a cart, pulled along by two gentle giants, while he masterfully guided them up and down Sweetwater road. Long after the rhythmic snoring of his daddy began, Jesse's mind was still on the future with all its possibilities.

Had he been able to see what lay ahead, it would have energized him even more. While they never did get the oxen, they did buy a horse. Tug was a beautiful and highly intelligent bay, with an incredible spirit so gentle and kind that the family came to love him, almost as much as they had Mike.

Indeed, the next few years would prove to be both challenging and charming. Mid-summer days spent eating green apples, sometimes so sour they turned his face side-ways. He and six or seven others could often be found hunched over their comic books, and munching away.

The coldness of winter held for him an entirely different kind of thrill. He would shiver in ecstasy after rushing from the glowing heat of Wade's fireplace to a fodder-lined outdoor privy. Once there he secretly gloated over having such a warm cocoon to shield him against the howling winds, while taking care of business.

He also relished the countless hours he and Max played football with their friends in the front yard. Without helmet or pad, they still battled like pros, oft times reeking from the mixed smell of sweat, grass and chicken-crap. Usually, they had so much fun it took the dark of night to drive them indoors. Cherished most, perhaps, was the delicious taste of forbidden fruit, especially that to be found at the swimming hole. Forbidden, because of a scourge called polio, its deadly virus lurked in a million hiding places. However, for Jesse the temptation was always worth the risk, even those times he got caught. It was most fortunate, indeed, that a leather strap to the backside was all it cost him; others were not so lucky.

Then there were the taffy pulling parties, the dew soaked mornings to pick berries, and raids on the grape vines. Of course, eating black cherries while sitting perched atop an ancient tree limb, it some seventy-five feet up provided its own excitement.

No, had he known of these and a thousand other delights, he would have quickly brushed aside the cobwebs of a sleepless night, to go racing madly toward the sunrise of his future.

CHAPTER 18

Bound to earth from our birth
Yet yearning to be free
The adolescence of our soul
Believes that it can be

"Jesse, if you're going with Ma this morning, you'd better jump up!" Edith said, sounding impatient. Since it was Saturday, she had let him sleep as late as possible, yet now his breakfast was getting cold. Once awake, the twelve-year-old hardly needed further prodding, however. Quickly dressing, he slid into a pair of overalls while ignoring the need for shoes and a shirt. At the table, Edith watched with amusement as three of her cathead biscuits vanished within moments of his arrival. *Just like moths disappearing before the mouth of a big frog*, she smiled.

Jesse glanced across at Ma as she nudged a platter of sliced country ham toward him. "Child," she crooned, "It's a just a little bite, but it'll go good with that red-eye gravy. Mae would have eat it all up if I hadn't set this aside for you."

Untying her apron, Ma used one of its tattered edges to wipe clean her chin before continuing. "It's awful pretty out this morning, and, no doubt, the mail-boy will be crowded, so try to get ready just as soon as you can." As usual, they would be riding the mail car into town, and that meant being at the roadside before it arrived. "I want to be sure Jesse gets a good seat," she said. "Last time that sorry Fred Ranger sat humped up in the back seat like a big catbird and this little feller had to ride in the trunk. I thought, my lands, what a shame this is." She then added a solemn footnote. "So, Edith, if it's the Lord's will and we get to go, Ed will have us back home sometime around four-thirty."

Sand along the road, cooled by kisses stolen from the morning's flirtatious breezes, felt pleasant and satin-like beneath Jesse's summer toughened feet. Staying well ahead of Ma, he trotted along as his gaze searched the hazy blue of mountains on the far horizon. It was then his thoughts left their terrestrial moorings, and soared to worlds yet untouched and unsullied by human hands. These were orbs filled with adoring maidens, girls with silky-flowing hair, and all of them clamoring for his attention. However, being pure and aloof he walked along their flower-strewn path teasing them with just a smile. Sighing at his bulging biceps, they gasped in astonishment when he burst the buttons from his shirt, this by merely taking a deep breath. Then finally he saw her, the loveliest of them all, the one who alone was worthy of his attention. Never, it seemed, could he remember a time when she, with her long flaxen hair and sad, beautiful countenance did not fill his every reverie. This time he saw them standing near a crystal-clear stream, and beneath the bowers of a giant spreading tree, pledging their love, eternal and true. It was while seeking the nectar found only at the surface of his beloved's lips that the unthinkable happened.

Unfortunately, a cut, as cruel as any ever rendered by the guillotine, severed Jesse's day from his dream. It arrived on the sharp edge of derisive laughter, sounding exactly like a hyena. Jesse knew immediately this could emanate but from one source, and that was the dark maw of his despicable cousin, Raymond Reece. Better known as Gutch, all six feet and one hundred twenty pounds of this twelve-year-old was, to Jesse, a recurring nightmare.

While Eden had her serpent and apples have their worms, Jesse Gernon had Gutch. His dislike for this contemptible wretch ran deep and bitter and he based it on several very solid reasons. Among them was the fact that Gutch hardly ever attended school, and they let him get away with it, too. Also, he smoked cigarettes and did so right in front of grownups, making it obvious he lived the life of a modern-day Huck Finn. In addition, he was a head taller than Jesse was, or anybody else his own age, and being part Cherokee his dark, good looks seemed to make him irresistible to girls.

"Well, I'll swear if it ain't *little Jesse*," Gutch's black eyes sparkled. "Where's your Ma, Son?" He asked, talking baby talk. "I know she must be nearby, 'cause if you needed to pee, who'd be here to hold your little hand?"

Jesse felt his anger flare, but he could not afford to let Gutch know, otherwise he'd never let up.

Gutch continued to laugh, if that is what was, while Jesse cursed his luck.

Silently he began praying that God would forever ban this scarecrow from his vineyard. *I can't let him know he's getting to me, I just can't,* Jesse gritted his teeth in determination. "Yeah, well, Son, you talk awful big for somebody who's scared of the dark, but you ought to be, the way you go around cussing all the time. The devil going to get you one of these nights, and he'll roast you alive!"

Raymond appeared unwilling to waste his time with such nonsense, besides there were plenty of ways yet to get Jesse riled.

By now, they were in sight of the mailboxes and Ma would be glad to know that no one else was there ahead of them. Jesse, however, did not feel like rejoicing since he knew Raymond would not let up.

"Let's see how good you can grip," the big boy demanded. Jesse was afraid of this, Gutch was back to badgering him again about it. Lately, every time he saw Jesse, he had been pestering him to do it. Actually, what Gutch wanted to do was crush his hand. The truth was hard to admit, but had to face up to it; he was more than just a little afraid of this freckled-faced tobacco worm. Jesse had watched him bring much larger boys than he was to their knees, some crying in pain. Towering over him, Gutch belied his age and appeared to be much older than he really was. Even more threatening, however, was his way of spouting cuss words. He seemed to take great delight in intimidating contemporaries by using a much-tried and well-practiced method. Scowling menacingly, he would lower the pitch but not the volume of his naturally cantankerous voice and then proceed to sear the eardrums of anyone within range of his scorching tongue.

"No, I don't want to," Jesse said. This while shaking his head to underscore a firm resolve. However, such resistance only served to spur the long-legged donkey on.

Reece scoffed, "By golly, I knowed you was scared of me! All you Gernons are nothing but a bunch of cowards. Why, I could run the whole lot of you off the head of Sweetwater with nothing but a crooked stick." To prove his point he reached down, and, in an air of exaggerated deliberation, selected the most twisted branch he could find. Jesse probably would have confirmed his claim and fled like a craven coward, had it not been for one notable fact. Gutch just happened to mention Ma in his tirade of insults.

"Your old Ma ain't no account, neither; she goes around clattering her head off and telling everybody what a great wonder you are. Just babying you to death," he sneered. "Now, you'd better get from here, Boy, or I'm liable to whup that butt for you."

That was it; that is all it took! Gutch might well ridicule him and walk all over the family name, but he was not going to besmirch Ma like that. Not and get away with it.

"Grip!" Jesse bellowed. His voice sounded hollow and strangely detached. Whether it was from the tone of voice or the quick change in attitude, that will never be known; but a look of alarm crossed Gutch's face. Nevertheless, he extended his right hand.

Adrenaline in great gushes flowed through Jesse to supply him with an enormous rush of power. It surged into the hand that held Gutch's, and he squeezed as though wringing milk from one of Dun's teats. Surprisingly, Jesse felt no pain; perhaps the injury was so severe that his hand was too numb. He did feel, however, something warm and wet falling onto his naked shoulder just as Gutch jerked loose. Jesse looked up into two brown eyes that only seconds before had beheld him with scorn. Now they were overflowing with great drops of pain.

"You're just a bully," said the tear-soaked words that somehow washed away Jesse's moment of triumph, making him feel ashamed. "Son, you got mad and really hurt my hand while I was only teasing you. It takes a real crappy sport to do that! So, we ain't going to be buddies no more… Nope, I ain't never going to play with you agin." He tossed the parting words over his shoulder, but not in time to get away before Ma caught up with them.

"What was that all about?" she asked, looking more than a little concerned. However, Raymond did not stop to answer her, but moved quickly away, fleeing like a shadow before the sun. Speaking from the heart, Ma's head swung gently from side to side as pity poured forth. "That poor young'in," she bemoaned, "why, he ain't never had a chance in this world. Not with that sorry daddy of his being gone from home all the time and then there's his poor mother, my goodness, Alma wouldn't know what it was to draw a well breath."

Fortunately, the soft hum of Ed Jennings' '46 Chevrolet spared Jesse of further remorse. Nevertheless, it was just as Ma feared; he already had a near full load of passengers. Taking into account that he recently had upped the charge to twenty-five cents a head, made this quite remarkable. Wanting to accommodate as much as possible, Ed would pile them in or on his automobile, just as long as they kept coming. To help with this, his car had undergone several unique modifications. One of these was to enlarge the luggage rack, thus freeing up trunk space for extra seating. In addition, a makeshift running board, recently attached to the right side, now provided a place for the standing-room-only patrons to ride.

Today, with four already in the back seat and two besides himself in the front, Ma expressed doubts about room for anyone else. Ed, however, smiled a big tobacco-stained grin and quickly swept aside such nonsense. "Pshaw, Ellie, Jesse there can ride in the trunk and I've got plenty of room for you right here beside me. We've still got to pick up two or three more at Stumpy's, so, no Ma'am, you get right in and make yourself comfortable."

Jesse knew well that she did not approve, but he really did not mind it at all. Hurt frowned Ma's face when Ed lifted the trunk lid and propped it up with a broom handle. Cut just the right length, the stick, no doubt, would hold the lid securely in place. Actually, he felt right at home nestled in his own private compartment. Unknowingly, Jesse was now on his way to what, ultimately, would prove to be one of the most incredible days of his life.

From this special berth, he watched as twin spirals of dust swirled upwards and back down again before gently settling into their new but uneasy resting places. The two-mile stretch to Stumpy's was quickly covered and upon arrival, they discovered that, indeed, other passengers were there waiting, just as Ed predicted.

Stumpy's was a typical "old-timey" store, well stocked with a full line of merchandise that ranged from farm implements to dry goods, seeds, patent medicine and groceries. His store, set central to the community, had a higher calling than merely providing food and work materials to a mountain village. It was also the post office and gossip center to a sizeable portion of the county. The well-to-do and the ne'er-do-wells could gather here and share common ground. Gossip was gospel until proven otherwise, and few there were who doubted.

Ed cheerily announced he would be there for about ten minutes and advised they make only "necessary" visits. For several days now Jesse had been craving an RC cola and he knew exactly where to find it; therefore, very little of Ed's precious time would be wasted.

Once his tears cleared, brought on by the chilled carbonate, Jesse looked around the dimly lit store to where he saw two elderly men, both, probably in their mid-forties, grinning at him. He immediately recognized the thinner one to be Jack Woodcock. Jack lifted his brows in salute while poking an elbow into Fred Ranger's rib. "Fred," he wheezed, "I'll swear if the back of that boy's head didn't cave in a little bit there while he was a pulling on that bottle. Did you see it, too?"

Fred snickered and then drew his big Barlow knife open, being careful to wipe the blade clean by dragging it across the knee of his overalls. After thoughtful contemplation he finally spoke up, "Can't say I did, Jack, but you know them Gernon boys are all awful thick-headed. I betcha if he'd a wanted to, he could've sucked the bottom out of that thing, getting to the last drop." Something sinister accompanied Fred's wink at Jesse as he neatly trimmed the corner off his tobacco plug. Tucking a large chew halfway back into his jaw, he rhetorically asked in a husky grunting voice, "You Wade's boy, hain't you, Son?"

Jesse was not at all certain why the question came up; Fred knew exactly who he was. He never liked the man before and certainly did not now. Feeling suddenly hot and flushed despite the RC, his throat began to close up on him. Swallowing hard Jesse nodded and tried to speak, but all that got for his efforts was a squeaky voice that surely must have belonged to somebody else. Instantly, he detested the sound. "Yeah, that's right, Fred, I'm the oldest." He had been out of the car for less than five minutes, yet he wondered now if the trip had really been necessary after all, and quickly decided no. If he had a single doubt left, it immediately evaporated to the sound of dry, raspy laughter that followed him through the door.

It surprised him not at all to learn that he and Fred would be riding together in Ed's trunk. Jesse could not help but feel a little smug; after all, it was comforting to know that Fred would not get a seat inside, either.

Meanwhile, Jack jumped onto the running board and hooked his arm through the open window as Ed pulled out. They moved along, slowly at first, and then gained momentum as Ed shifted into higher gears. When you stop to think about it, his car carried the weight of ten passengers, three bags of mail and a driver. This was no easy feat, not by any means!

As they neared town, the familiar sight of tall metal towers appeared off in the distance. Stretching as far as the eye could see, these glistening spires carried enormous quantities of hydroelectric power to an outside world. They looked like an army of steel giants tethered together and marching single file through the mountains. In their presence, Jesse suddenly felt small and insignificant; did that somehow portend an omen for what lay ahead?

CHAPTER 19

Historic Robbinsville sits prominently on a long, low knoll that overlooks the confluence of the Cheoah and Tallulah rivers. As both the county seat and business center, the hamlet in 1948 was very much like a young woman in love. After twenty years of denial through depression and another world war, she now was ready to live. Graced by majestic mountains, blessed by nature and nature's God with a superb climate, she was ripe for the good life. The returned service men were her darlings and they could do no wrong. Some of them may have had their fling in San Francisco or been infatuated with Paris, but none knew real love until they got back home. Streets, long silent and empty, now resounded with activity. New businesses sprang up everywhere, causing a slight ill-of-ease feeling amongst some of the better ensconced. One spirited citizen was heard to express his ambivalence with this observation; "Seems like the blue bird of paradise just dropped a big turd right in the middle of Courthouse Square and nobody knows what to do with it." Such was the Robbinsville that awaited a mail-car full of gregarious social seekers on that long ago early September morning.

Ed eased into a parking spot, and before they scattered, he reminded the passengers to be ready to leave at exactly three-thirty. Those with a watch checked theirs against his, noting the time to be precisely ten twenty-four. Obviously, they would have ample time to enjoy the many delights offered by this grand little town.

After taking but a few steps, Jesse looked up and saw the perfect reason for a spoiled trip. It seemed unbelievable, yet standing right before him was none other than Gutch Reece. He still looked exactly like a wretched scarecrow. Now, however, he was talking to the driver of a car, who, no doubt in some moment of misguided pity, had given the contemptible mendicant a ride into town. "Give me that duck," Reece demanded as he reached through the window to snatch a half-smoked cigarette from his benefactor's lips. Without further ado, he then hiked his pants, already three inches too short, and strode cockily away.

It was becoming increasingly evident that this day, which had begun with so much promise, had suddenly been doomed to failure. Jesse had seen it happen all too often, and perhaps fate has decreed it to be so, but if a bad thing happens once, it was bound to happen again and again. Yes, there was no doubt about it; Gutch Reece would prove to be the proverbial bad penny before this day was over. Jesse's heart sank at the prospect.

Saturday mornings, from early April until late October, were horse-trading days in Robbinsville. Traders and sellers alike brought their stock, often times in great herds, to town. Courthouse Square was the central arena for this activity and favorite sites were often vied for with a truculence that bordered on open warfare. Indeed, one of the main reasons the faithful came as early as daybreak, was to observe these many skirmishes. By September, however, most territorial disputes had been settled long before, so when farmers, loafers, eastern cowboys, and old men of all callings kept coming, it was in the hope of seeing something that would help to ease the passing of another long week.

Alas, as in the manner that flies are wont ever to torment horses, so was the blight of town boys always around to pester and constantly be underfoot while plying their odious ways. These street-urchins are never to be confused with the fine upstanding young men who sometimes occasioned into town for the sake of business or some other good purpose. No, these pests were a public nuisance, always in the way and acting as if they knew exactly how to tend to horses. Nothing could be further from the truth, however; they were there for the sole purpose of begging, stealing, or otherwise trying to take advantage of some innocent soul who might wander into their malevolent clutches. Even Gutch Reece had learned to be wary of their evil devising.

Not a person easily given to hyperbole, Jesse would still feel compelled to admit that the sights and sounds that greeted him on this spectacular autumn morning was a complete delight to him. A near carnival atmosphere accompanied this, the finest gathering of horses he had ever witnessed, and it had a singular effect on him. He now knew, without doubt, that he would not rest until one of these fine animals was his own.

When Jesse told Ma of his desire to go look over the stock, he watched bewilderment cast a shadow over her normally bright eyes. Obviously hurt, she responded with a question. “Why, Jesse, what on earth do you want to do that for? I thought you liked helping me do the trading.”

Not mentioned, but to her just as perplexing, was the fact that he would not be with her while visiting old friends. Still, being the kind-hearted grandmother that she was, Ma relented. Not before, however, extracting two promises from him; first, he was to watch out for the horse’s hoofs, and secondly, they would meet at Mayor Sluder’s house at eleven forty-five sharp. In parting, Ma had an added a word of advice; “Jesse, you just remember what our little preacher said about pool rooms; they’re dens of iniquity, and I expect you to stay out of them! Just keep in mind that good man knows exactly from whereof he speaks, because at one time he was a tool of the devil. But now, though, I believe his only desire is to serve the Lord.”

Perhaps it was due to the excitement or maybe from the twelve ounces of RC cola, but in any event, the young adventurer found he was getting more and more uncomfortable by the moment. Suddenly, his total concentration centered on one objective, finding a bathroom and finding it fast: he needed to pee. Fortunately, the courthouse offered public restrooms, so he made a beeline for the nearest door. Trouble was, the closer he got the more he hurt, so he began praying that no one would be ahead of him. Summarily, the answer came; however, it only served to remind him that one must always ask aright. For although the way, indeed, was clear, he still could not use the facility. Located top center on the door he spotted a typewritten note, but it was almost too high to read. On tiptoe, he managed to see a phrase that truly shook his faith. For him the words “out of order” spelled just one thing and that was trouble. The note, undoubtedly written by some compassionate and well-meaning soul, also suggested using the men’s room at the firehouse. Good advice, perhaps, but with such a vital service located over two blocks away, it may as well have been on the moon.

A big red oak tree, standing just beneath the steep bank and east of the courthouse, once again proved its worth. Many a suffering pilgrim had stood in the dense mass of ragweed and golden-rod, near the rugged base of this ancient landmark, and felt grateful for its presence. Moments later, shivering with relief, he was ready to have another look at the horses, so he readied himself for a run up the incline.

The low hum of male voices, however, stopped him in his tracks. Embarrassed, he pressed back into the underbrush and waited. From the sound of it, two men were in earnest conversation, and definitely moving in his direction. Knowing they probably meant to do him no harm, he felt secure enough to step forward, but that was before hearing a few of the muffled words.

"Charlie, I'm in bad shape, Son, and need to ask a big favor of you," said a voice pleadingly.

"What do you mean, Preacher?" was the reply, sounding harsh and unsympathetic.

Hunkering down in hopes of gaining better concealment, Jesse actually improved his view, allowing him to see them better. The younger of the two had reddish-blond hair, obviously thinning. After a moment, they moved a little closer and an amazing discovery was made; *why, he's our new evangelist the Reverend Claude Conway!* Jesse gasped silently. Again, he was ready to step forward, but something inside begged that he stay put. The two men slowly circled positions, allowing Jesse a better view of the other one. Much older that his companion, he resembled an ancient tree with its twisted trunk and limbs all knotted and gnarled. Obviously, here was a person who had endured many a stormy episode of arthritis. His wrinkled, leathery face framed a huge blade of nose and eyes that twinkled mischievously. His most notable feature, however, was a thatch of gray-streaked black hair. Jesse recognized at once that he was looking at his great-uncle and Beech Creek's very own, Charlie Ammons.

Placing a forefinger to his lips, Charlie leaned forward while staring directly into Conway's face. A sneer added tension when he repeated the question, this time using slightly different words. "Huh, do what? Say, just what kind of favor do you want anyway?" His voice, although low in volume, still sounded harsh.

"Dad burn it, Charlie, I need me a pint of likker." Thinking Charlie was hard of hearing he spoke louder than necessary, but that only brought him a look of disgust. Claude Conway was flustered, his red face and searching eyes indicated as much. Fortunately, he missed seeing Jesse, less than ten feet away.

When Charlie spoke again, Jesse noticed that his lips seemed hardly to move at all. "Ain't you supposed to be a man of God, Son?" Charlie's stare was so cold it caused Jesse to shiver again, much like he did at the tree. "And, what makes you think I fool with that stuff, anyhow?" He shook his head disgustedly. "The only thing any sorrier than a drunk woman is a drunk preacher, but either one will make you want to puke! They ain't no telling what kind of mess this might cause. Who sent you, anyway?"

Claude dropped his head in embarrassment. "Well see, I've got this nervous stomach, and old Doc Cranford told me to get a pint of good whiskey like you make. Said it would do me a heap better than anything he could prescribe. Now I'll swear that's the truth, Son. Oh, I could buy me all I want to from Jack Woodcock, but I'm scared to death of his."

The old man lifted his eyes and looked unto the hills from whence he had come. His gaze beheld the far horizon for what seemed like an eternity. Meanwhile, a fleecy white cloud drifted slowly over to dust off High Top's tallest peak. When its work was finally over, Charlie turned and looked again into eyes that pleaded earnestly for an answer. "Preacher, hand me a dollar, and then look over yonder under that piece of chestnut log," he snarled.

"Oh God bless you, Charlie, but please don't mention this to nobody. Why, if the word ever got out, they'd run me out of town. Fact is, and the Lord knows it's the truth, I'm a sick man."

Jesse had just witnessed an event that left him shaken. He saw Charlie finally smile, but it was only after the money changed hands. It amazed him to see how broad his great-uncle could grin while just barely moving his lips. More amazing still, however, was how much medicine the ailing preacher needed.. It took nearly one third of the bottle for his first dose. *Reverend Conway's a whole lot sicker feller than anybody knows*, Jesse thought.

Just the shadow of a moment, quicker than the hand of a gypsy, was all the time it took for the pair to absent themselves. They left nothing behind except a hushed goodbye whispered in the waving motion of the dense undergrowth. Unrealized until they were gone was just how tense Jesse had become during this. His left arm was asleep and both thighs ached from squatting so long in one position. However, he simultaneously felt a great sense of relief that it was over. Not able to understand what it all meant, he, nevertheless, believed that something evil had passed his way. The mere thought of it scared him.

One mighty rush for the bank quickly thrust him back into a surging tide of people. Immediately, he felt better again.

Drifting along with the current, he soon found himself at the entrance of Holly's Five and Dime Store. Of all the places in town, this was his favorite, but never had he been there by himself before. Full of magic, it held the pre-eminent location in town. Although one of Robbinsville's smaller shops, it was the first building noticed when approaching Main Street. Mainly, this was because of its white façade and bright red lettering.

Mr. Holly, proprietor, was a kindly, albeit nervous man with a rather severe attitude toward enforcing store policy. However, he and Mrs. Holly truly loved children, and over the years had developed a knack for displaying their wares in such an attractive manner, they succeeded to charm many a tiny heart to madness. This, in turn, became a tremendous source of power, allowing them to cudgel the most resistant parent into a submissive buyer.

Hardas' usual manner was to follow the youthful shopper at a respectful distance, but a quick eye might catch him artfully re-positioning his disturbed merchandise. Once he determined that the browser was most likely just a "lookers only" patron, he had a fine way of repeatedly clearing his throat, until the bogus customer left.

It was into this well guarded environment, so enchanting, that Jesse wandered while harboring the desire that he too, might reach a new level of imagination. In this, he was destined not to be disappointed. He ambled down the center aisle looking over the inventory until he neared the back of the store. It was there that the brightly painted walls suddenly turned into panels of deep, rich-red, velvet. They, trimmed in blue satin and gold brocade, seemed to hold a power that magnified the shop's special charm. Row upon row of dolls dressed in white, pink, or pale blue moved like ballerinas to the soft background music provided by a crimson-coated orchestra of specially carved figurines. Tiny hands of the dancers moved in unison to wave him toward a special door, a tiny one set within another door that was otherwise ordinary in both size and appearance. Somewhat reluctantly he took his eyes away from the minuet long enough to walk toward it. He had a strange feeling that he had seen it all before, yet at the same time knew that he had not. Probably it opened into Mr. Holly's back lot, so there would have been little reason for him to know about it. Still, its ornate and rather odd features provoked an overpowering need to take a closer look.

A feeling of gentleness and contentment began to wash over him as he reached for the handle of the smaller door. The larger one was constructed of common materials, but its smaller inset appeared to be made of a very fine wood, perhaps that of highly polished walnut. To the left side, a sealed crystal vessel, gleaming like transparent gold, contained a tiny key attached to a silver cord. Obviously, to loosen the silver cord and use the key, the crystal vessel must first be broken. The lock glistened and seemed to invite he open it, but suddenly a spirit of fear swept over him and he was about to turn away. That, however, is when he noticed a narrow slit at the top hinge where the small door was set. No power on earth could then have kept him from taking a peep. Just why he felt so intrigued he could never fully explain, for in verity all he expected to see was the backside of

Robbinsville. After all, that is where town sloped down and away from the shop. The slice of light passing through the crack afforded, at best, a very limited view of what lay beyond. It took rubbing his eyes and blinking several times before he could focus on the remarkable scene set before him. Rather than the eroded hillside, he gazed, instead, upon the loveliest and most tranquil panorama his eyes had ever beheld.

In wonderful array spread before him was a large valley, much wider than that of Sweetwater. Surrounding it were beautiful snow capped mountains with a wide stream meandering through the vale. Home to vast forests there were also scattered copses of trees standing tall and magnificent with their silvered green leaves glistening beneath an azure sky.

Mid-foreground to this living masterpiece was an evergreen, a spruce most eminent with its lowermost bowers gracefully embracing a grassy carpet strewn with flowers. On the top branch sat a great eagle with its wings outspread, prepared to soar. When Jesse gazed upon the scene, he thought surely this must be Eden and it was at that time he noticed a beautiful flaxen-haired woman. Bound about her gown of snow white was a golden girdle and atop her head rested a glistening tiara. Jesse was shocked to see that she was weeping bitterly and it was as if by signal that she looked up and directly at him, her voice rang clear as she lamented:

"O, must I forever weep
For those who are so blind?
Ask, and it will be given,
Seek, and you will find!"

"It's her, the one I always dream about!" he shouted. Reaching for the door to fling it open, he was astonished to find himself looking at one of Robbinsville's most unseemly back streets. He had opened the wrong door! In his great haste, he had opened the larger one. However, upon closer inspection he realized it to be the only one he could have opened. For gone was the little door within the door, also was gone the key within the vial, but most distressing of all, the angel too, was gone. Not gone however, was the deep sadness she left behind.

There is little telling how long he would have just stood there thinking on these things had it not been for Mr. Holly moving in behind him. First heard clearing his throat, he then spoke, but not too kindly, "Son, let's close that up, it's supposed to keep the honest folks in and the rest of 'em out. Here, now, let me lock it back and I'd appreciate it if in the future you didn't mess with my door."

Leaving the shop, Jesse brushed away several drops of moisture that somehow had gathered in his eyes. Noticeably, this improved his view of Bart Stevens seen piloting a large farm wagon past the clutter and chaos of Robbinsville's busiest day. Drawn by two powerful mules, Bart and his wagon was an established sight in town, going to and from the nearby fields he tended. The old farmer responded to Jesse's salute by cordially waving back. Little could either know, or even suspect, the extraordinary events they both must face before this day was over.

CHAPTER 20

Good as his word, Jesse kept his promise to meet Ma for lunch at the Sluder's. Arriving a few minutes early, he wistfully walked past the Joyce Kilmer Restaurant where he secretly had hoped they might dine. He and Ma had often enjoyed a meal together in this fine establishment. A tract of nearby virgin hardwood had been set aside in memorial to the great poet and his poem, "Trees." Of special interest to Jesse was the fact that President Franklin D. Roosevelt dedicated it on July 30, 1936, a mere three days before he was born. None of this, however, held much import for Jesse since he must now look forward to, as Ma put it, "one of Ida Sluder's good home-cooked meals." Trouble was, about all he ever got was "good home-cooked meals." What he really craved was some good store-bought kind, for a change.

Most people believed the office of Mayor to be nonpolitical with Mr. Sluder always running unopposed, this being de facto evidence of his unusually wily political instincts. He was so good at playing the game that much of the town was completely oblivious to the fact that he had them at all. For that matter, most could not remember a time when he was not their leader, yet they felt that his was a lifetime appointment, perhaps by Divine right.

The Sluder's lived in a huge Victorian house that was made to look even more massive by its chalk white exterior. The impressive structure was barely able to squeeze in between Holly's Dime Store and the Robin Theatre. Going inside was tantamount to taking a historical tour of Robbinsville. For it was there in that pale blue and pink striped wallpapered living room where many of the town's archives were on display. Included was the original town charter, dozens of photographs, deeds, and many other official documents. Above the white marble fireplace stood a Kelly green, oval-shaped, metal shield emblazoned with large script yellow letters that proudly proclaimed the title of "Mayor."

Despite efforts to keep the front room from appearing somber by the use of floral upholstered furniture and color-coordinated drapery, a definite funeral parlor ambiance still prevailed. Overnight guests were few, even though the mayor and his wife were among the most cordial of hosts. They often went out of their way to make folks feel welcome. Many locals said the house was haunted and Splinter Collins claimed his hair turned white within twenty-four hours after seeing strange lights spiral skyward from the manse. He recalled being alone early one Sunday morning while walking on the sidewalk in front of the structure. "It was about 2:30," he said, "when all hell broke loose." "Actually," he continued, "I wasn't feeling much pain when danged if I didn't see blue lights start shooting out the top of that old house. Looked to me like it had been struck by a king sized bolt of lightening; trouble was the flashes were flying straight up instead of the other way around. Must have lasted a good two or three minutes, but it sure seemed a lot longer, and it nearly scared the heck out of me. I guess I would have just stood there watching if it hadn't been for that big red ball of fire. I'll bet you that thing must have been a good three or four feet high and it come rolling off the roof right at me. Well, sir, reckon you can see I didn't hang around for the rest of the show, but it still troubles me a lot. I didn't know, and still don't for certain, but was the good Lord trying to tell me something, or what? Maybe He was or maybe it was because Jack Woodcock had just run off another bad batch. It's hard to say, but it don't pay to take no chances, so I'm a changed man now. The way I see it, life's just too short for that kind of foolishness. Charlie Ammons will get my money from here on out!"

While the town was about evenly divided over whether to believe Splinter or not, most would agree that there, indeed, did exist a very strange quality about the place. Interestingly, another mystery swirled around their beloved mayor, and it, too, remains unexplained. A lot like his home, large, open, breezy, and dedicated to the public, Bruce was always seen dressed in a medium gray suit and therein resides the enigma, for he never wore anything else. It always appeared to be well worn, slightly wrinkled and had shiny spots on each knee that never wore through. Bud Eller, sole dry-cleaner in town, emphatically denied that he had ever cleaned the garment or seen one like it. He certainly could offer no explanation as to why it appeared to possess such eternal qualities. Unfortunately, no one else could or would shed light on this grave secret and that is where it rests, even unto this present day.

Jesse and Ma found Mr. Sluder to be at his hearty best, he liked nothing better than the opportunity to entertain. They joined him on the large sofa while Ida busied herself in the kitchen. Before long, their gregarious host was plying Ma with questions about some of the many relatives they held in common. To Jesse, most of the names they bandied about were like disembodied spirits floating above his head, with no real attachment to this world. Politely pretending to listen, his mind began to wander back to the dime store, but that is when Mayor Sluder turned the spotlight onto him. "Now, you're Wade and Edith's eldest child, aren't you, Son?"

Answering silently, Jesse nodded several times. He hoped this would be the extent of his interrogation, not being used to such high-level attention. For some reason he literally detested the word "eldest."

"Speak up, Child, and talk to Bruce," Ma encouraged. "He's your first cousin twice removed on Matt's side."

Further probing led Jesse to believe that his distinguished cousin would not be satisfied until he got every detail of his life, including those about school. Still, and he would be the first to admit it, Bruce had such a warm way of making conversation that he actually began to enjoy the friendly exchange. Seemingly then, without either effort or precipitous modification to the dialog, this very articulate city-father moved an arid subject to a more verdant part of the vineyard.

"Dave Gernon," he reminisced, repeatedly rolling the name over across his tongue like a hot, but tasty morsel. Nodding ever so slightly, he then continued. "That old scamp's a real rascal and the devil's own man, but, I'll swear, you can't help but like him. I doubt there's ever been a better hearted person to live on Sweetwater." Hearing his grandfather's name mentioned came as no surprise to Jesse, and he rightly surmised that the good mayor was referring to Dave's belief system. In polite company, most folks would call him an agnostic, but privately the word "infidel" kept coming up.

Ma sensed Jesse's discomfort and picked up the conversation. "Why, I reckon he'd give you the shirt off his back if you asked him to, but he's still a wicked old man who needs to change his ways."

"Me and Dave used to get drunk together, back when we were just still house pups and lapping up every drop we could get. I reckon he's going to keep right on drinking 'til the day he drops; I just wish he'd learn to leave it alone. Dave's got a good mind and ought to be putting it to better use." Pity filled Bruce's words, but suddenly he switched moods to one that was much more optimistic. "It's been well over thirty years now since my last drink, Ella, and I would hope to die today if I ever touched another drop. No sir, it's all just a big waste."

Words spoken in haste sometimes have a way of becoming prophetic. These, uttered by the Mayor, would linger long in Jesse's memory to remind him of how much weight the Bible places on what we say. At this moment, however, Ida was the one who could claim title to a statement that held the most gravity. "The little bite is just about ready, so you'uns run in there and wash up, then we'll eat."

Soon they were at the big round mahogany table and holding hands, while Mr. Sluder asked the blessing. His voice, wrapped in reverence and aimed straight at Paradise, left little doubt as to his status with the one beseeched. Following the much-awaited "Amen," he then extended a most gracious invitation for all to partake. And how abundantly it was supplied!

Jesse had never seen the beat. He faced a veritable banquet that consisted of a variety of vegetables, roast beef, fried country ham, and a large chicken casserole. Accompanying this were side dishes of gravy, with pickles and condiments found thoughtfully placed everywhere. Ida also had baked fresh cornbread and prepared a big pitcher of iced tea, but by far the best part rested right in front of him. Strongly implied but not stated was the disappointing news that this centerpiece of her culinary art must wait until meal's end for serving. Actually, it was because of this utterly inane custom of saving the dessert until last that denied Jesse the chance to get even a taste Ida's delicious looking lemon meringue pie. In retrospect, however, who could have foreseen the untimely events about to unfold?

Lost now to memory was any of the disappointment Jesse felt about eating at the Joyce Kilmer Restaurant as he pursued the lusty leanings of his appetite. It was when he asked for a second helping that he chanced to look up and catch Mrs. Sluder's beaming smile. Obviously, the sight of her food evaporating like cotton candy was meat for her soul.

All but unnoticed by Jesse, the conversation had continued unabated, yet now it seemed to be picking up steam. "I guess you heard they've set an execution date again?" Bruce asked, referring to Guy Fowler and Lance Boyle.

Nodding, Ma frowned, but signaled with her eyes that he should continue. "I've got some real doubts here about the justice in all this, and if there's anybody in the world who wants to see that done, it's me and Ida. Of course, you know losing Earl like that has just about killed us both. My land, Ellie, Earl was Ida's favorite nephew. I'm just so very thankful that we got to see him at the family reunion in Winston-Salem… it was the Sunday just before he went to be with the Lord."

Offering butter all around before taking a generous serving himself, Bruce proceeded with the story. “Yes, we talked at length down there about some things that weighed heavily on his heart. You know, of course, that he and your son Keith had gotten to be rather close since they were going to be brothers-in-law. Well sir, and I’m certain you’re aware of this too, but Earl had collected some very incriminating evidence on a bootlegging ring that was operating right there in their midst. Obviously, we all know now that it was Guy Fowler and Lance Boyle working with Jack Woodcock. No doubt there were others too, but somehow they’ve slipped through the net.” Stopping to turn and blow his nose loudly into a big white handkerchief, he shook his head with the vigor of a Jersey bull before charging on, but Ma butted in.

“I’ll never believe, though, that Preacher Conway had a thing in this world to do with it, Bruce!” Ma’s bold statement caught her host completely off guard, thus giving her an opportunity to make a point. “Everybody says I ought not to be so trusting, considering what happened between him and Willard, but you should have heard the testimony he gave at church the other night. Confessed his sins and laid ‘em all on the altar, then told us about Earl and how much he loved him. Why, I’ve never seen a man so humble in all my life, come right up to where I was a setting and begged to be forgiven. He was crying and pleading so much that it reminded me of King David in the fifty-first Psalm. I don’t see how I could call myself a Christian and not forgive him, especially since he said the Lord already had.”

“Well, be that as it may,” Bruce dryly dismissed her comment. Perhaps Ma’s uncharacteristic assertiveness had caused him to lose his bearings. At any rate, he seemed to have lapsed into the role of town executive, and in that capacity was not accustomed to interruptions. Ida’s toe, however, found a familiar spot and promptly brought the big man back home again. “Oh, I’m sorry, Ella, I never really meant to give you a sharp answer. I guess I’m just not up to your spiritual level yet, but I do have my own ideas about that gentleman. You just pray that the Lord will have mercy on my soul and help me see him a little differently before I have to bid this old world goodbye. Regardless, however, let’s get back to what I was saying. Earl feared that something bad was about to happen. Said that Keith had got in the way of his investigation because, and, Ellie, you’ll have to forgive me for this, but Earl did say that Keith earlier had been suspicious of your daughter-in-law, Hester. He thought she might be interested in another man. To her credit, though, Earl did say there was absolutely nothing to it. But from what I hear that young'in of hers does look an awful lot like Conway, and that ain't helped the talk none."

"I need to tell you something, Bruce," Ma protested. "You know what the Good Book says about the tongue and all the evil it causes. Yes, little Claude Earl does have red hair, but that's the only feature that favors preacher Conway. Why, if you ever saw any of Hester's family you could see he looks just like them. A person needs to be awful careful about these things. Remember, we'll have to answer for every idle word in the judgment. I'm afraid you and Ida may have the wrong notion about Hester, she's a good woman and a good Christian, too!"

This admonishment did not sit well with Mayor Sluder. He took a deep breath and sighed loudly, "Ella, you and I have been close all of our lives, and you know I'm just being honest here... Earl certainly felt that her faith was real, and like I said, he thought she was being treated unfairly. Too, he assured me that he had full confidence in Claude Conway too, after all they were fellow evangelists. Now as far as I know, Keith never found out a thing to back up his suspicions, but still there had been an awful lot of talk and we'll just have to leave it at that."

"Earl said there was something else he'd uncovered, but he refused to talk about it. Whatever it was we'll probably never know, not this side of the Jerden anyway." Here he paused again, first to blot away the tears, then to study carefully the half square yard of handkerchief spread before him. Finally, he found just the right spot, and then snorted.

Ida reached over and tenderly laid her wrinkled hand on the back of his, their teary eyes met and held for one long, gold-filled moment of memory. Smiling gratitude, Mr. Sluder's face continued to show grief as he pushed back and away from the table. "I'm not absolutely certain who it was that took Earl's life, but I'm satisfied the two who are getting ready to pay the price are scapegoats. I went to the trial there in Gastonia, went every day, and watched it all from start to finish. It was plain to me that the prosecutor's office merely wanted to get this thing behind them. That's why I say they would've convicted the angel Gabriel if they needed to."

The medical examiner testified that according to evidence, the murderer probably struck him from behind, and then used a knife on him. Now recently I had an opportunity to read some of the official record and saw a lot of things there that didn't get brought out in the trial; stuff that seemed awfully relevant to me. Ella, those two men may be guilty, but if so, they're merely part of something bigger. I say there's certainly more to this than meets the eye. Why, they had no legal representation at all, just hogs headed for the slaughter pen, that's exactly what it was. I'm doing my best to get some of this before the press, but it's been an uphill climb every step of the way. Of course, you're probably aware that I testified on their behalf, in a closed-door session at the last hearing, but I don't hold out much hope. I solicit your prayers that the Lord may continue to give me strength. But even more than that, though, pray earnestly for justice to be done here!"

Ida broke in. "Ella, the Mayor needs you to do this, he's struggled for months now and I'm getting worried about his health."

"As I say, just ask the Lord for continued strength," he responded with a look of gratitude. He then invoked the name of Jack Woodcock. "That scoundrel was in on it, probably even the guilty party, but the shame of it all was that he cut a deal with the authorities. In return for turning state's evidence they gave him immunity against prosecution, and I say Earl's blood cries out for better than that!"

Jesse found himself running well ahead of everybody else and was at the point where good manners would dictate that he be offered some dessert. Suddenly, however, a light tapping sound occurred at the small white-curtained dining room door. It opened into an alley that separated the manse from the Robin Theatre, and over time had become an entrance for those seeking a private audience with the Mayor. It was as if the town's chief executive had anticipated this, and appeared pleased at the prospects of someone needing his help. Cracking open the door, he turned back to the table and smiled sheepishly. "I hope you folks will excuse me for a few minutes, I suspect there's a little town business here that needs my attention. Just enjoy your food, and I'll be back directly." With that, he was gone but not before Jesse caught sight of a face that made his hackles rise. Standing there in plain view was reason enough to make anybody feel nauseated, for staring straight at him was none other than Gutch Reece.

"You know I think I'll put this pie in the ice box until Mr. Sluder gets back. He always makes such a big to do over serving dessert to the young'ins." Ida's soft voice seemed to lend wings to the dish as she swooped it right out from under Jesse's nose. "Ella," she called back over her shoulder, "did you notice, was that the Reece boy standing outside there a minute ago?"

"Yes, it was," Ma yelled after Ida, but the hollering was unnecessary since her hostess stepped back through the door, just as the words rang out. "Yes, it was," Ma quietly repeated herself, looking embarrassed. "That poor child's awful pitiful and I can't help worrying about him. He's one of Jesse's little playmates and I know neither one would want me to tell this, but Raymond cried when Jesse left him this morning."

"Well, I swan; I'll say one thing for him though, he's cute as a button and if I was his age he'd be my beau."

Jesse, red-faced and busy counting cracks in the matched flooring, refused to look up even though he suddenly realized something. Nauseated as he was, he now could see it was a good idea that dessert had not been served. *Yep,* he thought, *right about now somebody would need to bring in a mop.*

The interlude of quiet that crept in to settle down around the table for a few moments proved to be a blessing for all. His ears had grown weary of hearing so much good being said about the great Gutch and the ladies were given time to regroup their thoughts.

Ida, however, could take just so much of a good thing. "What about Willard and Hester," she probed. "How are *they doing*?" The way she empathized her words left little doubt about an appetite for gossip.

A long moment ensued before Ma was ready to respond, and when she did, it was to the lazy-Susan. "Most of the time I reckon they get along fine, just about like anybody else. Willard loves that little Claude Earl to death and sees to it that he never wants for a thing. I notice though, sometimes he seems awful cold toward her, but it's been that way for a long time now. Hester's awful quare, acts like she worships the ground he walks on, but then there are times when she gets moody. Claims she gets the sick headache a lot. If she'd ever let you help her, that would be one thing, but no, she just piles up in bed and pulls the curtain down."

"Well, when Mr. Sluder and I went to the trial we heard her testimony about being at the meeting that night. Swore she didn't see a thing suspicious looking and that she left there right after Earl finished his sermon. Said she wasn't feeling well, but here's the funny part: she claimed she went back a little bit later looking for an umbrella she'd left there by mistake. Now I thought that smelled fishy; I find it hard to believe she would do such a thing just to get back an umbrella. Personally, I think the only reason she told it was to establish an alibi, that and the fact the bus driver remembered dropping her off. He said it was unusual to see her going there that time of night. Well, regardless, the prosecution accepted everything at face value, giving her and Conway the alibi they needed. Ida's voice trailed off, while she chased another thought. "Beyond that, though, Hester's testimony also helped establish a time frame and that, along with the state's prime witness, sneaky old Jack Woodcock was what got Fowler and Boyle convicted.

She swore they and Earl were still there when she left the second time. Jack then claimed to later seeing Lance throw his knife away. That was powerful evidence since it had the initials 'LB' carved on the handle. Three or four witnesses all said it belonged to Lance. Then with them finding Earl's watch on Guy Fowler put the icing on the cake, so in the end the state had for themselves a pretty tight case."

"You don't think they're the ones, either?" Ma asked, sounding unsurprised.

"No, no I don't, I'm just like Mr. Sluder about that; I believe they're scapegoats! I'll tell you directly, though, who I really think did it, but first let me say this. I don't know about you, but I never could stand that Jack Woodcock; always slinking around like an old egg-sucking dog."

Ida ducked her head down to where it was just level with the lazy Susan, and then lowered her voice while leaning forward. "Now don't you be angry with me about this, but frankly I believe it was Claude who murdered Earl. I say he was in on the bootlegging too, and was about to be exposed. Once he learned that Earl was working as an undercover agent, he's hatched up a way to kill him. You know, don't you that his mother was just an old hussy. Her husband left her years ago and took the other young'ins with him, all except Claude and she halfway raised him by herself over there on Painter Creek. Earl was just like you, Ella, and always thought Claude was ready for sainthood; but he was so blind, when it came to finding fault with a fellow minister. He was such a good soul, but really too good for this old world an I believe he in heaven right how."

Ma saw a chance to respond. "Ida, I've set here and listened to a lot of things that I could never agree with, especially what you just said about Reverend Conway! As far as I know he had nothing to do with that bootlegging business; if he had I think it would've come out by now. Remember, it was Boyle and Fowler, no doubt, who tried to break in on Edith that time. And we know for certain that it was them who jumped on Keith. So while I don't want to sit in judgment on anybody, they seem awful guilty to me, scapegoats or not!" Jesse marveled at her temerity, he had never heard his grandmother sound so human before.

Ida looked toward her china cabinet and stared for a long minute into the past. For her, it was an opportunity to re-visit a court scene that continued to toy with her sanity. "Claude managed to shed a few crocodile tears on the stand. Swore that when he learned Earl was working for the government, he'd begged him to leave it alone. 'Let Caesar take care of Caesar's business,' he said. Then acting so sanctimonious he looked over at Boyle and Fowler to slobber out, 'That's exactly what's going on here right now folks, Caesar taking care of business.'"

"Well, Ella, I don't have to tell you, but that made me so mad I nearly choked. Now may God forgive me, but I thought, you lying devil, the Lord takes care of business, too, and I can't wait to see you standing at the bar on judgment day. I take great comfort in that… Just knowing there's a day and an hour coming when all things will be made right."

Jesse could tell Ma was upset. This concern caused him miss the sound of Mayor Sluder stepping back through the door. He felt both surprised and pleased to see the big man glide smooth as a blimp back into his berthing slip. Somehow, however, he seemed changed, he was quieter now, and his eyes looked different. Normally blue sparkling and always smiling, they had taken on a glassy appearance. In addition, an aroma, not unlike the one he often smelled on Dave, was barely detectable. Clearing his throat, the Mayor coughed several times while Ida fetched in the lemon meringue. He brushed off her suggestion that he serve dessert with a rolling backward gesture of his right hand. Ma started a comment when a loud crash occurred. Turning toward it, Jesse was shocked to find Mr. Sluder had collapsed to the floor. Ida was on her feet in an instant, hovering over him while repeatedly calling out his name. Jesse suddenly found himself in another dimension, one where reality seemed to move in slow motion, and have a dream-like quality about it.

Facing Jesse, Mrs. Sluder spoke in a voice of surprising calmness while demanding that he go at once to get Dr. Cranford. However, he just stood there like a statue, with his eyes fixed on the fallen statesman. Once again, using the same controlled voice as before, she commanded: "Jesse, I want you to run and get the doctor, go get him just as fast as you can!" Perhaps paralyzed by fear, he still he did could not move. When Ida spoke again her words this time cracked like a whip, "Jesse, for Pete sakes move, Boy! Go now or I'll smack the piss right out of you!"

On the street, he ran at a fast trot down the sidewalk with her words still ringing in his ears. Trouble was he had only a vague notion where to go, but he headed for the Cranford Hotel knowing that it was located about a block down Main Street. Such a move was either a case of very fortuitous happenstance or else he was under Divine guidance. In any event, Jesse found his man. Seventy-seven-year-old Dr. Cranford, last of the horse and buggy doctors, practiced medicine out of an office located on the second floor of his hotel. Oblivious to the fact that he now was part of an unfolding drama; the learned doctor emerged from his hotel dining room moving along at a bare shuffle. Hearing the din around him, his only response was to raise one immense eyebrow in wonder. This bushy adnexia usually served to disguise an otherwise kindly and rounded face that always looked a little too pink. Yet, it perfectly matched a rotund body that many thought was the American duplicate of Prime Minister Churchill. Others, however, claimed this likeness was limited to the fact they both carried a cane and smoked cigars. Regardless, he appeared completely unruffled when Jesse blurted out the reason for his visit. Turning back to the dining room the physician seemed to be in no hurry as he carefully used a towel sized red-checkered napkin to wipe away all traces of food from his chin. This practiced ceremony irked Jesse to no end, could the man not see they had a real emergency here? Yet that was not all, it seemed to take forever to find his black leather bag and finally get under way. Even after that, however, they still moved along at the remarkable rate of a snail, barely inching their way up the street and toward the stricken mayor. Later, Jesse admitted that in all fairness to Dr. Cranford, the clock had ceased to measure time accurately, thus adding to his theory about another dimension. Later too, Ma confirmed this observation when she said that only about ten or twelve minutes actually elapsed from the time he left until they were back. In any case, Dr. Cranford dutifully made his way to the stricken man, while Ma led a reluctant Jesse from the room. Not, however, before he heard Mr. Sluder gasping out words that left him mystified. "Little foxes spoil the vines and our vines have tender grapes."

Just beginning to gather in, the crowd only moments later gave a hushed and awful sigh when Dr. Cranford made a sad announcement. "Dear ones," he solemnly intoned, "our beloved Mayor now belongs to the ages."

CHAPTER 21

The earth in all its glory is a shimmering blue jewel set just outside the boundary of eternity, yet at a point exactly central to where time enters space. It is at this unique juncture that future is turned to past in the white-hot flame of reality. In that created instant of being, there becomes an awareness of the present known as now. When such fusion ends, when the future no longer moves toward the fires of reality to beget a past, then all consciousness ends and life is over.

Ma did her best to bring comfort to a comfortless Mrs. Sluder; meanwhile, Jesse soared through a myriad of feelings, transported on the wings of several perplexing questions. Among them were, what did Mr. Sluder mean by, "Little foxes spoil the vines, and our vines have tender grapes?" What town business did he have that needed such immediate attention? What role did Gutch Reece play in all of this? And most puzzling of all, was that the scent of whiskey he smelled when the mayor returned? Jesse found himself in a state of disbelief. He felt disconnected as he searched through his thoughts while moving from room to room and using false smiles to greet people he didn't even know. Then he found himself staring at the Mayor's shield, an emblem once so proudly shining, but now just another piece of painted metal. Reaching up to touch it, he wondered why; was there hope perhaps that it might somehow transfer a little of the Mayor's magic to himself? If so, then he was disappointed for it possessed no such transcending quality. Yet the feel of cold metal did send a wave-like surge of sadness to his heart leaving him with an empty ache. He wished now he had shown more respect when responding to Mr. Sluder's questions. That and perhaps he should have warned him against such a dubious character as Gutch Reece.

Ma caught Jesse in the hall with her decision; he needed to leave immediately, but she would stay with Ida, at least until some of the closer neighbors got there. Ma had never seemed so serious and she spoke as if addressing someone standing a foot taller than he. They were to meet at the car as previously arranged, but by no means was it to be any later than the three-thirty time Ed had specified. "It won't do for us to miss our ride, Son," she said, "because we can't afford a taxi."

Town was in a state of stunned turmoil. People of all stripes had gathered in small clumps with most speaking in whispered tones of bewildered reverence. The people's mood was changing by the minute. Abruptly, it had gone from an air of near frivolity to one approaching that of a somber requiem and the difference was palpable.

Back on the street, Jesse could not put his finger on it, but he felt a need to seek distraction from the gloomy melancholy now shadowing his every thought. Interestingly, almost immediately he noticed a commotion going on in front of the courthouse. The county conducted business in a handsome structure that was only a few years old. Its designer, in departing from the traditional rotunda style, had created a modern edifice of hybrid architecture. Utilizing native granite, interspersed with limestone, he had then borrowed from both Federal and Southern designs to erect a magnificent building. From the start, it served as a centerpiece to the community, housing innumerable functions. In fact, it seemed that virtually every public event wound up occurring either in the courthouse or on the square. It was not surprising, therefore, when Jesse saw a sidewalk evangelist preparing his equipment for an afternoon sermon. What did astonish him, however, was to find that once again he was looking at Orr Branch Church's new pastor, the Reverend Claude Conway.

A shiny black '47 Oldsmobile sat parked by the curb. On its top were two huge bell-shaped loudspeakers, both pointing forward and slightly toward their respective sides, making the vehicle look a lot like a giant Mickey Mouse. Jesse immediately felt ashamed for even thinking such a thing. Reverend Conway was about ready to start, his speakers were set and pre-tested, a record of the Chuck Wagon Gang was playing, and he was getting the volume adjusted just right. One could see his head turning sideways to better catch a little of the golden harmony. That his efforts seemed satisfactory was demonstrated when he smacked hard the steering wheel, winked, and smiled approvingly. Jesse smiled too; obviously, his pastor was feeling much better now. Old Doc Cranford sure knew his business, but perhaps Charlie Ammons deserved a few accolades, too.

The Reverend emerged from his car still smiling and eager to shake hands with the many supporters now gathered about him. Then off came his suit coat. After neatly folding it, he took special care to check the inner pockets before arranging the garment on the back seat. One hand held a black leather-bound volume of the King James Bible, while the other rolled up the sleeve of his white shirt. A beautiful gold wristwatch flashed brilliantly in the sunlight. It was, as he oft times stated, an exact duplicate of Earl's. However, as he was always quick to add, he wore the timepiece only as a memorial to his dear friend.

Despite the prevailing mood, a large crowd had gathered. More would probably come if given time, so he put on another record to play. This time, however, a loud repetitive popping sound cut short the effort. Stepping smartly to the microphone, the speaker puffed into it several times, smiled broadly then launched into his message. "Friends, some of you know me as the Reverend Claude Conway, but I'm here to tell you right now, you ain't looking at who you think you are. No sir, who you've got standing before you ain't the same person he used to be, Praise God! The Lord took the old Claude Conway, jerked up his hood and slipped in a brand new creature! Now listen to me folks, I've been bought and paid for, but I ain't no trade-in model! No siree; I'm right off the showroom floor, shiny new and ready to roll. So, lets all get ready to praise the Lord together here this evening! Aman? Aman, and A-a-man!!"

A true transformation was in the process. He had gone from a smiling, gregarious sermonizer to a wired up orator of immense high-voltage in a matter of seconds. Jesse didn't know whether to be scared or impressed by such a manifestation. But he had very little time to think about it since Conway was just getting started. The preacher then proceeded to deliver a sermon that presently had shouted "Aman's!" resounding from every sector of the audience. After some twenty minutes of it, he stepped back from the microphone. His face, now covered with sweat, looked the color of a pickled beet. Using the side of his forefinger, he cleared away the perspiration before gulping water from a previously positioned container. Rinsing his mouth, he spewed the contents across the curb and up under the car's rear bumper. Some splashed so close to Jesse he felt the spray.

The speaker suddenly shifted gears by making an announcement. "Friends," he said, smiling broadly. "We're fixing to start us a revival up at Orr Branch, on the head of Sweetwater. It's sad to say, but before I accepted their call you could hear the death rattle in that little church. Now, though, with old Satan on the run, them bones are beginning to rise again. A-man? A-a-man! I'm asking each and every one of you here to come on up to Orr Branch and starting tonight we'll be having us a good time up there. Hey, I like that don't you? A good time up there! Ha! Ha! Yes sir, you're going to hear singing, and praying, and preaching to beat the band! We'll be casting out all kinds of sickness, health and spiritual both, just like they did back in Bible days. And yes sir, it won't be too much longer now 'til we'll all be having us a good time up there! ... I can't wait, can you?"

His demeanor turned serious again as he paused for the audience to catch up with him. "I've had something a laying on my heart for long enough now, folks. Most of you who know me, know just what a meek fella I am. Sometimes the Lord has to speak to me pretty straight before I'm willing to listen. But, praise God, I'm finally ready!! ... You've heard me preach against loose women, preach against hypocrites, against hard liquor and I've even preached against sorry preachers. Right now, though, I'm a fixing to preach against the worst of them all, and it's them old workers of iniquity. This may surprise some of you, but we've got one living not half a mile from the Orr Branch Church. Why it ain't no wonder them poor old saints are wore out. They've been abiding the presence of an old infidel right there in their midst. But by the grace of God, things are about to change. Now this feller claims to be a foxhunter, so we'll just see what happens when I sic the hounds of heaven on *him*. I believe they'll chase that old gray fox 'til they den him up in one of our Sunday school rooms, and then before you know it he'll be a setting in the card class every Sunday morning. Now, do I get an Aman on that?"

The air seemed to explode with loud outbursts of affirmations, with Jack Woodcock taking it one-step further; "Preach it, Claude; if Dave Gernon don't change his sorry ways, the devil's going to roast him alive." Jesse felt both shock and outrage, *Why, my goodness,* he thought, *it ain't right to name him like that!*

Although the preacher's zeal had just received a rousing boost, he was on the verge of losing a listener. *Dave ain't that bad,* Jesse's mind churned. *Besides, he ain't a real infidel anyway, he's a Roman Catholic, and I'll bet some of them are Christians, too.*

Exhaling loudly, Conway shouted back; "WHEEOUGH, IT'S A FEARFUL THANG TO FALL INTO THE HANDS OF THE LIVING GOD, AIN'T IT, FOLKS? Now listen to me, it takes a lot of money to do the Lord's work, and spread the gospel. So if I'm going to go after that old infidel, I need your help here. That's why I've asked these two fine men, Fred Ranger and Jack Woodcock to pass the hat. I know most of you have heard that we lost our Mayor today. There's no doubt Satan was done with Bruce and just cast him aside like a banana peel. You can be certain of one thing in this life, though; your sins *will* find *you* out. And you can be sure of something else too; this morning when Bruce Sluder got out of bed he never thought for a minute this would be his last day on earth. No sir… or that he would be facing the judgment, facing the fires of hell itself, and facing them same old sins he clung to all of his life. Here was a man who just held on to 'em too long, but now it's too late."

Anger throbbed with every beat of Jesse's heart. He wanted to shout at the top of his lungs, "No! No, that ain't right preacher, that ain't right a-tall!" But the tenor of the crowd was such that his nerve failed him and he slumped down sobbing. *I'm just another Judas*, he sighed disgustedly.

Meanwhile, Conway continued his appeal for financial help. "Remember folks, the devil's still got a lot of fight left in him; why, that old serpent could strike any one of us at any time, but you've got a chance now to strike first and make it count. All you've got to do is give a good offering and that way you can hit him where it hurts. So when Fred or Jack here hands you the hat, just remember the Lord is counting on you. He's looking into your heart, Friend, right now, right this moment. Not so much to see how much you give, but to gauge the spirit you give it in." With such a powerful exhortation, few found the will to resist; so, as the big wide-mouthed loud speakers overflowed with sweet melody, money burst forth like new wine from the presses. Jesse stood agape at seeing the amount garnered in; soon a brown paper bag looked strutted with greenbacks and silver. Then just as the crowd began to disperse, he saw Bart Stevens guiding his wagon through town again obviously, now on his way home. Waving farewell, Jesse felt a little chagrined at not getting even a nod back in turn. Perhaps, however, that was because he was just a face in the crowd, and too, the shadows were beginning to lengthen. No doubt, Ed was looking at his watch with the intent of leaving town on schedule.

Jesse picked up the pace once he saw that most of the others had already gathered around the car to wait. Since Ma was not among them, he felt perplexed. Guided more by concern than reason he was about to run across the street in an aimless search when the gates of hell abruptly opened up. That is when a loud cursing voice suddenly, and at the level of a thunderclap, blew the town apart. Hardly had it faded before another and equally disturbing outburst occurred. "HEY! HEY! STOP! SOMEBODY HEAD HIM OFF! GET THAT THIEF! GET HIM! GET HIM!" Then they heard the awful scream. If it is possible to verbalize pure agony, it occurred that day on the streets of Robbinsville. Another quickly followed but, truly, it was just an extension of the first, with both filled with utter horror. Pleas for help followed, pitiful, sobbing outbursts that could have come only from some unfortunate creature suffering unbearable pain.

A moment of quiet inexplicably ensued, yet it too proved to be unnerving. Was this merely an intermission between acts? Perhaps the first blast from Gabriel's trumpet will elicit similar drama at the end of time.

As it happened, the actual cause for this interlude was due to the earth pausing in its orbit long enough for shadow to synchronize with substance, or said another way, time enough to bring fear face to face with truth. In the tidal surge wrought by this suspension of the cosmos, people flowed like a mighty wave toward the breakers of peace. A circle quickly materialized around the center of agony and there, high above it all, could be seen two pairs of mules' ears. Mr. Stevens voice, although loud and clear, quivered as he bellowed out a series of commands to his team; "WHOA, WHOA, WHOA, BACKUP, BACKUP!" Some female, forever known but to God, seemed to be looking unto heaven while praying fervently. However, first reports of the horror came from Fodder-blade Roberts, "They, Lord have mercy, look at that pore boy. My gosh, would you look at his leg, GO GET DOCTOR. CRANFORD! SOMEBODY, GO GET DOCTOR. CRANFORD RIGHT NOW!"

Pressing forward, Jesse did his best to see what was going on, but a surging wall of onlookers rebuffed his efforts. Seemingly, it moved in unison to the erratic prancing of two frightened mules. Desperation drove him to look around; surely, there must be a better place than this. Suddenly he spotted a log truck parked across the street. By scampering up the hood and over the windshield, he found himself atop the cab, and from there his view was virtually unimpeded. While he now could clearly see the wagon and a crumpled form lying up close against the right rear wheel, he still could not quite identify the victim. Plain to see, however, was that some poor wretch had got his leg caught in one of the spokes, with it nearly twisted off. Although two men worked frantically, unfortunately, his position hampered their efforts. In addition, it appeared that if the wagon should move forward, even slightly, the leg might be lost. To complicate matters even further, the mules seemed determined to press ahead.

Seeing the plight of this poor soul touched Jesse in such a way that he felt driven to his knees. By being obedient, he came to see that when God makes the impossible to happen, a miracle occurs. He learned too, that with answered prayer, no one but the petitioner and The Petitioned can know exactly what has happened. Kneeling there on the truck cab, Jesse quickly and earnestly lifted up his request, and then believed with all his heart that it would happen. Upon opening his eyes, he saw the mules still struggling to press forward, however, they suddenly and unexpectedly moved back against the wagon. Those precious few inches proved to be just enough for the twisted limb to pop loose, and set the sufferer free! Many of those present were quick to herald the fortunes of Lady Luck and her smile, but Jesse knew better!

Within seconds, a car pulled up and the ovate figure of Dr. Cranford bumbled out. Some soul of kindness had used their vehicle to save precious moments and quite likely in the process preserved a life. The crowd parted to let the good doctor through and thereby afforded Jesse a better look at things. What he saw astounded him, for lying there on a carpet of greenbacks and writhing in agony was none other than Gutch Reece!

Perhaps almost as astonishing was the sight of the Reverend Claude Conway frantically contending with a host of youth for the money, blood spattered and strewn. Jesse allowed his attention to shift away from Gutch long enough to take in the spectacle. In that brief instant, his allegiance shifted. *Perhaps,* he thought, *I've been a way too hasty here in passing judgment on these fellas.* Suddenly, he found himself siding with them. Pejoratively referred to in the past, as "town boys," these intrepid keepers of the street deserved a lot better title than that.

Few people can logically expect to reach old age without having to contend with at least one chronic illness, and Dr. Cranford, giant of a man he was, proved to be no exception. His Parkinson's, over the years, had continued to progress, so that now he shook with gross tremor. The vibration was such that at times his whole body quaked, making many of his patients cringe in horror when he proposed to administer an injection. However, at those times, whether assisted by a Higher Power or from total concentration, he never failed at the task. Quietly, he surveyed the situation, and if touched by the pitiful condition set before him, he never let on. In calmness, he reached for his black bag and began to prepare the hypodermic. Slowly, he then administered a massive dose of morphine directly into the bloodstream, doing so with deadly precision. Meanwhile, not a quiver occurred in those hands so blessed for healing.

Narcotics require a few moments to act before they dull the mind against the reality of pain. It was during this time that Robbinsville's most respected physician demonstrated his considerable skills to the crowd. Drawing from a lifetime of experience, filled with both the art and science of medicine, he was able to comfort and reassure Gutch. Then with much gentleness, he lifted back the torn trousers to expose a leg nearly ripped off. Hardened veterans, even those recently returned from the hell of battle, gasped at the sight of blood, torn ligament, and shattered bone. He needed a blanket, but the request returned unto to him as empty as the stares that surrounded them. Jesse looked about, as if he half expected to see one come floating down from heaven like a giant snowflake. When it did not happen, he then lowered his sights. That, however, was the ticket! Merely by looking down, he saw a large blanket inside the selfsame truck he now stood on. Scrambling back down onto the hood, he had it in a moment and was charging the crowd before there was time to consider how to break through the perimeter. Valuable was the lesson he was about to learn; he would see that miracles are not necessarily just a one-time event. The Great Giver was about to give again and He did so by opening up a small hole for Jesse to plow through. Breathlessly, he handed over to a stoic Dr. Cranford that which he had asked for only minutes before. It was obvious he expected nothing less.

Although suspended, the Parkinson's had revived enough to prevent him from properly applying the cover. Jesse quickly sized up the situation and grabbed one side in an effort to help; once finished he glanced up to see a smile of gratitude. Forcing himself to look, he was shocked at what he saw. Gutch had his eyes closed and his teeth set. So grimaced was his face that he hardly was recognizable. His complexion, normally was a soft reddish tan, now looked a ghastly green. Mercifully, even while he stood there, Jesse could see that the morphine was beginning to take hold. Its influence on the central nervous system was becoming more evident by the second. Yet, it still was another five minutes before Gutch's dark eyes opened. They then became flitting black birds darting about and looking for a place to land. Alert to this, Dr. Cranford was quick to intervene and halt the search, his expert handling managed to conceal the worst of things from his patient's wounded quest. Then, however, Gutch turned and looked directly into Jesse's soul, past the tears, past the horror and past the fear to a place where he found a deep reservoir of concern that neither of them realized existed. Jesse, in turn, saw pain searching for mercy. They both suddenly understood that the bonds of blood and family are forever and that it was time now to bind up the wounds and let go of their old hurt feelings. Yes, it was time to grow up a little.

CHAPTER 22

Often, in the wake of disaster, questions of how could a God of Love allow such a thing to happen, arise. Unfortunately, it took much of Jesse's life to find an answer. "Surely," a Voice whispered; "you know that if man is to have a free will, then it is inevitable that imperfect choices can and will be made. Whether to deem the results of such an accident, or a sin depends entirely on the original intent expressed. God does not act to prevent or correct mistakes before they happen; else, we forfeit our free will. However, unless we expressly forbid it, He can and often does move to ameliorate such consequences." Could He do otherwise?

***

"Son, light me a cigarat!" Gutch said with enough audacity that it caused quite a stir with the crowd. Quickly the word passed from second to third hand, eliciting several shouts of encouragement. "DID YOU HEAR THAT?" It was Splinter Collins asking. "I'll tell you what; them old Sweetwater boys have what it takes. And they don't come no tougher than Gutch here!" He spoke for the crowd as was confirmed by a chorus of approvals. Seemingly, from out of nowhere, a cigarette suddenly materialized and it was ready for the smoking. Jesse slipped it between two lips that were pleading pitifully for him to hurry. He watched as the burning coal flared so brightly that it nearly burst into flames before Gutch would let it go.

Meanwhile, Dr. Cranford was busy arranging the patient's position to facilitate moving him. That was fortunate, because Ross Walters had just arrived, driving his new Desoto. Forced to move slowly through the ever-enlarging crowd, Ross literally had to push several rubbernecks aside with the front bumper of his huge automobile. Being the captain of the volunteer fire department, he felt it an honor to make an ambulance of this much-admired vehicle. Plans were already underway to have Raymond transferred to Andrews, where Drs. Van Gelder and Lyda would take over.

Before moving the injured, however, the Reverend Conway asked for a moment of prayer. Bending low, several witnesses would later claim that his face seemed to glow during the petition. Yet, had they been as close to Gutch as Jesse was they too might have heard words that sounded something less than heavenly. His low, guttural voice swore both a warning and a curse. "You little turd, see what happens when you try to mess with the Lord's anointed? If you tattle anything about what happened between me and the mayor, this ain't half what you'll get… You hear me?" Gutch did the best he could to nod. Conway then raised his voice to the throng. "PRAISE GOD, THIS LITTLE BOY WILL BE MADE WHOLE! I JUST LAID THE HAND OF HEALING ON HIM… AND FOR THE REST OF YOU STANDING HERE, PRAISE GOD, YOU WILL YET WITNESS THE GLORY OF LORD BEING MADE MANIFEST. THIS LITTLE LAMB WILL WALK AGAIN! SO LET'S ALL SAY AMAN AND AMAN!

As a former Navy corpsman who had served with the Marines on Iwo Jima, Ross Walters didn't look impressed. He brushed Conway aside while preparing the litter to move his patient. Gutch looked horrified when he called out to Jesse, first to ask a question, then to make an appeal. "Son, what do you reckon they'll to do to me? I'm scared they'll try to take my laig off, but you go tell Mama and she won't let 'em. I'm counting on you, Jesse, so you go tell her!" A desperate hand reached up to grab a cousin by the arm, but got a heart instead. Unashamedly, they both cried and then in broken words Jesse promised to do what he could.

Laughing through the tears, Jesse added a parting word; "I guess this ought to learn you the next time not to grip with somebody who'll put you in the hospital." Just as the big sedan pulled away, he felt a hand on his shoulder. "Son, we've got to go; you need to come on because we're already running awful late." From the pied-red look of Ed's face he had been feeling the heat from several of his impatient passengers. In the midst of it all Ma had made it to the car where she remained steadfast in her determination that they would not leave until the situation was in hand. Most agreed that she was right and settled back for the duration. However, patience is a whimsical thing with many considering it a virtue, especially when it's exercised on the behalf of others. To some, however, it is seen an act of obstinacy and even a means of control. To them it is a detestable thing. Ma saw patience as a virtue, while Fred Ranger and two of the others were squarely in the opposite camp. Ed Jennings, caught in the middle, was ready for the impasse to end. They departed late, just five minutes short of an hour, with everyone finding a seat inside the car but Jesse, yet he was happy. Many things were a lot worse than being nestled in your own private berth, especially after a day like this one. Propped up against the spare tire, he liked listening to the motor hum its mournful tune through the tailpipe. Remarkably, the sound of its low cat-like purr seemed to calm his nerves.

Once underway he began sorting through and re-arranging several of the bags placed there by the other passengers. Picking up a large paper sack with the name "Rose" printed on its side, he realized immediately why Ma had been late; she needed the extra time to finish her trading! Unfortunately, a huge stalk of bananas resting on top, just sat there tempting him to eat one. Usually Jesse could count on a will power he knew to be as strong as steel in situations like this, but he also knew there were limits. On second thought, with such a big bunch how could anybody miss just one? After three more, however, the cluster suddenly looked picked over and much smaller than it really was. Yet there were plenty still to make a good Sunday pudding and, after all, that was what Ma wanted, anyway. Digging deeper through the poke he made a startling discovery, giving him even more reason to love Ma, for that is when he found the latest issue of "Red Ryder." Now how in the world could she know this was his favorite comic book?

What a day! It was impossible to digest everything placed on his platter, but Ma's thoughtfulness had just provided the dessert. Yet some things were very perplexing. Poor old Mr. Sluder, and then the way they hollered Dave's name out to the crowd. However, Gutch's accident was what bothered him the most. *How did he get his leg caught like that? And the way Reverend Conway acted, now boy that was scary!* Recalling the gentle manner of Orr Branch's previous pastor, Harvey Jennings, (he liked to be called Harvey and not Reverend) left Jesse struggling to find respect for Conway. The last sermon Harvey preached, right before he left, was from the book of Matthew, chapter 24. Speaking on the Second Coming, he had warned the faithful against wolves in sheep's clothing. Using Jesus' own words, he quoted from memory. "Take heed that no man deceive you. For many shall come in my name, saying, I am Christ; and shall deceive many." Pondering this, Jesse stared at the buildings of Robbinsville as they faded from view. *Could this be a warning that even preachers might intentionally lead you astray?* Jesse found such a thing difficult to understand and would need more time to think about it. There was one matter, however, that didn't require a lot of thought and that was the need to be honest with one 's self.

Heretofore, his attitude toward certain contemporaries, including not only Gutch but also the town boys, had been grossly unfair. Now, however, all this was about to change. He had both envied and resented them, especially their ability to accept life the way it was. From the start, he realized he was different, but had become accustomed to believing that his way was the only way. To his mind they were the ones out of step, their drummer played to the wrong beat, making them to be the oddballs in every crowd. Hence, when their world collapsed, as most certainly it would, no tears should fall. But now his eyes were beginning to open, he could see that it was their life getting lived, not his. Jesse, in his ivory tower, had not, indeed could not, come to these conclusions on his own. They had proceeded from a heated dialogue that took place earlier between Truth and Reason. This while they sat enthroned somewhere high in his super-consciousness.

Spoke Truth: "He walks around acting like a big stick-in-the-mud, so it's no wonder he's lonely. Why, you'd think he was perfect!"

Replied Reason: "Jesse is not all that aloof, not anymore than you are, so just look who's talking. In his heart, he would really like to join in with the fun. Moreover, Truth, you ought to know this better than anybody does, he is painfully shy. Actually, with such a low self-esteem,, counseling is what he needs, almost to the point of it being mandatory. So how about showing a little mercy here?"

Truth responded: "Well, don't look at me; anytime I open my big mouth somebody gets hurt. But if you would quit trying to see everybody's point at the same time, then maybe you could be of help, too."

Reason: "There you go again, Truth, it's no wonder nobody wants to face you. Always pontificating about your name and nothing but; this while showing the world just what a big butt you are. I've penned Jesse a poem that might help a little; after all, he's a poet too, you know."

Oh, to the glory or is it shame
To board a ship and cross the main
Bound for a world where it might be
Peopled with people, all like me
All like me, the whole human race?
Heaven must be a heckuva place!

Suddenly Jesse was ready to accept that no matter how laudatory his ideals were, he still did not have right to pass judgment on anybody. This day's events had also shown him that life was far too uncertain to take it for granted, ever. In the valley the sun was setting, yet the gold crowned mountaintops seemed to glow even brighter in the gloaming. This day was not over yet, not by a long shot.

CHAPTER 23

Jesse's repeated efforts to read what promised to be one of Ryder's best episodes was proving to be quite a task. He struggled through several false starts before finally giving it up, but that was just as well since they now were nearing home. As expected, Ed had made excellent time driving up Sweetwater; he simply could not abide running late. It surprised Ma, therefore, when Ed offered to help get her things. From experience, he knew this was the most expedient way to get back on the road again.

"Jesse, Mr. Jennings says you can ride up here next to him up to Alma's. He heard what you promised Raymond and I know it's going to be awfully hard for you, but you're getting to be big boy now."

"Why can't I ride in the trunk?"

"No, I want you to set up front with him, so hop out. He needs to leave just as soon as I get my poke of stuff out of there."

Once the bag was in hand Jesse's heart sank at the look of disappointment he saw cross her face. However, Ma said nothing until she spotted Jesse with the comic book. "You'll have to let me have that back, Son, I got it for Raymond. Mr. Holly thought he'd like it and I figure we can send it to him at the hospital. After all, he is your little playmate and everybody talked about the way you stepped in to help him." The essence of admiration reappeared to stare at Jesse through a pair of bifocals.

Surrendering over the magazine looked to be far easier than it really was. A kite can literally lose its tail when falling from a great height, yet may make very little sound in doing so.

Unaccustomed to riding up front, Jesse sat beside Ed in silence, hating the thought of what lay ahead. After two miles of winding road, they at last reached the Reece home. Waves of dread beat unmercifully against his breast as he approached their front door.

"Why, Jesse? Oh what a pleasant surprise, won't you come in? As usual, the greeting was cheerful, yet this time a puzzled look clung to her smile. Alma, a handsome woman in her early fifties, had a most pleasing personality. Perky and plump, she wore her iron-gray hair in a tight bun enhancing her natural image: that of a good mother and grandmother, which she truly was. Mrs. Reece enjoyed teaching Sunday school and Jesse was not alone in believing he was her favorite student. Having visited here so often before, it seemed strange now to feel such apprehension, but this sentiment proved well placed, considering what was about to happen.

"Jesse, I'm sorry, but Raymond left early this morning and I don't know when to expect him back." A tiny smile traced her lips. "But I'll tell him you were here," she added.

Being in possession of absolutely none of the skills necessary to ease the impact, his only thought was to get the story told just as soon as possible. Unfortunately, once he blurted it out, all he could do was stand by and watch a massive tidal wave of horror wash over her. Jesse's first impulse was to run, but she had anchored herself to his shoulder.

"Oh, my Lord, oh no! No! No!" She screamed. "Jesse, what are you saying? Oh, I know," she said, looking confused. "You're helping Dave pull another one of his cruel jokes, aren't you?"

"No! They my goodness, no!" Jesse shook his head emphatically. "Ross Walters took Raymond over to Andrews in his car. And if you don't believe me, just ask Ma. Why, I'd never play a trick like that on anybody."

The look of shock returned, turning her face into a river of tears. Several moments of torment passed before she looked up again.

"Tell me," she sobbed. "Tell me everything." However, Jesse never got the opportunity, for suddenly she began railing about getting to a telephone.

"I'll have Daddy go get Nathan and he can take you," Jesse suggested.

"Oh, I know what," she said, squeezing his face between her hands. "You, run and tell Wade, maybe he can get Nathan!" Jesse was bewildered, had he not just suggested that?

With feelings of ambivalence, he left immediately; hating to, yet it seemed he could not get away fast enough. With his burden lifted, he suddenly was a feather wafting its way down the mountainside on the wings of a zephyr. Gliding through the evening twilight, he looked heavenward to a soft lavender sky where tiny nuggets of gold twinkled like evening stars in the firmament. *I wonder,* he thought, *are there other worlds up there? Maybe places with people and problems like those we have here...No,* he finally concluded; *stuff like that is just science fiction.* Yet, the idea still intrigued him.

A chorus of katydids suddenly brought him back to the here and now, serenading both sides of the road. Remarkably, his heart seemed to beat in harmony with the surrounding din making him feel one with the earth, as the earth was one with the sky. Now the fiery cosmos did not look so far away and the idea of a greater brotherhood seemed somehow to be a little less far-fetched. *Who knows,* he reasoned, *maybe the whole bowl of the heavens is just one giant cradle where God raises his young'ins.*

Once home, Jesse was shocked by the welcome he received. Ma had spread the word, telling everybody about his role in the day's events. Edith beamed with pride while Wade exulted; "I'll tell you what, I knowed he had it in him by Ned. Why, Jamup here is just a chip off the old block, but, Son, you'll have to learn how to kick your own hind-end first, before you can keep up with the old man!" Proudly, he proceeded to perform the trick on himself, doing so several times in quick succession. The sound of shoe leather smacking his backside never failed to get a good laugh and send spirits soaring.

Edith looked over at Jesse and gave her assessment of this dubious shenanigan. With one eye closed and her chin slightly lifted, she smiled impishly while nodding twice. "Wade," she said, "if you ever get to where you can't do it, I'll be glad to give you some help!"

"My Lord, Edith, I thought you had been ever since we got married."

"You can be awful smart, can't you? Well they ain't nobody here who appreciates it, so if I was you I'd just hush. Besides, don't you think it's time you went up to Nathan's for Alma? No doubt, she's a setting there waiting on him right now." The suggestion carried with it the sunset of a smile.

Since being laid off from Fontana Wade did not own a car, so he, like the rest of Sweetwater had to rely on Nathan for transportation. After the TVA projected ended, his work had not been steady enough for him to keep a vehicle. Interestingly, he made a trade with one of his fellow-worker's a few days before leaving Fontana. He found the offer of seventy-five dollars and a forty-pound hog just too good to pass up. Edith, when told of the swap seemed pleased with the money, but liked getting the pig even better.

"He's a dandy," she commented after a close look.

Wade concurred. "Yeah-h, I call him Roscoe, it's a good name, don't you think?"

"A lot better than Fannie," Edith replied. "Knowing *that* car, it could have been an old sow."

Mae was not impressed with Ma's story and forthrightly advised Jesse not to expect any pudding. "They ain't enough to go around now and Mother said you've had yours."

Jesse looked over at Max, hoping to get a little sympathy, but all he got was a steady gaze that met his own. "Son, other people like nanners too, but they don't go around acting like a big hog!"

Ma, along with Jesse, noticed the quiver in his dimpled chin. "Don't you worry, little Ikie," she consoled. "You'll get your pudding and you can have mine, too."

That night, long after the others had fallen asleep, Jesse lay awake listening to the few remaining katydids. Their seductive song sounded nearly sung now, love had once again found a way. Repeatedly, he replayed the day's events; starting with morning, he considered how much his life had changed. And, oh yes he must now face it; he, indeed, was a hero. However, more than that, much more, he was having trouble forcing images of Mayor Sluder from his mind. Yet when he did he started thinking about Gutch, and that was even worse. The mere act of swallowing nauseated him, causing a hollow, nebulous feeling to form in the back of his throat. *I may be a hero*, he thought, *but I sure don't feel like it.*

Right after he lost all hope for sleep, he finally dropped off, finding himself in a familiar world full of pearl-gray trappings. It was where his other self lived: A place of paradox where nightmares sometimes crept in, or where his most cherished fantasies suddenly sprang to life. Usually, however, the reveries were just humdrum and a little bit on the bizarre side. When forced to leave it he would probably do so with the same reluctance he had had in getting there. After all, it would mean having to start over again with a new tomorrow, while still holding onto yesterday. Somehow, the thought failed to inspire him.

"Church," was the only word he heard clearly, yet it woke him up.

"I've let you sleep as long as I could, Son. But if we're going to church at Sweetwater this morning, you'd better jump up!"

"Why? Why can't we go to Orr Branch like we always do?" he grumped.

Edith reached down to tousle a head of hair that only a Mohawk could appreciate with the coal-black mass sprouting nearly straight up from his pillow. "Well let's just say we like the pastor down there a lot better than this new feller over at Orr Branch. Besides, the Woodcocks will probably be there too, and you remember them, don't you? It's just best to dodge trouble when you can."

What Jesse recalled was that he could have saved them all a lot of trouble, if they had only listened to him in the first place.

Bracing himself for an icy sponge bath, Jesse bounced from foot to foot, protesting even the thought of it. His mother showed no mercy. "I think you may have left here yesterday without one, so I'm not taking a chance this time. Who knows, I may have to sit beside you in church." Meanwhile, after making up the bed she carefully draped his freshly ironed clothes over a chair-back. "Lather up that rag and scrub them ears!" She instructed. Why, it's a wonder you can hear yourself think with all that rust in there."

It took the countenance of a September sun to outshine the five faces looking toward church later that morning. Old Joe Pye weed lowered his head in respect as they walked past a roadside gilded with golden rod and ragweed. They arrived at the foot of church house hill just seconds before the bell sounded. It had taken longer than usual with Jesse dragging his feet most of the way. He kept protesting that he wanted to go with Ma and Keith because, as he put it, "Orr Branch was a whole lot closer." Other reasons, however, were much nearer to the truth; ones he really didn't want to discuss. Going to Sweetwater, as infrequently as they did, always meant being treated like a visitor, and he detested that. His primary objection, however, resided in the person of Cole Walker. Cole was the teacher and always took it on himself to be straightening up his collar and correcting his speech. Jesse never felt quite good enough around him. A World War II Navy lieutenant, he was stationed at Norfolk during the entire conflict, yet bragged as if he won the war single-handedly. Now an educator at Robbinsville High, he had joined his sister there two years earlier. Commonly known as a ladies' man, he seemed to enjoy the title, and many, but not to include Jesse, thought he favored Clark Gable. The fact he kept trim a black moustache did little to discourage this notion. Cole even spoke in that husky "frankly my dear," kind of voice that Jesse came to despise.

Today, as ever, Jesse could not help but feel a little awed as they stepped on holy ground. For, indeed, here stood an impressive structure! Conventionally built of white clapboard, the church stood gleaming high on a hill with its towering spire that seemed to touch Heaven itself. One would not have felt it at all odd to catch angels peeping out of the belfry. Just walking toward this imposing edifice always elicited the feeling of pilgrims drawing nigh unto the Holy Temple; such was its overwhelming presence.

Nearing the front door, Jesse saw only two boys that he knew and liked; they were Archie Phelps and Justice Edmonds. Sidling up to where they stood, he waited to be greeted, but got ignored instead. They had an intense argument going over which one had the better bicycle. Since Jesse did not own a bike and probably never would, he did not have the heart to hang around and listen. Quickly he rejoined the others, who now were talking to the pastor. "Well say, look here! We're blessed today to have the Gernons with us!"

"I see you're still drawing 'em in, Preacher," Wade's disarming smile made easy the welcome.

"Yes, the Lord has been good to us here, but lately we've missed you folks. I just hope you'll see fit to make this a habit."

Edith took the lead. "Well, we've been thinking lately about moving our letter back. You know they've just elected a new man up there at Orr Branch." Her knowing smile spoke volumes.

Pastor Hamilton nodded in response, but his eyes were on Jesse's left ear. Grabbing it as a handle, he led his red-faced victim, walking sideways and in a tight arc, to stand by his side. The preacher, though a man of great size, moved wonderfully well and seemed to float wherever he walked. Nearly as bald as Dave was, a lack of hair was not the only thing the two shared in common. Both men had a mature look of distinction.

One merely needed to hear his booming voice to know that here was a man born for the ministry. A good expounder of the gospel, Reverend Hamilton also genuinely loved people and it showed.

"Have we got us a Sunday school teacher for this 'un," the pastor beamed. "Son, just wait until you meet Mr. Walker, you're going to love that man." Speaking now to Edith, he kept her attention while shaking his head in disbelief. "Looks just like Clark Gable, everybody says he does." Three quick sounds of tooth sucking underscored his amazement at this remarkable quirk of nature.

"Brother Hamilton, she interjected, "you might like to know that Jesse here is something of a hero." Briefly then, she proceeded to outline the previous day's events and how he had been involved.

"Yes," sadness looked back at her, "I'd heard that about Bruce and my, my we've lost us a good old saint there, but I didn't know about the Reece boy. Truly, we're living the last days right now, and we all know these are just the beginning of sorrows. Now ain't that right, Sister Gernon?"

"Yes, I believe things are beginning to happen, Pastor, I just don't know what."

"Well," his face mimicked sunlight, "you folks go on in now and get yourself a good seat." With that, Jesse's ear got an extra tweak, while a broad sweeping gesture sent them on their way.

Sunday school, as expected, nearly burned Jesse out on Bible study. For the most part, he hated regular school, but even that was preferable to having to sit at the feet of "Mr. Clark Gable." Silently he was in the process of swearing, for perhaps the tenth time, that he would never be back when something quite extraordinary happened. For that is when he saw sitting on the front row, the prettiest girl he had ever seen.

Mesmerized, he could not move his eyes off her dark shoulder-length hair. Then she turned around and smiled. Twin beams from Flash Gordon's death-ray gun could not have stunned him more. Not only did he have to turn away to escape her bold gaze, but also his face was set on fire. Later, when introduced to the class, he forced himself to look at her again.

"Anna Marie Denton has just moved to Sweetwater. She'll be a regular member here from now on, so I hope you'll make her feel welcome," Mr. Walker said.

Never had Jesse been so affected, clearly she liked him, although for his own good it might have been well if she did not. Would that his head might clear long enough to think, yet handicapped as he was, he, nevertheless, fell to wondering; *My Lord,* he shuddered, *could this be love?*

Between services, he hurried to the safety of the sanctuary where he found a seat next to Mae and near an open window. Hamilton's voice rumbled across the congregation taking captive every ear except for the one he had tweaked. Jesse watched a shaft of sunlight creep surreptitiously over the windowsill and then move slowly across the floor. Persistent as a kitten, it moved forward until a favored spot was located, and then settled down to lie reverently until the sermon was over. Jesse's thoughts, however, kept drifting back to Anna Marie. Next time he would be better prepared; next time he would smile, too. No wonder he had been so embarrassed, she had caught him unaware. Suddenly, he noticed an unexpected change in the speaker's tempo.

"Friends, before I leave this morning I wish to bring to your attention a fine young man; one who is sitting right now in our midst. Often times the youth gets a bad reputation, what with the world being in the shape it is. However, this lad may change your mind about all that. I like to think of him as a hero, not only for his good works, but also for his attitude toward others. Oh sure, he could have easily spent his Saturday, just like everybody else did, but no, he saw a duty and did it. He put the needs of others before his own. Friends, now to me that spells just one word and that word is 'hero.'"

Oh crap! Jesse thought, shaking his head in disgust while looking down. *Why did mother have to say anything? My Lord, she knows how bashful I am, and no doubt, Anna Marie will be watching, too. If he says another word, I may just get up and run.*

"Yes," Pastor Hamilton continued, "I want this young fellow to stand up and be recognized. Stand up, Justice! Justice Edmonds, ladies and gentlemen! Justice, keep standing and let these folks see what a fine, good-looking young man you are. Justice came in here, him and his dad, and the two of them worked all day yesterday fixing that part of the foundation back there under the Sunday school room. Most of you know where it is, that rotted out place. Well, it ain't rotted out any more friends, thanks to old Justice here, and I reckon we ought to recognize his daddy too. After all you helped out a little too, didn't you, Ralph? I'll tell you what, folks, that place is sounder right now, than it was brand new. One final word, these fellows wouldn't charge us a dime for what they did, so don't be bashful about thanking 'em. Who knows, if we're real good, they might just be persuaded to move that membership back down here where it belongs! Aman?... A-a-man!"

The preacher lost Jesse right after the name Justice came up for the third time. He liked Justice; they were good friends that played together most weekends and all summer long. This, however, left him with an uneasy, queasy feeling; it was as if someone had jerked the rug out from under him. Yet at the same time, he felt relieved at not being embarrassed. Jesse did not know whether he ought to thank God or blame the devil for this event.

After services, he hurried out hoping to avoid contact with the "great imposter." However, he knew his luck had run out when Cole quickly moved up beside him.

"Jesse, did you hear what the pastor just said?"

"What?" Jesse asked.

"I thought not! Well anyway, I have a little homework for you; I understand that you and Justice are good friends, so I want the two of you to get together and let him teach you how to be a better team player. You know learn how to put other people's needs before your own. Remember now, I'm telling you this for your own good." While speaking, an eyebrow lifted and his voice now sounded husky. "But frankly, Son, I fear you don't really give a darn."

By the time they got home Wade was doing all he could to stay out of Edith's way. It was obvious that she was more than a little upset and he could not figure out why. All the way up the road, she spoke only when spoken to, yet even then, she sounded cool and detached. Such was not the case with Ma; however, her cup literally overflowed with praise. The services at Orr Branch had lifted her to a new spiritual high.

Edith, even in her present mood proved to be quite a maestro when it came to the culinary arts. Watching her cook was harmony in action and soon, with Ma's help, they had orchestrated a masterpiece. The only discordant note came from Mae when she reminded Jesse he would get no dessert.

"I wish you and Wade had been there to hear our little preacher," Ma regaled. "Reverend Conway preached the awfuliest sermon you've ever heard. Why, it had Viola Pilkey shouting all over the place, and you remember how sick little Onley Williams has been? Well, you should have seen him today; I believe that young man was healed. He sung the prettiest song you've ever heard and when he started picking his guitar, he broke every string on it. Before long everybody was bunched up around him a shouting and singing. Then the preacher got in on it too, and before you know it he'd preached another sermon. One he hadn't even planned on doing, and why I never seen the beat of it in my life. I truly believe that if the Lord had come right then, we'd all have been ready."

Ma used her apron to wipe the outside of a bowl before filling it with pickled beans. She then peered around the door to see if Wade was listening in, and since he was not, she lowered her voice to a whisper. "Preacher's gonna go talk to Dave this week," she smiled with an eye still fixed in the direction of her son-in-law.

Edith's quick nod, hardly discernable, demonstrated little interest in the matter. Well, that sorta makes me feel sorry for Conway then, not that he deserves it," she chuckled. Edith suddenly frowned deeply, an expression that resulted more from the rising steam than from her comment. Ma, however, misinterpreted it, causing her to be even more defensive of Conway.

"Well, he's got a real burden for Dave and I think we ought to be praying for him! The Lord is truly blessing that man!"

"I think Dave's got about as much use for preachers right now as I do," Edith responded while digging a potato masher hard into the spuds. Seeing such vigor was enough for Ma, she knew better than pursue the matter any further. They finished the meal in silence.

Wade, deep in thought, always perceived it as a threat when someone refused to talk to him and that went double for his wife. With care, he added the last chicken bone to a considerable pile before speaking. "Edith, I don't know what the devil's wrong with you, but I ain't putting up with it any longer."

"You've got about as much concern for your young'ins as a hog has for warts is all I've got to say!"

"Do what! They, Lord have mercy, would you listen to that? Are you out of your head, Woman? Why, I'd lay down right now and die for any one of my young'ins, and you know it, too." Aghast at her assertion, he continued to rant. "Would somebody please help me here?" He was looking to any person or agency, heavenly or otherwise, to step forward and help him out. "I'll swear to God she ain't got a lick of sense!" He shook his head disgustedly.

"Well, I reckon you thought it was all right then for Jesse to get slighted like that, didn't you? Preacher Hamilton heard me tell what a hero everybody thought he was, but no, not one word did he say about that. Them Edmond's, though, you'd think their crap didn't stink. It made me sick the way he kept bragging about getting a little carpenter work done. And that was just because he didn't want to pay for it. That's exactly what it was and you know it, too. But I ain't the kind of person you are, one who can go around grinning and get over things. No, I doubt I'll ever go back to that church again. Besides, it's as dry down there as an old camel turd; I'll bet you they ain't been a tear shed in that place since Hoover got voted out of office."

Relieved to find her anger not directed at him, Wade quickly found reason to take the young'ins for a visit to Dave's. Keith, dreading the thought of another family squabble, quickly left too. During times like this, he often sought the solace of church where he could sit quietly and listen to the voice of his soul.

With everybody but Ma gone, Edith felt the need to explain why she had been so disgruntled. Ma, in general, empathized with her yet also felt that Jesse probably did not need the attention, anyway. "Why, it could give him the bighead and you know what the Lord says about pride." Then with a look of wisdom, she took a step further. "I'd rather see the little feller slighted than have him wind up following after the world."

In an effort to change the subject, she began telling about her conversation with the Sluders. Edith listened politely until Ma finished. Then, like iron filings to a lodestone, Keith's name came up.

"If he ever gets his mind back, they ain't no telling what he's apt to say," she spoke wistfully. "You know, Keith's got to where he believes the Lord's going to heal him. He's been listening to that preacher again on the radio and last night even talked about going to see him."

"I don't know about that..." Ma frowned. "I'm afraid most of it's just for money."

"Yes, probably so," Edith agreed, sounding somewhat disappointed. "But maybe he *could* be healed, if we just had enough faith. I still wonder what was on his mind. He'd have told me, if that smart-aleck up there in Asheville had kept his big mouth shut!"

"I'd be afraid to talk like that, Edith. You don't know; he could have been a messenger from God."

"Yeah, or from the devil, and right now I don't know which. Anyway, I first figured it was about Hester, you know what with there being so much talk, and all. But the more I've thought about it, the less I think so. Why, if that'd been the case, I believe he would've just gone ahead and told Willard. Keith wouldn't have put up with that anymore than I would. Then I got to thinking, maybe it had to do with the bootlegging. You know he may've learned something by hanging around there so much. That makes sense, too, considering how those two jumped him, and then later coming after us. They've thought if Keith was an agent, he possibly had confided in me," she shuddered. "Now that's scary!"

Ma answered. "I'm satisfied it was them who killed poor little Earl, and I just can't understand folks trying to pack it on preacher Conway."

"Getting back to Hester for a minute," Edith seemed impatient. "Any part she's played in this thing will never be told, not by her, anyway. Another thing, too, it's time we all faced up to a few facts here. You know it and so does everybody else; Claude Earl does not belong to Willard, even if he does treat him like his own."

"Well, Earl told Bruce that Hester was not mixed up with anybody and he was right, too! Now Bruce claimed that Earl had learned something. Sounded like something big, and had learned it not too long before they murdered him. Now maybe *that's* what was on Keith's mind. But as for Claude Earl, bless his little heart, Willard accepts matters just the way they are and I think we ought to, too...

Edith, the Lord is not well pleased when we go questioning things like this." Ma's reprimanding look said it all.

"You may be able to accept it, but I ain't so sure myself!" Sounding more severe than she had intended, Edith decided to back off a little. First, she raked food scraps onto a plate, and then gathered up all the chicken bones left by Wade, getting a double handful. She found it hard to deal with the ambivalence: Wanting to move on while still harboring such deep feelings of loyalty. "To be fair though," she said, sounding now somewhat less hostile. "It's been several years since I've seen her, and I guess anybody *can* change, if they *really* want to." A large balloon shaped moment suddenly drifted into place, creating a voluminous pause. Finally, she spoke again. "The other day I got a letter from Hester saying they might come in for Christmas, but I don't know whether to look forward to it or not. I find it awful hard to trust somebody who may be an adulteress!"

CHAPTER 24

Burned out with the Sweetwater Church, Edith remained adamant in her determination not to return. Not Jesse, however, he could hardly wait to go back. Anna Marie filled his every thought and that suited him just fine. It seemed that every time he closed his eyes, there she was, but then for some strange reason it got to where he could not image her at all. It was during this time that he came to realize just how cruel Mae could be. She had incredible perceptive powers and began to use them against him. It was only after the second time Anna Marie's name slipped out that she noticed it; "Jesse loves Anna Marie," became her constant refrain and it dogged his every step. Even Max got in on the act, leaving him with no one to turn to.

Cole Walker played his part, too, by looming up unexpectedly in his mind like a giant Nasty-Bill to scare away the best daydreams he had. "Somebody" up there must have liked him, however, for it was only the next Sunday when he learned about Cole's promotion. So great was the demand for this Gable look-alike that they made him general superintendent of Sunday Schools.

Cole's replacement was Ollie Grindstaff, a widow in her mid-twenties. With her blond hair and deep blue eyes, she was truly an attractive woman. Slightly overweight, she, for some reason, seemed determined to appear older than she was. Left with one child to raise, her life revolved around this wisp of a weepy little girl with skin so fair that it looked nearly transparent. Having large, dark-circled eyes and a plaintive gaze, helped engender an orphaned-waif look that many found in her to be endearing. Laura, now five and a half, had resulted when her father and mother shared a cloistered three-day military leave in a motel near Fort Bragg. From the first grade, this soldier and his bride had been sweethearts, but always they smiled from afar. It was only after Glen answered the call to arms that he yielded to the call of his heart. Impassioned letters, both to and from Fort

Jackson, brought confessions of love that was strong enough to pledge forever. Therefore, they were married at the end of his basic training. The few blissful days they spent together passed in a swirl of intimacy, laughter, and tears. It came from a pent-up passion that could be unfettered at last. However, the winds of war soon ripped them apart, leaving two hearts torn and bleeding. She rode the bus all day in each direction the only two other times he had passes, just to be with him for a little while. Sadly, that is all the time they ever had together as husband and wife. Laura was born February 26, 1943. Glen learned about it right after landing in North Africa and her picture perished with him in Tunisia, six days before the German surrender there. Ollie never would, because she never could even consider marrying again, yet she became an incurable romanticist for everybody but Laura and herself.

Early on, Jesse found himself a favorite of hers, and thus became recipient to her many kind words of encouragement. Immediately, she noticed his interest in Anna Marie and of hers for him, which prompted a warning against being too faint hearted. Alas, however, for all such wisdom came to naught, because never was the fair maiden won; indeed, the effort was never even made. God has His ways of maintaining order in the universe and one those is to put altitude limits on the soaring flights of young swains.

On the way to Dave's with their daddy, Mae and Max chased butterflies knowing they were no match for Jesse's racing speed. He was the first to make it up the steps and onto the porch where his grandparents sat mellowing in the warm September sun.

Wade always enjoyed chatting with his parents and today they had a lot to discuss. First, though, they had aches and pains to compare, old ones to remember and new ones acknowledged. After that, there would be plenty of time for the news and gossip. Jesse found a favorite spot where he could sit and dangle his legs over the porch's edge while leaning back against a post. He had spent many an hour there listening to Dave weave his stories that were always interesting, and usually sprinkled with enough salty tidbits to make them funny. Dave's uproarious laughter, often red-faced and ribald, could slam the hillsides with the staccato of a flamingo dancer. Swirling mixtures of cuss words and favorite invectives were far too racy for many; however, he never used sexual expletives in the presence of children. Jesse could not help but suspect that Gutch Reece had acquired his stronger version of the mother tongue from Dave. With a syntax and word selection so uncannily alike, what else could explain the phenomenon?

"That was bad about Bruce," Wade stated sadly.

"Yeah, it was. He was a good man and a good mayor. Bruce will be missed and Graham County is a lot poorer place today, now that he's gone. He was highly respected across the state, both from lawmakers and law enforcement alike. When he was young, that old boy could drink a quart of whiskey and you couldn't tell he'd ever touched a drop. But then he turned against it, got to be so self-righteous I dodged him every time I went to town."

"Jesse was there when he passed away… said Bruce had left the house for a few minutes, but when he got back he acted kinda strange. Right before it happened, he mumbled something about foxes and grapevines. I figure he'd had a stroke, and was talking out of his head. Jesse smelled what he thought was whiskey on him."

"Uhm-m," Dave muttered. "Well, anyway, Robert Hyder was here this morning and brought the Citizen-Times with him. They wrote that there was some question about his death and probably there would be an inquest. If so, they may talk with you too, Jamup, but that ain't nothing you need to worry about. All you have to do is tell the truth; I've been asked to testify several times. Knowing Bruce, I doubt he was drinking, so just wait and you'll see there was some other reason for that smell. All they have to do is perform an autopsy and test his blood, but that won't show anything. Bruce was a teetotaler and I'd file an affidavit on it."

"You ought to have heard what Preacher Conway said about him!" Jesse chimed in, "Said he was already a facing the fires of hell, but he ain't, though ... is he, Daddy?"

"They Lord have mercy no, Jamup! Bruce Sluder was a *good* man and we don't ever go around saying stuff like that." Wade looked both perplexed and angry.

Jesse was not finished with his questions, however. "Is it okay to drink whiskey, for medicine?"

This prompted a spirited debate; Dave immediately took a strong pro stance while Wade tried to defend the con. The argument ended abruptly when Dave declared he was right and wanted to hear nothing more about it. Mary chuckled knowingly; she had seen a lot of sickness in her day.

That is when Jesse advised Dave to look for a visit from Preacher Conway, adding he had heard Ma whisper this to his mother. Wade snorted in disgust, "So, that's what it was, huh? Well by Ned, I knew they'as up to something, sneaking around the way they did!"

In an effort to divert the subject, Jesse referred again to his previous question. "Well, Preacher Conway uses it for medicine. I saw him take a big dose!"

"Oh ho!" Dave chuckled. "Well who's his doctor? I need me one like that."

Jesse tingled with fear. Oh *Lord*, he moaned, *now I'm in for it!* "No, no don't ask him, he'll cut my throat!"

"Don't worry, Son, if Conway ever lays a hand on you I'll kill him in a minute!" Wade reassured.

Wrinkles furrowed Dave's pate as he leaned forward from the two-legged prop of his chair. Slowly he got to his feet, meanwhile a Prince Albert cigarette that looked stuck to his lower lip waved wand-like with every word. "Jamup, when I get through with that feller the last thing on his mind will be whiskey. Now, if I'as you and got asked to appear before the inquest I'd keep my mouth shut about smelling whiskey on Bruce. Like I said, he didn't drink and it had nothing to do with the way he died." While Dave's conclusion was sincere, it was not entirely true.

He moved to sit beside his grandson where together they faced west, looking at High Top's smaller version. Today, as she had for millennia, the mountain stood waiting patiently for her beloved, the return of the sun to her bosom each evening. Only the night knew what joy they shared when darkness covered the heights. Dave sat quietly remembering Bruce, and the days when they were "just still-house pups." Sniffing loudly he wiped his eyes while Jesse thought about the serving of banana pudding Ma had quietly slipped him just before they left.

Dave suddenly looked up. "Oh, yeah, Robert said they shipped Gutch up to Asheville, but he didn't know if they were able to save his leg or not. It seems he grabbed Conway's money and made a run for it. But when he jumped on the back of Bart Stevens' wagon, he landed the wrong way and skidded into the spokes. I wish he'd got away with it, Gutch ain't half the crook that preacher is. People ought to be giving their money to help the poor, and not to some low-life like Conway."

Next morning Mrs. Stone's fifth-grade class sat waiting for their hero, but he arrived unsuspecting. After his experience at church, it pleased him to think it all that was behind him now. Such thoughts, however, only served to make the reception he got even more of a surprise. Walking through the door, nothing, at first, seemed any different, but suddenly he found himself at the center of attention. His face lit up immediately, becoming a bright red that pulsated to his every heartbeat. Mrs. Stone, kindness personified, knew his sensitive nature and, as always, made allowances for it. "No speeches," she said. "We just wanted you to know, Jesse, how proud we are of what you did. As a reward, indeed, as a reward for all the class, we're planning a party for the last hour of school on Friday."

Typical of Lowell Gernon, he had something to add. "I'm like Nathan Hale; I regret that we have but one hour to give for this party."

"Me, too!" Horace Rogers yelled out, "but I'll be *hanged* if I know why!"

With such enthusiasm, order resumed only after the good teacher threatened cancellation. Mercifully, however, things soon did return to normal and by Friday, Jesse was hoping he would never have to hear about it again.

Reverend Conway did not get to make a call on Dave that week; their success at the revival meetings left him with no time to make home visitations. Therefore, it was the next Monday afternoon when he finally got around to going. Jesse, finishing up an after school snack of blackberry jam and buttered biscuits, saw the big black Oldsmobile making its way up Grandma's dirt road. Its twin speakers at that distance looked more elephantine than mouse-like. To Jesse's eyes, it became a great behemoth nimbly picking its way up the rock-strewn lane. By a full minute, with Mae hot on his heels he beat the car to its destination. However, he arrived feeling somewhat perplexed. Running as hard as he could she still managed to match him, nearly step for step. "*She'll never know it*," he muttered under his breath. "*Besides, why does she have to be such a big tomboy for, anyhow*?"

Sitting on the front porch the Squire of Sweetwater was in the process of squirming himself into a more comfortable position when the car pulled into the yard. As usual, his straight chair was propped back against the wall. Logs, mostly chestnut poles free of knots and with very little taper, had been used to build a house that was now more than thirty years old.

Vertical lines dug deeply into Mary's forehead threatening to betray the dread she felt about an approaching storm. Wanting no part of it, she quickly repaired indoors, knowing that the sound of a howling wind can penetrate even the thickest of walls.

Claude sat piddling with his car radio for the first few minutes, this while harboring the hope that an air of anticipation might precede him to the porch. In so doing, however, he badly misjudged the outcome of such strategy. Unfortunately, anger, not anxiety was building up, and Dave was not one to control his temper.

In fact, a sudden outburst was his usual response to almost any provocation. The living epitome of Gernon fire, such a trait was as old as the name itself. Today, outwardly at least, he appeared to be at perfect peace with himself. To his way of thinking, this was his house and he set the rules here, any conflict that might arise would be on his terms and to his liking.

Claude Conway and Jack Woodcock, both well dressed and smiling, stepped smartly onto treacherous soil. Bent slightly at the waist, the preacher looked humble and even obeisant, as he marched forward.

"Mr. Gernon!" The greeting came both enthusiastic and friendly.

Dave sounded flat with his response. "How do you do Preacher, come on in."

You know Jack here don't you, Dave?" The two men nodded in mutual, but cool recognition. "Ah-h, I see you're enjoying this fine weather… Boys, you can't beat Sweetwater this time of the year, can you?"

A quick toss of the head indicated that chairs were there for the taking. Claude accepted his, but not Jack. He preferred the floor, sitting near the porch's edge with his shoulders pressed back against an end post. From there he could watch both men at the same time. Jesse sat with Jean at the other end of the structure while Mae, not willing to see a good seat go to waste, dragged it over and propped herself up next to Dave. "What can I do for you fellas?" Dave asked with a stare that was no friendlier than the sound of his voice. Great billows of blue smoke swirled up to hover fog-like around his grimaced face.

"Why, I reckon you've heard about our meetings over there at Orr Branch, ain't you? Well sir, we just wanted to stop by and invite you and the little Misses to come and enjoy some of the fellowship with us. We've been having us one of the best revivals you ever saw." His broad thumb rifled through a gilt-edged Bible; its spinning pages whispered softly that, indeed, there is a silent witness to all things, now and forevermore.

"Yeah, I heard about it, that and a few other things, too. But let me ask you something, Preacher, what the heck do you want with an old infidel like me over there, anyhow? Besides, don't you reckon I'm getting too old for the card class?" Feeling he now had gained the upper hand, Dave appeared ready for a little banter.

The look Conway shot at Jesse stunned him, it was the first time the minister had ever looked directly at him. "Ah-h, I don't really believe you're an atheist, Dave. In fact, it's hard for me to believe there is such a thing. Once in a while all of us say things we wish we hadn't and I bet you have too, ain't you?"

"Tell you what, Preacher; talk like that don't bother me one bit in this world. The way I see it, one man's god may be the next man's idol. Now, if an infidel is what you might call an unbeliever then I'd say you're right there, they ain't no such thing. Everybody believes in some kind of god or other and I guess money is it for most folks. The problem, though, comes when we start judging one another over who or what we believe in. You take me now, why heck, I'm a full-fledged Roman Catholic, yet most preachers around here think I've got some kind of disease. This tells me that if you don't think exactly like they do, then you ain't fit for nothing but firewood."

"Well David, what would it take to get you to come over and let me have a crack at changing your mind? I've got good reason to believe I could do it, but you'll have to give me a chance."

Jack was quick to agree. "A-man, Brother Claude ...Dave, the preacher here knows exactly how to turn your life around! Yes sir, you owe it to yourself to come on over and listen to him preach! I guarantee you'll leave there with a different attitude." Jack's eyes suddenly blared as he lifted his brow; it was a habit from childhood.

Dave flipped a tiny cigarette remnant toward the yard, but before it stopped spewing fire, another one was in the making. Jesse sensed that his grandfather was beginning to enjoy the company. "I've always said if I ever met a preacher who knows more about the Bible than I do, then I'd listen to him. So far, though, the only one I've found is Harvey Jennings, but I'm willing to give you a chance, too. What do you say about the unpardonable sin, Reverend?"

Claude looked at Jack with an "I-told-you-so-smile," before giving his exuberant response. "Now, Dave, you know it's not what I say, it's what the Bible says, and that's probably about the easiest question I'll ever get. Listen to me now, it's all made plain in the book of Matthew where it tells us that you commit the unpardonable sin by blaspheming the Holy Ghost. Here in the Savior's own words we're told that you can speak against Him or the Father, either one, and still be forgiven, but it's blaspheming the Holy Ghost that gets you in trouble. Now, I don't understand that, it seems like the Holy Ghost is set aside as special and in my opinion it takes a little more than just talking bad about Him. Most likely you actually have to curse Him."

"So you're saying that if I flew off the handle and cussed the Holy Ghost, I'd be lost forever. Is that right?"

"That's the way I read it, Son!"

From this rather inauspicious beginning, scripture was bantered back and forth like a tennis ball. While both sides got their points across, on this particular set Dave seemed to come out the winner. Claude thought to add to his initial statement by issuing a warning; "You've got to be awful careful here, Dave, because if you did there'd be no forgiveness for it, neither in this world nor the world to come! And that's Bible, Brother."

Obviously, Dave had a different take on the subject. He claimed that the issue ran much deeper than merely cursing a member of the Godhead. "If you read Matthew closely you'll find that Christ was being accused by Pharisees of casting out devils by the power of the Satan. In other words, they had become so sorry they were actually accusing Him of doing the devil's work. To do that, and do it knowingly, they either had or were close to grieving away the Holy Ghost. So what we see here is Jesus giving them fair warning. What you claim, though, could run a fella crazy; all he'd have to do is accidentally think a cuss-word against the Holy Ghost to find his-self on a one-way train to hell."

Claude answered him." 'Let this mind be in you, which was also in Christ Jesus.' Paul tells us that! So, yes, our thoughts will condemn us. Just read the beatitudes sometime… Aman, Brother Jack?"

Dave was unimpressed. "The book of First John tells us that God is faithful to forgive any sin we confess. So it tells us right there they ain't no sin that can't be forgiven. The key then is that you must be willing to confess it first, and then you'll be pardoned."

"I can see you've been studying up some on this, Dave, but I'm not here to argue Bible with you. I believe, though, I could get you to see things a lot different if you'd only give me the chance. By the way, why did you ask that for anyhow, you ain't committed it, have you?"

"Claude, I'm just an old fox hunter looking for a preacher who knows the Bible better than I do; so far, though, I ain't found one. But help me out on this; do you preach that only those who confess the name of Christ will receive salvation? That and about them ever-burning fires of hell. I need a lot of help there, because from what everybody says, that's exactly where I'm headed."

"Now, Dave, you know I preach that, every bit of it; why, if I didn't I wouldn't be true to the Gospel. God's word is sufficient here. Just remember; 'There is none other name under heaven, given among men, whereby we must be saved.' I preach Christ Jesus and Him crucified, if you don't accept Him, confess

His name, then surely you'll be cast into the ever-burning fires of hell. It's just as plain as day, Son, but I'm here trying to keep you out of that place. Think of it this way: me and Jack here are what you might call firefighters."

Dave extended the flat palm of his left hand to study it like reading from a text. "Would you say that God is not willing for any of us to perish and that he sent His Son so we might have everlasting life; just by believing in Him?"

"That's John 3:16," said Conway.

"Well sir, I'd like to know then how you'd square that with the god you preach about. The one you say is a god of love, yet created a world full of people destined to burn forever. That, for not confessing something they never heard of in the first place, so tell me, Claude, what kind of a god do you serve, anyhow?"

"Say what? Why that ain't the way it is and you know it! All you have to do is confess the name of Jesus Christ and then you'll be saved. That's the beauty of it, confess the name of the Lord Jesus Christ; take Him as your personal savior and truly, thou shalt be saved. Now, Son, *that's* the plan of Salvation."

"Then what about the billions and billions of people who never even heard of Jesus Christ, much less know His name; what about them? They's people right now, good honest people, who have no idea that such a man ever existed. Or even if they do they've been raised in some other kind of religion. Then think about the ones all down through all the centuries who died without ever hearing of Him; especially those who died before He was born. What do you say about them?"

"I don't have an answer that'll satisfy you, but you'd better know this; if they don't confess the name Christ Jesus, then they're condemned already. It's too bad if they happened to be born in the wrong place or at the wrong time, but that's just the way it is. Brother, that's what I read in the Bible and I'll take my stand on that!"

"Claude, that's foolishness!" Dave laughed scornfully. "You didn't read that *in* the Bible, that's what you read *into* it. Try reading it in context. And while you're at it, why don't you look at Romans, chapter 2, where it says that even though the Gentile don't have the law but does it naturally, they will be justified. It goes on to say that the law has been written on their hearts, it's there to guide their thoughts, and conscience's to do what's right. So if they know to do right and then do it, that's what they'll be judged on. Now, to me that sounds fair! And I say it's at the *judgment* where the ones who never had a chance to know Christ will at last be shown the plan of Salvation. They'll learn then that it was Christ who died for the whole world. It'll be at that time when, for everybody, it can honestly be said that indeed there is no other name under heaven, whereby you must be saved. *Then* is when every knee shall bow and every tongue confesses the name of Christ! Otherwise, if you were condemned already what would be the need of a judgment, anyway?"

Claude looked disturbed. "Hold on, now, I can't let you get away with this..."

Lifting one hip, Dave zipped a match-head hard against his thigh, causing it to explode into flame. After touching it to another cigarette, he simply ignored Conway's interruption and continued on. "The Day of Judgment is clearly shown in Matthew 25. That's where Christ has divided up mankind into two separate camps, the sheep and the goats. If you read it all, you'll see that the sheep are the ones who knew to do right and did it. The goats are the ones who knew to do right and didn't. He welcomes the sheep into His Father's kingdom saying they had fed Him when He was hungry, clothed Him when He was naked... and so on. But they ask Him when did they do these things, plainly showing they didn't know Him when they did it. And that's where He explains it; He says that if they did it even unto the least of these His brethren, then they did it unto Him also. The judgment pictured here is a place where *truth* is *finally* revealed, and not where only the death sentence is passed. Actually, it's a time when everything will finally be set right. In the Bible, *justice* and *judgment* come from the same word; something you might want to study up on."

"So you think *everybody's* going to be saved, do you, Dave? Well, boys, that would make a mockery out of the whole plan of Salvation!"

"Oh no! ...You're putting words in my mouth there, Claude. No, I've never said that! What I am trying to say, though, is that *everybody* will be given a chance. Besides, it's plain; 'Narrow is the *way* which leadeth unto life and *few* be that find it.' So that tells us right there that not everybody's going to make it. But the Lord also said that He was the *way*, the *truth* and the *life*. Then He promised that 'Ye shall know the *truth* and the *truth* shall make you free. Christ is the *truth* and at the Judgment He'll be revealed to the billions! Paul writes that every tongue *then* will confess Him. Now if you'll just take a good look at the Bible word 'confess' you'll find that one of its main meanings is *accept*. So, why is it you folks can't ever quite figure out that Salvation depends not on *when* you accept Christ, but it's *if* you accept Him. There's a big difference here and it's one that gives everybody a chance.

"We're getting on some mi-i-gh-t-y dangerous ground here, Dave, and I can't go there with you. That, in my opinion, would lead to a lot-t-t of false security." Conway nodded grimly at Jack

"Claude, I'm not saying I've got all the answers here, but I am giving you what me and Harvey Jennings come up with. What I'm looking for is basic fairness, something built on justice and not for some so-called *second* chance. If God is all good like everybody claims, then He must also be fair, otherwise His kingdom wouldn't stand. To condemn innocent people on an unfair standard would not be merciful. One of the main reasons Christ came to earth was to reveal the Father and to show His mercy. What's mostly preached around here, if you stop to think about it, makes Him out to be worse than Adolph Hitler."

Claude looked disgusted. "Well, you'll never hear me preach anything like that!"

"Let me say this too, if you'd look in the last chapter of Malachi it reads there that the *wicked*, now notice it's the *wicked* and not the ignorant or the innocent, who'll be made stubble, and the day cometh that will burn them *up*. Also in Revelation, if you studied it close, you'd find there that the wicked will suffer everlasting punish*ment*, not punish*ing*. Punish*ing* means that there would never be an end to it, but it says punish*ment*... in other words, it happens, then it's over and done with! What reason would God have to make Him want to punish people forever and ever for, anyhow? I believe the Bible says nothing about an ever-burning fire of hell and the preachers who know better, but still teach such a thing are in danger themselves of committing the unpardonable sin. Preaching such nonsense gives God the character of Satan and it's made more infidels out of people than any other one thing."

Claude challenged him. "Yeah, but trying to skirt around the plain teachings of scripture may be worse. I know you've read about the rich man and Lazarus; how do you get around that?"

"Truth is, Claude, you're talking about a parable. What would a man who is supposed to be burning up want with just one drop of water? Why, a thousand gallons wouldn't be enough! ... No! All that stuff about being tortured forever and forever is the invention of a man by the name of Dante who lived back during the Middle Ages and he made it all up to suit himself. Now, you can choose to believe in him if you want to, but if you do then you're putting his word before God's. So let me ask you, Preacher, who's the infidel then?"

"One other thing, something you might want to think about. Back a few years ago a feller brought my dog home after a car hit him; carried him all the way up here from the Shehan Cove. He told me then that there were three kinds of people in this old world; the ones who have *no use* for God… those who *use* God… and those who can be *used* of God. According to him it's all up to us and what we decide."

Early in the conversation, Jack had slipped a large knife from his front pocket and busied himself cutting notches into a well-seasoned piece of stove-wood. "You and old Harvey have just about got 'er all down pat ain't you, David? Yes sir, that was quite a little sermon there. The problem is, though, the Bible says it ain't for private interpretation."

"Yeah, well where do you think yours come from? Did it just fall out of the sky, or did somebody sit down and figure it out to suit their self? I reckon my version is just as good as yours, and with mine God turns out to be a pretty good Feller. Last time I read about it they was several hundred different Christian denominations and no doubt every one of 'em thinks they're right. So, who knows? Heck, I may just start my own brand… But say! I know you fellas feel bad about them two buddies of yours there on death row, don't you? Well, one week from tomorrow they'll be executed, that is unless something happens pretty soon."

The Reverend Conway appeared sad with his response: "I worked with Guy Fowler and Lance Boyle both for nearly two years before they murdered Earl. During all that time, I never once saw a thing out of either one that was wrong. Why, I treated them just like they were part of my own family, and Earl did too. But that just goes to show you, remember: 'That which seemeth right unto man leads unto death.' I loved Earl better than if he had been a blood brother and the way I see it, they betrayed a trust and will be getting exactly what they deserve. I have no doubt about this, Dave; if it hadn't been Earl it would have been me." Claude's face looked sober as his eyes searched the hills beyond.

An evil smile glinted on Jack's face. He was busy making thin shavings that curled and floated softly to the floor; obviously, the knife's blade was razor sharp. A long moment ensued before he finally spoke. "I hated to have to testify against 'em, it was the hardest thing I ever did, but a man has to do his duty. I told the truth and the court believed every word I said, but it's still a nightmare for me. I say anybody setting around trying to second-guess the courts needs to have their butt kicked!

"You boys wait here a minute, I want to show you a little something," Dave said on his way to the door. Without asking, a .22 rifle and a full box of cartridges mysteriously appeared in his hand. Carefully he loaded the weapon before asking them to step out into the yard with him. An air of anxiety had suddenly developed, but it was not the one hoped for earlier.

Dave thoughtfully selected three walnuts from a pile near the house; their thick hulls already removed left each about an inch in diameter. Tossing them into the air, they soared some twenty-five or thirty feet before three hundred bits of dust, like rain, began drifting softly back to earth. When Jesse looked around it surprised him to find their visitors gone.

CHAPTER 25

"Come on in, Jamup!" Dave announced the moment Jesse stepped up to the open door. Scorching hot from the afternoon sun, the porch would be unusable for at least another hour. Jesse liked spending after-school time with Dave; it helped delay having to do homework, something he hated even worse than the classroom.

Dave sat hunched up over his radio, but today he seemed more edgy than usual. "Set down and listen," he said while gesturing toward the set. "They're fixing to execute two men who may very well be innocent. Fowler and Boyle just got the word; their last appeal was denied, so it's the gas chamber unless the governor steps in, and I doubt he will."

"Surely not, not if they're..."

"Hush up, Son! Hush and be quiet a minute!" Dave was not kind in cutting him short and it hurt. Yet it came as no surprise since Jesse was well aware of Dave's addiction to the news. This compulsion took precedence over everybody and everything.

A familiar voice was describing what possibly could be the last few moments of life for two convicted killers. In a matter of seconds, they would be leaving death row for the last time. Public support had, over the years, continued to mount for them, yet to no obvious avail. Evidence, sifted through repeatedly, always resulted in disappointment. Moreover, no matter how promising at first, appeal after appeal always ended in failure. They were, it seemed, bound to die. Jesse stared at the clock with his gaze fixed on the minute hand as it moved just one quarter-tick at a time. What he saw, however, were lives once the size of huge icebergs now melted down to tiny crystals, soon to disappear altogether. But suddenly, a commercial broke the spell.

"They're liable to have a real riot on their hands when this thing's over."

Dave yawned while stretching both arms toward the ceiling. Although the act should have dissipated tension, skepticism continued to fill his words. "Best thing that could happen too! Heck, they should've been given life sentences since it was all based on circumstantial evidence. Why, you ought to have more proof than that to put a man to death."

Ray joined Frank and Jesse on the couch; curvilinear lines bracketed his lips, indicating deep concern. As usual, however, he had no comment to make. Frank seemed completely oblivious to the fact that his eyes were dancing wildly. Only Dave and Jesse chose to articulate their feelings. "A lot of people think it was that sorry Jack Woodcock who done it, and I'll betcha he'll get away with it, too!", Jesse said.

"Yeah, it could have been him, or maybe one of a half dozen others; but who knows? Trouble is, it'll all be over with in a few minutes, and when it is, this case is closed. After that, how are you ever going to know what the truth really was? Those boys are being executed without a dime's worth of proof and it's like I said, it's all circumstantial. I figure they're patsies for somebody; they've been set up to take the fall. Now, that's what scares the crap out of me. They ain't no such a thing as justice in this country; no sir, we've all been sold a bill of goods here. If you ain't got the money, Buddy, then you're just up the creek. This is getting to be nothing but a rich man's country."

Abruptly, with fingers fan-like and extended, Dave wave-signaled an end to the conversation. Word by word the listeners were ushered into the chamber of death. Suddenly, Jesse had a disturbing thought. In his mind's he saw them as they were, stripped of all hope and standing before a great precipice. Pitiful, though the sight was, it took this to expose one of the great truths of all time. To show that the real archenemy of all mortals is something most of us have, heretofore, considered as a friend. *Time*, because of its familiarity and label, had been able to get away with it for millennia. Devious to the core, *time* continually hides its real identity of being nothing more than a conveyor belt that constantly moves all of life toward the edge, and finally over into the abyss.

"Surely the Governor will stop this," he blurted out, as if caring enough would make it happen. A grizzled and grimaced face shot a dark scowl at him. He should know better than that. Jesse prayed and his faith pressed hard against the firmament. Sadly, however, the radio went silent; it was five o'clock and tears rolled down Dave's face.

Jesse quickly removed himself from the room, doing so without uttering another word. When on the porch, he looked deep into the sky: *The spirits of Guy Fowler and Lance Boyle,* he wondered, *are they up there now winging their way toward a Higher Court?* An aching void had replaced his heart, lasting long past the time his homework was finished.

Octobers are for celebrating; Mother Earth dons her gaudiest dress, the days are warm and the nights cool, but it's the sun-lit frosty mornings that are best, for that is when she displays her prettiest diamonds. Remember, it is party time! The harvest is in, the grain yellow, the fruit ripe and the air an intoxicating wine that quickens the senses of every breathing thing.

Jesse caught the smell the moment he jumped from the school bus, and it sent him straight for the back porch, since that was the quickest way to the kitchen. Apple butter was cooking on the stove, however, between him and it stood Shep, their Lassie look-alike who had very little regard for irrational acts. Yet, here Jesse was charging full speed straight at her. At the last possible moment, she decided to move, unfortunately, however, she took the wrong direction. The next thing Jesse knew he was in the air and looking for a place to land.

"WHAT IN THIS WORLD!! ...THEY SON!... WHAT IN THE NAME OF GOD *ARE* YOU DOING?" Edith was astounded; he seemed to appear from out of nowhere, doing so abruptly that she was beside herself. Busy washing jars to hold the apple butter; she was expecting everybody to lend her a hand. Picking up his books, the young acrobat, although somewhat chagrined, seemed unruffled. Peering through the screen, he could see Ma in the kitchen, hand on hip, and stirring away at the bubbling sauce. The ladle she used was nearly a hundred years old, having passed from mother to daughter down through the generations. The spoon-end, worn thin at an angle of about 45 degrees, had a big stout handle that still looked almost as good as new.

Although refused even a taste, nothing could dampen Jesse's spirits. Anna Marie had smiled sweetly at him in the lunchroom! She was in the other fifth grade class and for that, he was grateful. That, considering the nose-dive his grades had taken lately. Studying was hard enough without her being constantly around to distract him even more. A mere glance or smile could send his spirits soaring and right now, he was content just to think of her as his sweetheart.

Edith, organized as ever, set up an assembly line and quickly got production going. She did, however, amidst complaining, with much of that coming from an unusual source. To hear Max grumble was indeed odd; he, obviously, was not in a good mood today, nor was his friend and tonight's guest, Billy Todd Bates. As Max's classmate, Billy Todd was also 8 years old and a frequent visitor to Sweetwater. He talked so fast that when asked his name, he made it sound like "BigTuddBits," which had evolved into the nickname of Big Turd Bits. His thick black hair grew within an inch of a long and unbroken eyebrow that accented a pair of big sparkling brown eyes.

Something definitely was amiss here, so Edith felt the need to do a little probing. Since both boys seemed eager to cooperate, she saw her efforts quickly rewarded. "Yeah, they'sabigbullyinourroom, beengoingaroundbraggingtoo, sezhe'sgoingtobeatusup!" The unbroken syntax came at her like a rocket-propelled locomotive.

"Yeah, he's a bad'un," Max agreed. "Vince has whupped just about every boy in our room and it looks like he'll be setting in on us next!"

The confession was so heart-felt that Edith immediately empathized with their predicament. "Well, my goodness, can't the teachers do anything about this big bully? What's his name, anyway?" Implied was the need perhaps to make a serious inquiry at the principal's office, school board, or even the authorities about such abuse.

"Vince Jerdan," the answer came as a disharmonious duet.

"Well, tell me a little bit about what's happened."

"Like this morning," Max replied. "He come up at recess and grabbed the front of my shirt and made me give him my lunch money."

"He did what? Did he take your lunch money? That means you didn't have anything to eat then, did you? The indignant tone of her voice was obvious. "And what about you, Billy Todd, did he take yours too?" A pair of solemn nodding heads supplied all the answer she needed. Edith was ready to go on the warpath; nobody would treat a child of hers like this, not and get away with it. "How big is this Vince Jerdan, anyway?" She had been around long enough to know that chronic troublemakers caused most such incidents. Often, they were two or three grades behind the others, and cowardly when confronted by someone their size.

"Oh, goodness, he's a big 'un," said Max shaking his head in awe.

"Yeah! Yeah!" Billy Todd's eyes burned bright; the speed of his tongue now far exceeded that of his brain.

"Well, my Lord, just how big *is* he anyway? Here, Son, show me how high he is."

Stepping forward, her youngest possessed a quizzical look that quickly turned thoughtful as he gazed skyward with an unseeing eye. "Why, I reckon, he's about this big." Fully extended his arm was at 45 degrees, and with the hand semi-cupped, he appeared to be giving a heil-Hitler salute. However, when his estimate dropped down to below chin level, he looked at Billy Todd for confirmation and got it.

"Yeahthatsright! Godhesbigandmeantoo!"

Suppressing an impulse to snicker, Edith somehow managed to keep a straight face long enough to end the discussion. "You boys need to learn how to say no to this bully. Just stand up to him one time and I guarantee you he'll go looking for somebody else to pick on. If he don't, I'll talk to the teacher about him then, but I want you to try that first. Will you?"

Meanwhile, Jesse noticed someone had joined Ma in the kitchen. It was a man holding a saucer full of hot apple-butter. Moments later Ma and the Reverend Conway made their way onto the porch.

"Edith, look who's here to see us!"

Taken by surprise, she was unprepared and showed it. Edith looked down at her dress and then shifted her gaze furtively left and right before commenting. "You'll have to forgive me for not shaking hands, preacher, but I'm dirty and not dressed fit for company ...I really didn't expect to see nobody."

Conway dismissed the concern by graciously waving off her consternation. "Now, don't you worry one minute about *that,* Sister Gernon. Lord knows, a lot of people I drop in on won't shake my hand, but with them, it's mostly their soul that needs washing." Here he paused long enough to stare daggers across the meadow. "No, my dear sister, I know your heart and it's just as sweet and pure as this good apple butter here. By the by, Ellie, would I be imposing too much to have you warm me up a couple of them fine looking biscuits I saw there on the stove?"

Perhaps not all of Conway' daggers was on target, for one suddenly struck Jesse right in the heart. *Dang, those were supposed to be mine. H*e brooded darkly.

Talk continued at low ebb until Ma happily returned from her mission. She then asked the preacher to have special prayer for Jesse. "Tomorrow, the little feller has to go give his testimony for Mayor Sluder."

The two males exchanged glances; looking into his eyes Jesse felt the same queasy way he did once before when peering into a well that was said to be bottomless. *Did it really reach all the way to hell*? He wondered.

"Why, Son, of course, I'd be proud to pray for you. Now that's a very commendable thing you're doing; just be careful about what you say and you'll be all right. I gave mine the other day and really it was quite simple."

"You know, you've got yourself a mighty fine grandson there don't you, Ellie? My goodness, I saw him helping out with Raymond Reece that day. And, oh, by the way, I went up to the hospital yesterday and paid old Gutch a visit!"

"You did? Well, I'll say! ... Was he all right?" Edith was eager for news.

"Right now Raymond's still getting over his last surgery, had it three times already and there's more on the way. But yeah, all in all, he's in good spirits. Alma sits there with him night and day; I just plain don't know how that poor soul keeps holding up. She's awful grateful to the neighbors, though, them who took in the other young'ins. It eased her mind a whole lot when I told her that I'd dropped the charges against Gutch. You know he tried to run off with our offering, but I asked Sheriff Brewer not to take any action against him. Figure he's been through enough already; just pray he's learned a lesson from it."

"That was awful good of you, Preacher. Why, I've known all along that your heart was in the right place." Ma was still flushed with admiration when she turned to Jesse. "Son, go see if you can find them books we bought from that Bible salesman last week and we'll let Preacher Conway tell us what he thinks of 'em."

Conway's puzzled look led Ma to give a fuller explanation. "I bought two books from this feller that Jesse begged me to, and I wanted you to see if you think they're all right for him. I got to thinking, though, you can't be too careful these days, we all know not everything that passes itself off as Christian really is."

"A-a-man, Sister Rose!" the preacher's voice may have been directed at Ella, but his eyes were on Jesse. From where he sat, it was easy to look through the window and track him all the way back to the bedroom. Moments later Jesse returned carrying two attractively bound volumes. He loved books and already had read several chapters in one of them.

"Nu-ue...nue, nue, nue, Son! ...Oh ho-ho–ho! Nuue! Nuue! You don't want to be reading that kind of stuff, I can tell you that right now. You got a good fireplace in there, ain't you? Well... on one these cool mornings I'd be using it for kindling and that's just about all it's fit for. You start reading junk like that and pretty soon you'll be going to church on the wrong day. And then the next thing you know you'll be giving up that good ham meat and pork chops we all love so well. People who wrote that stuff don't even believe in the ever-burning fires of hell. To beat all, though, they even deny that the Resurrection changed our day of worship from Saturday to the Lord's Day. I'll tell you what, it's dangerous and the crowd who peddles it is evil!"

Remarkably, Ma's reply was to defend her purchase. "I understand they go to church on Saturday, the man who sold us the books told us that. He claimed Christ never changed the Ten Commandments, said that baptism by immersion was what symbolized the Resurrection and quoted Romans chapter six to prove it. The Resurrection, according to him, had nothing to do with changing the Law of God." Here she paused to tap her snuffbox thoughtfully before installing a tiny pinch, placing it just inside her lower lip. Ma's brown eyes twinkled with wisdom.

"Now, that just goes to show you, Ellie, see how slick these agents of hell are; twisting up the plain words of scripture like that."

"Well, Preacher, he challenged anybody to find one statement in the Bible where it says that the law was ever changed or that the Lord's Day is Sunday. In fact, he quoted Jesus claiming that He came not to change the law but to uphold it, and that not one jot or tittle would be changed before heaven and earth passed away."

"Well, like I said, I'd burn that stuff, wouldn't keep it in my house for five minutes. Now, that brings me to the reason for my visit this afternoon. Edith, I want you and Wade to start coming over to Orr Branch. Our folks miss you being there and they need you too, we all do. Now let me say something else while I'm at it; we've been having us some awful good meetings lately. Ain't we, Ellie?"

"Well, we've been thinking about it," Edith replied politely. "I'll admit I wasn't very happy the Sunday we went to Sweetwater. That meeting was so dry I stayed thirsty for a week. But Earl Cable and Harvey Jennings are fixing to run a revival down there and I want to go! Everybody knows both of them are called to preach and I've never seen anybody more spirit filled than Harvey Jennings. Why, I've seen him just stand in the pulpit and tremble all over, like a leaf caught in the wind. That's when the power of God comes over him. But to answer your question; yes, after that we'll probably be coming back to Orr Branch. I'll let you know ahead of time, though."

His answer was one that seemed to satisfy; yet before leaving he insisted on having another saucer of apple butter and a biscuit. It must have been very good, but Jesse had no way of knowing.

That night an evil shadow whispered dark threats at him.

CHAPTER 26

Indian summer, always fickle, gave no hint at sunset what lay ahead. For several days, the sky had been fair with the air warm and calm, however, by bedtime thick clouds moved in to hover low and rumble dark threats at the earth. Then with startling swiftness, the tempest hit, bursting with such fury that no mortal could have long survived it unprotected. However, just as quickly as it began it ended, leaving in the wake a feeling of incredible peace. Jesse slept the sleep of innocence until a few minutes past one. Normally easy to arouse, it was not surprising, therefore, that he awoke to the sound of a curious noise. The disturbance, not unlike that of twigs brushing against a windowpane, was persistent and annoying. Then he heard it again, sounding this time no louder than the sigh of a shadow. "Jesse!... Hey Jesse!... Listen here!" Fear was now in control, and his first instinct was to dive beneath the covers and hide. Unable to think, he lay that way for what seemed like an hour before his mind began functioning again. *Why, I've just had a bad dream,* he conjectured. Emboldened now, he was willing to take another step down the path of introspection. However, he then began to think the unthinkable; *why look at me, here I am being nothing but a big baby...No, a big coward is more like it. Well, I may be,* he admitted, *but I ain't stupid, so I need to prove something right here and now.* Sitting up, he peered at the window; obviously, his imagination had been running wild. *Heck, if I didn't know better, I'd think somebody was staring right back at me...* "IT IS!!" he shouted at the night. Abject terror suddenly tried to rip his heart out. This was no dream, and now he knew it! Every muscle immediately locked into place, even his eyeballs were incapable of moving.

"Hey! Hey!" Angry words rasped the silence. "You'd better be listening to me, Boy! Now you keep that mouth of your's shut tomorrow and say you know nothing about Mayor Sluder or Gutch Reece, either. Just one peep and I'll cut your throat... Now tap on the wall and I'll be gone."

As a zombie might respond to its master, Jesse smacked the wall so hard it aroused Wade in the next room.

"Hey! ... What was that? Huh? What! ... What?" He sounded startled.

The stirring woke Edith up too, "Wade, for crying out loud, will you hush? You're going to have everybody in the house awake if you don't settle down. You're just having a dream, so go back to sleep! Don't you talk enough in the daytime without doing it all night long, too?"

Except for Jesse, all those who had been disturbed dropped back off almost immediately. For him, however, his night of rest was over, although he did manage to garner a few fitful moments from time to time. Dawn, if it existed at all, was only some phantasmal hope at the end of an eternal night. After an indeterminate amount of time, measured by half-life quotients of the fear factor, he forced himself out of bed. The light of a full moon invited him to gaze upon its face. With dark, spirit-like clouds soaring past, there was a definite feeling of Halloween in the air. Had it all been just a nightmare, yet one so real that it left him drained of all rational thought? The morning sunlight found him still groggy and feeling uncertain about just how much of this had been real. Two things he did know, however; one being that he would volunteer absolutely nothing at the inquest; nor would he ever mention the whispering to anybody. These were secrets that would forever remain locked away in the deepest vault of his soul.

Legal counsel and a court appointed clerk were present to hear Jesse give his deposition. It greatly relieved him to find that the clerk was Ollie Grindstaff; her presence made all the difference. Indeed, he began to feel more relaxed after she explained that he needed to answer only a few rather perfunctory questions. It had already been correctly surmised that he had very little to offer, beyond helping to verify the sequence of events. When finished she rubbed his shoulder and commented. "You did just fine, Jesse, a lot better than your cousin, Raymond; we saw him yesterday, and he acted scared to death." Ollie's companion wasted no time in indicating his displeasure at this breach of legal etiquette. A tight-lipped shake of the head and an uplifted forefinger served to remind her that she was not to be sharing such information. Bending over to plant a kiss on Jesse's forehead, she inadvertently left the wet feel of warm tears on his face.

Jesse was one of the first to reach church Thursday night and he still just could not believe it, nobody had asked him to come forward yet. Five meetings straight he had been at the Sweetwater revival, sitting through sermon after sermon, hoping for an invitation. Listening to hymns while sinners were being brought to the altar, made him want to cry out, "I'm here, too; take me, I'll go!" Night after night, the saints had swarmed around other lost souls, praying and begging they come forward and confess their sins. Some went up on their own at the open invitation, but not Jesse; he could never be so bold. Here he was, longing to give his heart to Jesus, yet nobody seemed to care. Obviously, he was either invisible or a pariah for not a single person had approached him. His age was not it; every night the evangelists spent time displaying other members from his Sunday school class as trophies. After such shabby treatment, he was about ready to give it up; it was now evident, they just plain did not want him.

Friday morning, in a fit of rage, he flung his New Testament to the kitchen floor. He had carried in his shirt pocket since Ma gave it to him at Christmas. Disgusted and frustrated, he was ready to announce to anyone who would listen that he had given up on church. "No more waiting to be a Christian," he moaned. "I'll just be a Roman Catholic like Dave; may even be a priest, too!" This he added, recalling Anna Marie's recent cool attitude toward him.

Nightfall found him back at church, but not in a very good mood. Edith begged that he give it at least one more chance and he agreed to, but with the attitude that it all was "just one big waste of time." Little said during the sermon touched him; he was too busy brooding. A*ll those words and not one meant for me,* he seethed. Next, while sulking through the hymn "Pass Me Not O Gentle Savior," he barely added his voice to the sound. "Somebody ought to listen to what they're singing," he muttered. "They'll never ask me, they never will." Remarkably, however, they did!

Reverend Cable headed straight for him immediately after the invitation and seconds later, the two were kneeling at the mourners' bench. In Sweetwater's lamp-lit sanctuary, the front row of seats was where sinners surrendered their souls to Jesus. There was no need for a crowd to come and plead with Jesse; he was ready to make his commitment. Unfortunately, that is when all the doubts began. Was it possible to receive forgiveness after harboring such dark feelings about the church? Moreover, why was he not filled with joy as he expected to be; or paradoxically, grief-stricken and bawling like some of the others? He had felt neither emotion. Could it be that now, after the church had finally accepted him, God would not?

Edith refused to abide such nonsense, yet expressed certain reservations of her own. "Jesse, are you just doing this, trying to act grown-up? … If so, I'm not a-tall sure you've been saved!"

In his heart, Jesse acknowledged that she might be right, but quickly denied the allegation. "Well, I felt like it was what the Lord wanted me to do, so that's why I went up with the preacher." The words he spoke were actually much nearer to the truth than he realized.

His baptism would be at Orr Branch along with the converts from Reverend Conway's revival.

Never was there a setting more favored than this for such an occasion. An October sky, blue and serene, vaulted the brilliantly colored hillsides surrounding the vale. Grass-carpeted, the baptismal pool was actually an old sunken roadbed, flooded with water diverted from a nearby mountain stream. Beside it stood a great black walnut tree with a few scattered clumps of walnuts glistening like burnished gold in the sunlight. Jesse would never read this from Psalms: "And he shall be like a tree planted by the rivers of water," without this scene coming to mind.

The air was warm but the water cold. He watched pilgrim after pilgrim enter the pool, only to return blue-lipped and shivering. Remarkably, some did not seem to notice it, but usually they were the ones who came forth shouting and singing praises. Secretly, Jesse hoped he would not be one of those; it would be too embarrassing. *Maybe,* he silently prayed, *if I feel it just a little bit, that'll* be *enough to let me know whether I'm saved or not.*

A crowd of seventy or more had gathered to witness the event and to fill the glen with joyous song. Jesse saw much of his family standing nearby, including Ma, Keith, Grandma Gernon, uncles, aunts, and cousins, but not Dave or Mom. Being one of fifteen, he stood next to last in line. Edith had insisted that Reverend Jennings be the one to administer the rite for she had known of his true witness most of her life. When Jesse stepped into the icy stream, he felt his breath nearly slip the bonds of earth and return to the One Who gave it. Then into arms open wide he walked, going as a lamb to its shepherd, and the chill went away. While Jesse searched for faces in the crowd, the preacher sought the face of God. After uplifting his right arm and speaking to the sky, he then plunged the boy into a watery grave. Cold and dark, it received him and covered him, but he arose again to the light of a new day. Jesse's eyes had opened while still under water and perhaps that explains it. For instead of finding the scene he left behind, there now were hundreds of shiny beings everywhere, with one standing right beside of him. All were clad in robes of snow white. Physics possibly would offer that droplets of water had formed tiny prisms on the surface of his corneas, creating an optical illusion. Certainly, that is a plausible explanation when you consider that after only a few blinks the real world came back into focus again... or did it? Nevertheless, what could explain the musical words made audible only unto him that said, "Oh my dear little friend, today I am so very pleased with you." Regardless of the answer, Jesse knew at that moment all his doubts, like the chill before, just somehow went away.

CHAPTER 27

Jesse noticed it right away, yet, in truth, there was not that much to see, just a muddy spot on the ground.

He and Wade had been hard at it for most of the day, trying to finish clearing land for a new cornfield. "Daddy thinks I'm just playing-off," Jesse muttered. "But, heck, I'm tired of all this old work; He knows I ain't used to grubbing like this."

After listening to this all afternoon, Wade had finally heard enough. "Son, if it'll make you hush, go find yourself a big rock somewhere and just set on it 'til I get through!" He was exasperated and they both knew it.

Although it was early December, the sun still felt hot, so Jesse began looking for shade instead. That is when he discovered the grotto. Actually, it was nothing more than a shallow excavation with scrubby sprouts all around its exterior. Probably, the dry weather of late was what made finding the muddy spot seem so odd.

Wade soon finished his immediate task and moved up to where Jesse was sitting. He felt sorry for his words, after all, Jesse was a good boy, even if he did do his work begrudgingly. "Jamup," he spoke softly, "sometimes I get too busy and forget that you're still just a boy, so Son, why don't you take the rest of the day off?"

Tickled at the opportunity, Jesse jumped to his feet, but before leaving pointed out his finding. "They look a there" Wade said while reaching for his axe, "You may have just found us something here!" Using the dull bit like a mattock, he started removing big chunks of dirt, and seconds later had a bubbling fount of crystal-clear water flowing from the site. He then let out a war-whoop, "Son, we've got us a brand new spring!"

The gushing sluice soon had Wade chasing after it, trying to guide the stream away from the middle of his new-ground. Meanwhile, the spring had cleared itself of trash, allowing Jesse to be the first one to take a drink from it. However, that meant having to lie in the mud and sip directly from the stream.

Not only did he find the taste invigorating, it was cold enough to make his teeth ache. Even more remarkable, however, was the way it set him to tingling all over. After another deep swallow he stood, ready to leave, when suddenly, coming from high above, he heard a great rushing sound. Something huge had swept perilously close to his head. Unnerved, and at a loss to explain it; Jesse knew that whatever it was, it had entered the cave. Alarmed and feeling uncertain his first impulse was to turn and run, but then curiosity took over. Moving cautiously to peep in, it surprised him to learn that the grotto actually penetrated even deeper than he first perceived. Although still scared, he decided to see if he could find some clue as to what had happened. Brushing aside the shrubs all he saw were a few tiny bones lying scattered about; nothing else was immediately evident. Pushing deeper into the cavern, he could still make out most of the interior, even though the light grew dimmer with each step. Great granite boulders created the walls, except for the left side next to the entrance. There, bushes had grown so thick that he had to struggle in order to separate the branches. After doing so is when he got the surprise of his life.

A dark gaping fissure lay directly before him and it appeared to reach far into the mountainside. Startled, he stepped back; this would be a great place to explore, but he would need others to help him do that. *Boys, just wait until old Ray and Frank hear about this! But we'll need us a big flashlight and lots of rope to go any further,* he conjectured. Jesse turned to leave, but the sweet sound of music stopped him in his tracks. It was an experience beyond beautiful, eliciting a vision of radiant colors that came in rapturous waves of swirling melody. Torn between fear and wonder, he pushed forward and past the bushes, going deeper into the opening. If he expected the way to be dark, he was in for yet another surprise, for immediately after making a sharp right turn and then a left; he found himself in a well-lit, long passageway. Meantime, the music grew louder, giving it even greater control over his will power. If a soul has DNA then the notes of this lilting rhapsody resonated to his every chromosome and gene.

He paused for a moment, hoping to gain enough courage to turn back. However, a verse from scripture, followed by a word of counsel suddenly came to his mind. "Be not afraid, Jesse, for, lo, I am with you always, even unto the end." Then, "Continue that which you have just begun and be not afraid, for rest assured you will be amply rewarded."

Although still frightened, he now felt emboldened enough to move a few more steps forward and toward the sweetest sounds he had ever heard. The way sloped gently downward, and soon he found himself approaching what appeared to be the antechamber to a large cavern immediately beyond. However, once he stepped inside of it everything instantly changed, causing him to panic. Suddenly gone was the music; gone was the light and gone too were all his hopes for survival. Unashamedly, he railed bitterly against the darkness, yet it all was to no avail. At last, after reminding himself of the promises just given, he began to pray, asking for deliverance. The darkness remained, however, leaving him to feel more alone than ever; had some sinister force lured him here to die?

Squatting down in an effort to collect his thoughts, he tried to figure a way out. But he had become so disoriented that he had no idea which way to turn. He was completely at the mercy of whatever power had brought him here. In desperation, he turned his head slowly back and forth hoping to peer through the blackness, yet absolutely nothing was discernible; or was it. Now, fully dark-adapted, he for a moment thought he saw a tiny glint of light coming from somewhere off to his right. Moving with extreme caution, one baby step at a time, he inched his way forward while half-expecting to step into an abyss at any moment. After what felt like an eternity, the tiny glint had grown into a shaft bright enough to light up his world. Once there he saw a much smaller replica of the structure that led him in. It would be a tight squeeze, but, "By-doggies, I made it!" he exulted after stepping out into the bright sunlight.

Blinded, he still felt helpless, yet now he knew it would be but momentary. Rubbing his eyes seemed to help, yet there were more surprises in store. Looking around, Jesse fully expected to find himself on the backside of the ridge from where he had started. Today, however, his guidance system was obviously off. And although he had never visited a beach before he knew one when saw one; and there it was, a vast stretch of snow white sand curving gently around an inlet of brilliantly tinted aquamarine water. The ocean lay beyond, its deeper hue of the same color stretched as far as the eye could see. A blend of azure sky, the blue green of water, and gold borrowed from the sun had emblazoned a rainbow onto infinity's far horizon. He had never beheld anything so beautiful.

If he expected to see palm trees, then he again was disappointed. Instead, an even more decorative tree was present and it was a delight to behold. Scattered hither and yon, these glorious flower-like giants bloomed in both pastels and brilliant hues. Most were in the shape of Lombardi Poplars and covered with orchid-like shoots that made them reach heights of fifty feet and more. The fuchsia and lilac-colored ones quickly became his favorites, yet he liked those of iridescent scarlet, also. Their perfume, blown by a warm southerly breeze, was intoxicating. Had not the sound of a male voice distracted him, he may very well have wandered right out into the sea.

"Like it?"

"Mike!... Uh-h I mean Mr. Goodman," he sputtered.

"I'm surprised you remember!"

"Oh, Dave still talks about you... just what did you say to him, *anyway?* Everybody still wonders."

"Nothing that pertains to you, but I'm not finished with Dave yet, so let's just leave it at that. Say, aren't you a little curious as to why *you're* here?"

Something caught Jesse's eye, causing him to glance up to where a great golden eagle could be seen navigating its way through the sky. Only an occasional fluffy-white cloud dotted the otherwise resplendent expanse. "I'm still trying to get over my scare when the lights went out." He said. "What happen, anyway?"

"Son, it's hoped that you learned something in there. Remember, as long as you could drift downhill by a well-lit path, everything seemed fine. However, just as soon as things changed you began to hurl insults at the darkness. First, let me say that had you continued on the way you were, you would never have made it. In fact, not too far ahead was a maze so confusing that, indeed, you would have become lost and perished. Nevertheless, it took the darkness to help you see the light and it took the light to set you free. Thus shall it be in your life. Jesse, your Heavenly Father will use the dark times, and there will be many, to redirect you and strengthen your faith. I know you felt alone and abandoned in there, yet nothing could be further from the truth. You would be amazed to know just how many were there surrounding you in your hour of need."

"It was a test then?"

"Yes...sort of"

"Well, did I pass?" Jesse asked optimistically.

"If I were your teacher, you'd get a C minus," he laughed. "But I'm not and this was pass-fail, so I guess you did! That's not why you're here though; we've got other turf to plow."

"Hitch up your mule then!" Jesse quipped, sounding much bolder than he felt.

"Let's move over to the porch and talk a bit first," Michael suggested. He then nodded in the direction of a small log cabin previously unnoticed by Jesse. It occupied a grassy rise just a few yards beyond the beach's beginning margin and overlooked the narrow inlet. Simplicity gave the structure elegance.

"Boys, I'd like to live there!" Jesse exulted.

"Oh, it's not much, but I like it," Michael smiled, looking pleased. "Grab yourself a seat, Son." Indicated was a rocker; Michael took one, an obvious favorite by the way it fit his frame. The two just sat in silence for a few moments enjoying the warm breezes that skipped playfully across the sand. Finally, when Michael spoke again he sounded much more business-like than before.

"Do you remember the time your daddy rescued those little chicks from the toilet hole?"

"I sure do," he laughed. "That was really something, wasn't it?"

"Well, a lesson was to be learned there, also. It's important for you to look closely at any experience, but even more so at the ones where the innocent are involved. For instance, in this case God demonstrated His perfect plan of Salvation. The little chicks represent humanity trapped in the excrement of the world, and placed there by an enemy. Remember, Satan tricked Adam and Eve, and they were innocent, too. Your earthly father heard the cries for help and that was not unlike what your heavenly Father hears from a dying world. Thus, as He reached down through His Son Jesus, so did Wade reach down with a hoe to save those below. Think of the hoe as a symbol of Jesus. However, even though help was there, it still was not enough for the little biddies; they had to have a light to show them the way. That's why you have the Scriptures; they are a light unto your path and without it all mortals would die in their sins."

"Gosh, I'd have never thought of that!" Jesse marveled. "Do you reckon God let it happen just to teach us a lesson?"

"No, Jesse, no! God never is party to a sinful act. But the world you live in is fallen, and yet He has given you a free will. That means bad things are bound to happen and when it does He works then toward salvaging something good from the situation. Often times this comes in the way of a lesson. There's one other instance I'd like to talk about, then you'll have to go back home."

"Not yet!" Jesse protested. "I'm getting to really like it here."

"I'll just bet you are," Michael grinned. "But that's not up to me. By the way, have you noticed that time seems to be standing still?"

"So, that's what it is? Well, I knew something was different, but just could not quite figure it out. Boys, I'll tell you what though; I feel the best right now I've ever felt."

"It's called the *eternal now*," Michael explained. "People from time immemorial have tried to explain the concept of eternity. Unfortunately, they nearly always reach the conclusion that it's like a circle. Carried to the ultimate, that would mean life was a repetitive process, leading to reincarnation and nothing could be further from the truth. Actually, where God dwells, at the very center of His Kingdom, there is no movement of time; however, as a creature of time and space you cannot yet understand that.

"Now here's the good news! When you return home, it's possible to begin experiencing some of this present joy even there; that is, if you truly believe. Jesus taught that the Kingdom comes not by observation, but that it dwells within you. The depth of this great truth is still unsounded. By totally surrendering your will to His, the Kingdom will come and with it, the unending bliss of now is yours forever. Even though you remain bound by all the laws that rule your existence, your soul will be set free. You experienced this joy at your baptism and it can be yours again, just don't let the world keep robbing you of it."

"So, what you are saying then is that I can take some of this back with me?" Jesse asked, looking hopeful.

"Yes, and here's another thought, too; if you will be faithful, some day you can bring it back. At that time, though, you'll be coming to stay."

"Ain't what you've been talking about, something pretty much impossible to do?" Jesse queried further.

"It would be on your own," Michael confessed. "But help is always available to all those who fully surrender. Also, I suggest that you learn how to be thankful for all things, and that means both the good and the bad; but that, too, is impossible if you try it on your own"

Suddenly, the same incredible sounds that had worked its magic before was heard again. Now, however, he had an even dozen reasons to change his focus; and he did, for never before had he seen the beat!

Twelve beautiful maidens, all dressed in white with a golden sash tied around their waists, had mysteriously materialized at the water's edge. Although they looked to be some thirty or forty yards away, the glistening tiaras that adorned each head were easy to see. At once he was taken by the grace and rhythm of the lovely performance, it was like nothing he had ever witnessed before.

"It's called 'ballet,'" Michael stated in answer to Jesse's thoughts. "Someday you will come to truly appreciate it. Observe their poise and grace; it is the melody of music made visible. Just as you cannot see the wind, only its affect, so it is with ballet to music. Every note, every movement is choreographed to the composition; this work, by the way, is a simple one by Beethoven and its called *Ode to Joy*."

Jesse contented himself to just living in the now until he suddenly recognized one of the performers. "Why, she's the one I saw there at Hollis' Five and Dime!" he exclaimed. "Yeah, that's her, it sure is!" he reaffirmed to himself. By then, however, he was standing up and appeared to be on the verge of dashing forth.

"Hey, wait a minute, Rooster! Sit back down, of course, you recognize her, but that does not mean you can go barging up to her like that. There's a time and place for everything and your time will come, but, believe you me, this is not it."

From the instant their eyes met, he continued to behold her face, which had brightened at the connection. Unfortunately, just as it started the performance ended and the dancers began to move away. Before they left, however, Jesse's special one waved goodbye. It saddened him to watch her cheerful countenance change into one of sorrow, as they moved beyond view. "Who is she, and why does she always seem so sad," Jesse wanted to know.

"Those question are not mine to answer," replied Michael. "Only she can do that and who knows, maybe someday she will."

"Well, what's the big secret anyway? At least you could tell me what her *name* is, couldn't you?

"Even in your realm, Jesse, names are very important and that is even more so here. Divinely given, they denote not only the bearer's personality, but also their unique assignment in the grand design of things. You cannot possibly understand this now, but you and your angel have always existed together in the mind of God. Earthly bonds are but for a season, while spiritual ones last forever. Your part is to choose life and thus to make it so."

"I still don't see why you can't tell me; I know what yours is so what's the big deal?"

"No," he chuckled. "No, you don't know mine. All you know is my 'handle' and that may change from time to time, all according to what the situation dictates. Speaking of time, though, yours is about up, so let's get ready to go!"

"I will if you'll let me come back," Jesse bargained.

"Coming back is entirely up to you; however, it won't be under these conditions. Too, like I said earlier you can carry the joy of now back with you."

Reluctantly, Jesse followed the footsteps of Michael as they skirted around the cabin to move up the hill. Soon they were back at a place that looked familiar. "Well, Son, I guess we're here!" Michael announced, sounding a little sad. "But before you go, there's something else I need to say; when you get home there will be some of this you won't remember. Yet it will be embedded in your deeper thoughts, in a place called the subconscious, and it's put there to provide you guidance for the future. All the rest, though, will seem like a vague, yet compelling dream."

"So, I guess this is it, huh?" Jesse pouted.

"Don't look so sad; remember you've seen things today that very few mortals have ever been allowed to. But look, I've got a little souvenir for you." Michael then presented Jesse with a flat, wafer-thin object that looked to be about three inches in diameter. It was circular in shape.

"They, golly-bum! Would you look at that!" Jesse brightened. "What is it anyway?"

"It's called a 'sand dollar' and if you look closely you'll see the interesting markings it has on both sides. Later on, take time to learn their significance and they will become a blessing for you. Right now, though, suffice it to say they are similar to those found on the dogwood blossom. Stick it in your shirt pocket so it doesn't get lost," he admonished.

Jesse's smile looked insincere as he moved toward the fissure. Remarkably, it now matched the size of the one he had first entered. His initial steps, however, led this time first to the left and then sharply to the right. Expecting darkness, he instead found himself caught in of a heavy clump of bushes. By pushing them aside, he suddenly was back in the little grotto. Any doubts as to where he was, immediately vanished at the irascible sound of Wade's voice calling his name. "Jesse," he yelled. "Are you deef, Son? Come down here a minute." Before complying, however, Jesse wanted one last look at the opening, but it was gone! All that remained was a solid wall of granite.

Jesse made his way down stream to where Wade stood waiting. By then, however, his mood had reverted to its usual good humor. "I didn't mean to hurt your feelings, Son, but I had to holler two or three times to get your attention. Boys, we've got us a dandy little spring here, and by the looks of them clothes I'd say you took a sup too, didn't you? Well Buddy, I'll tell you what, it's so cold it made my teeth hurt. What I wanted to say, though, is that we can go on to the house now since they ain't a whole lot left to do… Say, what was you doing in that hole up there, anyway?"

Jesse felt unsure of just how much to say when he remembered something. “Look what I found,” he said, holding up the strange object Michael gave him.

“They, what on earth… Why, that’s a sight, Son. What do you reckon it is?” He asked. He found tilting it to one side made the star-shaped markings easier to see. “Well, if that don’t beat all! Off-hand I’d say it’s something the Indian’s made, but I don’t know for sure. You may want to ask your teacher about it; that thing could be worth a fortune.”

The moment they stepped through the door, Edith, was onto him like a hen after a June bug. “Jesse, I’d like to know where you’ve been to get all that mud on you,” she ranted.

“To a little cabin in the corner of Glory Land,” he sang lustily.

“If you’re going to act like a smart-aleck, you can do your own washing, and then we’ll see just how glorious that mud is.”

Later, he shared the story, telling her all he could remember, and then ended it by handing over the souvenir.

Edith remained silent until he finished, then had her say. “Jesse, sometimes I don’t know where your imagination leaves off and the bald-faced lying begins. There is something about this, though, that has the ring of truth to it and I am trying hard to believe you. Some people have visions and that’s what this could be, but I just don’t know. Myself, I’m willing to give you the benefit of doubt, but if I was you I wouldn’t go around blabbing this to just anybody, you could end up in a straight jacket.

“What we have here is called a sand dollar, its something like a seashell. In Kannapolis, my schoolteacher there had one and she told us about the legend. On this side is an Easter lily with a star at its center. The lily stands for the resurrection of Christ and, of course, the star represents the one that led the wise men to Bethlehem. On the other side is a poinsettia to remind us of His birthday. Now, if you broke it open, they say five little doves will fall out. They help us to remember that He is the Prince of Peace. There are five holes in the shell; four of them show what the nails did to each of His hands and feet, while the fifth represents His spear-pierced side.”

That same evening, just at twilight, Edith saw several birds spread their wings in perfect unison to land just outside the kitchen window. Her curiosity peaked to wonder when she counted them. Twice she did so just to make certain and sure enough, there were exactly five, five mourning doves in all. *Hmn-n*, she nodded with a smile. *Glory Land mud, huh? Well, how about that!*

CHAPTER 28

Although bits of sleet pelted his face, Wade remained the epitome of good cheer. "Boys," he jubilated, "we'll have us a white Christmas yet." This, however, was all but lost on Jesse and Max since they were too busy rabbit hunting. This, the first Saturday afternoon since school let out for the holidays, was a trip they had planned on for months. A rabbit hunt this time of year was tantamount by many of Sweetwater to be a little bit of heaven on earth. Actually, at such times the two places seemed to meld together so seamlessly that a man and his dog could walk from one to the other without ever noticing the difference. After tramping over virtually all the Gernon land without luck, they now found themselves on a neighboring farm. So far, however, they had bagged not a single bunny. Leading the party, with her tail spinning like a helicopter blade, was Brownie. Part Beagle, part Feist, she had a well-earned reputation of being a good rabbit hound. Brownie possessed all the credentials it took to be in charge of the hunt. Hit by a car when she was just a pup, the accident left her crippled. However, as so often is the case, a handicap can become an asset. Quickly she learned to relish both the sympathy and attention the exaggerated limp brought her, it becoming especially evident when audience was present. At other times, the defect was hardly noticeable at all. Shep wanted no part of this outing. While she loved a good chase, she harbored a deep fear of guns. Just the sound of a firearm or firecracker would send her to Grandma's, where she would crawl up under the floor to lie shivering in fear for days on end.

Brownie left nothing to chance by darting around and sniffing out every possible hiding place. She showed no signs of discouragement, knowing that perseverance usually provides its own reward. They were drifting down the mountainside, following the ruts of an old sled road when Brownie exploded with excitement. She alone had not abandoned hope and now felt justified as evidenced by the mellifluent tones heard lilting forth. Brownie voiced the opinion of all loyal canines that have doubting masters; they should learn to trust and better appreciate their truest and most faithful friends.

Wade responded immediately by pumping a 12-gauge shell into the chamber and firing at a patch of white before it disappeared into an old stump. Working the action again, he pulled up another round, but this time there was no target to shoot at. With an eye still trained on the spot, he carefully set the safety lock, taking time to make certain it clicked "on." Moments earlier, they were ready to quit, but now everything had changed, leaving the hunters feeling both excited and perplexed. Wondering aloud what next to do, they stomped out a path around the lair. Not Brownie, however, not a second was lost before she dived headfirst into the hole and started sending back great heaves of dirt. Spraying it between her legs, she sent it straight into Jesse's face as he tried to peer in. Right away, they surmised that such efforts would ultimately prove futile, leaving Jesse with the unpleasant task of trying to pull her out. Meanwhile, Max had spotted a well-worn path leading to a hole underneath a fallen tree trunk. By being located some ten feet below the stump, this obviously was a well-engineered escape hatch!

Wade shouted his order. "Boys, run get me some twigs and leaves, and by Ned, we'll smoke him out!" It was a simple plan with lots of promise, yet it, too, was destined to failure. The damp weather made it virtually impossible to get a fire started, so after several attempts they had to abandon the project. Still buoyed up with enthusiasm, they discussed other strategies before ultimately deciding on the use of scare tactics. Whereupon, Wade kicked and stomped the stump while all three yelled down into the hole. Unfortunately, all they gained for their efforts were empty stares from each other. "Boys, I'm about ready to give her up and go on home. Besides, we've got to go look for a Christmas tree and get it up by this evening. Edith will be waiting." Plainly, he was ready to call it quits.

Jesse and Max, however, had a very different perspective and were nowhere near ready to leave. After all, this was only the second or third time they had ever been hunting with their daddy and such rare occasions deserved more time. "Let's try scarin.g him again." Max urged.

"Yeah, Daddy, you keep beating on the stump while me and Max throw rocks down in the hole, maybe that'll scare him out," Jesse added.

"Well... okay, boys, we'll try it just once, but if that don't work we've got to go." Wade, obviously resigned to failure, yet would deny his own feelings in deference to theirs. Using both hands to hold the barrel, he lifted the gun high above his head and slammed the butt-end hard against the stump. The resulting blast left such a loud roar that it would never fade from their collective memories. Weakened by the shock, a moment passed then two more before they dared to look at one another. Actually, each had been reduced to just a huge pair of eyes that stared in wonder. Wade dropped the gun and grabbed both boys, pulling them up close, "Oh, my goodness," his voice trembled. "I could have killed one of you! Oh, my Lord!" he breathed disgust at himself. A fallen log offered a place to sit while his shoulders began to heave. Moments, terrible moments of deep introspection, slowly passed as he covered his face and sobbed. Events had happened so quickly and with such potential for tragedy that Jesse and Max just stood there searching the silence for answers. Words were entirely too inadequate to even attempt.

Later inspection of the gun revealed a defective mechanism. It took only the slightest vibration to move the safety off its locked position, allowing the gun to fire inadvertently. Such a flaw, when coupled with a hair trigger, produced a weapon readymade for horrifying results. Wade was completely oblivious to these quirks since he had merely borrowed it for the day. Even more disturbing, perhaps, was the looks of Wade's hat with one side of the brim blown off. When the gun fired, it blew his Stetson into a nearby briar patch; the full load had passed within half an inch of his head!

Standing up again, Wade brushed clinging bits of wet wood particles off the seat of his britches. "Boys, it's only by the grace of the good Lord that my life has been spared! By Ned, I'll tell you what, though, we all need to change our way of doing." He then lowered his voice to a near whisper before pulling them up close. After placing big rough hands across their still trembling shoulders, he had one further word of caution to share. "Listen to me, boys; don't go to the house telling Edith about this. Why, it'd just make her nervous and they ain't a bit of need in that!"

Seeing his point, they grimly nodded in agreement, both would keep mum, and he could. count on that.

"Wade, where's your hat?" Edith asked the moment he stepped through the door. The question was reasonable enough, considering that he never left home without wearing it.

"Aw heck, Edith, when Brownie treed that old rabbit it got knocked off and ruined. Best one I had, too! Unfortunately, his sheepish smile only severed to alert a person who had the instincts of a border collie.

"Yeah," Max chimed in, hoping to help. "They's a hole in it as big as your fist!"

"Well what in the world put a hole in it?" Edith asked, now certain she was onto something. Being one who would persist until she got the full story, more questions quickly ensued, but what she learned left her dumbfounded. Desiring to bring an end to th discussion, Wade insisted they go look for a tree before it got dark.

Having been reclusive for most of the day, the sun finally stuck its face out from behind the clouds to smile weakly at the pee-colored sedge grass, turning it to gold. Grandma's house was nestled just beneath a long, sloping knoll where a few good cedars had begun to grow. Something that had come about since Wade's unsuccessful foray several Christmases earlier. Since they contrasted sharply with the bare-bone trunks and limbs of hardwood, it was easy to spot them and soon one found its way into their living room, near the fireplace.

"Prettiest 'un we've ever had!" Jesse exclaimed after adjusting the last string of lights to Edith's satisfaction. Electricity had just arrived, and with it a new way of decorating for Christmas.

Wade flipped a cigarette at the hearth and agreed. "Every year they get a little prettier and, dad-gummit, I think we ought to just leave this'un up. Makes you feel good, just to sit here and look at them pretty lights. "

"Yeah," Edith replied, her eyes twinkling, "and the next thing I know you'll be hanging up a stocking too. Maybe old Santa Clause will bring you a new hat if you promise not to shoot it."

Except for the early years, this Holiday season proved to be one of the most memorable of Jesse's life. This, no doubt, was mostly due to Clark's failing health and a vague feeling that this probably was the last time all the siblings would be together as a complete unit.

Outwardly, the gathering was for Dave and Mary's benefit, yet virtually everything related to the holiday took place at Wade and Edith's house. The tree was there, much of the food was prepared there, but most of all, the spirit of Christmas was there.

Upon arrival, each member added a unique flavor to the mix. This was certainly true for Howard when he launched into one of his sermons. Virtually everyone who knew him felt that he should be in the ministry, yet somehow he had managed to either deny or suppress the call. Usually, after just "a taste or two," he would set aside such inhibitions long enough to belt out one of the many homilies stored away in his soul. Using a style characteristic of the area, his messages always contained several nuggets of pure gospel gold, and he presented them with such earnestness that his audience always left in a state of wonder. Most found it hard to define their feelings, but one perplexed soul said that it perhaps was not unlike going to church on Sunday morning, only to step outside into a rip-roaring Saturday night. Hearing the word preached so effectively from the lips of a half-drunk saint was, to say the least, a most remarkable experience. Dave, on the other hand, claimed that Howard should have been a priest, that he was a natural for the job. No one knew exactly whether this was in reference to the alcohol or to the vow of chastity.

Wade and Edith had other houseguests too, for just as promised Willard and Hester brought Claude Earl in from Gastonia. Tall for his age and good looking with dark auburn hair, he quickly latched onto Max. The two soon became virtually inseparable.

For Christmas Eve, Edith waited until late afternoon before putting on a big pot of hot cocoa. It brimmed with fresh cream. Wade kept the fireplace popping and cracking a cheery welcome to all who might draw near its warmth. The glow of candle, tree, and hearth created a scene worthy enough to inspire a dozen Christmas cards.

Only by the force of will was Ollie able to bring a reluctant Laura to the party. She pouted all the way; it had been her plan to spend Christmas Eve at a friend's house playing games. However, something truly amazing happened the moment she spotted Claude Earl. Suddenly her attitude made a complete change. He was outside shooting firecrackers with Jesse and Max when they walked by. Both she and her mother looked fetching in their new coats. Even in the gathering dusk, there was light enough for Claude Earl to catch the flickered smile that Laura cast his way. So sheer was this fairy-net allurement that it took him captive long before he knew what had happened. Proof of this was demonstrated when he, like a pup, dutifully followed her inside.

At the door, they met with an exuberant greeting. The air, heady with the scent of oranges, candle wax, and evergreen, contributed to Wade's spirited welcome. His voice, coming from the living room, sounded both friendly and flirtatious. "Come on in, here you pretty things, Willard's a fixing to play us a tune on his banjer!.

"I will be if I can get Keith to help me," Willard replied. His wry smile seemed to take on a new glow now that he had others besides an all-male cast of lethargy-laced braggarts to look at. Soon banjo and guitar were inspiring carolers from all over the house to come and join in. Jim Gernon sat parked on the couch next to Wade wearing the face of contentment. It was obvious that he was there to stay until the party was over.

"Son, let's have one of your smokes," he announced while reaching for Wade's package. A freeloader by profession, Jim preferred cigarettes to any other form of tobacco, yet never considered buying them himself.

Why bother even mentioning it? Wade wondered as alien fingers rifled through his shirt pocket seeking a pack that was always be there. Then in a noticeable departure from his usual demeanor, Jim sat quietly through the next song with a look of thoughtful contemplation on his face. He seemed happy to just sit and admire the tree, but looks can be deceiving.

"Rose," his voice knifed through a haze of blue smoke, "I reckon that whupping you give old Conway must have bobbed his tail good for him. He's been trying to pastor over there at the little Orr Branch Church, but you don't hear much out of him anymore. I guess you know that Dave set his butt on fire, too, don't you?"

Willard, with deliberate care, began to put his banjo away. The instrument brought him purpose, contentment, and joy; without it, his soul would soon wither and die. He harbored no illusions about that.

"What happened between us was very unfortunate, Jim, and it's something I'd prefer just to forget." Sighing softly, he suddenly brightened up, "But I spoke with him a few months ago and we agreed to just bury the hatchet. You know they ain't no mileage in letting a thing like that ruin your life."

"Amen, Brother!" Wade agreed. "It's always best to put stuff like that behind you. My Lord, I'd never know a minute's peace if I didn't believe in that old saying of live and let live, considering all the Shivalay drivers we've got around here!"

Not happy with where this was going, Jim was prepared to offer them a bone with more meat on it. "Hey, fellers, not to change the subject or anything, but ain't you glad they finally got around to putting old Fowler and Boyle to sleep?" With almost any discussion, Jim thrived on taking the opposing side to any popular view. Obviously, he loved a good argument.

Hester looked horrified. "My Lord, Jim! How can you say that?" Having just joined the singing, she was not about to let the comment go unchallenged. "I know they were an awful sorry lot, but I also believe they were innocent. And if there's anybody here who ought to know, it's me! Willard has watched me cry my eyes out over this for years, being so close to it and all. Actually, I thought they both were despicable, but the law has yet to come up with any real evidence to show they did it. No, Jim, I can't imagine why you brought this up, and I don't think you know what you're talking about!" Nearly blinded by tears, she pushed past Edith and ran in search for a pillow to bury her face in. Jim had just ruined Christmas for Hester.

Everybody but Jim looked dumbfounded, yet he sat smiling smugly and beaming with pride. "Well, by Jacks, I do know what I'm talking about here, 'cause I know what I've been told!" He was unstoppable; the smell of blood had invigorated his appetite for more. "It seems like to me folks are awful quick to blame just about anybody, except the very ones who did it!" Concocting bizarre theories was his forte and on rare occasions he would uncork some obscure fact that flew in the face of all current knowledge; this appeared to be one of those times.

Screwing up his mouth in an attempt to look thoughtful he dropped what he hoped would be a bombshell. "Folks, it was a deputy sheriff down there in Gastonia who blew the whistle on Akers. That's how they learned that he was the agent; yes sir, one of the deputies tipped them two off so they could lay a trap for him. If the law hadn't done it, Boyle and Fowler would never have known who to turn on."

If Jim's intent was to gain attention, then he had it in spades. Suddenly the house went silent with all eyes now turned on him. Beaming with pride, he underscored his next comment with a smile. "So, they set their trap and when he fell for it, they sprung it. No doubt, they figured getting rid of him would keep them out of jail. But their little plan backfired on 'em when Jack Woodcock pulled his double-cross… that and with the knife turning up like it did."

Often called "Shady" for obvious reasons, Jim was now ready for the coup d'etat. "But there's something else, though, and I'll bet they ain't a one of you here who knows about it. While fighting for his life, Akers was struck over the head several times and that's what probably killed him, not the blood loss. Now that's what the doctor said; he claimed Akers didn't bleed a whole lot, not to where you could see it, anyhow."

Ollie looked puzzled. "Oh my Lord, Jim, I never heard the beat of this! Who told you such a thing anyway?"

Now a force to deal with, Jim had his answer ready. "I'll tell you who it was; it was Bruce Sluder! Yes sir, the big man himself told me that, did it just three days before he died. We got into a big dispute over the way it happened and that's when he told me. He figured there was just one of 'em, but I argued, and still do, that when a man's a fighting for his life, it'd take two or three to hold him down. Old Bruce bought me a Co-cola to keep my mouth shut about what he told me, but now that he's gone I figure the deals off."

Ollie's resignation accented her next remark. "Shady, what you just said is absolutely preposterous! I'd say Bruce was merely repeating some wild rumor he'd heard; it seems like there's a new one every day."

Edith backed her up. "Why, yes it's all just pure baloney coming from people who have nothing better to do than set around speculating. Now, I'm not saying Bruce Sluder was like that, but he was human like everybody else, and may actually have believed what he told you. By the way, Ollie and I'll hush about this in a minute, but have you heard anything from the inquest?"

"I reckon it's alright now to tell this since they released the news about it yesterday, but I still ask you not to quote me on it. I think it's well known that I've got the worst boss anybody ever had, and he'd like nothing better than to fire me." Her voice abruptly dropped to a level just above that of a whisper before she continued. "Mr. Sluder's tests all showed that he didn't have a drop of alcohol in his blood and the only trace they found was some on his right coat sleeve. The autopsy did show, though, that he passed away from natural causes; actually, it was from a massive stroke. Personally, I believe that was as a result of all the excitement caused by a confrontation he'd just had."

"Oh, I think we all know who Bruce had it out with, but I ain't going to say; besides, he'd just lie about it anyhow." Edith watched another piece of the puzzle fall into place, making her even more determined to see the complete picture. More and more it appeared that the mystery locked inside Keith's head somehow was part of the murder. Someday she hoped to have a talk with Kathleen; *who knows,* Edith conjectured, *she may be the very one to bust this thing wide-open.*

Turning to Jim, Edith severely reprimanded him. "You ought to be ashamed of yourself, talking the way you did around Hester. She's been right in the middle of this thing ever since it happened and I don't know how in the world she's stood it. I'm giving you fair warning, Jim Gernon, keep your big mouth shut about this around her!"

Something inside urged that she go to Hester and offer her comfort, but never having felt this way before she did not know how to deal with it. *Why, if I did, she'd just resent it and that would make matters even worser,* she reasoned.

Again, the voice of Mercy went unheeded.

Suddenly Christmas returned to center stage when they learned it was snowing. For nearly half an hour heavy clumps had been silently piling up like rose petals beneath a bush. After that, it continued until over four inches was on the ground. Snowstorms in the southern Appalachians, on occasion, can be fierce, but nearly always, they arrive unannounced and then quickly depart. Mae was the first to discover that they were in for a white Christmas.

"Daddy was right!" She yelled. "Everybody come look! He said it would snow for Christmas and it has." Her words affected their mood much the way live current does to a light bulb; things lit up! Not all the response was positive, however, when the younger set went from being rowdy to riotous. Edith was willing to put up with it for a while, but enough was enough and a line had to be drawn somewhere. Since Ollie would not do it, she dealt with the problem directly and called Laura down. "You're getting to be a way too big to act this way around boys. Claude Earl ain't used to girls behaving like this!"

"Well, he acts worse than I do, because he keeps trying to court me," she giggled.

."That young'in is more like Hester than Claude Earl could ever be," Edith whispered to Effie. "Just mark my word, she'll bear watching!"

"Oh, I think they're just being young'ins and showing out." Effie smiled. "But I'm glad Wanda Ann ain't like that, she's always been such a little lady. Wanda was Howard and Effie's only child; sweet and beautiful, she never had cause to want for anything.

Christmas morning arrived much too early, but seeing the world turned into a winter wonderland made it easy to get up. However, just as with the snow, so also the days of the season, both melted away all too soon. When it came time for Clark and Lorraine to leave, felt but not expressed was the sentiment that this probably was his last visit home. The last time he would gaze unto the mountains, places of the heart that would remain there as long as it kept beating. Unfortunately, that would not be long now, just a few more months. Turning then to those gathered around the car, he bravely smiled goodbye. Sunlight made a cameo of his face and a blue-black raven's wing of his hair. Words spoken were few, for there are times when love is better felt than said. After all, it's in the reflection of a tear where the soul can best be seen. For eight months, he fought the good fight, but July brought bad news and August was when he looked toward a place far higher than any mountain could ever rise.

They were with him at the end, all his immediate family except for Edith. She offered to stay home and take care of things there. Dave's foxhounds and other livestock needed feeding, cows milked, and eggs gathered, all that and so much more. Edith mourned deeply the sickness that was unto death, and it showed in the grim lines of her face. Muggy days, dreary and tense, were fear-filled with a deep dread of the inevitable. As they dragged on, the heavy hand of sorrow seemed to press the life out of Sweetwater's soul. Jesse joined Mae and Max to sit on the porch and mope for hours. Normally, this would have been a time for comic books, green apples, and romping in the swimming hole, not watching the sky and wondering if Gabriel was about to sound his trumpet. They felt that the end of time was very near.

At first, they stayed fulltime at Dave's house since that seemed the expedient thing to do. However, before long they began to feel alien-like and out of place. Nothing seemed to go right; no rain to cool the day, no dew to refresh the morning and at night they sweltered in a heat that allowed them to sleep only fitfully. Because of polio, the swimming hole was off-limits, so little or nothing was available to relieve their languor. It was the hottest August in memory, causing Edith to grow increasingly edgy with each passing day. She did not like cooking in someone else's kitchen, so they ended up eating at one house and sleeping in the other.

When word finally came, even though expected, it struck like a thunderbolt. Three days later a family, heartbroken and crushed, arrived back home. Jesse was perplexed at the changes he saw in his daddy. It concerned him that this transformation might be permanent and to some extent, his fears were well founded. Yes, Wade seemed different, now oddly quiet, but perhaps it would be better to say he seemed resigned. He again had come to grips with the inevitability of mortality, yet this time it took him to his knees. However, it is from that perspective, as some have so aptly noted where one may see their way the best. Wade proved to be no exception, and with time was able to find much of the peace there his soul craved.

CHAPTER 29

November brought Raymond home after spending fourteen months in two different hospitals and undergoing eleven separate surgeries. Now eager to resume life where he left it, he was pleased to find most of Sweetwater welcoming him back. Following a short period of sniffing each other out, he and Jesse felt ready to attempt a friendship. No more badgering this time, and certainly the subject of "gripping" was altogether off limits. While away, Raymond had no other choice, but to attend school; now, however, he was more than anxious to drop the habit.

Raymond's high-stepping limp soon became a familiar sight moving up and down Sweetwater road. At almost any hour of the day, he was on the go. His ordeal had endeared him to virtually everybody on the creek, prompting many to show their support by taking him into their homes. His favorite place to stay, however, was at "Wade and Edith's." No other spot was quite like theirs, for he found he could show up there and enjoy all the amenities of home without having to pay dues. Thus he stayed, night after night for weeks on end.

Despite Edith's many requests, several months passed before he was willing to talk to her about his ordeal. In the meantime, a few scattered details had slowly emerged.

"Finish up supper boys, and then you can have some butterscotch pie," Edith's words of promise painted a portrait of ulterior motives.

Pushing back from the table Gutch responded in his typical brash manner. "If I eat another pinto bean, it's liable to set off an explosion they'll feel in Robbinsville. And just look at Jesse there, why heck, he's as dangerous as a cocked Winchester. Heck, Edith, go ahead and give us some of that pie before we both go off!"

"When you stop that cussing I might, but not one minute before. You know

I don't allow talk like that at this table. Have you ever heard Jesse use such language?"

"Well, I've heard Dave do it, but if it'll make you feel any better, I can say I'm sorry."

"Gutch, you feel about as much remorse as a buzzard does for road kill"

"Well, don't worry about it, just hand me that pack of cigarettes over here. I need one to go with a cup of coffee and that butterscotch you promised."

Jesse sat behind the table on a long wooden bench that his daddy had made years before. Inching closer, he hoped not to miss any of the action. His mother was obviously up to something and it would be interesting to watch the fireworks.

"Raymond Reece, you'll get no coffee from me, not for supper anyway; besides I ain't a short-order cook, even if everybody thinks I am. You'll get a cigarette alright, but it'll be after I hear about what really happened the day you got hurt."

Quietly Gutch finished his dessert, leaving Jesse to wonder if the game was about over, but once again a little patience was called for. "Okay, Edith, I'll take that smoke now," he said belching loudly. Several wispy tooth-sucking sounds followed to signal his impatience.

Edith was onto his game, however. "Not until you tell me what happened between Mayor Sluder and Preacher Conway, you won't! You've been dodging me over this for long enough now."

"I told the law all about it, so why the heck don't you ask them!" Such hubris was rare on Sweetwater.

"With that smart mouth you'll be lucky if I don't run you off… then what'll you do?" She watched him squirm, his dark eyes darting back and forth before filling up with tears.

"Edith, I'm scared to death; why, I could get my throat cut over this."

Well known to play loose with the truth, this time, however, Raymond was not lying. He truly was a frightened young man.

"Listen," she said, wanting to reassure him. "What you say here will be kept private, and you can bank on that! Besides, it's important that the get truth out. Who you're talking about would be afraid to try anything after it is."

"Well, give me that duck then, and I'll tell you all I know, but I can guarantee you one thing, though: you're going to be disappointed." Here he paused to rub the table top with the tip of his fingers, unconsciously going back and forth while remaining deep in thought. Edith's chin rested at the apex of a triangle formed by the outspreading of her elbows. She nodded her head at the ashtray, indicating the half-smoked cigarette was his, if the deal was on.

"Jesse knows a lot too; why, he even heard the Preacher threaten me after I got hurt, so he may be in danger, too… Are you sure you still want hear this?"

"Stop making excuses or give me my cigarette back!"

"Ah-h heck, well let's see now, I guess it all started when Conway paid me a dime to go get Mr. Sluder. See, in order to hold services on Main Street he had to have a special permit. Anyhow, I went to the side door to get him and it sure surprised the crap out me to see Jesse a setting there too, acting like a big shot, or something. The Mayor, though, he seemed glad to see me, so we hurried on across the street to the courthouse where the preacher was waiting. Mr. Sluder said a special permit would cost him five dollars and you could tell that didn't set too well with the Preacher, but he paid it anyhow. About that time I needed to use the bathroom, so I took off down the hall and that's when I found this note saying it was out of order." Raymond stopped talking long enough to break off a piece of cornbread, and spread it thickly with mayonnaise; the huge morsel disappeared with one gulp.

"I've got to stand up for just a minute, my laig's starting to hurt;" the wily fourteen-year-old said as he squinted one eye and grimaced to hoist a stiff knee out from beneath the table. Once afoot, he then used a crutch to propel his six-foot, four-inch frame toward the hall door.

"Hey! You take just one more step and I'll break that other leg for you!" Edith warned with a reprimanding eye.

"Let me see Mae and Jo Nell for a second," he chuckled, having spied the two girls when they passed through the hall. Shrieks and giggles followed his unannounced foray into the front room. "Gimme a little sugar," he begged as they tumbled over each other, trying to escape his long groping arms. Jo Nell, a pretty redhead, lived nearby and was a good friend of Mae's. She, too, was fourteen.

"Acting like this you can just forget about another cigarette," Edith warned. And as far as Preacher Conway goes, you'd better be scared of him. So let's get back to business here and finish up."

"No! No! Don't talk like that. Up in Asheville the minute Mama stepped out of the room he showed me a big knife, and said he'd cut my throat if I ever said a word…. Now, Edith, you know you promised!"

Seeing the need to explain, she recounted her previous statement. "Gutch, for heaven's sake, it's like I said; getting this out to the public is the best possible way to protect yourself!"

Snuffing twice, he made deep snore-like noises to clear his pharynx, and then impatiently wiped several tears away with the palm of his hand. Suddenly he glanced up, a huge wet grin glistening brightly. "Hey, wait a minute, Beautiful, here's something for you!" Lips smacked loud against his fingertips as he blew a kiss. "I love you, Honey," he hollered as she disappeared from view. "Jo Nell's going to be my sweetheart," he bragged to a blushing Jesse.

"Gutch, puh-leese, let's get back to this!" she said, now fully exasperated.

"Um-m, let me think for a minute," he said. "Where was I, anyhow? Oh, yeah, the bathroom, it wasn't working so I just busted in anyway. You know, when a feller's got to pee, he's got to pee! Thing was though, they'd lied about the bathroom; it was working just fine. They'd already fixed it and I reckon since it was a Saturday they didn't plan on opening it back up 'til Monday. When I finished, though, I didn't flush because I heard Reverend Conway and the Mayor just outside the door and I wanted to listen. Since I'd had to break in, the door was slightly cracked, so I could hear every word they said. At first, they just talked about the two men facing the gas chamber, but then Mr. Sluder brought up the blockading and moonshining. He asked Preacher Conway, with all that going on right there under their noses, why wasn't he suspicious. Claude mumbled something about it not being unusual a-tall to have two or three hundred people there at a time, and bootlegging was the last thing on his mind. Said Earl probably wouldn't have known about it either if the law hadn't tipped him off. He sounded kinda smart-alecky with his answers, saying that after all, it wasn't like the Wild West around there. He did say, though, that right near the end he did notice some strange things happening. He claimed there was no reason to suspect them two of anything, since they just worked there part-time. And that Jack had come to the meetings, off an on, for years like a lot of folks did, so there was no reason to think anything about it.

"Preacher Conway sounded awful sad when he told how he had begged Earl to stay out of it. But, boys, that's when the crap hit the fan. Mr. Sluder was quick to tell him that Earl was too good a Christian to put up with nonsense like that. You could tell the Mayor was mad as fire by the way his voice got louder and louder. I think he was letting Preacher Conway know just how little he thought of him. The Preacher got mad, too, and started cussing, but it didn't take long for the Mayor to call him down. 'You've been drinking, ain't you? Yes, sir,' he said, 'I smell whiskey here, why you're nothing but a low-down, lying hypocrite.' That's what he called him and it set off a scuffle. I was too scared to look, but you could hear what sounded like them a wrassling around out there. Then after a minute or two Bruce let out this funny sounding laugh, one just like daddy does when he catches me doing something. 'By heavens I was right!' he said, 'and would you look a there, a bottle of likker in your pocket all this time!'

"He must have took the top off because they started a scuffling again and, buddy, you could sure smell it then, all over the place. So a minute or two later I heard Claude crying and begging the Mayor not to tell on him. Said the only reason he had it was for his stomach. Claimed Dr. Cranford had prescribed it for him and if he didn't believe it, to go ask the doctor. Claude sounded real pitiful begging like that; especially when he said people would run him off, even if they knew it was just for medicine.

"I think Mr. Sluder must have felt sorry for him because it seems like he settled down after that and sounded quieter. He said, 'You need to quit it, Son, look at what it's done to your brother. Just because it runs in the family, you think you can't quit, but I'm here to tell you that you can.'

"The Reverend said he ought to be ashamed of himself for talking like that, and since he'd been raised pretty much as an orphan, to leave his family out of it.

"Mr. Sluder was quick to tell him he was no orphan and it was time he quit trying to hide behind such nonsense.

"Things then seemed to settle down for awhile, but next the Mayor started accusing him of being a womanizer. Said, from what he'd heard the main reason Claude had stayed out of the bootlegging was because he was too busy chasing after women. You could tell Preacher Conway got puffed up over that, even though he didn't say much. I guess he figured the Mayor had enough on him not to argue the point. Finally, he said, 'Yes, it was true he had been accused of running around with Hester Rose and that a lot of people had been quick to attack him, even though they knew it all was just a big lie. Truth was,' according to him, 'Hester and Earl were the ones who needed to be watched.' Well, boys, you should've heard the Mayor then, he wasn't about to listen to that. So, Preacher Conway started boo-hooing again, and claimed that nobody ever loved Earl like he did, that they'd been just like brothers."

Impatient to finish his tale, Raymond suddenly closed both eyes, and then like a snorting bull, began slinging his head back and forth wildly.

"I thought it was kinda funny that the Mayor sounded more like a preacher than the Preacher did. Especially when he quoted the Bible where it says something about foxes and grapevines; I can't exactly remember what. After that, about the only other thing said was the Mayor asking why he'd ever let Earl get that deep into stuff without being there to protect him. That's when they walked on down the hall to where I couldn't hear anything else. I knew it wouldn't be a good idea to get caught listening, so I just laid low for another minute or two. I didn't figure on Jack Woodcock, though; I reckon he must have been standing around the corner a listening too, because there he was, arms folded up and leaning back against the wall. He never said a word, just blared them old ugly eyes at me and I tell you what, I got out of there right then. Now, by golly, let's have that cigarette like you promised."

"Hold on here a minute, we're not done yet and you know it too! Let's hear what else was said about Hester; they didn't just let it drop like that."

"Nope, that was it, word for word and you may just as well quit asking me. I believe after all this; you owe me another slice of pie too… Oh, crap, well, yes, maybe there was one more little thing. But after I tell you that, you'll have to hush. See, when Claude was talking about her and Earl, he called her a name that sounded pretty bad.

"What kind of name?

"I don't know, it was one I'd never heard before!"

"Well, when did he say it?" Edith probed.

"Right before the Mayor quoted that Bible verse, I think. But what difference does that make?"

Gutch was now riled; leaving Edith to wonder if she could get him to answer one last question. "Anything else…" Her eyes squinted knowingly as she asked.

"My goodness, Woman," he grumbled, "this is worse than going to school. Hold on a second and let me think…What was it, anyhow!… Oh yeah, I heard him say that it took an old fox to outfox a little'un… And that's it, Sister! That's all she wrote, so now you know everything I do!"

"Who said that?," she asked.

"Said what?"

"What you *just* said!" She sounded testy.

"Why, the Mayor! Who else? Now listen to me, I'm starting to get a sick-headache over this, so how about forking over my smoke!"

"I just wanted to make sure," she murmured, looking pleased. "I know this all fits together, somehow. I just can't quite see it yet, but I will," she nodded confidently. "Yes, in time it'll all be clear."

Jesse watched it disappear, the last piece of the best pie he had ever tasted. Made from a recipe only his mother knew with such ingredients as fresh butter, honey, and pie filling mix. The best part, however, was magic and she would never share that with anyone.

Later, Gutch and Jesse stayed up listening to "The Grand Ole Opry". Abruptly, Gutch began talking about his misfortune. "Remember, how you jumped in and tried to act like a bigshot when I got hurt? Well Son, you'as just as full of crap then as you are right now. And I heard about how you tried to steal my comic book! " he chuckled derisively.

"Well, I didn't run off with somebody else's money, did I? What a hair-brained thing to do!"

Coarse laughter preceded an abrupt paroxysm of raspy coughs that could have easily been mistaken for a case of pneumonia. "Heck," he wheezed, "if I hadn't got my laig hurt it would have been worth it just to watch old Conway act like a cat covering up crap, grabbing for that money! After Jack Woodcock and Fred Ranger took up the collection, they put it in a paper bag, and then just laid it there on the courthouse steps. So, when nobody was a looking, I just retched down and snatched it up. And, boys, was it full; stuffed to the gills with greenbacks. I figured then I'd hit the jackpot and, Son, you don't know how good that makes you feel." Jesse was amazed at the look of pride he saw in his face.

"Heck," Gutch exulted, "It was just as much mine as it was his'n, 'cause he'd stole it, too. I stuck it up under my arm and started easing off; I'd have got away with 'er too if Fred Ranger hadn't spotted me. That idiot started squalling out at the top of his lungs; but it didn't stop me, though."

Suddenly Gutch pointed to the radio. "Wait a minute, Son, I want to hear this, it's Chet Adkins!" Naturally gifted in music, Gutch knew Jesse begrudged him of this talent. Any tune Raymond heard immediately became his own, and one he could reproduce at will. This ability far exceeded Jesse's kin or, indeed, his willingness to accept. Another conundrum to Jesse was why such a scoundrel as Gutch could be so blessed, while he, a baptized member of the Orr Branch Church, couldn't even whistle "Dixie" without it sounding like "Yankee-Doodle." *Perhaps,* he reasoned, *the angel in charge of handing out talents needed a good laugh, and did things like this as a joke. Yes, that could be it,* Jesse smiled at his sudden insight.

Gutch waited until the last round of applause had faded before resuming his monologue. Considering the hour, and the fact that they were the only ones still up, Jesse felt they should turn the volume down. It would not do for Wade to be awakened, else Dave be put to shame when it came to pitching a fit.

"I nearly got away with it, too," Gutch boasted. "Why, nobody but Preacher Conway and those two other idiots tried to catch me. I cut across the courthouse lawn and headed for Bart Stevens' wagon. I allowed maybe I could jump on the back, and ride that thing to glory. But with me sailing through the air, it must have spooked them mules, because I missed where I'd aimed for. After hitting the left back corner, I skidded straight across into the wheel. From then on, everything just seems like a bad dream. I do remember you and Dr. Cranford being there and what preacher Conway said. Cussing me like that, and then turning around to pray loud enough for everybody in the county to hear him. But I'm glad Ross Walters was there, 'cause I think he heard it, too. Ross told me on the way over to Andrews that if I'd just say the word, he'd beat the heck out of him. Said Conway was a slacker and had started preaching just to stay out of the war. You could tell he had no use for him."

Saturday nights on Sweetwater, spent listening to the Grand Ole Opry was a tradition that dated back to the 1920's. Family and friends would gather at each other's homes to make fudge, dance, laugh and sing along with the radio. By the 1940's they were meeting regularly at Wade and Edith's, since their place was always open to the community. Usually Claude and Lilly Edmonds acted as co-hosts, while Bill and Maye Morrow, Walter and Sue Roberts, Don and Dolly Pierson were the regulars. In addition, many drop-ins made impromptu stops, some that lived as far away as Robbinsville and Stecoah. Tragically, like so many other good customs, this too had to end, and when it did the passing was hardly noticed at all. Ironically, it took several years to realize that something truly special was gone and there was no way to bring it back again. They traded a precious jewel for the gaudy glitter of television.

At first, the seducing power of the new medium was overwhelming. It drew crowds much larger than radio ever did, and did so nearly every night of the week. So many came, in fact, that there were never enough seats to go around, leaving the overflow to sit on the floor. Rows of eyes staring in the black and white twilight at incredibly uninteresting shows, right up until the test pattern drove them away. However, this situation did not last, either, for soon every home had one. Now they could sit and let their minds slowly molder away in the comfort of their own easy chairs. Sadly, it was when ionized sepulchers began to appear before the face of man that the world became a much duller place in which to live.

CHAPTER 30

It was a good time to turn fourteen, the summer of 1954, and a good time to spend a month on Sweetwater. Claude Earl felt fortunate, indeed, and especially liked the freedom of being out from under his mother's watchful eye.

Jesse, a rising senior at Robbinsville High, had taken a temporary job with a small sawmill located nearby. He hoped to earn some money now that he had a driver's license and limited access to the family car. Such privileges made for exciting times, but they came with a price. There were trips to the drive-in in Andrews, Saturday night movies, church, and, of course, parties. Without work, however, he could do none of it.

Claude Earl wanted to spread his wings and Laura wanted to be his sky. Right from the start it was Laura; she never left his mind and it was evident her feeling ran much the same. Starting with the first Sunday at church they found a seat together, then it was long walks in the afternoon that later led to holding hands. On the evening before he left they lingered awhile at the bridge in front of her house. Claude Earl felt a great lump in his throat and seemed unwilling to say very much, but not so Laura. "You'll forget me this fall when you see all those pretty girls at school," she teased. Without warning, he suddenly pulled her close and for the first time they kissed. As they turned to leave, a full moon over the mountain glistened in the tears of their eyes.

Edith, long before, had grown weary of hearing about Laura, but just bit her lip and did not let on. "It's nothing but a bad case of puppy love," she wrote Hester. "They ain't a bit of need in worrying, why it'll pass before the summer is over." Although Edith's words offered comfort, Hester still worried. Meanwhile, Ollie's concern over Laura mounted daily. Everyone knew Ollie doted on matchmaking, yet such talent was for neither herself nor Laura. The upshot of it all, however, was that Claude Earl and Laura must "simply" forget each other. They were "much too young for such silliness," and as far as them writing to each other, "well that was just out of the question."

Traveling back home Hester spent much of her time reminding him that he was different. "Remember," she emphasized, "I dedicated you to the Lord, so above all you must never let carnal feelings get in the way of your calling. There's a special purpose for your life and I know it just as well as I know my own name. Now, what that might be we've not been shown yet, but we will. Our part is to keep the faith and be ready when He calls." The family had heard all this before, and to a person felt convinced she was just "full of beans," but that is putting it politely.

"I always wanted to go back," sighed Grandma. "But now I doubt I ever will." She and Jesse were enjoying the afternoon sun from her front porch. Recently, he had felt the need to spend more and more time with her, yet could not understand exactly why.

"Will and his daddy did three times before Charles got too weak to go. It's a hard trip back to Bad Creek; why, it took us nearly two weeks to move here." Will and Axie, Jesse's great-grandparents had moved their family in 1903 from Mitchell County to Graham, traveling the one hundred and fifty miles by both train and wagon. They built their house to face northeast so, when seated on the porch she could always gaze in the direction of "home."

Jesse quickly realized her mood was a little different today as evidenced by the look in her eyes. Although a kind and deeply caring person, the eighty-five-year-old was not one to show a lot of sentimentality. All of her life a strong and resolute will had sustained her though much hardship and adversity. Thinking to get away with it by pretending to wipe away what she called "matter," Grandma smiled weakly at her handkerchief. This did not fool Jesse, however. *Homesick,* he thought, *after all these years and she's still homesick.* "Why did you'uns ever leave there anyway?" He probed. "From what I hear you had a fine place there on Bad Creek."

"Will and Charles got a big contract to supply Springfield Arms with wood to make gun stocks. The timber they needed was a lot more plentiful here, so they decided we'd just move. No doubt, it was a good opportunity, giving us a whole lot better chance at making it. You know, we had a big family then, and after Charles made the first trip to look it over, he came back all excited. All he could talk about was us moving here. I guess in the long run he was right, said there was some good farms for sale with the kind of trees they needed. And too, we wanted to find a place where people could get along. I was born the year the Civil War ended and I know you've heard them old blood-and-guts tales; nothing but fighting all the time. It all started on account of so much hate left over from the war. Half the people there were for the North and the other half for the South and I doubt even now it's much better. Everybody for the North was Republicans while the Democrats fought for the South.

"My mother used to talk about them old out-liars. They were a bunch of outlaws and the sorriest trash on earth who didn't fight on either side. Worse than the home guard, they just roved the countryside a robbing and murdering. They took advantage of the situation, knowing that the men folks were all off fighting. They killed the livestock, burned farms and houses, and were known to take food right out of the mouths of little young'ins, leaving then to starve." Suddenly her words turned bitter when she told how they sifted even the dirt from under their smokehouse to get enough salt to survive. "You have to have salt or your meat won't cure, it'll just rot," she said. "Why, our people didn't have nothing to live on, and a lot of 'em didn't make it neither. Trouble was," she continued, "even after the war ended, times didn't get much better. There were so many scores to settle. Why, right up to the time we left there you couldn't hold an election without somebody getting hurt or killed."

Listening to this, Jesse realized why she clung so tenaciously to her convictions. Moreover, just as uncompromising as she was about politics, so was her devotion to the Methodist Church. Emphatically, she made this point when Dolly, her youngest and perhaps favorite child, announced her intention to be married. Upon learning the political and religious leanings of the prospective groom, Grandma immediately expressed her feelings. "Well, go ahead and get married if you think you have to; then join the Baptist Church and become a Republican, and that'll make you just a *big… nothing*, but see if I care!"

Jesse liked spending his nights there, and especially enjoyed awakening to find her sitting before the hearth, rocking in her chair. The front room was large enough to accommodate three featherbeds and the one he slept in had a good view of the fireplace. With the smell of coffee perking, hot biscuits in the oven, and a sizzling pan full of ham he found it easy to get up. More often than not, however, he preferred to just lie there and gaze at the profile of a goddess whose hair was so white that it gave light to the light, and yet she was never vain or pretended to be anything. Grandma met life where it was, embraced it, loved it, and left it without regret. She was a very special lady, and everybody on Sweetwater but her knew it.

"Grandma," he pressed, "all my life I've noticed that you and Dave don't get along good; and yet I've never understood why."

For a long moment Jesse felt the emptiness of silence, he had stepped onto forbidden turf and found it frightening. Mercifully, his elder recalled she was dealing with naiveté and softened a gaze that suddenly had turned hard. "That's not the way I ever wanted things to be; why, Dave is my oldest, and in many ways the one I had the highest hopes for. He's bull-headed, though, and always has been. He was a good boy growing up and worked like a dog right up until just before we moved. He used to pick flowers and bring them to me, mostly wild ones from the woods. But once, though, he brought me a handful of rosebuds! Well, without thinking I scolded him for not waiting until they were in full bloom. Later, I realized I'd made a mistake and told him so, but he never brought me another flower.

Then after he got a little older, it seems like overnight he turned into a real smart-aleck, wouldn't help out none around the place, and wanted to be gone all the time. Before long, he started drinking and laying out all night foxhunting, with never a good word for anybody. Claimed me and Will made a big difference between him and the others. By the way he acted, I guess we did, but our feelings for him had not changed, not one bit, and he knew it, too!"

"What do you reckon happened?" Jesse asked.

"I think he let the devil take over. Now here's something you never heard about because everybody's always been too ashamed to talk about it, but one time he came within a gnat's whisker of murdering your Grandmother Mary." She paused long enough to let the impact of this sink in before continuing.

Jesse was stunned. "Mom?" his voice quivered.

"It was back when your daddy was just a baby and Dave had been laying out drunk for nearly two weeks. After running out of anything to eat, Mary, I guess, finally decided she had put up with it long enough and was fixing to leave him when he came storming through door. The first thing he did was to demand that she get in kitchen and fix him some breakfast, but when she informed him that there was nothing to cook, he took a fit. He called her every name in the book and threatened to beat her head off. Without a word she picked up little Wade and started for the door. At that, Dave grabbed his .22 rifle and pointed it straight between her eyes; told her if she made another step, he'd pull the trigger. Well she just sunk down and started crying, holding your daddy up close to her breast. Dave gave her a big shove and she almost fell, but was able to steady herself by grabbing a strip of ceiling-panel that for some reason she'd put there the day before. It helped get her to her feet; however, by now Dave seemed determined to kill her. Again, he pointed the gun at her and she could tell he meant business, but right when he fired she slung the board at him. Miraculously, it struck the barrel just right to deflect his aim, causing the bullet to whizz past her head. In a flash, she was out of there and running as hard as she could towards our house. I figure the shock of what he tried to do must have hit home hard enough that he didn't take out after her. Well, she and Wade ended up staying here with us for about a month, but when he finally did show up, I really balled him out. I told him then, and he knew I meant it; he was not welcome here, and wouldn't be until he gave up his drinking and started acting sensibly. He let me know right away that he was done with me and all his brothers and sisters, too. Said none of us had ever treated him right or as part of the family, and that he had no use for any of us.

"I've heard him say that a lot of times," Jesse nodded. "He also says you cheated him out of his rights to the land, once you divided it up."

"I gave him exactly the part he always claimed!" Grandma responded firmly. "On the day we bought this place from Noah Rice he staked out a piece of ground up there under the Oak Field Ridge. Now, though, he wants some of the bottom land, too, but it's too late; it's all been deeded out."

"When did Mom go back home," Jesse asked, hoping to change the tenor of things.

"Oh, she went back with him that day he showed out here with me, with both of them acting like nothing had ever happened. After that, she treated me just as cold as he did; you'd think I was the one who caused it all. Wade, though, young as he was, wanted to stay with me and did every chance he got. The little feller would slip off and come over here to stay for weeks at a time... Why, I wound up nearly raising that young'in."

"I guess then you and Dave will never be able to patch it up will you?"

"Lord, I forgave him a long time ago and I think he has me too, but it's awful hard to start back over without opening up old wounds. I wish it was different, though," she sighed wistfully.

CHAPTER 31

Light comes in many forms and manners, it being primordial to creation and the source of all energy. Every living thing, whether plant or animal, owes its existence to this presence. In the purest sense, light defies definition in the same manner that infinity does limits; therefore, it may be useful to employ certain parallels when discussing its effect on the physical, mental, and spiritual realms. An example would be the phenomenon of insight, something we usually think of as occurring suddenly, in a flash of revelation. However, sometimes it takes place slowly; much like the dawning of a day, and certainly, this is the way it was for Jesse when he came to realize just how his grandmother meant to him. It takes the power of love to light up a heart.

She was there from the beginning, quiet and unassuming with her music playing softly in the background. Jesse loved to tag along behind this frail shadow, plying her with a million questions. He sensed in her a source that others seemed to have missed. She, like the woman at the well, drew from the deeper cisterns of life.

Mary wore her long black hair wound tightly in a bun, thereby hiding her beauty. Conjecture alone explains why she chose to do this. Perhaps it was from having a poor self-image, but more than likely it was to appease a jealous husband. Quick, furtive movements and a sharp mind would always be part of Jesse's memory of this beloved figure. She suffered from chronic headaches caused by an injury to her right eye that happened when she was only three. Willie, her younger brother, accidentally stuck a fork into the cornea, causing it permanent damage. With proper medical still far in the future, she had to endure the pain most of her life. In time, Jesse learned how to manage such conditions; unfortunately, this ability came much too late to benefit her.

Often, she would treat him very special. Once she gathered up scrap pieces of cloth and sewed them together to make him a book bag for the first grade. Another time was when he spent a week with her in early March during the second grade. He had decided to stay the night but awoke before morning with a fever and vomiting. At sunrise, it was obvious that he should remain in bed and not try to go home. Consequently, he ended up recuperating there, with the episode ultimately leaving him with a host of pleasant memories.

Mom cooked from a limited larder, yet somehow still managed to come up with some very tasty treats. First, she made him a layer cake with hard fudge icing that was so rich it tasted like candy. Another snack was thin slices of Irish potatoes placed on the stove eye and cooked to a crispy brown. When salted, they tasted far better than anything did from the store.

To some extent, Jesse felt guilty about Mom because he had always taken her so much for granted. Being quiet and unassuming, she never sought attention and it was only after he left for the Navy that he came to realized just how much she meant to him. His high school years came and went with remarkably little of the turmoil that so often accompanies the rites of teenage passage. Perhaps this was due, in part, to the fact it was the 1950's. The world was quieter and more naïve then. This is not to say, however, that he lived such a cloistered life that none of earth's finer allurements did not tested his mettle. There were seasons when he fell in and out of love several times a day. He learned how to play pool, poorly, and even tried the bitter taste of Budweiser once or twice. For him school was merely an obstacle to get past on the way to his real goal, and that was to join the Navy. Therefore, he left for boot camp and Great Lakes Illinois early on Monday morning, following Friday night graduation.

Before departing, Jesse spent Sunday afternoon with Dave and Mom. For a time they just sat chatting amiably and remembering the old, mostly good times together. Laughingly, Dave retold the story of Jesse's birth and, as expected, new, and even more interesting details emerged.

"When do you leave?" Dave asked.

"We have to be at Topton by 9:30 in the morning. Arnold Roberts is taking us."

"Who's going with you?"

"Max Roberts, Pug Calhoun, Mack Crisp and Don Buchanan; we're such a motley crew I hope the Navy survives us," Jesse laughed.

When he stood up to leave he watched surprised as their demeanor suddenly changed. Until then Jesse had assumed they would be excited too; after all, this was their oldest grandchild getting ready to spread his wings. Instead, it perplexed him to see Dave drop his head sobbing. Even more troubling, however, was when Mom covered her eyes and headed for the bedroom. Tilted down, the face of this spirit-like essence became a fount of tears as she faded from view.

Shortly before leaving, Dr. Parker gave him the bad news. Jesse had high blood pressure and that could keep him out of the Navy. After asking for something to keep it down, he received two "nerve" pills to take with him. It was at Fort Jackson where he faced the now suddenly all-important physical. Miraculously, however, the medicine worked! That evening he and four of his classmates climbed aboard a Pullman bound for the shores of Lake Michigan. On the way, they partied day and night, celebrating with dozens of others who joined them along the way. The revelry grew in strength through Atlanta, Cincinnati, and Chicago before they finally arrived at their destination. Slaphappy grins quickly turned into looks of sober-faced wonder once they stepped through the gate and greeted by the sentry. Actually, his exact words were, "Okay, Suckers, you've had it, your heart may belong to your girl friend, but your butt belongs to the Navy!" Later an old Chief Petty Officer extended to them a very personal welcome. They spent the first hour listening to all the reasons why they no longer should think themselves as being part of the human race. Remarkably, by the end of his lecture, the presentation was so good they bought it. Most, if not all, now realized they were the lowest form of life known to man.

Benumbed and stripped of all self-worth, they suddenly found themselves in a world that most had never dreamed existed. The new "boots" were given temporary quarters in an old World War II barracks where they tried to settle down and figure out just what exactly had gone wrong. None, it seems, realized that another and even more exhaustive medical exam lay just ahead, this time administered by the Navy. Army medics did the first one and they recorded Jesse's systolic pressure at 148. He was shocked when a corpsman informed him that it now read 180. Immediately, they set him aside for further testing. Six weeks later, after learning that he had a congenital heart condition; they mustered him out with an honorable discharge. After leaving Sweetwater with such high hopes, he suddenly was back and feeling like a boat up the well-known creek without an oar.

Nevertheless, while at Great Lakes he fought one of the epic battles of his life, and did so completely unprepared. Immediately after being separated him from the others they sent him to a purgatory-like place called the "holding company."

Here he was destined to remain until all health issues were resolved. Usually this took about two weeks, but true to form, things did not work out quite that way. It was during his first week there that a huge boil popped up on his buttock. The angry sore continued to develop, in both size and pain, until he came to a state of near desperation. Despite fervent prayer that it would just go away, the sore continued to worsen. Finally, in desperation he asked for permission to visit the sick bay. One look by the doctor was enough to warrant hospital admission. Up until then Jesse had felt perhaps a few pangs of homesickness, but by keeping busy, he was able to keep it in tow. This changed, however, after he found himself confined to bed. Hour after hour, he had to deal with the heavy hand of boredom. Unrelentingly, it kept bearing down, threatening to crush the fragile shell of his optimism. Once cracked, it was just a matter of time before the germs of despair invaded his soul to leave him fevered with homesickness. Nor did it help him to know that others, too, had the infection as he listened to them sobbing. His own ability to sleep became increasingly difficult since a wounded heart tends to hurt worse in the dark. They cried throughout the night, then laughed and joked all day, putting on a brave face that helped them to exist, but only by becoming hypocrites.

Jesse soon reached the lowest ebb of his life; the tide was out, and he could see debris from his few short years strewn and scattered all across the shoreline. Wasted and empty shells of dreams, once treasured for their taste, had become stale and were worthy now only of the trashcan. Suddenly, exposed, these embedded hopes and aspirations now lurked dangerously as he waded unshod among them, their sharp edges cutting deeply into tender flesh. It was while amid this flotsam that better memories from a happier time washed across his soul, causing him to lose his footing, and great was the fall. That is when he cried, too.

Contrary to conventional thought, heaven is much closer to us when sought from the valley, than from the mountaintop, and Jesse was right where he needed to be in order to learn this lesson well. Previously, he had read the Bible, studied it, and prayed, but now a spirit he never knew existed before was helping to facilitate his efforts. He moved through the Gospels, several chapters at a time while developing an entirely new perspective of what was there. In one place he read that, "If you believe, you will receive whatever you ask for in prayer." In another, he found this: "What things so ever ye desire, when ye pray, believe that ye receive them and ye shall have them." He discovered these and dozens more scattered throughout the scriptures.

Suddenly, Jesse had an epiphany; he saw that by focusing his thoughts on a definite place in heaven, the Christ of the Bible became personal and real. This lasted but a second or two, yet during this instant of time, he sensed the living presence of Jesus! This, he realized, was the "now" that Michael had spoken about.

He had heard that successful performers know that when they *feel* the words of a song, it transforms their music to a higher level. Two unrelated concepts, perhaps, yet they began to fuse in his mind. Could it be that by imaging the reality of deity while mentally experiencing the answer to his prayers, faith truly does become "the substance of things hoped for?" If so, then by faith he soon would be going home. Thus, it became an accomplished fact and he accepted it as such.

Wade and Edith were shocked when he unexpectedly showed up, yet it saddened them to learn the reason why. They, too, had shared in his dream for a career in the Navy and although happy to have him back, they felt perplexed. For Dave and Mom this was not the case, however. As sad as had been the departing, so now was their delight in having him back. Grandparents have the luxury of being able to enjoy the moment without being overly concerned about the future. Perhaps even nature itself is teaching them that they are drawing nigh unto that day when the "now" experience will be theirs forever.

CHAPTER 32

A vast and uncharted domain is the future, and it alone has right to the title of "final frontier". For it is within the confines of this unconquered territory that our fondest dreams and highest aspirations lie. Entering it, however, is not without risk, yet whether to do so or not has never been an option. Merely to live means that the quest is sine qua non. There will be a resting place, however, and beyond that the isle of paradise. It is on those celestial shores where the soul will wait before One who yields not to the vagaries of time and never shall, for to Him the future, like the past, is forever now.

Without a job to go to, Jesse, for a time, merely existed. However, it only took a few days of this before boredom began to set in. "*Life is passing you by,*" claimed an ill-defined feeling. And when the whippoorwills sang what he heard was, "n*e're do well... ne're do well... Jesse is a... ne're do well.*" The country was in recession, yet for the most part affluent America was quite content during the Eisenhower years. For those fortunate enough to have a job times were not at all bad. It did not pay, however, to be without work experience, and everywhere Jesse went all he got for his efforts was word that they were hiring skilled workers only. Caught in a closed loop where work was not available without experience and yet there was no way to get that without a job, so he floundered. Unable to afford college, he worked for several months at odd jobs and dreamed of the day when he could start living again. Without money or a car, he decided just to put girls out of his mind. Perhaps he should take Dave's advice and join the Catholics; that way if he became a priest he would then have a good excuse for living such a celibate life.

Although it was a time of trial, he ultimately came to realize that it all had been preordained. Such a day and hour, from the beginning, had been his destiny and even a gift. Such a philosophical view, however, did not arise immediately, coming later from the perspective of maturity.

During this era, he and his mother developed a much deeper relationship than ever before. This, by using the opportunity to do things together such as planting flowers, visiting neighbors, fishing and being content just to be able to sit and watch the world turn through its seasons. She, in her greater wisdom, knew that this gentle time would not last. Indeed, after just one short year it abruptly ended when Dave's health took a turn for the worse.

"Doctor Parker told me I'm a dying man, Jamup."

"He's said that before, Dave; let's just hope he's wrong this time, too." They were pulling away from the clinic with Jesse driving. It had become his routine to take Dave every Saturday afternoon to the doctor. "How high was it?" he asked, referring to the blood pressure.

"My systolic was too high to read, but the diastolic was 130. He told me with a pressure like that and with my coronary heart disease it's just a matter of time."

Having suffered for decades with extreme hypertension and heart disease, Dave's last few months proved to be ones of pure agony. By-pass surgery was yet to be developed; therefore, little was available, except Demerol and morphine to ease the pain. Jesse quickly became adept at performing the necessary procedures it took to maintain him, including administering IV injections. Dr. Parker taught both him and Ray how to give around the clock coverage and it became quickly apparent that they were the designated caregivers. Before long, the demands of such a schedule began to extract its toll.

"Jesse!... Jesse!" He cried. "I'm hurting awful again, Son; would you give me another shot?"

"Let's try to wait a few more minutes, Dave; it's just been two hours, and Dr. Parker said no more often than every four."

"Lord have mercy, Son! My arm's a killing me, can't we go ahead? After I'm dead it won't matter no how!"

Sleep came at a premium. Dave called out for help at all hours, day, or night; many times, though, it was just when the caregiver had dropped off. For months after he died, Jesse would still wake up to a voice yelling out his name, begging for assistance.

Dave suddenly took a turn for the worse, and it was during this time that he seemed to resign himself to the inevitable. Now, however, instead of pleading for more pain medication, his pleadings turned toward addressing a higher need. At first, they were simple prayers, heard almost indiscernible above that of mere muttering. Then their fervor intensified, almost as if he stood naked before the bar of judgment without hope or recourse. This continued for hours with his body lathered in sweat. Repeatedly he begged for forgiveness, both from God and from his fellow man. On and on he called the roll; naming names and confessing wrongs, he had committed against them, until finally he asked for Mary. "I've made a mess of our life together and never told you what I fool I was that time I tried to kill you. I can't go to my grave with that on my conscience so I'm begging you now to forgive me."

"They Lordy mercy, Dave, you know I do! So why don't you try to be quiet and get yourself a little rest," she suggested.

"One other thing," he continued. "I'm not able to get up and do it myself but I want you to talk to my Mammy and tell her how sorry I am about everything."

Turning then to face Jesse, he appeared now to be much more at peace with himself. "Jamup," he said. "You're a good boy; son so you remember that time I brought you home with me and you ate that big bait of rabbit eggs?"

Jesse nodded solemnly with a faint smile outlining his lips.

"I guess you remember then that feller Mike Goodman who brought old Dugan home, don't you, carried him all the way up here from the Shehan Cove? When we went outside to talk, he was straight with me and didn't mince words. I was convinced then, and still am, that he wasn't of this world; he said that me and Nasty-Bill was two of a kind and had been making life miserable for just about everybody. That he couldn't do much about that old gander, but he expected a lot more out of me. I doubt anybody noticed it, but after that I did try to do better, even quit cussing so much."

The next morning, with Dave seemingly on the mend, Ray took Jesse aside and told him to take a few hours off, to get away for a while. This was the first break he had had for months, so he quickly got up with Roy Dees, a long time pal, and they headed straight for the Georgia line where beer was available. Two dollars was enough to get a six-pack of king-sized "Bud" and after making it back to Roy's place on Beech Creek, they each had one. One was all it took to make his head spin like a top and he was still trying to slow the world back down when he started for home. Driving up into the yard his heart began to pound at the sight of a small crowd that had gathered near his front door. Max met him with the word;

Dave had just died! While the shock was unbelievable, it was the feeling of guilt that overwhelmed him.

Dave lay in state at Wade and Edith's house for two days, making it impossible for Jesse to sleep. He kept telling himself that if only he had stayed home none of this would have happened. Worse, however, was the knowledge of something else, something he could never share with anyone and it kept haunting him. *Lord, here I was half-drunk and not being where I ought to be and now just look at what happened.* Worry made Jesse so sick he barely made it to the funeral.

Just before they closed the casket, Grandma requested to have one last moment with her son. Tenderly, she leaned forward, tears spilling onto his face like wax drops from a candle, to place a tiny clump of rosebuds over his heart. *I wonder,* Jesse mused, *who, besides me, knows that the breach is now repaired.*

After the service, four unopened cans of Budweiser took flight to somewhere deep in the woods.

In time, Jesse's guilt would fade, doing so much like an old garment losing its color. The stain to his life, however, was permanent. Never again would he feel comfortable at turning loose of the controls, lest the world fly apart. He learned that of all things on earth, guilt has the highest specific gravity and no power, save that of Divinity, can lift it.

Dave died in December; February found Jesse working in Macon Georgia for the same company that Wade did. At last, he was where the river joined the ocean and as a young salmon, he now was ready to make his run. With a steady income, the first thing he did was to buy a car and some new clothes. The six-year-old Ford ran like a tent revival, spirited, loud, and on lots of faith. Pride brought him back to Sweetwater every other weekend and the new clothes gave him enough confidence to start thinking about girls again.

While working at District Memorial Hospital in Andrews, Mae had made many new friends there. Among them was a beautiful young woman with the name of Maggie Lominac. Soon Maggie and Jesse were dating and from the start, he found it hard to stay away from her. He quickly became so enamored that he loved even the essence of her perfume. "To a Wild Rose" lingered in the car on his shirt long after they parted, making him miss her even more. After seven months of courtship, they were married in the Andrews Methodist Church at four o'clock on a Saturday afternoon. A September sun slanted its long golden rays through the stained glass windows, illuminating the altar. Four others, including the pastor and his wife had gathered there to witness them pledge their vows. Immediately, they left for Myrtle Beach, however, they spent that night at Chimney Rock. A tiny apartment in Macon, Georgia, became their first home soon after the honeymoon was over.

With prospects not good for meaningful employment, they soon realized that more education was their only hope for a brighter future. Jesse discovered that a proprietary school Asheville offered a fifteen-month program in medical lab and x-ray technology. Best of all, he would have an almost absolute guarantee of getting a good job once his training was over. He also learned that by doubling up on courses the diploma could be his in just one year, and what a year that turned out to be!

Asheville's long history of housing shortages forced them into buying a new mobile home. Fortunately, they were able to locate a quiet, well-kept lot just off Merrimon Avenue to park it. Maggie went to work for one of the more prominent physicians in town as his secretary-receptionist, while Jesse found part-time employment at the Country Club of Asheville.

While their income was meager, they were able, by careful planning and budgeting, to get by. For instance, even though the weather that winter was severe they stayed comfortable at a cost of about one dollar per week. Jesse watched for oil company ads with special come-on offers for the first few customers. He would race to get in line, buying it, oftentimes, at ten cents a gallon.

In October, Theresa was born and when Jesse saw her, it was love at first-sight. To him she was the prettiest, and nearest to perfect baby, he had ever seen. Surely, the angels must have made a mistake by leaving one of their very own in her place. He was at the nursery every time they opened it for viewing. Hospitals at the time maintained very austere rules about keeping new fathers at bay. They allowed only a teasing 15-minute glimpse of the babies, twice each day. Broadway never had a production that generated more excitement than the one that played before those windows. When the curtains finally parted Jesse had to scramble, nook and crane, just to beam his adoration at a tiny pink bundle that now contained his heart.

Feelings of pride, unlike anything he had ever experienced before, swept over him when they finally left the hospital for home. Now they truly were a family and the small compartment of his car gave a cozy, warm feeling to the moment. However, joy sometimes can be elusive, and unfortunately, this happened to be one of those occasions. Without warning, their elation suddenly turned to near panic when they simultaneously reached a troubling conclusion. How could they, with virtually no experience, ever be able properly care for this tiny fragment of life? The voice of reason offered them very little encouragement with its statement that this was a high time to be thinking about that now. With Theresa already demanding her bottle, expert guidance was what they most needed, not some "I told you so" lecture coming from their collective super-consciousness.

"Didn't they tell you how to make the formula?" Jesse asked, sounding a little irascible.

"That and at least a hundred other things, too!" she shot back. "They gave us enough to last through the day, but you're going to have to start helping me out a little bit. I can't do it all by myself!"

They rode in silence for the rest of the way, each secretly wondering about the other's lack of wisdom.

Edith was present for the delivery, yet had to leave after a few days; Wade needed her at home. Maggie felt she could and should have stayed a day or two longer. While relief comes in many packages, it nearly always is something pleasant to experience, and it was there waiting for them at home. Maggie was the first to spot her parents standing by their car in the driveway. Shortly thereafter, the hands of experience took over, and the future began to look bright again.

"Oh, would you look at that!" Mary exclaimed as she reached for her granddaughter. "With that black hair she looks just like her daddy. Jesse, you'll need to go get her a pacifier; I saw a drug store right up the street."

Back with the purchase, Jesse beamed while handing over the package. Suddenly, however, his exultation turned into chagrin.

"Jesse!" Maggie giggled like a schoolgirl. "That's a teething ring, not a pacifier, and I don't think she's quite ready for it yet."

Seven months later, they were living in Highlands, NC with Jesse working at the hospital as their chief lab and X-ray technician. In September, Ma suddenly took sick; she had liver cancer and after only two months was gone. That she had lived such a selfless life with devotion to both family and God left little doubt as to her eternal destiny. Yet, her passing brought Jesse hurt that could never be assuaged; tender and cherished were his memories of her. Emulating the ways of the Holy spirit, she had always been there hovering near, nurturing, guiding, and lending him wisdom.

Love is the true staff of life, not just a sentiment, for feelings merely reflect its presence.

One year, almost to the day after he started work in Highlands, Lisa was born and the world changed forever. She arrived kicking and screaming with such fervor that they wrongly assumed she did so as an attention getter. After more than a few sleepless nights, the doctors found she could not tolerate milk, thus she flourished once given a suitable formula. However, Lisa was not one to fade into the woodworks, this fetching little angel with a teary face, nor would she accept being born second in birth order, meant playing second fiddle to anyone.

Becky arrived just nine days before the Kennedy assassination. They lived at the time in Milledgeville, Georgia, where Jesse worked in the laboratory of a pharmaceutical firm. Endowed with a thoughtful and pleasing personality, this beautiful child learned early how to profit from the missteps of others. So rare were her transgressions that Jesse and Maggie often questioned what it was they were finally doing right.

Having regarded the year they lived in Asheville as the best one of their marriage, Jesse and Maggie set their sights on going back. They lived nearly five years in Milledgeville, yet every day while there, he prayed that something would open up in Asheville. One sleepless night he felt particularly impressed to seek help, the same way he did at Great Lakes. It nearly took his breath away, when within days the Buncombe County Health Department contacted him about a position. True to form, however, his faith seemed to wither in the face of success. It had thrived when odds looked their worse, yet now here he was wondering. *You reckon this wouldn't have happened anyway? I'd say it's probably just a coincidence; after all, why would God care about something like this?*

Never before had he enjoyed working like he did at the health department. It involved testing milk and water, solving food poisoning outbreaks and diagnosing communicable diseases. He loved it so much that he would often be there after hours, working on his own time. Later, upon reflection, he realized that these were the happiest years of his life. Unfortunately, not all memories from that era were pleasant, especially those associated with a particular religious cult.

The decade of the sixties was a time unparalleled in American history. It was a period of such riotous turmoil that many sought to escape its influence through spiritual retreat. Great excitement accompanied the "hippie movement" and Jesse quickly discovered that a lot of it was much to his liking. A revolution was in the making and he felt a close kinship to many of those involved. Folk music was his genre, and he appreciated society's apparent willingness to accept everyone into the mainstream, regardless of his or her social, racial, or financial status. Somehow, it seemed right when many of the barriers, heretofore insurmountable, began to fall and he often wondered when and how the "establishment" would ultimately bring it down. Unfortunately, many of the naive and pure-in-heart believed that this beautiful flower was a perennial, not an annual.

Jesse soon came to realize that not everything it espoused was good, however, not by a long shot. Drug use, illicit sex, licentious behavior, and causes not worthy of the title, soon destroyed much of the genuine altruism initially espoused. It seems this grassroots phenomenon was doomed from the start, because by placing both the guns and ammunition in the hands of death-squad pseudo-moralists, its demise was certain.

Tensions developed with much of it racial in origin. Many then, even as now, were not willing or able to accept the inevitable. They were the same ones who claimed allegiance to the Lamb while speaking for the dragon. Satan has a loud voice that always drowns out the opposition while complaining bitterly that Truth gets the better press. He knows that the human ear is whimsical and tends to believe anything its told, if repeated often enough. Deadly, indeed, is the big lie when religion and nationalism are combined, because God and Country are always right!

Why is it so? And ever shall be
That truth must wait on history

Revealed then to the unconcerned
Truth delayed is truth unlearned!

In the South events moved quickly to center stage, with Jesse so close to the action that he could feel the board's quake beneath his feet. After rebuffing an effort by the KKK to recruit him, he began a search for more and deeper spiritual moorings. Following the Kennedy assassination, he often wondered if the Second Coming was imminent.

He felt most of the pat answers offered by pastors to his many questions did not seem to square with the scriptures. But suddenly he had a source that could provide more answers than he had questions for, and it was just as close to him as the radio. At the time, Thomas H. Livermore dominated the airwaves with his daily program entitled *The Age to Come*. Jesse soon became a daily listener and, before long, a steady stream of literature was filling up his mailbox. He could hardly wait for the next issue of *The Real Truth* magazine to be printed. New revelations were being unearthed daily and old teachings no longer seemed relevant. Satisfied that he had tapped into the main conduit of God's will, Jesse rejoiced in his discovery. Heaven had a true church on earth and it was *The Radio Assembly of Yahweh.*

Reading letters from like-believers in the monthly magazine served to strengthen his faith and before long, he was sending in a tithe to the organization. Such of course, bonded him even closer to the program and after awhile he felt comfortable enough to request a personal visitation. Several weeks passed without a response then one day, while home for lunch, a new Chrysler pulled up in front of the house. Two associate pastors wearing expensive suits, stepped up to the door and knocked.

"Good afternoon," exclaimed the larger man, obviously in his mid-thirties. "We are here representing the World Wide Assembly of Yahweh."

Jesse was ecstatic. He had just learned about the church's name change, and here they were already calling on him. "Come in, Gentlemen," he sputtered, "I'm really glad to see you. My little girl has an earache and she's running a fever, so I wonder if you would mind anointing her for healing?"

The visitors seemed eager to oblige, but spent their first few minutes in cordial conversation. To say the least, Jesse was impressed and felt an immediate fellowship developing. After all, this was his first face-to-face encounter with real people from a church that heretofore had existed only in his imagination. All previous contact had been either through the mail or by broadcast, but now an actual organization had materialized and he was anxious to become a part of it. Trouble was he had just learned he and his family would soon be moving to Asheville.

"No problem," the big sandy-headed man laughed. "We've got a very active congregation up there and I'll have David drop by sometime after you're settled in." No sooner had they left than Maggie remarked that Terri's fever was dropping; she seemed surprised, but not so Jesse. Back at work, he was more convinced than ever that Livermore, indeed, was a prophet of God with a special message for these, the final days of earth's history.

Jesse learned early that the church did not approve of smoking, so he and Maggie quit cold turkey. Bit by bit he was allowing himself to accept teachings that at first seemed odd, but by following Livermore's study guidelines, he found them to be in harmony with the scriptures. Especially those written in the Old

Testament; they stopped eating pork and all unclean meats, accepted Saturday as the seventh-day Sabbath, substituted "pagan holidays" for "God's Holy Days," believed that foot washing was part of the holy communion and that baptism should be by immersion. Since none of these points of doctrine offered much of a challenge to their lifestyle, the transition went smoothly for a while.

For the move to Asheville Jesse rented a U-haul truck and Max offered to drive. They left Milledgeville late in the afternoon and drove all night, reaching their destination at daybreak. Sometime after midnight, Jesse felt he had deliberated long enough over a pack of Max's cigarettes lying between them, so he fired one up. Immediately, he became a slave again, this time, however, for only three or four a day. Previously, he smoked up to three packs daily; so he felt at this level it would probably be okay with Livermore. Boy was he in for a big surprise!

Not too many days passed before they got a call from the local "Assembly" minister saying that he and his partner would be stopping by for an initial visit. However, when they got there Jesse was not favorably impressed. He detected a definite attitude of criticism in their opening statement. "We are here to evaluate your level of commitment, and to determine whether we issue you an invitation to our church services, or not." Next, they demanded to know what percent of their income went for rent and other personal items; then they asked why a second tithe had not been forthcoming. This caught Jesse and Maggie both by surprise, since neither had ever heard of such a thing. A modest cut in pay had attended the move back to Asheville, so the family budget was already under stress and any additional outgo, especially of this magnitude, would be devastating. Jesse tried to explain that he was completely unaware of a "second tithe," but David, the taller one, nearly exploded. "We've wasted our time coming here Wayne, these people are not serious. They're just playing games with God, so brush the dust off your feet herewith, and let us depart this house, immediately!"

Jesse was aghast. "Wait a minute," he pleaded. "How can I be held accountable for something I never heard of? There's not one word about this in your literature, or the Bible either, as far as I know. The minister there in Georgia never mentioned it, either, so let me and Maggie pray over it and then we'll look at our budget."

"Oh it's in the Bible all right and looking at your budget has absolutely nothing to do with it. Either you have faith to obey God or you don't!" His eyes were as flames of fire and his voice rang like steel striking steel. Jesse had never met preachers that acted like these. "We'll be back in a few days to see if you're sincere... And if you're not," he warned. "It will be our last visit here, and make no mistake about it!"

One week later to the hour, David and Wayne returned. They were in a hurry, however, and seemed somewhat more conciliatory this time, staying just long enough to extend an invitation to their church the next Sabbath. It would be a trial visit. "Keep the services strictly confidential," David warned, "otherwise, that will be it!"

Growing up in a small, family-like church had ill-prepared Jesse for the type of service he encountered at the Greek Fellowship Hall. He and Terri found their way to the rented facility, where a crowd of over three hundred had already gathered. Later he learned that many of these had driven a hundred miles or more to attend. Laity seemed a happy and friendly lot, standing in sharp contrast to the leadership. Wayne presented the sermonette where he painted an ominous picture for anyone who might choose to backslide. "Once you turn your hand from the plow, you then face eternal damnation," sternly, he warned. "The mere fact you're here today means that you have been chosen to be part of God's coming government. He has called you to do His special work at a time when the world is in total darkness; all the other churches have apostatized and are in gross error. *Come out of her, my people*, He says. God grants enlightenment for a purpose, and with it comes great responsibility. To flag or fail now could earn you excommunication and eternal damnation, banning you forever from the gates of paradise."

Livermore constantly advertised that all his material came, "Free, and without cost or obligation ever," that it had been "paid for by others." Jesse was about to learn what the cost of "free" truly was.

David began his part by spending the first few minutes ridiculing the local dialect, and then he launched into a sermon. "Brothers and sisters," he intoned. "I bring before you a very serious matter this morning. Sister Buchanan over in Yancy County is near unto death; that, despite our anointing her and the laying on of hands. This dear woman is willing to go on to her rest if that's the Lord's will... and, yes, her faith remains strong! The family, however, is fighting us all the way by insisting that she seek medical care. Thank God for her strong witness in the face of this!"

He continued to give more details while Jesse slowly came to realize that this middle-aged housewife was dying from gallstones. It tortured him to think that such a common and easily treatable malady might prove fatal. He had seen many dozens of such patients thrive after surgery and could not understand the lack of common sense in play here.

Obviously, David anticipated such heresy and addressed it straight on. "Anybody here not agreeing with God's handling of this is free to get up and leave right now! But I warn you, I had better not hear of you discussing this with anyone outside the sound of my voice. They found the last person who did that dead in his garage one week later. He had committed suicide. I'll tell you what, you don't tempt the Lord your God like that! No, not Him or His anointed ones, either!"

Jesse and Terri stayed until the service ended, but did not wait for the potluck dinner. Suddenly he had no appetite. Maggie was livid when she heard the details and was ready to "chuck the whole mess." Not Jesse, however, he felt there was still something here of value. After all, he had learned so much from Livermore and perhaps these particular ministers were just renegades. Maybe if they could stick it out for a while, new ones would come. Maggie, however, was not quite so generous. "Jesse, now that you've developed a taste for crap, you just have to keep going back for another nibble, don't you?"

If she was right, then he got it the next Friday night after supper. After finishing two Sloppy Joes, Jesse took a long drag off his cigarette. He had been looking forward to this moment all evening, since it was his third and final one for the day. That is when he heard a loud, almost menacing knock at the door. Quick furtive glances indicated that both were in the dark as to who it might be. The mystery, however, quickly resolved itself when Maggie opened the door. Right away, Jesse knew he was in trouble.

"Do I smell cigarette smoke?" David demanded. "Yes, Wayne we've caught him red-handed! Still playing games with God, are we, Gernon? Well, He's sick and tired of it and so am I!"

"Oh, I see what's going on here, that little white tube of tobacco is your god, isn't it? Then why didn't you just tell us that to start with? Everybody has a right to serve whom or whatever god they want to. So why don't you just bow down and pray to it? It's already ruling your life, but here you've been passing yourself off to everybody that you're a Christian." His voice had softened to a taunting, mocking jeer while his face took on the look of utter contempt.

The minutes ticked away, yet they really seemed like hours. Later, thinking back on it, Jesse vowed he'd rather die than ever be ridiculed like that again. He heard repeatedly, just how weak and unworthy he was. David was unsparing with his rebuke. The grilling reminded Jesse of the "cussing out" he got at Great Lakes;

then, however, it was far less personal and did not leave him feeling alienated to God.

Abruptly as they came, they left, leaving Jesse to sit quietly in a near catatonic state; the stupor lasted until late Sunday evening. During all this time he barely spoke to anyone, he did not eat, sleep, bathe, or smoke while slinking as far back into his cave as possible. Then suddenly he burst forth! Coming from the tomb as one reborn to freedom; "I ain't going to take it any longer," he announced. "When I started this it was a quest for the truth, but I was ignorant and very gullible. These people have been spoon-feeding me from just a thin slice of God's Word, while the rest of the Bible is there as a great banquet to feast on. You'll notice they repeat the same things over and over using a few selected scriptures, that, for the most part, come from the Old Testament. Why, it's like being brainwashed against almost anything that comes from the Christian era!"

"I wondered when you'd ever see it," Maggie agreed. "And I'll tell you something else, too; they don't want people going to a doctor because that takes money away from them. Remember, any money spent on healthcare means there's less for them to get their filthy hands on. Hell ain't going to be near hot enough to suit me for that bunch!"

The next Tuesday evening another knock at the door once again caught Jesse by surprise. Wayne and his wife were ushered into the living room where they received a cool, but respectful greeting. Uncertain as to how her husband might react, Mackie felt a little apprehensive. His body language suggested a readiness, even a desire, to do battle. Could it be that the spirit of Dave Gernon was alive and well?

Her pensive mind did not have long to wonder. "Where's your buddy?" Jesse asked, not too kindly.

"David wouldn't come tonight; he's given up on you. But I wanted to leave the door open, at least enough to try and reason with you."

Jesse recognized immediately they were playing the "good cop, bad cop" routine. "I was hoping he'd come so I could say what's on my mind to both of you. I want to see no part of you or that gospel you preach according to Livermore around here any longer. Yes, I believe in the Ten Commandments, including the seventh day Sabbath and a few other things, too, like clean and unclean meats. But a lot of that stuff you preach was for ancient Israel and only pointed toward the coming of the Messiah. It's not consistent to equate those laws with the Ten Commandments; the Commandments are eternal. The others, however, were only temporal until Jesus came. Stuff like requiring a second tithe is just a form of extortion using God as a club to get your hands on a little more of that filthy lucre."

A look of confused amazement filled the faces of both visitors, yet neither said a word.

"You make such a big to-do over people observing Christmas and Easter, saying how wrong it is. Then you go ramming those so-called holy days down their throats. It's no wonder Christianity can hardly be recognized in the holidays anymore. What with there being so much commercializing on the one hand and fanatics like Livermore on the other trying to put a curse on anybody who keeps them. But like I said, I want no further part of your organization and just ask that you leave us alone."

"Well I don't quite agree with you, Gernon, I think we've all got off on the wrong foot here and I can't see turning you and your family over to Satan, not without a fight. And, besides, you've come into some privileged information here by attending our church."

"Let me tell you something, Wayne, you're not leaving me or my family to Satan. No, quite to the contrary, you don't have that authority. From this day forward, I'm putting my faith in the Lord Jesus Christ and not Thomas H. Livermore. We've talked it over, and decided to start attending another Sabbath-keeping church. It seems to us what they teach is far closer to the Bible than what you're doing."

"Oh, I know what sect you're talking about, well that so-called prophet of theirs is a fake and one they consider to be infallible, just like the Catholics do the Pope."

"No, that's not right, they don't have a prophet in the sense you do with Livermore. I think you're referring to her writings, but if you find anything there that doesn't agree with scripture, then I pray you point it out. In fact, it's said that these works are just a smaller light that leads to the greater light, which is the Bible. They go on to say if one is not consistent with the other then, by all means, you should always accept what the Bible says. But I'm yet to see anywhere they claim infallibility for anybody except Christ."

"Gernon, you're hopeless! No man is so blind as he who chooses to be!" Equal parts of disgust and pity filled the hollow sound of Wayne's voice.

"Let it be known that my wife and I are hereby witnesses to your abominable decision to go whoring after an apostate church. That denomination is a synagogue of Satan, just as verily as are the Baptists and Methodists. Merely keeping the Sabbath will not save you from the wrath of God. The Bible requires a witness from two people when you appear before the judgment seat. Know this, Jesse Gernon; you are right now facing your two witnesses. May God Almighty have mercy on your soul!"

"And, Wayne, my wife and I will bear witness against you at this attempt to intimidate us, but you know it and I do, too, what you just said is nothing but bull. God allows no man to judge another in these matters, for we all stand equal before His eyes and only He knows the content of the heart. Christ alone is worthy to be our judge, so for you to try and assume that role borders on blasphemy." Jesse's reply came with equal solemnity. "Neither you nor your idol Thomas H. Livermore, who by the way claims to being infallible, could save a piss-ant. But the truth is, you're not really interested in the salvation of souls. You're just interested in salvaging every penny that can be extorted from good-hearted people like us, who you consider to be nothing but hillbillies."

"I'll see you at the judgment bar, Gernon!"

Like so many other victims of a cult, Jesse soon learned that merely severing the tie that binds does not fully set you free. Subsequently, he came to appreciate what Jesus taught when he declared, "Ye shall know the truth and the truth shall make you free." It took nearly four years of intensive Bible study, using every resource available, to find satisfactory answers that refuted all the error he had learned. Early on, Mae, using her prized multi-lingual concordance, had argued that he was on the wrong track. She now directed her efforts toward assisting him with his new search. A little later, he and Maggie joined a denominational Church. Thomas H. Livermore remained on the air for a few more years, however, his organization ultimately died shortly after he did. It splintered into several disparate factions, all of which lacked the coercive forces it took to keep their flocks in line.

CHAPTER 33

"I like it," Jesse said, "the price is good and it's just big enough."

His comment came as no surprise to Maggie; she had heard it at least a dozen times in the past month. They were out searching for a house to buy.

"I don't know yet, let me think about it," she grimaced. "Did you notice the water heater; I'd say it's pretty old and probably needs replacing."

"The thing for us to do is ask the owner about it. Tell him we won't buy unless he puts in a new one. The roof looks awful good, though; I'd say it's less than five years old," Jesse hedged optimistically.

After several months of weekend looking, this white two-bedroom bungalow in West Asheville proved ultimately to be the one. They lived there for nearly four years, but with each passing day, it became increasingly evident that more room was necessary if they planned to keep three growing girls comfortable. Hence, the search was on again. But this time it didn't take long before they located a new white fiesta stone French Provincial. It was in east Asheville, just off Old Haw Creek Road and loaded with virtually everything they wanted in a house. Two questions were immediately apparent, however; could they afford it and would it stay on the market long enough to sell theirs first? Probably the answer to both would have been a resounding "no" had it not been for a very remarkable woman named Mildred Bowdin.

They moved in on Christmas Eve, 1970, which proved to be quite an experience in itself. Maggie felt uncertain that they could qualify for the loan, but Jesse suffered no such doubts, not after talking with Mrs. Bowdin. This optimistic builder-seller was a person with the heart of a saint and the mind of a horse trader. Quickly she worked out a swap between the two properties, and then pulled just the right strings at the bank to get a loan through. She had made a promise to have them in the house by Christmas, and Jesse believed it. So positive was he about the deal that on the day they were to hear from the bank he began making plans to move. Maggie, however, was not quite so certain.

"Jesse, you're jumping the gun," she said, looking skeptical. "Just settle down and at least wait until we hear. This is Christmas Eve and there's absolutely no way we can be moved in, in time to meet that deadline you and Mildred set. Personally, I think that was very foolish on both your parts."

"Yeah, well back in October it looked then like we could, but where are you headed, anyway?"

"I've still got a few things to get; that is, if we plan on having Christmas this year. I'll be back directly, so just cool your jets, and settle down!"

She had hardly left the driveway when he mobilized the troops. Since the girls were not present to hear any of the previous conversation, they were eager to join in and did so with gusto. When Maggie returned, she found at least half their belongings already packed. Sitting down on the sofa, now positioned out on the front lawn, she was beside herself. She saw twelve years of marriage under the Sword of Damocles, it now hanging on the whim of some unknown banker. Fate, however, seems always to favor those who live with danger. Jesse, though, would never again listen for a phone call with such intensity as he did this one. Worry, somehow absent until now, abruptly surfaced to fray his every nerve. When the phone finally did ring, just by the sound of it he knew immediately who was calling. Maggie took it, yet said very little at first, leaving him to relax only after the taut lines about her lips began to soften.

Remarkably, they managed to move last piece of furniture into place just seconds before midnight. Mildred Bowdin's promise had been kept.

Haw Creek became for Jesse a place of the heart and even years after they had moved away he continued to dream of it as home. Such attachment created a dilemma that perhaps cannot be resolved, for it reached much too close to the taproot of his being. Without forfeiting the house, he could never have accomplished what he did, and yet by so doing a portion of his soul was lost.

His work at the health department had become increasingly more important, especially now that he was Lab Director and a certified Public Health Microbiologist. Such a promotion came with a private office and a secretary; therefore, it seemed his future was finally on solid ground. Perhaps so, had it not been for one particular hot and humid afternoon in August. He had been mowing the lawn for about 30 minutes when an unseen finger tapped him on the shoulder.

"No," Maggie said "He didn't get tapped on the shoulder; touched in the head was more like it."

Jesse had long felt it was his ultimate destiny to gain higher education. Yet he knew not how this could possible be when all his resources were already committed to the needs of a growing family. There had been many times when he, for months, would pour over classical literature, study discarded college texts, review science papers, read biographies; on and on, with the idea that someday it might come in handy. Recently, however, doubt had begun to cloud his dream. "Jesse, what on earth are you thinking?" the dark demanded to know. Unbeknownst to him, however, others agencies, behind the scenes, were hard at work to make it happen.

Occasionally, images of this vision would flash before his eyes, and even though he was not privy to the big picture, they seemed always to re-inspire his hopes. Such an event occurred early the previous year when an office secretary told about reading where college credit was available, merely by taking tests based on life experiences. Keenly interested, he immediately sent away for further details. After several weeks passed without getting a reply, he soon all but put it out of mind. Once in awhile it would cross his mind, but the initial enthusiasm had faded, and he was at the point of thinking that probably it was just another fraud. He had just reached this conclusion when a large manila envelope packed with information arrived. From it, he learned that the College Level Equivalency Program, located in Princeton, New Jersey, had started a new program. Since they also administered the Scholastic Achievement Testing, their credibility was obviously well established.

While very excited to learn that such a vehicle existed, he still lacked a road map and a clear destination to head for, nevertheless he was rearing to go. It seems nothing in life moves in linear fashion, so it would be the next March before another event hove into view. It, too, popped up unexpectedly, this time while he was attending a public health seminar. A presentation designed to recruit health department personnel for a new advanced-degree program at Chapel Hill intrigued him. He was surprised to learn that fellowship grants were available at the UNC School of Public Health there.

One of the speakers that day was a doctoral candidate in the program who was ready to graduate. Jesse let his mind wander to a world of fantasy. *Was it possible that he too one day might reach such a level?* Before leaving, he ventured even further onto the timorous turf of imagination. When no one was looking, he slipped a brochure into his pocket. However, the pamphlet offered very little, except a telephone number.

Jesse had a fetish against using the telephone when talking to strangers, so he asked Maggie to do it for him. Reluctantly she agreed, insisting that they wait until lunch the next day when he could be there in case of follow-up questions.

A very friendly professor at the University took her call and was quite helpful. They chatted amiably for several minutes; meanwhile Jesse sat waiting anxiously to hear what surely must be some good news. Hanging up she smiled encouragingly, "Well, I guess that puts an end to that. You have to have a BS degree before they'll even send you an application. But even if you had one, you'd have to live the first two years in Chapel Hill, then two more at the CDC in Atlanta. It's no wonder they can't get anybody to take their programs!"

Jesse rolled it over in his mind, but rather than be discouraged it only fired him up even more.

It was months after this when the mowing episode occurred, and, as previously noted, the afternoon was typical for August. Although the sweat running into his eyes had left him nearly blinded, he still was able to see Lisa leaving a friend's house for home. *Her daddy's a doctor, and I could be one, too; but will it ever happen?* He questioned himself. Lifting his gaze toward the sky, it was as by looking up his thoughts would generate enough fervor to penetrate the firmament; "*Lord, you know this better than I do; I've just turned thirty-six, so it has to be now or never!*"

To his amazement, an immediate answer was forthcoming.

"I've been waiting on you, Jesse, but it's all up to you. What you must consider is do you have faith enough to stay the course? You learned a long time ago that all things are possible... if you believe. So, ask yourself: Do I truly believe?"

Jesse was stunned, he stopped the mower and leaned up against the big chestnut oak dividing his property from that of his neighbors. *Did I hear what I think I did, or is it just this heat getting to me?* While, indeed, it was oppressively hot, he had no answer for the peace he felt. Could it be that some celestial agent, an angel if you please, had just favored him with their presence? The thought scared him, yet he desperately wanted to continue the dialogue. "Yes, Lord, again and again You have shown me that Your word is true and I believe it. I also know that You always answer prayers according to our best interests. But how can I possibly do this? How can I afford to go to college when I've got a family to support? I don't really have any money or even know exactly what it is You want me to do. I just know that if it's Your will, then I'll try to do it, no matter what."

The answer, in a voice so sweet that it surprised him, came even before he finished. "Jesse, I am but a messenger and a fellow servant sent by the Father so do not address me as Lord. If I told you everything, the way you'd like, then where would there be room for faith? I am authorized to say that there will always be light for your next step, but no more than that, ever. Furthermore, I promise to be with you all the way, for great will be your discouragement and many times, you will suffer it. Yet, if you remain faithful and hold to my hand, I will lead you to victory. Now, do you accept my word on this? I urge you to count the cost very carefully before answering, for you are one given to being impetuous. If you truly believe and accept this offer, then the doors of opportunity will immediately begin to open, and will continue to do so one by one. However, if you reject it, then the invitation will close forever, and things will be as though this never happened. The decision is yours and yours alone."

An enormous weight immediately fell upon him, one so oppressive that he could hardly breathe. Yet somehow, he knew that once he made the decision, it would quickly lift. This, he now realized was the defining moment of his life.

Turning his face to the sky, he sought the Creator, "Yes, Lord, I do trust you, and pray that you will supply me with faith enough to finish what I begin here today!"

Indeed, not only did the weight at once lift, but also he immediately felt a surge of new energy. Thrilled with excitement he blurted out to Maggie what had just occurred and the decision he had made.

At first, she was appalled to think that he would even consider such a thing and would have no part in discussing something so preposterous. However, Jesse's enthusiasm was so overwhelming that rather than waning in face of skepticism, it continued to soar. Whether it was the fervor that finally won her over or she merely elected to appease him is still unknown. In any event, she agreed to sleep on it, but if she expected that dawn would bring sanity back to their household, then sunrise held a huge disappointment for her. If anything, he was more animated than ever; causing her to wonder if he closed his eyes at all during the night.

Not willing to let time slip away, he quickly set the ball into motion by seeking out his best friend, Bob. Bob Lamb headed up the Air-Pollution Laboratory and had an office just down the hall from his. As a dedicated Christian with lots of contacts, he recommended that Jesse talk to a professor he knew at one of the local colleges. This was someone he went to church with who was capable of offering a lot of guidance. Meanwhile, Jesse felt impressed to consider going to dental school since he knew there was a dearth of practitioner's in the area.

Taking Bob's advice, he scheduled an appointment with the professor; however, the school secretary recommended that Jesse see one of their counselors first. Unfortunately, he garnered little in the way of encouragement there, being informed that competition for placement in all the health professions was extremely keen. They further explained that even for recent graduates, gaining admission was nearly impossible and for someone over thirty it might very well prove to be out of the question. However, Bob's friend, who turned out to be the head of the science department, gave Jesse some unexpected good news. This very kind and learned professor had the insight to recognize that Jesse's work experience and present position were valuable assets. He expressed confidence these factors could contribute significantly toward his goal.

"Yes," he smiled broadly, "it is hard to get into those schools, but not impossible. I had two students last year accepted at Duke. There's no accounting for intangibles like motivation and desire and I perceive you have them both. Tell you what, if you enroll in one of my advanced classes and pass with a grade of B or better, I'll give you full credit for the introductory portion, as well. This would mean you get four hours for the cost of two, cutting both time and money in half. Of course, the college requires that you take two full semesters of core subjects first, and unfortunately, there can be no exceptions to that."

Jesse left the campus feeling both encouraged and discouraged. Paradoxically, he was more convinced now than ever of ultimate success, but not in a conventional manner. That way would mean giving up his job and going to school fulltime, and, of course, such was out of the question.

On the way home, while pondering what to do next, it hit him; why not look again at the CLEP program. Could this not be the first door of promise to open? The real question was, however, did he have faith enough to walk through it? Regardless, there was light and, yes, it was enough to make the next step. Proceeding meant he would have to work and study hard for tests, the result of which might not be acceptable to an accredited school. It was definitely a high-risk proposition requiring an immense amount of effort that could easily end up accomplishing absolutely nothing. This, while wasting a lot of time and money he could ill afford. Moreover, even if he was able to pass all the tests and subsequently receive full credit, would there then be a professional school, anywhere, willing to accept such an unorthodox approach toward meeting their requirements?

"Keep in mind," a voice whispered, "There will always be light enough for one step at a time, but it is up to you to take it."

The material from CLEP, he learned, had been prepared so that one test equated to two semester hours of work, therefore, he opted to take three exams each session. The small private college that would administer them was about seventy miles away. After several weeks of study and review, he felt ready to take the initial series. Except for the math portion, he felt good about his efforts. This came as no surprise, since he had a long history of struggling with its concepts.

The entire CLEP episode, first the study phase and then the testing, lasted for well over a year. By the end of the process, he had passed them all with an average score well above the ninetieth percentile. By adhering to this schedule, he was able to gain two years of college while remaining fully employed. Once the medical director at the health department learned of his efforts, he became enthusiastically supportive, and later wrote letters of recommendation for Jesse to the professional schools.

Meanwhile, Jesse learned that the State University of New York recognized CLEP credits and would grant a two-year Associate Degree in Science, with suitable scores and documentation.

While CLEP had brought him thus far, he was still short of the goal, and it now looked next to impossible to go any further. Without a baccalaureate degree, all of his work would be in vain. *Am I like Peter after walking on the water*? He fretted. *And how many miracles do you get before they run out*? Jesse suddenly found it most disconcerting to realize that his very existence now depended on faith, especially since his own seemed to be trickling away. He was still to learn it is not how much faith you have or how pure it is, that gets you across the rolling waves.

Two doors had opened; one got him two years of college while the other provided an accredited institution to accept it. Remarkably, a third suddenly materialized right before his eyes. From early on, Jesse had set up some very strict study guidelines that allowed him only a limited amount of time away from the books. Yet he did claim one minor exception each week and that was to take time off long enough to read the Sunday paper. It and a cup of coffee while everyone else still slept was a simple pleasure he greatly cherished. That is just how it was one cold and frosty January morning, when quite unexpectedly the next door swung wide open. The event reminded him of the door set within another door, seen at another place and time; oddly, this one, too, beckoned that he move closer.

Section C of the Asheville Citizen-Times contained an article about certain institutions that had embraced a concept called "Universities without Walls." Shaw University in Raleigh was one of these *and* they had just opened a campus in Asheville. Jesse knew a smattering about Shaw, remembering it to be a Negro University with a highly respected national reputation.

Since they listed a telephone number, he called the next day and set up an appointment with their representative. Enthusiasm stored within the wineskin of flesh was about to burst forth with new vigor, and was that the Promised Land off there in the distance? Oh, swing-low sweet chariot! Is the way Jesse felt after talking to Mr. Johnson, a huge black gentleman with a heart the size of a mountain.

"Mr. Gernon!" His voice rocked Jesse with a friendly greeting. After a few moments of polite conversation, the two were ready to settle down and talk business. Three hours and more passed with both parties being surprised at how well their separate agendas seemed to agree. Jesse presented copied transcripts from every school and certified courses he had taken since high school. Mr. Johnson was surprised at such preparedness and promised to submit it right away. The two seemed equally anxious to get a quick evaluation and learn just how much credit Shaw would allow him. Jesse got the definite impression that his eagerness had become contagious.

Six weeks later the appraisal was back; Jesse had acceptable academic credentials and life experiences enough to get him within one semester of the B.A. degree. However, he still must complete certain course requirements first. Fortunately, he could do this in Asheville without it interfering with his employment. Jesse was still learning that He who made the waters, can also trace a path across them.

While still pursuing his undergraduate degree, Jesse began the process of applying to many of the dental schools. However, that required he take the Dental Admission Test first. They were given twice yearly at certain designated locations and were said to be quite formidable. Of more immediate concern, however, was the fact that he would be required to break the Sabbath in order to do so. By looking closer at the details, however he learned of special exceptions. Merely for the asking, he could do it on the following day in Chattanooga.

His resultant DAT scores were quite impressive, in fact well above average, but discouragingly, it all seemed to be of no avail. By being flooded with applicants, most dental schools, he learned, were not accepting anyone over the age of twenty-seven. Since Jesse was now thirty-eight, this came as a splash of cold water. Further research finally located just two schools without such restrictions; however, in both instances their tuition and fees were prohibitively high. Had he come this far over the waves, only to flounder and drown? If that were true, then why was the fire still raging in his soul? He still could hardly sleep at night, so great was the glow, and it seemed brighter now than when he started. "Yours," a sweet voice whispered, "is to take but one step at a time, doing so by the light you are given. It will always be there if you believe."

Could it be that the light was trying to lead him in a direction other than where he thought? The answer was not long in coming.

Just why or when he requested information from the American Optometric Association remains, even to this day, very much a mystery. However, Jesse does recall seeing a large white envelope that arrived in the mail. Pushing it aside into a mass of other unopened material, he gave it no more than a curious glance. *They must be needing applicants,* he thought, *I guess it's no wonder, though, what with everybody headed for dental school.*

Jesse must wait yet a little longer in order to learn just how wrong he was about this. Presently, however, he was torn between feeling despondent and remembering that nothing could deny him of victory. Such dichotomy, while painful, was to be his constant companion, and the sooner he got used to it the better. Unfortunately, from early on Jesse had made the decision to savor a little of doubt, this even while the fruits of faith still lingered on his tongue.

Moping about the house, he spent an entire weekend deliberating over whether to continue or just give it up and quit. His mumbled prayers became such an incessant refrain that he, no doubt, tried even the patience of angels. "Please, dear God," he pled over and over, "just show me what to do and I'll do it."

"Oh, ye of little faith," lamented his companion loudly, but Jesse's ears were now attuned only to the sounds of frustration.

Late Sunday afternoon his eyes began to open; the light that had been there all along, but he could not see it through the gloom of self-pity. It was while sifting through a stack of discarded college catalogues, application forms and other material when he saw it again, the large white envelope. After reading through the basic information, the thought of practicing optometry suddenly sent a wave of renewed optimism surging through his soul.

Included in the dossier was a list of all domestic schools and their academic requirements; remarkably, none mentioned age as criteria. Since the pre-admission requisites for medical and dental schools were essentially the same as those for optometry, he was already eligible to make application. Their entrance exam, the OAT, also was available for Sunday testing, but unlike the DAT, they allowed local proctoring. Of course, this meant not having to make a four-hour trip to Chattanooga.

Jesse actually enjoyed taking the OAT; it covered material much closer to his natural interests than did those in the DAT, and his scores proved it. With the exception of math, his overall ranking was in the mid-ninetieth percentile, but weaknesses in trigonometry and calculus were ominous harbingers for the future.

Wasting no time, he made applications to all the schools that listed contracts with the State of North Carolina Medical Care Commission. This was imperative since contractual schools meant funding and that, in turn, meant lower tuition and fees. Jesse was already looking toward admission, knowing that many challenges lay yet ahead to test his faith. Probably the first would be to find enough money not only to meet school needs but, more importantly, to keep his family solvent for four long years. Such a daunting task would easily overwhelm him if he tried crossing that bridge before he got to it. Always he had prided himself in not being a prognosticator, but now he was beginning to like this, "one step at a time," thing. Living in the now had definite rewards if one could ever manage to get a handle on it!

Thinking that optometry suffered from a shortage of applicants was a gross error on his part. He quickly discovered that they, in fact, were so inundated with candidates that little encouragement was given to anyone with a GPA lower than 3.5 on the 4.0 scale, and scores on the OAT must exceed the eighty-fifth percentile level. After applying to four schools,

Jesse received an acceptance letter from Southern College in Memphis. However, it contained a caveat; he could not matriculate for another two years. He went into a tailspin. "Well, what good is that?" he asked. "Being accepted two years ahead of time don't help me none!" he bemoaned. "Here it is February and that means it would be September of next year before I could even hope to get started. Why, I'll be forty years old then and I ain't going if I can't enroll while I'm still in my thirties." Jesse had sent in his applications the previous November since most institutions listed a cut off date of December 31.

"Well, then maybe you'll be accepted by one of the other's," Maggie encouraged. Yet, he did not think it would happen. He knew Southern had a large beginning class and looked very favorably upon those from North Carolina. Other schools tended to take students from their own region and those, he correctly surmised, would barely give him a passing glance.

Much the same way optometry became a part of his lexicon; an application to Indiana University made its way to Bloomington. For him to take a cold and blustery February afternoon off from work was, to say the least, quite unusual; after all, who in their right mind wanted to use up a day of precious vacation time in the middle of winter, just to stay home? Besides, he was there alone since Maggie and the girls were either at work or in school.

Tooling about the house, he decided to give it one last shot. Several times already, he had searched for a school that was still accepting applications. So far, he had met with no success, yet he felt compelled to look again. That is when he spotted a catalog from Indiana University; it was one he could not remember ordering. Interestingly, their cut-off date was March 31, and they did not require an application fee. Most asked fifty dollars or more, and that fact alone was getting to be a sore spot with Maggie. "I'm getting kinda tired of sending these schools my hard-earned money just so they can write you a rejection letter," she carped.

Quickly gathering up copies of necessary letters and documents, he completed the form and hurriedly placed it all in the mail; barely finishing, before Maggie and the girls came rolling into the carport. Just two days earlier he'd made them a promise when he said, "Well, it's all in the hands of the Good Lord now, and if none of those I've applied to don't accept me, I won't try anymore." Credibility is a swinging door that easily comes unhinged by misplaced trust.

It was a typical day for June when he and Maggie arrived home for lunch. The weather was hot and humid, leaving neither he nor Maggie in a very good mood. Besides, he was still fretting over the latest rejection letter he had received two days earlier. "Let's get the mail on the way in," he grumbled. "They ain't a bit of need in walking back out here in this heat."

Maggie, as the driver, reached for the box and tossed several pieces onto his lap. An Indiana University letterhead immediately caught her attention. "When did you send them an application?" she asked scornfully. "Another fifty dollars down the drain I didn't know about!"

"What's the use in opening it," he said, trying to evade her question. "I can read it even before they're opened. They all begin the same the way, 'Dear sir; We regret to inform you that ....'"

Now, however, he had it open, "We are *pleased* to inform you that you have been accepted to the Indiana University School of Optometry, in Bloomington. Classes will start August...

Merely to say he was flabbergasted would be tantamount to claiming man's walk on the moon was like a stroll in the park. After having lost all hope of making it into school, this left him breathless. In truth, he never really expected to hear from them, since no fees were involved. Too, and this was significant, he knew that with such a tiny beginning class, his chance for acceptance was miniscule, if it existed at all. Considered by the profession to be an elite school, Indiana accepted only sixty-seven student's total, with just twenty-five of those to come from out-of-state. Furthermore, nearly 950 applicants were vying for those few favored slots, so odds were definitely not in his favor.

Exhilaration abruptly turned into near panic when reality finally struck home. Until now, all of this had been an elusive dream, a quest for the impossible and an odyssey of the mind. Now, however, substance had replaced faith. "But isn't faith the substance of things hoped for?" a voice whispered.

Words from Maggie also echoed in his ears, "You'd better be careful what you pray for, because you're liable get it!" Her next statement sounded almost like a complaint. "Lord, I hate to always be right."

Smiling wryly, he shook his head in wonder; "Boy's that's one you'll never hear out of me!" He said.

CHAPTER 34

Roiling continuously from birth to death against the rocks of chance, circumstance, and power, the soul of man is as restless as the sea. Yet, after the struggle is over, peace will finally come where it all began, in the nether regions of that great ocean called unknown. Were all these strivings worthwhile some may inquire? "No, not if you must ask," answers Wisdom.

"Son, you're making a big mistake," Wade asserted. "Here you've finally got yourself a good job, a fine house, and now you're fixing to throw it all away with this school thing, blamed if I can see it."

Not wishing to cause more worry than necessary Jesse had waited until it he could deliver the news in person. It was nearly dark on Friday when they got there to drop the bombshell. "Well," Jesse countered, "I told you and Mother what I was up to three years ago. Remember that time we all went up to Mitchell County looking for Grandma's old home place? I think it was in September, right after I decided on it in August. But I reckon you, like everybody else, figured it wouldn't happen."

"I guess a feller has to do what he thinks he does, but dad-burn it, Son, you needn't count on me and Edith to help you out, because we ain't got it. Being retired, we have to live on what little we've got… you can see that can't you?"

Jesse laughed uneasily, "No, that's not what I'm here for; I don't expect anybody to help me like that. Why, I wouldn't even think of going if that was it. Counting what we get out of the house, my state retirement fund, school grants and loans… that and with Maggie working, we ought to be able to make it just fine. Why, look at how far we've come already. When I started this thing I didn't have a college credit to my name, and from what it looked like there was no way of getting one, either. But by going on faith, I took tests and it was like one miracle after another happened. I ended up getting two colleges that would grant me the degrees I needed. So, next I took and passed the entrance exam, getting a score that was more than good enough to make me eligible. To top it all off though, I've just been accepted by probably the best school in country, doing it against odds you wouldn't believe. You need to understand, though, this is not of my doing; it all came from the hand of God. So, the way I look at it, if He wants me to do it, then my part is to show a little faith and go."

Jesse left for home the next morning with a heavy heart. Wade and Edith, deeply concerned, could not bring themselves to bless such an endeavor. Unknown to Jesse, however, was the strong ally he had in Mae. She went to bat for him immediately, trying to allay their fears while admonishing them to trust his judgment. "Ain't he always been level-headed before," she asked, and, besides, you know good and well he won't do anything foolish."

"I don't know," Edith replied skeptically. "He's got an awful lot of Wade in him and that's what bothers me."

The two-hour drive back to Asheville allowed plenty of time for a frank discussion. "Even with everything that's happened I'm still scared," Jesse admitted to Maggie.

"I've been scared a long time," she confessed, sounding a lot more negative than he liked. "We've got to be awful careful here that we don't throw away everything we've worked for. Besides, the girls are getting up to the age now where they'll need all the support they can get. Whatever we decide or whatever happens, we've got to keep that in mind."

"Yeah, it's been on my heart, too," he sighed. "You know we can't possibly go without getting our money out of the house. Without that, there just won't be loans and grants enough to do it. You finding a job in Bloomington should be easy, and, of course, you'll make as much there as you do here. If this comes together, like I think it will, though, we ought to be able to make it just fine. So, the girls won't really be denied all that much, not from just making the move."

Maggie sniffed twice, but noticeably did not nod in agreement. "I think the smart thing to do is go ahead and put the house on the market. That'll give us about six weeks for it to sell, and if it truly is God's will for you to go, it'll move by then."

"Yes, that's it!" Jesse agreed. For the first time since getting the letter, his mind seemed at ease. The couple had just made a three-way pact without consulting the major Party involved.

Instructions in the letter from I.U. stated that in the event of acceptance, the successful candidate must file a notice of intent. Compliance to this request was immediately forthcoming, notwithstanding the harbored doubts that accompanied its submission. Subsequent calls and letters made it clear that a trip to Bloomington was mandatory, and it must occur during the early days of July.

Although it was mid-afternoon by the time Jesse and Maggie were able to leave Asheville, they still made it to Scottsburg, Indiana, by bedtime. The next day they ate lunch in Bloomington and upon reaching the city's edge Jesse was awe struck by the sight. Massive limestone structures were everywhere, but one huge building dominated the scene. Framed in limestone, a curved wedge of glass, sharply defined the skyline; it was the beautiful Tulip Tree apartments and home to many foreign students. With considerable effort, the School of Optometry was finally located, however, by that time they knew most of the campus. Dr. Epperson, Dean of Admissions, met them with a warm handshake and smile. It took only a matter of moments before Jesse realized that he was in the presence of a truly brilliant man. Dr. Epperson's memory was phenomenal; he was able to call visitors by name merely from speaking with them on the telephone. Without notes he recalled the minutest of details about Jesse's application, even to the unique manner he used to meet pre-admission requirements..

In response to Jesse's query as to why did they picked him, Dr. Epperson responded thoughtfully. "In addition to your excellent grades, one of the main reasons was that we wanted to see you finally get a break." A shy smile accompanied the remark; giving Jesse reason to appreciate that at the center of this great institution, beat a heart of compassion. How could he now not enroll? How could he even consider denying himself such a destiny? Did not this demonstrate once again that light was still there to make his "one step at a time" journey possible?

While in Bloomington, they were able to get a good estimate of total yearly costs, including tuition, books, fees, and housing. At the same time, by talking with the Bursar's office, they learned about school grants, loans, and scholarship aid. Leaving for home, both felt encouraged and optimistic about the amount of money available. However, it would take a lot more than that, before everything was in place.

The following Monday morning found Jesse in the health director's office. He, not wishing to be clandestine about matters, recognized the need to share with administration all that was going on. If a cold reception was expected, then he was pleasantly surprised when Dr. Terry, the new medical director, heartily congratulated him. They discussed the fact that a final decision depended on finances, and agreed that a month's time would be an adequate period of notice. A tentative date was then set.

Kathy, Dr. Terry's secretary, was privy to the conversation and on his way out spoke encouragingly; "I'm not trying to influence your decision, Jesse, but we all think very highly of you here, and would hate to see you go. I believe, though, from what I've heard, you're a man of faith. My advice: listen to what He tells you. And, oh, if you don't mind I'd like to come down later and have prayer with you." Jesse was a little surprised at this, knowing that she was the current first runner-up in the Miss Asheville beauty pageant he wrongly supposed her to be anything but spiritual.

Having prayer with her along with Glinda from the lab became a morning routine during the next two weeks. Meanwhile, letters, phone calls, trips to Raleigh and Charlotte secured commitments for enough funds to pay school expenses during the first year. However, the biggest piece of the puzzle was yet to fall into place; the house had not sold and without that, they could not go.

Jesse felt increasingly helpless as the day of decision drew nigh; this, while waiting for the first potential buyer to make an offer. On the final evening, he and Maggie waited until the girls were in bed before sitting down together. "Well, we laid out the fleece, and the house didn't sell, so I guess it's not His will I not go!" Jesse lamented.

"I'm not so certain about that," Maggie argued. "Maybe God didn't feel a part of this; remember we didn't ask Him. I've watched this thing for three years now and seen stuff happen I never dreamt would. Don't take me wrong here; I've still got my reservations, but nothing like what I had to start with. You know me, I wouldn't say this if I didn't mean it, but I believe the house *will* sell, given enough time, and when it does we'll follow you to Bloomington. It's up to you, though, do what you think is right; if you decide to go, then we'll support you all the way. On the other hand, if you decide not to, I don't want to hear you harping on it for the rest of your life... Is that understood?"

Jesse understood all right, perhaps too well, for what she was asking was a tall order, indeed. To come this far, and give up without a whimper, just wasn't in him; *and she knows it, too*, he thought.

"You may just have something here," he replied. "Yeah, it's something to think about all right." A wanderer lost in the desert had just found a compass. "We'll sleep on it tonight and maybe by morning the way will be made clear." Unfortunately, the new day brought only light and not a map for direction; on top of that, he now was dealing with exhaustion. Very little sleep is possible when indecision decides to spend the night with you

"Do what you have to," Maggie admonished from behind the wheel. Her voice sounded just as flat as he felt. Standing in the health department parking lot, he had just exited the car, but was still holding onto the passenger door.

"Tell me what you'd do," he begged.

"Tell you what to do? No sir, that's a decision you'll have to make on your own. All I can do is say I'll back you, one way or the other... So call me at work and let me know!" With that, she pulled away, headed for her office across town.

Bypassing the usual ritual of morning greetings, he headed straight for his desk. It was 8:28 and the workday would begin in two minutes. This left him just enough time to appeal heaven once more for guidance. It surprised him not at all that he got exactly the same help from there that he got from Maggie. He felt totally abandoned. Then suddenly he had the answer, and it was final; I'll *not go,* he decided. *No, I didn't get a clear sign saying what to do, so I'll call Kathy and tell her.* Nevertheless, even as he reached for the phone his conviction shifted. "No, I'm going! I've seen too many doors open, just to ignore God's hand in all this!" Unbeknownst to him ears pressed hard against the office door had suddenly been rewarded for their efforts.

"Now wait just a dad-burn minute," he mumbled. "I've got to be awful careful here." One hand held the phone while the other was poised to dial. Interestingly, at that very same instant, another important decision was in the making, and it, too, could have profound consequences.

***

Drumming his fingers on the countertop served only to break the silence, but he did no seem to notice, frustration creates its own world. "Heck," Claude Earl snorted, "I don't know what to do! Here I am acting more like a teenager than a thirty-five-year-old, but I just can't seem to shake this thing." Words, laced with feeling, danced through his mind like leaves in a winter wind. This mental conversation was a habit he brought home from Vietnam; *Man, what a trip that was,* he brooded. However, memory often takes wings and is renowned for its ability to fly in any direction. His quickly found a perch in the summer of '54.

That's when I knew for sure, his head nodded in tempo to the inner music. Love is a song found in every soul. *No... it was before that, the Christmas we went up to Wade and Edith's, 1948, I think. I knew it then, the first moment I laid eyes on her. Laura does something to me and always has. And, oh yeah, that time I went up there after graduation; drove my rod up the next day. Boys that was one fast '40 Ford; thought I'd have to fight old Wade just to keep it.* He chuckled softly, but suddenly his thoughts turned serious again*; broke my heart, though, seeing her like that at the drive-in with another guy. You could tell It shook her up, too when she spotted me, and boys I'll never forget the way she looked. Just like a deer caught in the headlights. From what I heard, she ended up marrying him, but I can't blame her for that because even before the summer was over I'd got married, too.*

Thank God, we weren't like them, though, and wound up with a young'in. It just goes to show you that marriages made in hell have about as much chance of making it, as a flea fart does at setting off an avalanche.

"Had a little boy from what I heard," he continued, now mumbling aloud. "But they didn't make it, either," a hint of satisfaction bled through the grim half-smile seen distorting his face. *That Aunt Edith, though. Wow! She must be some kind of psychic. She picked up on how I felt about Laura right off the bat. If it hadn't been for her I'd have lost contact with Laura years ago, but not the way I feel, though. God, sometimes I wish I could just forget her!* Why, *she didn't even bother to answer my letter? She could have at least acknowledged it to let me know one way or the other. Being a Navy Corpsman and stationed with the Marines in Saigon was a nightmare; Lord, what a mess! It's been five years, right about now, since Edith wrote that Laura was getting a divorce. Said she'd moved in with her mother and seemed awful lonesome.*

I wrestled with this then, wanting to get in touch but knowing it would be awful risky. Playing the fool, I went right ahead and did it; just poured my heart out in that letter. Told her how much I loved her, that I always had and always would. I guess the most embarrassing part was where I asked her to wait for me… now that was just about the dumbest thing anybody could ever do. My goodness, why it had been years since we'd even seen each other, so just how silly can one human being be over another? "No excuses this time, Claude Earl, about being so far from home, that won't cut it! Not, when you're about to make the same mistake again; no sir, I think it's a lack of brains. No wonder I never heard from her; who wants to be involved with a fool? The thing I can't understand is why all of a sudden she's popped back into my head again, and it's been that way all the time lately. I've been dreaming of her every night, sorta like she's reaching out to me, her heart seeking mine."

Remarkably, Claude Earl was not alone with this experience. Inside the domain of human love there operates an energy that far exceeds finite understanding. Sometimes, also, the ticking clock of biology may help facilitate matters. Laura was well aware of this. Recently she had been unable to close her eyes without seeing him. Claude Earl was not a man that most would think of as being truly handsome, yet to here, he was extremely so.

Perhaps for the millionth time she wondered why he had never bothered to answer her letter. She'd written him right back, seven pages in all, doing so within hours after reading his words of love. Her own echoed those of his, they were sentiments she had felt since that Christmas eve so long ago. Had she appeared too eager by answering back so soon? Perhaps he was like many men and felt threatened by an overly anxious or aggressive female. However, she wished to be honest and not play games; war did not allow for such tactics even if she had been so inclined, and she was not.

My goodness, she reflected at the mirror, it seems like yesterday, but it's been five years now. Mom took my letter with her on the way to work, so I know it got mailed and oh how I waited and waited for his reply. At first I feared he might have been injured... or something maybe worse. But I couldn't stand to think about that, so when Edith told me he was home again, I nearly died.

I can't understand why he's been on my mind so much lately, it seems like every night now he's in my dreams. it's over though; in fact, and this is the truth, we never really got started. I think he had a bad case homesickness and just needed somebody, maybe anybody, to write to. Yes, no doubt that was it.

While certain angels may be addicted to humor, most, by far, are not. Seraphs in the main are much more given to romance and it pains them greatly to see love go unrequited. Behind the scenes they struggle mightily to constrain themselves when watching the confusion that so often results when mortals delve into the realm of human passion. Thus challenged by Claude Earl and Laura, they had been prompting the subconscious of each with dreams and feelings. Yet what they desired most was to take Laura by the hand and lead her gently upstairs, where in the attic she would find an old mildewed leather clutch bag with a letter stashed away at the bottom. She would quickly discover that the stamps on it remained unmarked, since her mother had not seen fit to post it. Who better than Ollie could know what it was like to lose a husband and a soldier, so at all costs she would spare Laura the pain. By accomplishing this, however, three empty spaces now occupied spots where three hearts used to beat.

"Just to satisfy my mind I guess I really ought to go see." Claude Earl scowled. "I *could* drive up tonight." However, as an EMT who had just finished a 72-hour shift, he was in no condition to make such decisions. "Darn," he sputtered. "Here I am ready to make a fool out of myself again, but it'll pass. What's needed now is a little common sense for a change. Besides, a man's gotta think of his pride, don't he? No! I ain't going."

***

Kathy?...Yeah, it's me. Yeah, I've definitely decided, and this is my notice; one month from today and I'll be in school!" Jesse sounded the epitome of confidence, yet felt none of it. The decision had remained open right up to the moment he opened his mouth, surprising him just as much as it did Kathy.

"Oh, Jesse," she sounded disappointed. "We'd all hoped you wouldn't do it, but it sounds like you're determined. So congratulations, my dear friend... and may God go with you!"

CHAPTER 35

Immediately, events began to move with lightening speed. Another trip to Bloomington was mandatory, this time for registration, orientation, and, of course, to secure a suitable place to stay. Actually, everything went far better than Jesse expected, with the exception of housing. The sixth floor of Eigenmann Hall would be his new home and the thought of having to live in this huge graduate dorm caused him a great deal of concern. Maggie tried to cheer him up, "At the longest it'll probably only be for a month or two," she smiled weakly.

Lest there be some misunderstanding here that Jesse may suddenly have become apprehensive about the future, please then, herewith, put that matter to rest. Actually, he quite taken with Bloomington, a beautiful town drenched in an ambiance of the 1940's. Like a time warp, it transported him back to the days of childhood and he happily looked forward to living there again. Enormous beech and maples seemed to grow everywhere, trees that had watched many a generation come and go. Giant bowers that had witnessed it all, proud peacocks strutting by, angels kissing and cry-baby recent virgins still in wonder how it happened; yet these sylvan sentries stood ready again to open wide their arms of welcome. Oddly, he recalled a dream from adolescence picturing him wearing a brightly colored toboggan and racing across the campus of some major college or university. A veritable blizzard of leaves, orange, yellow, and red swirled all about him with the show set and choreographed in a glory that only a mid-western October could produce. Hence, he felt right at home, where fate, obviously, had destined he be.

However, one nagging question kept chipping away at his optimism; did he have transportation dependable enough to make the long trips back and forth? Since nearly five hundred miles separated Asheville from Bloomington, it was something they needed to discuss. Two years earlier he had bought a '72 Vega for their second car, doing so never dreaming what tests it ultimately must face. Friend and family alike, heaped scorn on him for making such a purchase. So intense was their ridicule that he finally depicted them all as being like a bunch of tumblebugs in a pile of dung. "How," they seemed to rejoice in asking, "could you be so foolish, Jesse?"

Wade took it worst of all; "My gosh, Jamup, what in the world were you thinking about?" Belief in his oldest son had been shattered. "Son," he paused to swallow, but found it hard with a mouth suddenly gone dry. "A Vega, I can't believe you bought a Vega. Why Jesse, that's the sorriest Shivalay they ever made, and you won't find one that can make it for more than twenty-five thousand miles. How many has it already got it?"

From the ruins of a smoldering spirit there arose just a wisp of response; "Nearly nine thousand when I bought it and I've put on another eight hundred since then." Jesse felt bolder now; a flicker of the old Gernon fire suddenly flared up to re-vitalize him. "Look! I just bought it for running back and forth to work and the salesman said it'd be fine for that. He did mention, though, it would be a good idea not to drive it too-o hard. I'll only be putting about twenty or thirty miles a week on it, so I figure it'll hold out for several years like that. You'd think I ought to be took out and horse-whipped, the way everybody's acting!"

"Well, I sure wouldn't push it anymore than I had to." Wade seemed satisfied now that he had made his point.

About a month before hearing from Indiana, Jesse had given up all hope of going to school, so he had decided to console himself with a new Mercury Marquis. Obviously, this unwise decision was now putting additional stress on the family budget and it came on the whim of an impulse.

"I'll take Vega to Bloomington," he piped, sounding a lot more confident than he felt. It'll be a lot cheaper to drive and now with gas selling at 50 cents a gallon, we have to think about stuff like that. You just watch that thing, it'll cruise up to Indiana and back like a big 707; why, I'd rather fly it any day!"

That settled it then, he would drive the Vega. Therefore, early the last Sunday morning of August found Jesse loading up the little compact in preparation to leave. The day had dawned both bright and beautiful, with a sky that looked far away and more like early fall than summer, and yet it was typical for Asheville. Weather this nice usually set him to singing his off-key version of *Carolina in the Morning*; but not this time, not with Indiana on his mind.

Despite an eagerness to leave, reality suddenly set in rendering them all nearly incapable of saying goodbye. Standing before the couch and lined up in order Maggie, Terri, Lisa, and Becky all tried to look brave, yet their smiles were not enough to hide the teardrops. Never before had he been away from them longer than a few days at a time and now here he was leaving on a four-year pilgrimage that was both ill defined and potentially dangerous. They were all about to learn that life is more than just a chain of experiences linked together by circumstance.

Going north for the third time in just over a month seemed almost anti-climatic. It was an uneventful trek except for the occasional pang of homesickness that urged he turn back around and go home. However, he knew that was impossible. "It'll go away after I start class," he reasoned. "Besides, it would be abnormal not to feel a little blue." Seeking to gird up his mind, he decided that if he did not stop thinking aloud, he soon would have a very lively conversation going on with himself.

"I hope you'll remember that your age and wisdom could be intimidating to some of the younger students," his moral side admonished. "So try to be gracious."

His ego was quick with an answer. "Hmm-m –I hadn't thought about that. You *may* be right, especially when you consider all my experience. Yeah, I'll go easy at first, but they'll catch up in a semester or two... don't you think?"

Jesse felt better now. After all, it does not hurt to clear the air once in awhile.

When he got to Eigenmann the first thing he noticed was how hot it was, much worse than he had expected. Then to make matters worse, he soon learned that not only were both elevators not working, the air conditioning was also out. Great lines of graduate students had formed in the foyer with their luggage scattered everywhere. Jesse took one look and decided to carry his things up the seven flights of stairs. Although his room was on the sixth floor, numbering did not start until above the ground level. With the stairwell hot and crowded, he encountered much frustration and delay, but after four trips and fifty-five minutes, he finally was in. Unfortunately, the air conditioning was still not working, and to top it off the check-in clerk told him to expect a roommate. This obviously meant having to put up with a stranger, and who could relax knowing that? By taking a few moments to survey his situation, however, he began to feel better. After all, he was safely in and the opportunity to bed down early seemed most appealing.

Supper, on the other hand, held little interest for him.

Next morning he was up early and ready to start class at 9:30. The first two days passed quickly enough and things seemed to be going pretty well, except for the occasional twinge of homesickness. This, he soon realized, was most apt to occur when he was alone or had time on his hands. Oddly, these episodes made him feel alienated and strange, as if he was a visitor there from another planet.

By Thursday, he had met his roommate and with someone to talk to, his situation slowly began to improve.

Mark, a handsome young graduate student from Indianapolis was a Business Administration major. Soon after moving in, he told Jesse that it was nothing personal, but he would be leaving the dorm in a day or two. His name was on a list for off-campus housing and he was just waiting for the nod. Jesse found Mark to be most helpful in showing him some of the ways of campus life. He took time to explain such basics as using the dining room, getting mail, and applying for a telephone calling card. By the time he left, Jesse had come to appreciate this good-natured Hoosier, feeling that a kind Providence had placed him there. It was nearly a week after Mark left when Dave showed up.

David James from Warsaw, Indiana, was both a little older and more mature-acting than Mark. There to earn his Master's degree in Audio-Visual Technology, he was a serious student. It was at lunch when they met and an instant friendship developed. His dark red hair and blue eyes defined rugged good looks that reminded Jesse of Claude Earl, and even their demeanor seemed much the same. Dave's modest stutter in no way hampered his ability to communicate; he was a fine conversationalist. Coming from a farm and near a large lake, his stories about rural life gave them much to talk about, and they liked sharing their Christian experiences with one another. After comparing schedules, they quickly realized their paths would rarely cross, and while this was ideal for study, it left Jesse with far too many hours to be alone.

His initial concern about overshadowing his classmates soon dissipated once he met them. Never had Jesse been in the company of such a bright bunch before. They were not only bright they were brilliant, enough so that he began to fret. *Son,* he told himself, *you might have stepped in it over your head this time!* Truth was, his advanced classes in anatomy and physiology were a snap, yet when it came to geometric optics that was quite another story. G.O., he soon discovered, was a bane to every first-year optometry student. As an advanced study in physics, it still holds many challenges for science. In fact, branches of this discipline continues to defy the best efforts of philosophers and scientists alike to comprehend it fully, as it has done down through the ages. The profundity of Light, as heretofore discussed, is an essential entity for every living thing. As stated elsewhere "God is Light." Yet this must not be taken to mean that light is a definition of deity. No, it is merely a useful metaphor and nothing more.

The study of geometric optics presented Jesse and his classmates with problems so devilish, so teasing, and yet so unfathomable that many of the top students found themselves praying just to get a passing grade. Rhetorically; if those who obtained their pre-optometry courses at this self-same university were struggling, consider then what anguish Jesse must have suffered by having so little higher math to draw from. When accepted by I.U. he had agreed to take five hours of calculus during the next summer session. Unfortunately, math was the "language" he needed then, considering that it is the mother tongue of physics. Without it, he constantly felt like a nudist at a cookout for cannibals.

Before leaving for Indiana, they decided he would try to stay a month before returning home. However, by the middle of the second week he came to realize just how foolish and unrealistic this decision had been. Accordingly, right after the G.O. class Thursday morning he was on the road and headed home. The trip took him back through Brown County and Nashville, then on to Columbus. All along the way, the scenes he enjoyed of early September Americana were ones that Norman Rockwell could very well have painted.

CHAPTER 36

The weekend came and went so quickly it seemed he hardly got unpacked before it was time to leave. The trip back was dismal with heavy, menacing clouds that hovered low all the way.

He promised to stay this time for two weeks and did so, yet the ordeal nearly killed him. Another two-week cycle followed that one, and he was beginning to get into a routine. With the midterm exams now imminent, Jesse found it hard to explain why he dreaded them so much. Obviously, what he feared most was failing, and yet he had difficulty articulating his situation to Maggie. By seeking help from others, he could solve many of the textbook and lab problems; however, the lectures were what worried him the most. After a lifetime of learning by rote, a professor who demanded that his students think for themselves bewildered him. From studying old exams, Jesse knew that the questions would come from the global presentation and not from any single source, making it mandatory that he learn the underlying concepts.

Poor math skills, no doubt, played a big part in his dilemma, but there were other factors as well. Most, if not all, the other students had joined study groups where they could pool their speculative powers for potential questions. These groups had coalesced around long-standing friendships, developed during their undergraduate years. Although Jesse invited himself to a few of these, he actually benefited very little from the experiences. Usually they formed spontaneously, and, more often than not, at some off-campus location. Another major handicap was his inability to take good notes. Here, however, he had lots of company and until he wised up and copied those made by others more skilled at the art, his grades would continue to flounder.

Maggie did her best at encouragement, believing he would do better than he thought. Jesse, however, knew better; she was wrong and he proved it by doing far worse than anybody expected.

The professor of G.O., an unusually learned man, held doctorates in both Physiological Optics and Optometry. He taught by the confrontational method and from the perspective that everyone there was at or near his level of understanding. For those fortunate few who may have been, they no doubt profited greatly by this approach, but not so Jesse; it devastated him.

Each lecture period became for him a desperate time of extreme anxiety, causing paralysis to his very thought processes. Never could he give a correct answer when called upon in class, making him feel like a bonehead. Scenes from his first day in school with Miss Walker kept coming back to mind. To the credit of this good doctor, his objective was not to intimidate, but rather to get them to where they could think on their feet. After all, nothing less is expected from an eye doctor. To show that it was not personal, he would, after a few attempts, call on only those who were obviously keeping up. Many, however, were not doing so as demonstrated by their test results.

In handing back the papers, starting with the highest score first, Jesse realized immediately how poorly he had done. When his eye caught the score, he was devastated, for never, not even in the worst days of high school, had he gotten a grade so low as 19! A wave of nausea made him want to vomit, and then his mind blanked out. Not one word said after that got through. By the time the class ended it did not matter to him any longer because he had given up. "You've got to quit and go home," screamed a voice inside his head. "Here's all the proof it takes to show what a grave mistake you've made by starting this. God did not want you here in the first place; it was all your idea and nothing but a big ego trip for you. If this truly had been His will He would never have allowed you to become embarrassed like this. 19! Why, my Lord, 19 is probably the worst score anybody ever made in G.O!

While more than willing to listen to all this, his ears were insensitive to what others were saying. They, too, had reason to complain with their own poor showing, yet that aspect never penetrated his psyche. Walking alongside them on the way to the parking lot, he seemed unaffected by what they said. It was clear, no other choice remained, but to quit and go on home; a grade this pitiful, so shameful, and so humiliating was beyond discussing. Never mind his good grades in the other classes; that did not really count, for, after all, optometry was about optics and he had just made a spectacle of himself. Again, moments from the first grade suddenly flashed through his mind; he had quit then, too. *Looks like my early instincts were right after all.* He nodded, looking bitter.

With a finger poised to dial, Maggie was surprised when the phone rang. Lifting the receiver to her ear, she immediately realized they were in trouble. A weak voice, almost inaudible, informed her of the decision; "I'm coming home," he said. "I can't take it anymore; God knows I've made a bad mistake. I just wish I'd stayed on at Buncombe County."

It took less than thirty minutes to pack everything; TV, books, clothes, all of it he piled into the car. David happened to be present and after a brief explanation, they exchanged words of goodbye. A low hum from the Vega helped to drown out his ex-roommate's admonition; "If I were you, I'd give it just a little more time." Jesse's sorry state was not such that he missed hearing the sound of concern in David's voice.

Nightfall found him at home, yet the darkness in his soul far exceeded that of the eventide. He and Maggie talked well into the morning hours, since sleep was impossible for them both. They reviewed, repeatedly, every aspect of this great and disappointing venture. The thought of giving up a good job after working so hard to get it, tortured him. He had thrown the opportunity of a lifetime away and now had nothing to show for it. He could not go back to the health department; they had already hired a replacement, and, in addition, after the big send-off there, it would look pathetic to show up again with hat in hand. No, he would have to look elsewhere.

Next morning, Wednesday, he and Maggie left the house early, seeking the services of an employment agency. It was while there that he experienced a sense of even deeper discouragement. He saw right away they had nothing that came even close to what he had left behind. Almost in tears, he talked it over with Maggie. While supportive, she could offer him little more than sympathy. Half dead, both from grief and a lack of sleep, he looked at all the reasonable options and decided to go back. "Maybe," he said, "if we pray hard enough God will forgive me for this. I realize I have been selfish, but I know this, too, I thought I was doing his will. Always before he has been able to bring good out of bad, so let's give him another chance. Pray, too, that he'll strengthen my mind so I can pass the next test. You know, they give two midterms and let you throw out the lower score. Heaven only knows, I should be able to beat a 19."

"Well, you just didn't happen to mention that before, did you?" She scolded. "This puts everything in a whole different light. Anyway, look at it this way; somebody has to be last. Besides, it's better to be brought low like this than to lose your health or maybe something worse. I told the girls the morning you left that it was all up to us now; to remember that I was in charge and reserved the right *to always be right*. Well right now, that advice applies to you, too, so I'm fixing to speak my mind here. You may not want to hear this, but you need to anyway. Jesse, I think you're just feeling sorry for yourself and that's because you're spoiled. Here it is the first time that things get a little rough and you're ready to chuck it all and quit. Do you think it's been easy on us? We still have to put up with the same old crap we did before you left. But here you are running back with your tail tucked between your legs and blaming God. I ask you, what kind of signal does that send to the girls? And it's all. because-you-didn't-do-so-well-on-a-test. Well, I say welcome to the real world, Buster! You need to buck up and take your lumps like the rest of us. God ain't the one who's give up here, it's you!"

At precisely ten past two that afternoon, he was on his way back to Indiana, the second time in four days. The Vega continued to be true to its calling and never missed a beat for another five hundred miles. It got him there at five minutes before ten. David helped with the unpacking as he negotiated the seven flights of stairs, three round-trips to move back in again. "I was praying you'd do this," he smiled. After all, from what I hear, it's awfully hard to get into optometry and, why, I'd stay until *they* asked me to leave. My advice, Jesse: wait until *they* say go; leave that up to them, but I believe you have what it takes to make it!"

"It was amazing, David, coming up the road I heard a song by Tennessee Ernie and I felt like it was aimed right at me! I forget what the name was, but the words helped me to understand that passage in the Bible where Jesus was asleep in the boat with His disciples. Remember it was storming and they thought they were about to drown, but He spoke to the sea and it grew still. So, I thought, here I am in a boat, too, one that looks like it's ready to sink, but if He's really in it with me then there's nothing to fear. Truth is, and it's hard to face, but fear of failure has just about replaced what little faith I had."

Next morning Jesse returned to G.O. praying that his mind would somehow suddenly flash in a divine synapse. However, it did not happen, not that day, at least. Near exhaustion, his brain had become so insensate that he found it impossible to answer even a softball question tossed his way. Later, he realized that it had been offered as a means to boost his spirits, but, by playing the game of self-pity he managed to foul out instead.

'Tis a sad but true commentary on the sport of life, that the prize we covet most is often lost because of the games we play in our mind.

Somehow, he muddled through the day, then after getting a good night's sleep, Friday morning dawned to a brighter looking world, not bright enough, however, to keep him in Bloomington for the weekend. Even the thought of it seemed unbearable. It depressed him to think that the best he could now hope for was four years of the same misery he'd just experienced. He needed to get away and try to sort through it all. Yes, he would agree, he had acted childishly, but this trip would be different. Driving would give him an opportunity to seek guidance and find perspective. *By the time I make it home,* he reasoned, *I'll know then just what to do*. Unfortunately, this never came even close to happening.

Again the Vega proved its worth by getting him to Asheville in less than eight hours, this at a time when fifty-five mph was the national speed limit. Sunday found him on the road again pushing a motor that most would swear could not take it, yet it got him back in near record time. However, he still faced the task of moving in again since he'd taken everything along, just in case. Too tired to plan further trips, it was time now to face a few facts; he had to either do something or get off the pot. There simply were no other options left.

Somewhere along the line, it occurred to him that this made three complete round trips, almost 3000 miles in a week! "Perhaps," a still, small voice whispered, "if you put half as much time into studying as you do on the road, it's just possible you might make better grades."

The advice, while completely sound, went mostly unheeded. Remarkably, however, Jesse did manage to stay two weeks this time before going home. The Sabbath he was in Bloomington found him doing something he'd promised earlier to do; attend church. Located just off campus, it was a nice structure with a friendly congregation. The sermon contained words that came alive when the pastor looked straight at him and quoted from First Peter, chapter 5, "*Casting all your cares upon him, for he careth for you.*" Jesse's spirit caught the uplift and soared. *He careth for you, he careth for you,* the Word echoed from new heights. With the pastor's eyes still on him, a synapse finally occurred, yet not in his brain, but in his heart. At that instant, he knew it; he had just received a personal touch from the Master. He who opens doors and gives light enough to take one-step at a time, added to more to the message: "Remember," he said, "I'm always in the boat with you, and never do I slumber nor sleep; and although the wind and waves may roar, they still obey my voice.

Of all that he had done since arriving in Bloomington, going to church proved, by far, to be the most profitable. He quickly made new friends that were there when he needed a fresh touch with reality. Obviously, this did not become an instant solution for all his problems, nor that suddenly they all just vanished away, not by a long shot. As the semester progressed, he quit so many times the actual count was lost. Nevertheless, on one particular occasion an event occurred that would linger in memory. Dragging in from class one Thursday evening he was so completely discouraged that he could see neither rhyme nor reason as to why he should continue trying. Now totally bereft of all hope, he once again made the decision to quit for good and go on home. "I may as well quit punishing myself," he grumbled, "and the sooner the better." Best thing to do, he determined, was pack up and be gone before David got back; however, he'd begun to leave the TV and heavier items behind... just in case. By taking only clothes and books, Dave would not know whether he had quit or not and that would save a lot of explaining later if he decided not stay. Jesse was learning a lot more than he cared to admit.

Life is full of the unexpected as events of this night were about to prove.

CHAPTER 37

October, that siren of months and seducer of senses had beguiled the evening with another incredible harvest moon, yet its magic was all but lost on Jesse. "Oh, dear God, just show me what to do," he prayed, "You know I'm failing again and there's nothing I can do about it. For some reason you've not helped me one bit with this G.O., so please send me a sign that it's Your will I be here." Seeking an omen, he ventured further. "Show me one of your wild creatures between here and Nashville, something beautiful and innocent, and then I'll know you want me to stay."

Once previously, after a similar request, a big marsh hawk had manifested within a mile or so; but that was just a coincidence. This time, though, he had hardly uttered his petition before the largest red fox he had ever seen suddenly dashed out of the forest to run ahead of him down the highway. Tossing its head flippantly over a swaggering shoulder, it looked straight back at Jesse, and rakishly laughed in his face. It was too much; there was nothing to do but slow down and take in the show. Starting with a tripping ballet, the animal performed magnificently in the moonlight. Jesse watched incredulously as it stood upright doing a roguish boogie-woogie before hitting all fours and sashaying seamlessly into a graceful foxtrot. Suddenly, it leapt high in the air while doing a full-turn spin, and then repeated the feat twice more. Obviously, here was a veteran trouper; however, previously it had always danced only for the wild things.

Moments later, it abruptly switched back to ballet. Meanwhile it dawned on Jesse that he was witnessing an event that probably no one would believe.

Unfortunately, just as quickly as it started, the presentation was over; a switch of the tail sent the performer scurrying into the broad cornfields of Brown County. Merely another coincidence was it… perhaps so, but what a show!

Anyone spending this many hours on the road would naturally cause his or her grades to suffer, yet not all was a complete loss. Jesse soon learned to put much of his travel time into good use; mile after mile became opportunities to work on G.O. problems. At his goodbye party, one of the gifts the health department staff had presented him with was a small hand-held calculator. Still a new tool in 1975, it was banned by most universities since they perceived the device to be a shortcut to learning. However, the time for such technology was at hand and it was inevitable that they, too, the great bastions of higher learning, would ultimately capitulate. For Jesse this proved to be a most fortunate turn of events. He had never fully mastered the art of using a slide rule, and without a calculator, his time at I.U. would probably have been a matter of days. As it was, he wore out two his first semester, doing so mostly on the long trips home. Working intensively while driving, two or more hours could slip by without him being aware of the passing interval. Once, after leaving Louisville, he became so oblivious to the changing landscape that he and the Vega might very well have ended up in Florida, had it not been for a traffic tie-up in Knoxville.

Whether it was by answered prayer or because of dogged determination, such is unknown, but his mind slowly did begin to open. At first, it was barely discernable, a shaft of light breaking through into a space previously occupied by nothing more than a few dust particles. Suddenly myriads of them danced sprightly in the golden ray of insight. The turning point came after he decided to review one of his old algebra and trigonometry books. By spending just a few minutes there each day his efforts began to pay off. On the second mid-term exam, he scored a whopping 37! Not the best, but not the worst either and by being graded on a curve he felt that this time he actually may have passed. Only time would tell.

Considering that he had focused more than ninety percent of his efforts on this one subject, he had put other disciplines also in jeopardy. Such was not the case, however. Actually, when the semester ended he clearly had passed everything except G.O. where he received an incomplete. A final grade there would depend on his passing part two the next semester, but at least he now had a fighting chance.

Christmas was bleak with so little to celebrate. Much had failed him since starting school, his courage, his faith and his hope, but not the Vega. Sometime in late November, he had watched the odometer roll past the twenty-five-thousand-mile mark, a point where natural death could occur at any moment. A quiet miracle was in the making, yet he was oblivious to it. Jesse was so preoccupied with what had gone wrong that he found little time to consider all that was going right.

Earlier, he had prayed much for their house to sell, but now, after trudging so deeply into the valley of the shadow, he was exceedingly glad it had not. To have it sell at this point, with the future so uncertain, would be more than he could bear. Who but heavenly agencies are caring enough to protect us from the bedevilment of our own devising?

I. U. offered two classes in G.O. with each being uniquely difficult and challenging. However, the one Jesse had taken was considered by most to be the harder of the two to pass. Now that he was better informed, he was determined to switch to the one taught by the School Dean. Even though he was a tough educator, his methods of instruction were more traditional and straightforward. The Dean and Maggie had spoken at length on the phone during Jesse's initial crisis, whereupon she arranged a conference between the two. After listening sympathetically, he laid an arm across the stooping shoulders of his troubled student and assured him that not all was lost. He then related a story that sounded eerily similar to Jesse's ordeal, telling how another student had also struggled mightily with G.O. and wanted to quit. "Ultimately," he said, that student went on to graduate with honors." With a twinkle in his eye he continued, "Son, you are looking at him right now." His head went moving slowly back and forth, as he added; "We're not going to let you give up, Jesse; your wife's counting on you, and so am I."

Knowing that competition was extremely keen for this class, they left for Bloomington and early registration two days after New Years. Flakes from a light snow silently struck the windshield before vanishing, as they rode along in the Mercury. Wade was with them, although he dreaded making the trip, knowing what the weather forecasters had predicted.

After passing through Knoxville snow began to accumulate by the roadside, on cedars, and other evergreens. However, once they reached the Cumberland Plateau, the scene changed dramatically into one of a winter wonderland. This unusual stretch of highway spans a region that never failed to intrigue Jesse. Starkly beautiful at any time of the year, its huge out-cropping of limestone overlooks deep valleys below. Much of this high ground had lost its natural beauty to strip mining, yet amazingly, the contrast created a charm of its own. Felt here were sentiments one might experience by looking into the eyes of a street urchin, seeing hope mingled with hurt.

A place where the sky hovers near
And the Great Spirit can be found
Although scarred and badly torn
The Plateau is still Holy Ground.

Kentucky lay directly ahead. A state with so much coal, that it, in places, fills the ditch lines and the proud people there still holds high the great name of Daniel Boone. Even now, with a little imagination, one might see a ghost-like figure moving stealthily through the shadows, hog-rifle in hand, headed for the "gap." At Lexington, the snow was beginning to accumulate in earnest. Three hours later, they found six inches of it on the ground in Bloomington.

That night temperatures dropped dramatically, and when Wade awoke, he complained bitterly. "I reckon I must to have slept five minutes last night!" Such news caught the other two by surprise, having listened to several hours of snoring.

After a look outside, he had another observation to make. "Say, Jamup," he asked, "are you sure you want to come back up here into all of this? If it was left up to me, buddy, I'd say give this place back to the Eskimos."

Maggie shot a glance at her father-in-law that fortunately he did not see. Jesse did, however, and winced at her anger. He knew she saw four months of hard work, both at encouragement and cracking the whip, about to go down the tube. "Most of the time the weather's been real nice here and what you're looking at this morning is the worst I've seen it," Jesse defended. Besides, Daddy, you know I can't quit now because when a fellow takes a row he has to hoe it to the end; you've always said that."

"Tell you what, by Ned, it's going to get a lot worse here before this winter's over; you just wait and see, and I still can't figure out why we had to make this trip, anyway; it's awful dangerous out there. It'll pay you not to be running up and down that road too much, that's all I've got to say."

Wade probably never knew just how sage his advice was. However, getting there to register early did pay Jesse dividends, since he got what he wanted.

He also got a room to himself, which was both good and bad. Good that it gave him more privacy, yet bad in the sense that he and David would but rarely see each other again. The last time they did was just before spring break; David would soon be graduating and had accepted a job in Indianapolis. He was very excited about the prospects and promised to keep in touch. Unfortunately, this never materialized.

Failure, or perhaps the fear of it, was what set Jesse to packing so often during the first semester. Not this time, though, now it was just plain homesickness. Undeniable and unrelenting this cursed malady drove him south nearly every weekend. He harbored little hope that his family would soon join him in Bloomington, so he made every effort to make it home as often as possible. Thus, for better or worse, with some manipulation of schedules he was able to arrange it so that none of his major lectures fell on Friday. Obviously, that meant after his last class on Thursday he was free to go and it all worked out fine, just as long as the weather cooperated. However, by mid-January, he was literally slipping in and out of Indiana on the cuff of miracles. Severe weather seemed ordained to arise early in the week, and then clear out by Thursday giving him a narrow window of travel time. Jesse realized this could not go on indefinitely, making him fear the worst; and sure enough, the inevitable finally happened.

Heretofore, fate had been kind, yet in retrospect, such seems to have been solely for setting a trap for him. To do that, however, a paradox must first occur by creating a sucker-punch, if you please.

Indiana's weather suddenly turned much warmer near the end of January with many claiming that it was the anticipated thaw. Jesse left for home on a high note; it would be a great weekend. Forecasts called for temperatures in Asheville to reach the high sixties and since he was accustomed to morning lows of zero or below, this would seem like a trip to Florida. Blue skies and sunshine were all he could see ahead with Friday and Saturday both expected to meet or even exceed these readings. By early Sunday morning, however, matters were beginning to change. Lulled into complacency he had not felt the urge to keep up with the weather and that is why it shocked him to hear the morning report. It told of a massive cold front that had formed quickly and was dipping down across the Great Lakes, pushing south rapidly and bringing with it snow and ice. The chill already covered northern Indiana, and probably would reach deep into Dixie by Sunday night. Jesse immediately realized the problem he faced and began making plans to leave at once. Normally he would stay until around noon and get back to Bloomington by about eight. Knowing this time he could not afford to wait, he packed and was ready to go at 10:00; the extra two hours would prove critical.

Actually, driving was not too bad until he reached Louisville. However, once he crossed the Ohio River he saw a landscape that looked both familiar and yet remarkably different. Although it was still Indiana, the scene could easily have been mistaken for one near the Arctic Circle. Radio advisories told that all Interstates remained open, but many of the lesser thoroughfares were impassable except for vehicles equipped with chains. Jesse switched from station to station hoping to get word on state route 46, the stretch between Columbus and Bloomington. His efforts went unrewarded, however. The further north he pushed the deeper the snow was, yet just as perplexing were the "No Vacancy" signs he saw beginning to flash. By the time he reached Columbus no new precipitation was falling, and traffic seemed to be moving well in all directions. Even though he was leaving the interstate, he did so with renewed hope while pointing his Vega west toward Nashville. It disturbed him, though, when accelerating to find the car wanting to fishtail. Then he realized it; he was gliding over at least four inches of packed ice! *How long will I be able to keep this up?* He worried. Then almost in the same thought; *I'll end up in a ditch line if I try to turn around, so I'd better just keep trucking.*

Despite skimming along on the surface of a two-lane iceberg, he still marveled at the sight set before him. Tawny brown clouds rising above the horizon shimmered gold-edged between alternating bands of sunlight and shadow. Although beautiful, he still felt inspired to start praying. Somehow, he knew he needed to make it beyond Nashville before darkness set in. It would be close but with a little luck, he could do it.

Twilight came earlier than expected, bringing with it special memories from the long ago. Headlights from the on-coming traffic reminded him of Christmas candles casting their yellow glow across in the snow. For one splendid moment, he was back on Sweetwater again, back to the warmth of Wade and Edith's hearth and waiting for supper. However, moments like these were side trips he could ill afford; a check on his driving skills lay just ahead, and it would demand his full attention.

Between Nashville and Bloomington there are a series of steep hills and sharp curves that in winter often tests the skill of drivers. Already, he had passed several abandoned vehicles, cars, pick-ups and, remarkably, even a few four-wheelers. He drew comfort, however, from the presence of a huge black Mercedes immediately ahead of him. Its driver appeared to be in full control of the situation and able to plow them both a path all the way into Bloomington.

Although subtle at first it, nevertheless, was there gnawing away at his determination, that archenemy of all human achievement called doubt. Its sharp fangs suddenly hit an artery, causing his confidence to hemorrhage profusely.

Maybe I'd better turn around and head back, he reasoned. *If I go much further, it'll be too late then, and besides, after I cross over the first hill, I won't be able to make it back. Still,* he pondered, *turning around is no answer* either, *since all the motels between here and Columbus are full. No, if I have to sleep in the Vega, I'll be better off getting as close to Bloomington as I can.* Too troubling to think about were the inherent risks associated with spending the night in a car so utterly ill prepared for such conditions.

Rather than dwell on that he decided to take comfort from his wealthy escort, this while appreciating the faithful hum of his own car's engine. Although the tires slipped and slid several times, he was still able to crest the first mountain, and just beginning the steep descent down when he watched the Mercedes flounder. The last he saw of it, the big vehicle was jammed up against a guardrail with its driver angrily motioning him to go around.

Another mountain to cross, but this one proved to be a little easier, yet Jesse knew that the true challenge lay further ahead. It was the last one before Bloomington and had the longest, most precipitous climb of them all. Since it faced north, the road, no doubt, held much more snow and ice than thus far encountered. He felt rather than saw the slope beginning to rise.

Words from a familiar song suddenly came to mind; "But this time, Lord, you gave me a mountain… a mountain you know I may never climb." It was a refrain that had coursed through his mind almost incessantly during the past semester. Somehow, he had been foolish enough to think its relevancy was finally behind him, but now he knew better. "It isn't a hill any longer. . You gave me a mountain this time." Mustering up courage, he felt brave enough to make up a few words of his own, "But now, you are with me… and you're driving this time. So, Lord, there isn't a mountain… That together we can't climb!"

There it was dead ahead and looking more like a ski-slope than Route 46; headlights marked the way from vehicle to vehicle, they being sideways in the ditch or otherwise stuck. Jesse took a long deep breath, "Okay, little Vega," he muttered, "we've had our fun, but now this is for real."

He attempted to accelerate just a little, but that served only to turn the car halfway around. Remarkably, he felt the tires bite suddenly into something that gave him traction, and then for nearly a hundred yards the tiny car was able to skim over the crusted ice and snow. He was on his way! Unfortunately, his speed began to drop again forcing the need to downshift. When he did, however, the wheels started spinning. His optimism, just on the verge of burgeoning, now dropped faster than the car's momentum. Suddenly, stalling out or perhaps plowing into a snow bank loomed now as a very real possibility. "Oh, no, no. No!... Oh well, so much for answered prayer!" He ranted.

Anger pressed the accelerator hard against the floor causing the smell of hot rubber, smoke, and exhaust to fill his nostrils; this while the fumes swirled all around and even past him. Temporary blinded, he could not possibly see that several young men had put their shoulders to the effort. Slowly, the car began to pick up speed and miraculously start moving again! As the air cleared, so did his vision, leaving Jesse humbled at the sight of complete strangers doing their best to help him! Two beeps of the car horn acknowledged his gratitude, but quickly he applied himself to the task still ahead.

Now halfway up the incline, he had already passed dozens of stranded vehicles, but straight in front sat one stuck in the middle of the road! To get past meant squeezing between it and the ditch-line. That would be a tall order, indeed, and one fraught with danger. Getting too close on either side meant putting an end to his efforts. He ran the risk of either sliding into a snowdrift or crashing into the side of a BMW, with neither option being acceptable. Straining at the wheel, Jesse and his car seemed to shrink and meld into one as he drew a short breath and held it between clenched teeth. General Motors had a lot to be proud of with their progeny, for never did an automobile perform with more precision. They slipped by with only inches to spare on either side, but that was enough!

Nearing the crest, he again saw the need for help if he made it. That is when they stepped forward, student angels wearing winter garb decorated with the I.U. insignia. These agents, all, no doubt, bound for celestial realms; obviously enjoyed their work as they pushed, applauded, and cheered. Their reward seemed to be just in helping some mortal gain the victory. Jubilant with enthusiasm, it was contagious enough to infect Jesse; he could not have felt better by winning the Indy 500!

"Hot dang!" he banged on the seat beside him. As far as he could tell, his was the first and only vehicle to do it. "By golly," he exulted, "the best doggone driver in Indiana may just be an old boy from North Carolina." This mood kept him going as he covered the next few miles into town. Nevertheless, that is when it happened. He was approaching the first stoplight on a street shiny with ice when suddenly he realized that his brakes would not hold. Merely touching the pedal was enough to send the car spinning out of control and into the curb. At five-miles-an-hour the foot-high impediment rebounded him smartly back onto the roadway, but it happened so fast that he felt dizzy. Not so quick, however, that he did not recognize a message when he got one. *Well, maybe I'm not really the best driver in Indiana, after all,* he confessed. *But I know that God is.* Suddenly, words from his version of the song softly played back through his mind again, and that is when he had an epiphany. "*By Ned, I think I finally did it; I just high-geared the mountain!*"

CHAPTER 38

The first harbingers of spring brought with them a powerful uplift to Jesse's spirit; and after another round of mid-terms, this was exactly what he needed. While his G.O. scores showed definite improvement, they still were quite disappointing. Poor grades, however, were not the only reason he felt blue. To gaze continuously upon a never-changing landscape of gray and white was enough to dim the brightest hope. Yet, what else could one expect from a sky so jealous of the love between earth and sunshine that it conspired daily to keep them apart? Mid-western winters are very different from those in the Tar-heel State, causing Jesse to recall Sir Walter Raleigh's famous proclamation that North Carolina was the "Goodliest land under the sun."

On his first trip home in March, the trees were just beginning to bud. This was especially noticeable along the banks of the Kentucky River where the view was unbelievable. Dark verdant swellings at the tips of bare branches stood in stark contrast to the lingering drab of winter, and this followed the river wherever it wound. Springtime, that great painter of life, was just beginning to splash its colors all across the hinterland on a canvas illuminated by the brightest sun he'd seen in months. It reminded him of Hoot Owl Hollow when the world was still fresh from creation. Wonderful is the splendor of earth during its vernal renewal, an unfinished masterpiece for the soul.

It probably surprised Jesse more than anybody when his final grades in G.O. showed that he had not faired too badly. In fact, he did well enough to receive credit for both parts. Thus, he now was free to concentrate on meeting the entrance requirements. Admitted to I. U. with deficits in calculus and Spanish, he agreed to remedy this during the summer between years one and two.

With UNC-Asheville less than five miles away, it was the obvious choice to accomplish this. Back home by early afternoon, he usually headed for the den with one eye trained on his studies and the other on a new TV program called Mary Hartman Mary Hartman. Considered by many to be rather avant-garde, he could do little to dissuade the girls from watching it. Indeed, they sat glued to the set until their hour was up, then it was his turn, so he insisted they join him in viewing the PTL Club. This show, hosted by Jim and Tammy Bakker, had real redemptive value and, at least, it featured no tawdry romantic affairs to pollute the young and impressionable mind.

Butch, their overweight Boston bulldog, did not approve of either production. It was his habit to spend the afternoon spread out across the top of the recliner watching for his soul mate, Maggie, to come home. They shared exactly the same sentiments about daytime television, with neither having much use for it. The moment Butch spotted her driving into the carport he would leap from his perch, going for the door and often times just skimming past the top of Jesse's head. This never failed to prompt a fight between the two, with the Boston being the one most likely to draw first blood.

"Well, at least Butch is glad to see me!" Maggie would claim, once she opened the door. "What's the matter, Boy, has Daddy been mean to you again? Look at that, his tongue's a hanging out; poor little fellow."

"Yeah, and look at that big grin; he thinks he whipped me," Jesse complained. "Here, let me wash my hand, this will probably leave a scar I'll carry to my grave. I'd get rid of that meat grinder if it was up to me!"

Song titles and lyrics from the era defined the summer for it was almost like a song, but it all ended too soon, putting Jesse back on the road again. The house still hadn't sold and with no buyers in sight his only option was to continue to rely on the Vega.

Quickly it became obvious that his second year would be far different from the first. He held no illusions this time, however, knowing that neither the school nor Maggie would tolerate anything less than success.

Yet, he somehow still managed to make it home two weekends out of three during the semester. The weather continued to cooperate unusually well except for two occasions; the first took place at Thanksgiving when he spent Sunday night in Louisville. A deep snowfall kept most traffic from proceeding further north for the night. However, next morning it was as if a miracle had occurred; a warm rain during the night had melted most of it, allowing him to make it to Bloomington before the start of his second class.

The next event occurred the first Sunday morning he was back in

Bloomington, following the Christmas break. He had returned a day early hoping to start the new semester feeling rested and fresh. He awoke a few minutes past eight and just lay there marveling at the sight of sunlight streaming through the window. In January, this was a rare sight indeed. *Looks nice,* he mused, *I may go out and take a little walk this afternoon.* He then switched on the radio.

"Downtown Bloomington, at ten minutes past eight, has thirteen degrees below zero," the announcer clicked off each word. Remarkably, during the next six weeks not once did the thermometer move above the freezing point, and every night the temperature dropped to below zero.

Finally, the second years ended, yet long before it did plans were well underway to move the family to Indiana. The house still had not sold and no evidence existed that it ever would, so it was time to act accordingly. They would seek suitable tenants and rent it, hopefully for enough to meet the monthly payment.

Driving home the last day of the semester proved to be an experience equal to his first trip back. All of nature seemed to be celebrating with him; a lovely fragrance filled the air, birds were singing, and the trees and grass had a glow about them that bordered on the surreal. Jesse found it astounding, but the Vega drove like a new car, handling with unbelievable power and precision. It did, that is, until he got within sight of home and that is when things went haywire. A sudden backfire set it to bucking and bolting like an irate Brahman bull. Now barely able to move along, the motor wheezed and sputtered out just enough power to make it into the carport before conking out.

"Hey!" Jesse yelled. "What's the matter with this pile of junk, anyway?" The fact that he had been in such a good mood earlier probably saved his foot, for otherwise it may have been broken over a piece of plunder that refused to move another inch.

Next day it hit him while listening to a mechanic say what he already knew, the engine had blown. "How many miles this thing got on it?" He asked while rolling a soggy cigar around on his tongue.

That is when he saw it. *Well, I'll be dogged,* Jesse thought. *The last trip it would ever have to make and it got me right up to the front door!* He felt compelled to refocus back on the mechanic, and what he had to say.

"You don't mean to tell me it's got over seventy-two thousand miles on it? Well, Son, you'd better get that thing put in the Guinness book of records, because nobody's ever had a Vega to do that before. Nope, you've got yourself one-of-a-kind here, buddy!"

"Yes sir," Jesse agreed. "You're right there! It's definitely a one-of-a-kind, and the best car I'll probably ever own."

Although driven hard with no extra maintenance, the little sedan had traveled almost three times its expected mileage without once failing him. Averaging twenty-eight miles to the gallon, the vehicle had still yet another redeeming factor; it rode comfortably or else how could he have ever stood it? Most remarkable of all, however, was the fact that it traveled just as far as it needed to, right down to the inch.

The summer of '77 was a time like none other. It was both the happiest of times and the saddest of times.

It was the happiest because the family could now be together full-time again. In addition, Terri graduated high school and they found renters ready to move in as soon as the townhouse in Bloomington was ready.

It was the saddest of times, because Elvis died. That and what happened between Claude Earl and Laura.

Max had long been extolled by the residents of Sweetwater for his fish-fry cookouts. He and his wife, Gayle, liked to move their gas-fired cooking apparatus onto Wade and Edith's lawn and start cooking. This was especially true on summer holidays such as the Fourth of July. In many ways, these events were reminiscent of the Grand-Ole-Opry Saturday nights.

Folding chairs were scattered across the lawn to form a wide semi-circle around Mae's husband Johnny and their two boys, Steve and Robbie, as they, along with several neighbors, played Bluegrass and Mountain Music. Wade, as usual, was right at the center of things. "How about you boys playing, 'Faded Love' for me; I'll dedicate it to my old girl friends, because most of 'em still feel that way about me."

"I'm sure they do," Edith smiled sweetly. "I've always thought of you as being a little lackluster, myself!"

Laura came early, bringing with her both Ollie and her son Ralph. Unfortunately, a first cousin named Eric had tagged along, too. Considered as quite the ladies man, he lived in Chattanooga, however, his good looks and charm tended to get him into a lot of trouble. He now was working on a third divorce. With three kids and two ex-wives to support, it kept him a trifle worried about maintaining the lifestyle he had become accustomed to. However, no one would have ever suspected this, not the way he kept horsing around with Laura and the other females present. How he saw it was that any woman who wandered within reach of his busy hands was fair game. A noticeable halo of "white-lightening" constantly surrounded his persona.

Eric had just pulled Laura over into his lap when Claude Earl, Willard, and Hester drove up; Edith gasped at the sight. It had been her hope to get Laura and Claude Earl together during the weekend, but not after this. By the way, no one should ever think of Edith being a matchmaker; she merely felt the pair belonged together and wanted do her part.

Claude Earl helped his mother find a seat next to Maye Morrow and Dolly Pierson. Hester had recently suffered a heart attack, yet she refused to allow anyone to give her more than a minimum amount of assistance. Her strongly expressed intention was to make a full recovery, and she intended to do it on her own. That was when Claude Earl spotted Laura and Eric and for a moment, he was stunned. Quickly, however, he snapped out of it. "*By golly, I don't have to stand around here and look at that, not by a long shot.*" Moments later, he was gone.

All night long he brooded in the "sugar-shack," a two-bedroom bungalow set just around the curve and above Wade and Edith's place. Arnold had built the place for weekend and summer use, yet it worked equally well for pouting sessions, too. Feeling shell shocked, his insides were about as numb as the time a two-hundred-and-ten-volt power line had knocked him senseless.

Laura never realized what had happened; she saw him drive up, but then he was gone. The episode seemed so strange and perplexing that it left her feeling empty. He *always manages to do that*, she grumbled. *Maybe I'm wasting my time thinking about him anyway, and the way he acted; why it was like he didn't want to be around me. He's probably embarrassed about* that *letter, but I had to be myself and be honest. So, I guess if he doesn't like honesty, things wouldn't have worked out anyway."*

Momentous events may seem to move in a linear fashion; however, in general this not true. Indeed, they tend to occur much more sporadically, having extended periods of dormancy followed by frenzied episodes of activity. Such, it appears, was the case involving Keith's secret and all matters related to it. Instinctively, Edith realized this and seemingly was content just to let the years roll along with the expectation that the truth would ultimately surface. Little did she know that the period of latency would soon be over, and like the lilies of springtime, how welcome would be the bloom!

CHAPTER 39

Two days following Elvis's death Wade and Edith, on their way to Marion, stopped to stay the night with Jesse and his family. It was customary for the couple to spend a few days in August with Edith's brother, Arnold, and his wife, Inez. On this trip, however, their travels would serve an additional purpose. Edith had an appointment with "a specialist" in Asheville, a referral by her doctor in Robbinsville.

"What's it for?" Maggie asked, feeling uncertain how best to phrase the question.

"Greed, that's what it's for, pure and simple greed. Doctor Jensen no doubt's a good friend of this feller and I figure he's pushing her to send him a few patients. Now, don't take me wrong, I love Doctor Jensen to death, but they ain't a thing wrong with me that a good dose of salts wouldn't cure."

Next morning they left early, Wade wanted plenty of time to reach the medical park where her appointment was scheduled.

Stepping from the car, Edith wasted no time in admiring the beautifully landscaped surroundings of Dr. Smithfield's office. Her wrinkled brow had been that way since the first light of dawn, "Looks like it could start any minute," she scowled. "They's some bad looking clouds up there and the weatherman said it might storm." Standing just inside the noted Endocrinologist's door she was waiting impatiently for her husband to catch up, "Wade, for Pete's sake, will you please hurry, I don't want to get caught in this."

"My lord, Edith, I've never seen anybody like you. They said there was a thirty percent chance of rain today and, besides that, we could use it. Ever since we left the house yesterday, you've been looking for a storm and it's starting to get on my nerves. If I was you, I'd quit worrying about it; you ain't no more liable to get hit by a tornado than anybody else is."

"Well, you ain't me and common sense tells you to be careful when it looks this way. I wish you'd quit acting like you ain't never been off Sweetwater before, and for goodness sakes hike them britches up!" Her voice had changed into a loud-chiding whisper.

Once inside, the pair moved past several people seated in the waiting room, making their way to the glassed-in front desk. The petite occupant, a blond woman in her mid-forties, did a good job at ignoring their presence. Dressed to look much younger than she really was, the receptionist seemed intent on spending a few menopausal minutes beating her typewriter into submission. Edith, unaccustomed to such treatment, dealt with the matter directly; "Excuse me, Miss, but I need you to serve me."

The typing stopped in mid-stroke; the operator snapped to her feet, brushed off the back of her pleated skirt, and then wheeled sharply around to confront another pesky patient.

"I'll have you to know I'm not a waitress and they don't pay me enough to be treated like one either. What do you want, anyway?" The steel in her voice had a razors edge.

"Oh, I'm sorry about that, but, Honey, you just keep looking and someday there'll be a *good* job for you." Sympathy accompanied every word, but Wade knew better.

"Oh, please!" she glared. "Just use the sign in sheet, or do you want me to 'X' it for you?"

"No, but thank you, anyway." Edith then lifted the pen and pointed it like a dart, waving it back and forth. "Now, right there's the trouble; you just learn how to read and write and before you know it one of these cafes here will put you on. You just wait and see!"

Wade had heard enough, "Edith, I think I'm going back outside and look around a little bit. I may even go get myself a pack of cigarettes, I'm just about out." With that, he was gone, leaving Edith to find a seat near a pleasant-looking woman about her own age. They exchanged smiles, but no words until several minutes passed. Edith was first to break the silence. "Excuse me, but do you live here in Asheville?"

"No, actually, I live down near Belmont, but my daughter lives in Marion. She's a nurse over there and thinks there's nobody like Dr. Smithfield. You know, she wouldn't give up until I made myself an appointment with him."

Nonchalantly, Edith used the back of her hand to brush away a spot of previously undetected cigarette ash from her black polyester slacks. "Our home is over in Robbinsville, but we have a son who lives here in Asheville. We come up yesterday and I didn't sleep a wink last night. Never can when I'm in a strange bed, especially when it's stormy weather. Well, anyhow, my doctor at home made me this appointment because she thinks I'm too negative, but personally I don't think so. She's got me on a lot of blood pressure medicine, too, which I probably don't need, and they ain't no telling what this feller will do. What did you say you come for?"

"Oh, I'm a diabetic and as far as I know everything else is all right, but you know how children are when they think you're getting old, especially if they've already lost a parent. Why, I feel and act as good right now as I did twenty years ago."

Nodding in agreement, Edith would not be satisfied until she dug deeper. "I used to know a family there at home who moved to Belmont; did you ever meet anybody by the name of Grindstaff… Junior or Melba Grindstaff?"

"No, I don't think so...well, now wait a minute maybe I did know some people by that name, but that was so many years ago. Yes, they moved in next door to us, but we only stayed there a little while. My husband and I hadn't been married very long and we were just renting the place. Why, I doubt that we lived there for more than two or three months. As I recall it, though, they were nice folks who worked at one of the mills; times were awful hard back then. Now that you mention it, however, I do remember them saying they were from the mountains. What was the name of the place you said you were from?"

"Robbinsville."

"Yes, that was it, we talked about that because at one time I was engaged to a boy from there. He got real sick and never could get over it."

Edith felt chill spreading goose bumps down her arms. The receptors of an innate sixth sense queued up for action. "If you don't mind me asking, what's your name?"

"Kathleen Allen, but why do you ask?"

"Did it used to be Akers?"

"Yes, as a matter of fact it did, but how in the world could you know that?" Kathleen's rising sense of curiosity matched that of Edith's. "Why, you're the girl Keith was engaged to… Keith Rose, my brother."

"Well, my goodness gracious! I can't believe this! So you're the sister I never met. You're, now let me think a minute, you're... Edna?"

"No, Edith."

"Edith... Why yes, of course it is! Please forgive me, but it's been a lot of years and I never did get a chance to meet you. You know with Keith getting sick and then us losing Earl, all at the same time was more than I could take. Then later I met Hobart and gradually just lost touch with everybody, but you know there's hardly been a day I haven't thought of him; he was so pitiful. By the way, how is he?"

"He's at the Oak Forest nursing home in Marion, I try to go and see him two or three time a year. But Arnold and Inez are close by and can go about every week or two. I guess you don't remember it, but we did meet one time just briefly there at the hospital."

"This is getting to be stranger by the moment. My daughter Luella is the director of nursing and the administrator at Oak Forest, and, oh my goodness, she's always talking about this little gentleman who she thinks is so sweet. I recall her saying that he'd lost his memory and was real religious." Kathleen finished her thoughts while searching through a large black leather pocketbook for Kleenex. When found, it took several tissues to shore up mascara that was dangerously close to eroding away. The silence of the next few moments said more than a thousand words could. Only the soft sounds of sniffling passed between them.

When Kathleen spoke again, it was to change the subject. "Edith, before we part could you tell me about Hester. I've thought about her so many times and the burden she's had to bear."

This was the opening Edith had hoped for; "Well, you'll have to tell me about that, but as far as Hester goes, she's not doing too good. She's had one bad heart attack that we know of, and maybe another'n. Hester won't take care of herself or listen to what anybody says. Sometimes I wonder if she wants to die. Her and Willard have just one child, a boy named Claude Earl who still lives with them there in Gastonia."

"So, she and Willard stayed together then, and I guess their boy was named after Earl and Claude. Well I'm glad they didn't seperate. Sometime before he got sick, Keith was suspicious that she'd been stepping out on Willard, so he took it on himself to do some spying. I didn't know what he was up to until later, but by that time he was satisfied she wasn't involved with Claude Conway, who he suspected. Now, I have to say I didn't approve of him doing that, and told him so, too. However, that's when Earl revealed to Keith about his being an agent for the

Revenue Department and how Hester had been helping him with the investigation. Actually, he had to tell Keith this to keep him from ruining everything. Of course, Keith told me, knowing I could keep a secret, and I have too, right up until now." Kathleen chuckled softly, temporarily she had run aground on a sandbar of the past, but a wave of reality suddenly washed her back to the present, buoyed along by Edith's response.

"Well, I'm glad he could trust somebody, he certainly didn't feel that way with me!"

Kathleen wisely chose not to wade in where the water looked so troubled. "Well, anyway, Earl let Keith know just how dangerous this thing was, and that he may have already tipped the suspects off."

"He may have," Edith agreed, remembering the attempted break-in.

"The law had reason to believe there was some kind of tie between the evangelistic ministry and a moonshine operation. Almost from the start, they knew Earl wasn't involved, and so they enlisted his help. Now I'm supposing this, but Earl, no doubt, figured that since Hester was their most faithful member she knew just about everything that was going on, so he's asked her to help. Before long, though, things got so hot he made her quit, probably saving her life."

Edith agreed. "It very well could have, but the worry from all this has really changed Hester… I doubt you'd even recognize her now."

"That's why I mentioned a burden. She may know absolutely nothing, but I believe she does. Just think about it; the poor woman was right there in the middle of things. Personally, I don't think the two they executed were the *actual* murderers; they've played a big part no doubt, but the real one may still be on the loose. If so, then for Hester just to open her mouth could've got her killed, Willard, and their boy, too, for that matter."

Edith nodded in agreement. "With the passing of time and since nothing else has happened they've probably thought she knew very little and just let it go. That could've been her salvation."

Kathleen kept the thought moving. "Looking back, I firmly believe they meant to also kill Keith, if he hadn't got sick. With him snooping around on Hester, they thought he was spying on them."

Edith smiled grimly, "You probably never knew this, but even after Earl lost his life Boyle and Fowler kept their eye on Keith. It's obvious they thought he was an undercover agent, too, and even made a trip to Robbinsville. Remember Keith been there before he got sick and I guess they thought he might have confided in me. Of course, once they learned he was permanently brain damaged, and I never came forward they lost interest in us both."

"There's something I need to ask about, Edith; do you know anything about Earl's Bible? Keith and I gave it to him for a birthday present not long before he died. It had leather binding with gold lettering and gilt-edged pages. Fowler and Boyle claimed Earl still had it with him when they left that night, but when they got back it was gone. If that be true, then it means whoever killed Earl must have done something with it. They had no way of proving this, and the state claimed they merely destroyed it; hoping to manufacture an alibi. Now, my question is; why would they have even mentioned it if it wasn't true. They weren't smart enough to come up with something like that, besides it would have been a weak alibi, anyway. In my opinion, the whereabouts of Earl's Bible could very be the key to this whole thing."

The conversation suddenly lagged, leaving Edith time enough to formulate a question that she now felt was hardly worth the asking. "Keith was bothered over something just before he got sick and I've never been able to learn what." Quickly, she then outlined the entire episode before posing her inquiry. "Do you have any idea what it was?"

"No, I'm afraid not, but remember just before that he'd been concerned about Hester. However, like I said, he satisfied his mind about her, so I doubt that was it; otherwise I can't help you. By the way, whatever happened to Jack Woodcock and Claude Conway? After the execution, I tried to put it all behind me and pretty well lost contact completely. I do know that Jack got off relatively light, but as I understand it Claude Conway was never charged with anything."

"About three years ago Jack died of liver failure; drunk his-self to death, I reckon. Claude Conway, though, the last I heard of him he'd moved back to Gastonia after living in Robbinsville for several years. Took a church there to pastor, from what I hear."

Kathleen forced a frown that definitely was at variance with the twinkle in her eyes. "Even at his age, I'd bet he's still trying to keep the ladies happy." Suddenly her demeanor changed; "But I determined a long time ago that Jack probably was the one who did it and just left it all in the hands of the Lord. I knew that even he would have to face the judgment someday."

"Vengeance is mine, saith the Lord!" Edith nodded to a cadence of her own. Kathleen reached for her purse again, this time to dig around trying to locate a large tube of lipstick. Edith waited until she found it before continuing; "I've always felt Preacher Conway had a lot to do with it, too; truthfully, I never liked the man myself, even though an awful lot of people seem to think he's a saint."

Pursing her lips after a light touching with the reddener, Kathleen's response was finally forthcoming; "At first I was suspicious of him, too, I guess, though, in fairness, I was of everybody back then. Nevertheless, the more I thought about it, the more I realized he was just a womanizing hypocrite. Now, Aunt Ida though, she went to her grave believing he was the one. Without question, Claude could have done more to protect Earl, but in my opinion, he was interested only in saving his own hide. What Earl saw in him I'll never know, but he liked him and that's just the way it was. The law felt he was innocent, and I did, too… no, I'm satisfied now it was Jack Woodcock; that man was evil." A coarse shudder suddenly reverberated through her entire upper body, leaving in its wake a trance-like stare. She quickly recovered, however, asking, "Did you ever see Earl's picture? I have one that was made the night he died."

The black and white photo handed to Edith was of obvious professional quality; she positioned it beneath the table lamp for better viewing. Pictured was a handsome, blond haired young man standing beside a podium with a smiling Reverend Claude Conway on the other. Both were holding their Bibles. "My goodness, wasn't he good looking, and oh what a shame! Is this the Bible you mentioned?"

Kathleen answered with a nod as tears seeped to the surface from a wellspring of an endless supply. "I'll never get over it if I live to be a thousand and I miss him every day. To your question, though, yes that's it. In the enlargement I have at home you can see the special script in gold lettering; it's unique to this edition. You know they were starting a new revival and had asked a photographer to come by after the meeting. They'd planned on giving an autographed picture to anyone who pledged financial support. The newspapers heard about this picture and tried their best to buy it; that sorry Claude Conway would have given them his copy, but we wouldn't release it. Mother even hired a lawyer to keep him from doing it. For us that would have been unfaithful to Earl's memory, doing something like that just for the publicity.

Perhaps it was because of Kathleen's emotional state that she jumped so noticeably when a voice from the front cracked over their heads. The sound of it was not unlike that of frozen timber breaking in a forest; "Miss Allen, Dr. Smithfield is waiting for you!"

Rising to her feet, Kathleen received back her treasured print, but seemed flustered. "I need to get your address, Edith; would you just leave it at the front desk?"

"No, I don't trust that woman for one minute; here let me write it down. Do you think you might go by and see Keith at Oak Forest?"

Kathleen looked troubled when she answered. "That's something I'll have to pray about, Edith. I just don't know… "

Edith now had her purse balanced on both knees and was producing the requested information on the back of a used envelope. That is when she noticed the presence of others in their midst. One was a tall and very handsome man with a full head of reddish-blond hair, and he was in the company of a most gracious front-desk clerk. She was barely recognizable now, however, so dramatic was the change in her demeanor.

"Michael," she gushed, "you don't ever stop and talk with me like you used to, and you know how hard I work getting you in to see the doctor. Now when you leave you're always in such a hurry, so what do I have to do to get you to slow down for a few minutes; it gets lonesome out here." Fixing an icy stare on Edith, she continued; "And you'd never believe how rude some people can be."

"We'll do lunch one day when my schedule permits," the big man laughed. "Then you can tell me all about it; but look, you've got this nice lady waiting here to see Dr. Smithfield." With that, he bowed slightly, twirled around with a gesture that invited her to enter as he held open the door. Kathleen smiled and accepted his offer gracefully, an act that was not favorably received by the front desk.

"I'll hold you to that," she called back while in pursuit of Kathleen.

Michael looked over at Edith, and then flashed a dazzling smile that exposed an enormous array of beautiful white teeth. "Oh, the hazards of the road and one can never know what dangers lurk there," he bemoaned. Sitting down on the spot recently vacated by Kathleen he hastily scribbled out a short note before folding it neatly.

Edith stared at the well-dressed representative long and hard before speaking, "You look awfully familiar, have I seen you before?"

"I wouldn't be surprised," he responded warmly, "I've been to a lot of places in my day. I don't mean to be nosey, but did I see Robbinsville written on that envelope you just gave the lady?"

"Well, yes you did, actually, I live on Sweetwater; do you know where it is?"

"I should say I do, spent some of my best days over there when I was just a pup." The sparkle in his violet-blue eyes matched perfectly that of his laughter. "By the way, read this when you get time; it may mean something to you." With that, he handed her the note and was back on his feet. "Say?" He asked. "Is Jesse fixing to move his family to Indiana?"

"He will be in a week or two. But how did you know that?"

"Oh word gets around; there are no secrets here in Asheville! Look, I don't think Jesse would take any wooden nickels from anybody, but he does have a weakness for sand dollars, so I think we all better to keep an eye on him."

Edith looked puzzled. "He'll bear watching," she agreed.

Michael glanced at his watch. "Well, I'll be dog-gone, would you look at that, and I'm supposed to be across town right now."

Edith watched as he, briefcase in hand, reached for the door, but there was one final word forthcoming. "Be sure and say hello to Jesse for me, and tell Wade to stay out of those rock and roll places, like Fontana, he could be playing with dynamite." Without further ado, he turned and left. For a long moment, she just sat in stunned silence thinking. *This has got to be the strangest day of my life.* While slowly shaking her head in wonder she continued her thoughts; *and how in this world does he know who Jesse and Wade are?* Recalling the note, she read it aloud.

Thou must go to the valley
And walk the dark glen
Seek ye the Light
To be found therein.

With eyes now blind
Yet shall you see
Quickened by the dark
To the Light seeking thee.

Why, that's the poem Keith showed me right before he got sick, but I can't remember it having a second verse. Suddenly it was as if a light came on, causing her to rush for the door. She ignored the lightening that coursed across a blackened sky to hurry outside. "Oh, he got away," Edith murmured, "well dog-gone." Now with a wide smile cleaving her face she repeated the words, but this time they came much more slowly, "well… dog... gone."

CHAPTER 40

Ultimate success in any endeavor requires action, and Einstein said; "Nothing happens until something moves." Although completely oblivious to such rarified thought, the Gernons, nevertheless, took action and made the big move. Remarkably, when they did the population center of America shifted slightly to the direction of Indiana.

Maggie, longsuffering and harried, stayed close behind the van that ferried their furniture north, and although they pushed hard, the trip still took nearly 10 hours. Jesse watched with anxious eyes; he had arrived two days earlier to make certain all the utilities were on and to get the townhouse ready for occupancy. Nearly an hour before they got there he drove out to the city limits and waited, hoping to give them a cheery welcome. Terri would not be with them, she had just enrolled at UNC-Asheville. *Things will never be the same.* He began to brood. *I should never have started this, and we'd all still be together*. It took conscious effort to push aside such thoughts, and that turned out to be a good thing. For after driving five hundred miles and listening to Wade, Lisa, and Butch harp at each other, Maggie was not in the mood for it. This became evident the moment she stepped into a house where the humidity and temperature both hovered around the one hundred degree mark. "Whew! Why, it's like an oven in here," she complained, "we can't stand this; let's get some windows open!"

Hot weather and tempers are a bad mixture, with rational behavior usually becoming the first casualty. Accordingly, they unloaded the truck in near silence with only an occasional hurt look or curt nod passing between the two principles.

Some thirty minutes before dark, one of the worst electrical storms they both had ever witnessed took place. For over an hour, the sky flashed unceasingly, four to five jagged streaks at a time, creating thunderous explosions immediately overhead. "Pretend it's the London blitz," Jesse cracked.

"Humph," Maggie responded with a look that could clabber milk;" I fail see anything funny about this."

August in the mid-West can be brutal, but so can November, as Maggie could attest to later. A few days before Thanksgiving she stepped off the city bus, and by the time she had walked the two blocks home her hair and outer garments were a glaze of ice. However, Mother Nature's most spectacular production was yet to come. Jesse, busy in his clinics, was now the most content he had been in two years and except for a brief encounter with the flu, had no complaints.

It was late January when the customary bitter cold arrived, bringing with it daily accumulations of new snow and ice. Still, the weather was not truly bad until the blizzard hit. For several days, all the newscasts had been predicting it, yet school administration pooh-poohed the expected impact. In the face of mounting concern, the dean of schools sent out the following memo: "Indiana University, with its long history and dedication to higher learning, has never yielded to the whims of nature. Therefore, we do not anticipate any interruption to our regular schedule of classes due to inclement weather. All faculty and students are advised to plan accordingly." Bravely stated, the word went forth just one day before the storm hit and Jesse prepared to do as instructed.

The next morning, a Tuesday, he was awakened at 5:30 by a call from the school. "Jesse?" an excited voice almost shouted. "All appointments have been cancelled! They've just closed the University because this storm is far worse than anybody expected."

Snow fell hard all day, and by nightfall, the wind had picked up. Never had they heard it roar like that and at times shriek eerily like a siren. All agreed that going to bed early was a good idea and when they did, it was with a thankful heart that still had power and heat. It was around 2.00 a.m. when Jesse awoke to the unmistakably sound of breaking glass. Immediately, he knew it came from Maggie's room. Stepping through her door was tantamount to walking into a meat-locker; yet even more disturbing, was the noise. The wind was a howling monster. One of the windowpanes had blown out, allowing the fingers of a horrible blizzard to reach in. Desperate measures were obviously called for, lest the chill quickly overwhelm them. Since only snowmobiles could travel, rescue would be a long time in coming.

Providence can peer beyond the shroud of time and had already arranged for a solution to be in place. A large piece of heavy cardboard lay at his feet and even though his fingers were already numb, he awkwardly managed to cut it into three rectangles, each larger than the opening. Gale forces exceeding 80 miles an hour were screaming to get in while he taped the sections into plies, hoping they would be strong enough to hold. Meanwhile, Becky and Lisa kept trying to push open the door, thus distracting Maggie from her effort to help. She was not kind when swooshing them out into the hall.

With pellets of ice striking the floor like BB shot, it took only moments for Jesse to realize he had never experienced cold like this before. Ungloved hands, now completely unfeeling, were barely able to fold the cardboard and pass it through the opening. Once he began pushing against the wind's extreme pressures it did not appear he could do it, but that is when, from some unknown resource, the strength he needed suddenly materialized. The makeshift pane slid precisely into place shutting the storm's awful fury outside. Minutes passed in relative quiet; the dreadful noise now sounded further away and although still unbearably cold, the air somehow seemed less hostile to life. Fortunately, the fix continued to hold, yet in an effort to isolate the room they pressed quilts down and against the door to seal it off. Jesse's sleep was fitful from that time until dawn.

Daylight brought with it the silence of a tomb. Nothing was moving and what he saw outside was unbelievable! Before him lay a frozen ocean, one complete with motionless breakers that stretched as far as the eye could see. Waves of alternating troughs and crests completed the scene of perfect white. Looking straight down from his bedroom window, Jesse saw a six-foot snowdrift in front of their front door.

Lisa came forward with a tearful confession; the evening before her curiosity had made her do it. Seeing a frosted over windowpane in her mother's room, she wondered what would happen if she barely touched it, despite having been warned against doing such. According to her, she had struggled long and hard with the decision, but at last she did it and that is when a tiny crack appeared. At first, the hair-like fracture was barely evident, but it grew and grew until the break extended from top to bottom. Still, the window looked just fine. It was keeping the cold out as good as ever, so she went on to bed without giving it another thought. Rising with a guilty conscious, she solemnly vowed, "It won't ever happen again, I swear I've learned my lesson this time!"

Jesse and Maggie could not help but notice the big know-it-all grin pasted on Butch's face; he had heard that one before.

During the final week of his second year, Jesse took Part I of the National

Board Exams in Optometry. Though not mandatory, he, like most in his class, did so in order to avoid the daunting task of facing all three parts at once following graduation. When the results were back he was elated, not only had he passed all sections, he did so with room to spare! The best news, however, was what he made in "Theoretical Optics," G.O. included. He was at the eighty-eighth percentile level, giving him a score well above the average.

Much of his third year revolved around clinical instruction, in both theory and practice, a time when he finally could see patients. It was expected that third year clinicians would spend up to four hours doing just a single eye exam. Since they did not make their own appointments, it was merely by luck of the draw that Miss Frazier came to him. Mary Frazier at age forty-seven was experiencing reading difficulty. *Here's a chance to prescribe a pair of bifocals,* Jesse surmised after reviewing her chart. He felt lucky; this was a rare opportunity in a clinic where most patient's were students from the university, and obviously not old enough to be presbyopic.

Greeting her with his best smile, a warm hand was extended in welcome, "Good afternoon, Miss Frazier, it's a pleasure to meet you."

Ignoring his hand, she asked curtly, "You're not the one I saw last time, are you?" Then without pausing, she proceeded to answer her own question. "No, I see you're not. Well, you better not have been. I told that little snip at the front desk how badly I was treated last year. But she assured me that it wasn't you; well, let's get on with it then; I've dreaded this long enough."

Jesse heard his name paged from the front, so he quickly excused himself. He found a forth-year student waiting nervously at the front desk. "I thought I'd better warn you about this one," he grinned. "Last year I never got to first base with her; she's an old maid and a real pain in the butt. We got into an argument over the bifocal; she wanted one that would last her a lifetime, yet when I tried to explain that it didn't work that way, she had a fit. My advice, Jesse: give her what she wants; just tell her what to expect and then let it be her decision. But you'd better get it in writing," he warned.

Jesse felt both perplexed and glad, perplexed at having to handle such a difficult person, yet glad for the tip. His approach the second time was much more circumspect. "Miss Frazier, as you know our patient information sheet is quite thorough and I see that you've noted special dietary habits; would you mind elaborating?"

"No, I don't mind telling you, I'm a vegetarian, but I don't understand what not eating carrion has to do with eyesight. I know this much, though, the minute I leave here you're going to start making fun of me!"

" Oh, no Ma'am!" Jesse quickly replied. "The fact is, I'm essentially a vegetarian, myself. Besides, it would be most unethical to disparage a patient, ever. I assure you, Miss Frazier, you have nothing to worry about there!" Seeking then to find foundational data made of something less slippery, he stepped onto the well-trodden path of employment history. "I find, too, that you didn't specify an occupation; what should we write in that space, please?"

"*None*," she responded. Although she used only one word, it was enough to brighten Jesse's corner for it gave him a handle on things. Here was a fellow believer.

"Oh, *Nun*... well, how nice." Having known no other Catholics except Dave, Jesse, nevertheless, held them in high regard. Besides, only recently he had read somewhere that certain nuns could leave off their habits; perhaps Sister Mary was one of those. "May I say, Sister, that it's indeed an honor to serve you?"

"What are you talking about? Are you ridiculing me?"

"Oh, no Ma'am; you see, I need to make a confession, well perhaps that's an inappropriate phrase here, but I grew up not knowing Catholics; so should I call you Sister Mary? I just want to be respectful to both you and your calling." Jesse felt edgy, serious doubts were beginning to surface about his patient-management skills.

"My goodness," she exclaimed. "You think I'm a nun just because I marked on there I'm not married; so you think I must be an off-duty nun. Well let me ask you, buster, since when did nuns start wearing makeup, anyway?"

Jesse saw that he now was in too deep to wiggle out gracefully, so he tried slithering by sideways; "Miss Frazier, I don't know if nuns wear make-up or not; I never knew one. However, I think I've made a big mistake here. It's all my fault and I apologize, but I thought I heard you say N-U-N was your occupation, when actually is was N-O-N-E; now, can we please just start over?"

They, indeed, did, and remarkably, the exam went quite well from that point forward. At the end, he honored her request by prescribing a "lifetime" bifocal, but only after warning of the likelihood that she could get headaches from wearing such strong lenses. He also explained that bifocal power needs at the age of forty-seven are far less than those worn by the elderly." The last he saw of her was at the front desk where she stated matter-of-factly, "I don't know whether to feel insulted or complimented by being called a nun."

Jesse said. “I meant nothing but to be complimentary, Miss Frazier. A bright countenance like yours could fool anybody.”

To his amazement, he watched a lie turn into truth; her face brightened for a moment, but slowly the glow began to fade. *Maybe she’ll remember how good it feels to be happy and let it happen again,* he smiled.

CHAPTER 41

Bloomington, the epitome of a college town, is an exquisite place. Yet there is a need for more than structures and streets to create the heart and soul of an academic community. There must be bookstores, patched sleeved and pipe-puffing professors, libraries, bicycles, stadium, and gymnasiums. Even more, however, there must be that raucous, life sucking, and hell-raising presence of the student; otherwise, it would have no reason to exist at all.

During Jesse's last year he came truly to appreciate three of his fellow clinicians, while they were externs at the Fort Campbell U.S. Army Hospital in Kentucky. Pat, from St. Louis, had plans to be married soon after her graduation, and Jesse thoroughly enjoyed listening to her talk about it. Jan was also from I. U. and a great conservationist while Brenda was the only outsider, coming from Southern College of Optometry at Memphis. Housing was in a pre-World War II facility where each had a private room. In truth, these were little more than tiny cubes of roach-riddled steam baths. After spending just one night there, it became obvious that in order to survive they would need to purchase individual room air-conditioners, along with an array of bug-sprays and poisons.

The building's central lounge provided place at night where they could talk eye care and discuss problems encountered during the day. More importantly, however, it afforded them an opportunity to support one another during the low times. Discouragement and melancholy are twin thugs that often prey on dreary souls when away from home.

Whether or not to stay on base for the weekend was never a serious consideration for any of them, even though it would have made good sense. Yet even the idea of such seemed alien to their thinking. In fact, they were all so eager to go that by Friday morning their cars were packed and ready for a quick get away. Nonetheless, Jesse liked his time at "Campbell," especially the fact that he could patients there much like he would in a private office.

Major Richardson, the clinic director, often invited them to his home for cookouts and volleyball. The contests actually proved to be neighborhood events that bordered on blood sport. His wife, the consummate host, had a knack for making her guests feel both right at home and very special. She enjoyed finding out what their favorite music was so she could play it during the dinner hour. Once, when invited to the officers club for a "beef and burgundy night," Jesse was amazed to find wine spouting continuously from a huge silver fountain. After taking just a curious sip, though, he found himself not nearly so impressed. The most spectacular event of the summer, however, turned out to be a tornado.

Watching a cyclone on the prowl took the prize for drama and it happened late one afternoon when the four were on their way back from the town of Hopkinsville, Kentucky. On occasion, they drove up there to a steakhouse in an attempt to escape the many hazards of Army chow. Pat saw it first causing her to breathlessly point toward a long cylindrical tube hanging eerily from the sky. Black as midnight, it gently swayed back and forth, as a giant snake would before striking. The phenomenon seemed even more sinister by the fact they were outside the storm path and driving in bright sunlight. Since it obviously was five miles or more away and moving in a northeasterly direction, they felt no direct threat, yet, just by seeing it left them awe struck and shaken. Temperatures, just hours before above one hundred degrees, now suddenly dropped into the low seventies, adding to the chill they felt. That evening they had a lot more to talk about than patient care.

At the end of his third year, Jesse took Part II of the National Boards, and once again, his efforts paid off. By passing all sections thus far, he could now begin to study for Part III, the most difficult portion of all. Of course, earning a license to practice was the ultimate objective and most states, including North Carolina, required passing scores in all three parts as a prerequisite to taking their own boards. Prior to his final year Jesse had given little thought to this aspect of his training, but now it loomed ominously on the horizon as a serious threat to his future. Would he wind up finally meeting all the academic requirements only to fail the state boards? If so, then all his work would be for naught. He knew there had been those who had suffered such a fate, and it could happen to him, too.

Increasingly, North Carolina had become the place to practice optometry. New licensees were attracted there in droves, since optometrists there could prescribed both diagnostic and therapeutic drugs. By force of law, only they and those practicing in West Virginia could do so. Ultimately, all states would gain this right, but now it was a powerful inducement to locate there. With so many applicants, the Board was averse to admitting any but the very best, thus the failure rate was exceedingly high. Such odds did not deter Jesse, however, since he did not intend to practice anywhere else. He clearly saw his only option was to dig in and begin the most intensive study session of his life.

On Wednesday night, a week before the Nationals, he was deep in the books when the phone rang. Normally, Maggie usually took such calls and he rarely paid them any attention, but this time was different. Edith had been sick for days, to the point of hospitalization, and it was this knowledge that had him on edge. By cocking an ear, he heard the dreaded words he had half-been expecting all day. "Wait a minute, Doctor Jensen, and I'll get him."

Jesse knew then the caller was Robbinsville's premier physician. "Jesse, this is Elaine Jensen. I'm sorry to bother you, but Mae asked me to call and tell you about Edith."

"Yes," Jesse answered nervously, "I appreciate so much you taking the time to call. How is she? I know she's been sick now for several days and I've been worried about her, but I'm studying for the boards and everybody said I wasn't needed." He felt guilty and it sounded that way.

Sensing his dilemma, Doctor Jensen empathized but continued with her report. "Your mother's seriously ill, Jesse. As you know, we had her in the hospital last week with pneumonia, but she made enough progress that I could send her home. Now, however, she has taken a turn for the worse. I looked at her latest chest film this afternoon and found that the upper right lobe is almost fully obscured and I'm afraid it's cancer. While we haven't done a biopsy, her cytology certainly indicates that probably we're dealing with a malignancy. So I strongly recommend that you come down right away, in order to see her alive. She'll appreciate it and I know the rest of the family will, too… With these conditions you can never know just how much time we've got."

Jesse was devastated; even with four years of work at stake he knew it all meant nothing when compared to this. By setting out at first light, he reached Sweetwater sometime near mid-afternoon and once there noticed immediately that his mother's demeanor was very striking. Although poor in color and looking weak-eyed, she had retained a spunky attitude. "Why, they weren't any need for you to make this trip, Son, I'll be all right. Every time somebody gets one turned crossways, these doctors throw up their hands. It's nothing but a little gas that went the wrong way; I'll take me a big run of salts tonight and be better in the morning, you just wait and see."

Actually, she worsened during the night, making it fortunate that she already had an appointment with Doctor Jensen for 10:30. Jesse insisted on going in with her and when shown the X-rays, he was overwhelmed. Never had he seen a chest film that looked worse. When it was time for the three to talk Edith showed more grit than the other two combined. "Doctor Jensen," she said, "I'm not one bit scared because it ain't my time to go, and I ain't giving up until it is."

This boldness, coming from a woman who had lived most of her life in abject terror of a storm cloud, was stupefying.

"We'll do everything it takes to keep you comfortable, Edith; do you want me to put you back in the hospital?"

"For crying out loud would you listen to this," she protested." Only the sight of a sallow face kept her words from conveying more weight. It was well that she did not catch the slow shake of her doctor's head moving back and forth in sad disbelief. On the way home, Jesse felt an overwhelming need to pray for healing. It was only after he silently agreed to obey the urge that it let up.

"Mother, would you mind if we put this before the Lord when we get home?" he asked. Jesse feared it might serve to undermine her courage, but he need not have worried.

"No, not if it'll make *you* feel better I won't." A weak smile accompanied the peaked look that stared at him. Once in the living room, they knelt together before the couch where Jesse lifted up his petition. It is unfortunate, indeed, that no one else was present there to witness the remarkable event that subsequently took place. When he prayed the words of love were simple and elegant, yet filled with power. For an instant the "now" experience was his again, while scenes from paradise flashed before his eyes. The supplication was short, but when finished the two arose in victory, knowing that she had been touched! Now no longer haggard, her face suddenly radiated a healthy pink; Edith knew it and Jesse did, too. She would live!

Her response should not have surprised him. "Why, I knowed I'd get better," she reveled. "I never had a doubt."

Pleased with this display of faith, Jesse complimented her on it.

"Oh, it ain't that," she smiled. "I just happened to run across something this morning; something you probably forgot about a long time ago, but I want you to have it." With that, she handed him the object; he stared at it for a long minute before dropping it into his shirt pocket. "It was all the sign I needed to know that everything would be all right," she continued. "Besides, I've been thinking about what Gutch said and I think maybe I've got something else figured out, but I can't prove it yet. I will, though, it's all just a matter of time and mine won't come until I do!" she declared emphatically.

Jesse left for Bloomington the next day with one hand clutching a miracle and the other grasping at straws. With less than a week to go, how could there be time enough now to prepare for both the boards and the midterms. The answer to that lay in yet another miracle, one already on its way.

Seeking the isolation he needed, Jesse pulled away from everybody and everything, to hole up in his room. His intentions were to leave the books only long enough for bathroom visits and a quick snack now and then. For three days, he kept at it until he began to feel confident again. Still, he did not take it kindly when Maggie tapped on the bedroom door. "Come on in!" he snapped hatefully.

"You won't believe this," she smiled, "but Mildred Bowdin just called to say she's got us a buyer."

It took a moment for the news to sink in. "Do what?" he asked incredulously. "You mean to tell me that after all this time, and with just a few weeks of school left, the house has actually sold? Well, can you beat that? And it's right at the when we need the money, too."

"Not only that, but we're getting considerably more for it now than we would have four years ago. Heaven only knows, though, how much we need that money right now. I guess we serve an 11:59 God, that's all I can figure. I guess too, this means we won't be living in Asheville, I really believe if He wanted us there, it wouldn't have happened this way. While you've been studying I've put a lot of time into praying that it would sell; you know, if it had sold four years ago that money would all be long gone by now. If we've got it, we'll spend it, and you can bet on that," she remarked pointedly.

Nodding in agreement, knowing looks passed between the two, each knew the truth about the other.

Events suddenly took on a life of their own, midterms, the dreaded national boards, and then the finals, each taken at their appointed time. Subsequently, Jesse felt that his head had been swirled through a cesspool. "I think I've ruptured my brain," he half complained, half joked when it was all over. Graduation lay just ahead and he faced it with absolutely no enthusiasm; somehow, it seemed anti-climatic. Ironically, the very moment he had lived for was finally here, yet the two hundred and ten volts of his previous enthusiasm could now barely power a flashlight.

CHAPTER 42

From the floor of Assembly Hall, the view looked so surreal he had to try hard just to focus on a few of the many thousands of faces gazing down at him. From where he sat, they seemed to stretch all the way to heaven. A cloud of witnesses had gathered for the event; so many, in fact, that it was almost impossible to make out any single person. With the governor, two US senators, and other fine dignitaries only a few feet from him, he could easily see them, but not the ones who really counted. Over five thousand graduates were present, yet not for individual recognition. Each school in the University had done that earlier.

Inevitably, the sweet-sadness that ever attends donning a cap and gown began to envelop him. Jesse's mind wandered back to another Sunday afternoon nearly four years earlier, making him chuckle at the thought. "Now, wasn't that a trip," his inner voice chided, "and here you were so concerned about the younger classmates! My goodness, with such superior knowledge, it's a wonder you needed to go at all." Slowly, his smile began to fade after recalling the hot humid air of Eigenmann Hall and reliving those old familiar feelings again.

Now look what I've done, he grimaced. *With all this rummaging around in my mind, I've pulled up a nightmare... What 's more this was supposed to be my moment of glory, too!* Here was G.O, that slimy monster, was struggling to re-emerge from his subconscious again. Although that age-old dragon had long before tasted the sword, the mere thought of it still made him shudder.

Knowing that we have no problems except those we *think* we do, Jesse stood the idea on its head and decided life could be pleasant if he *thought* it was. This, he found easier to do by focusing on something tangible, which turned out to be the sand dollar Edith handed him on the day of her healing. Fingering it delicately, he, for one golden moment was back to the day they discovered the spring. Again, he could taste the sparkling water that coursed his tongue. *Light for another step; I see it!* His spirit soared. Popping his eyes back open, he suddenly knew exactly where they would be going, Andrews, North Carolina. That settled it then, Andrews was where they would move. Until the house had sold, where to practice was not a question, they just naturally assumed it would be Asheville. Since then, however, exactly that had been the subject of much conversation.

Before moving, however, they must tarry yet for another month in Indiana while waiting on Lisa to graduate from North Bloomington High. The exercises took place at the prestigious IU Eli Lily Auditorium five weeks after Jesse's big day. Afterwards, the family spent the rest of the afternoon just roaming around the IU campus at a time when it was almost deserted. Unexpectedly, this became an unfettered opportunity to explore the beautiful grounds, walk among splendid trees, and laze about the gazebo. It dawned on him that he had never allowed himself to appreciate this great institution the way he should have. Fear of failure is a powerful intimidator. Still, his fondness, his pride, and his love for this marvelous University had never been more evident than it was on this day, the day before he left it forever as a student.

What is a school?
Is it the yards, the rooms, or the names
Could it be the smells, the books
Or, heaven forbid, the games?
A place once feared
But now revered
And, oh yes, memory may get bent
When recalling days long spent
But what is a school? Why, it's a dunce's stool
Where this fool was blessed to sit!

In early April he got the news, he had passed Part III of the boards. He read and re-read the results aloud while standing outside in the chilly air of an overcast day. Although it was not unlike the two dozen that immediately preceded it, the sky suddenly turned golden. The mailbox, located some fifty yards from the house, was a place Butch loved to accompany him to every day, but not merely to check the mail. He loved to trot cockily alongside Jesse while making it obvious to everybody watching that while the world belonged to bulldogs, it was his personal oyster. This time, however, it would be hard to tell who had the biggest grin, he or Jesse.

During the first week of June, they moved to Andrews after finding an older house there. State boards were set to begin in mid-July, so he had ample time to prepare for the week of testing. It would begin with orientation, and then end after a grueling contest that pitted newly educated minds against those belonging to the best optometrists in the nation. With such progressive optometric laws, the profession was under extreme scrutiny by its severest critic, and they all knew it. Ophthalmology would like nothing better than to see optometry give license to some dolt who would then turn around and make a big mess of things. In fact, eye surgeons were sparing no effort when it came to bewailing the hazards of allowing "non-physicians" prescribe "dangerous and potentially blinding" medication. Nevertheless, such discordant tones sounded flat when their own record was exposed. Perhaps, as was proffered by some of the more advanced thinkers in both professions, if a more cooperative spirit could develop, then everyone would benefit; perhaps even the patients. Thus, the gauntlet was down with no quarter asked or given. It all began in the selfsame city, and on the exact day, that Jeffery MacDonald went on trial there for murdering his family.

Better stars than those of the former Green Beret must have determined Jesse's fate, however, "six weeks must pass before he learned of it."

"Oh, no, so that's what they wanted," he would exclaim to the dark at three in the morning. This after thinking through, for at least the hundredth time some obscure question that lingered on to torture his recollection. *Now I see what they wanted. Oh great, well I missed that one, too, and I'll bet you a dollar I've failed the whole thing.* Still, he and Maggie proceeded forward by leasing office space, and to even buying equipment, and interviewing prospective employees, acting as if they already had a license. Maggie must have amazed the angels with her patience, but by the time August 23 rolled around they both were suffering night sweats. Ironically, Wade had just pulled into the driveway when he heard her shouting. She, being the first to reach the mailbox, had just read the results. Not only did they celebrate, but their neighbors, Cecil and Barbara, did so as well. Literally, there was dancing in the street!

Wade, however, had not come with good news; he was there bearing another message. "Me and Max are fixing to take Edith out to Marion Sunday, and then we'll drive her on down to Willard's Monday morning." His face, mere moments before alight with joy, now suddenly turned somber and grave; "Yeah, well you know Hester's had heart trouble now for quite some time. She had a bad attack last year, right after Keith died, and that nearly killed her. Well, she's just had another'n and the doctor said she ain't going to make'r this time. Anyway, she called Edith last night and asked her to come down there."

Here, he stopped for a moment, but unlike some men was not afraid to show his emotion. He had to wait, however, until his voice could grow stronger before continuing. "I can't figure it; her and Edith have always acted like they couldn't stand each other, but last night they must've talked for an hour. She's made up her mind to go, says Hester wants to tell her something that happened years ago and she thinks it might be about Keith. You know, if it was me, why I'd have give up on that thing a long time ago, especially after the little fella died. Now that's a strange thing, too; you know the woman who Keith was supposed to marry before he got sick? Well, she and her daughter showed up at the funeral. The daughter was a head nurse there at the place where he stayed for so long. She's an awful pretty woman."

With Wade carrying the word back to Sweetwater, the news would soon be out; Andrews was getting an optometrist and Jesse was the man to see. That, however, must wait until they returned from Gastonia.

CHAPTER 43

"Willard said to tell you he's sorry not to be here today because he'd promised a neighbor to take him over to Stanley to see his daughter. The old fellow's getting feeble and it ain't safe for him to be driving. But you know how Willard is, always wanting to help. This has worked out good though, because we need some time to talk, and what I have to tell you, Edith, it wouldn't do to have anybody else around."

Lifting back the covers, she twisted around in an attempt to reach the lower shelf of the bedside table to retrieve a beautifully leather-bound Bible. If she didn't have it already this grabbed Edith's attention, "I figured you did and if I was you I'd want to clear things up, too. It's got to do with Earl Aker's, ain't it?" X-rays could not have penetrated deeper when blue eyes met brown.

"Edith, let me have my say first, and then if you feel like you need to, that'll be the time to pass judgment. All I ask is for you to listen with your heart as well as your mind. Sometimes there are things that just can't be told until they can. So much of what I have to say is so shocking that if it'd come to light any sooner innocent lives would have been destroyed. Now, could I get you to light me a cigarette, Honey?"

"Hester, you know what the doctor said about smoking and besides, you're under oxygen. They say it's awful dangerous to do that!"

Giggling like a teenager, a moment was all it took for Hester to pull the clear plastic tubing from her nose and twist shut the valve behind her right shoulder. "I guess that takes care of that, don't it? And as far as what the doctor says, well, you know as well as I do his orders don't make a lick of sense. My goodness, this old heart's so bad it ain't going to make it for more than a week or two at best, so I might as well go happy."

Edith's face reflected pain. An unfiltered Pall Mall sketched thread-like curls of blue haze between them as it traded hands. "I don't know, Hester, but I believe if you'd listen to him you might make it longer than you think. You owe it to Willard and Claude Earl to at least try."

Shaking her head in a manner that left no room for discussion the dying woman answered back, "I've already accepted it, Edith, and have talked it over with both of them. They understand as best as they can and accept it, too. I've been sick a long time now and have suffered so much that I don't want to go on any longer. I'm right with the Lord, but you know years ago when I got saved nobody believed me; well, maybe Ma Rose did. Things like that don't bother me now, though, not like it used to. See, I knew that my heart was right, and the One Who owns it is true, so I just trusted in him." An impatient hand, multicolored blue, brushed the tears from her eyes. "Oh, heck, I'd better get on with this if I'm ever going to; I'll start at the point where I was helping Earl in his undercover work with the revenue department."

Edith nodded knowingly, but made no comment.

"Well, since you are already aware of most of it, I won't waste my breath on stuff you already know about, except to say the bootlegging had obviously been going on for some time. They were pretty slick." Eyes met eyes again, this time, however, merely to confirm that rapport was still intact.

"Not knowing whether they were onto him or not, Earl merely asked me to keep an eye out for anything that looked suspicious. He didn't exactly say, but I finally figured it out, he was watching Lance Boyle and Guy Fowler. With Jack Woodcock, though, Earl was right upfront about him. Said he had circumstantial evidence that showed Jack was operating a still out of Lincolnton and making several trips a year back and forth from Robbinsville to run off a few batches. Not only was he making whiskey, it was bad at that, and dangerous to drink. Of course, the Feds didn't have proof enough to get a conviction or else there would have already been some arrests. Anyhow, I kept my eyes and ears open for a while, maybe for about a month and did notice a few things that looked suspicious. All this time, however, I never caught Claude doing a thing wrong; of course, now I know that just like a fox he was very sly."

Coquettish looks searched the face of her sister-in-law, "You and Keith thought he was too busy messing with me to be involved with anything else, didn't you?" Edith's gaze was non-committal as she responded with a question of her own.

"Didn't Earl set the record straight with Keith about that?"

"Well, yes he did and we'll talk about that later, but at the moment I'm much more concerned about you. I hope when you leave here today you'll do so with a completely different opinion about me. Looking back, I guess I did do a few things that looked questionable. Still, however, it really hurt to have Keith going around spying on me like that. There were times when I could have just slapped the fire out of him. Problem was, all it did was make Lance and Guy think he was snooping on them and that liked to have got him killed. In any event, let's get back to Earl. He got nervous and said that I couldn't help him anymore because he was afraid they were getting onto us. Now we know, too, that at the time he had just about enough evidence to make a case, but what the Fed's wanted to do was catch them red-handed."

"The night it happened, all during the sermon he kept sending me a signal to leave there as quickly as I could. He kept referring to Psalms 11, verse 1 where it says, *Flee as a bird to your mountain.* Every time he quoted that, he'd look straight at me as if to say; *get away from here.* Well, I don't have to tell you, I got message and it scared me. Here, let me show you something."

The pure gold of gilt-edged Holy Writ glittered in the morning sunlight as its spinning pages stopped at the desired text. Hester asked Edith to read what she said Earl had underlined, and then waited for the passage to makes its impact before continuing. "When I walked into the tent that evening he whispered that things were headed for a showdown. Now he didn't tell me this part... it came out later, but he'd overheard something between Jack and the other two that a load was due in around midnight and, of course, that's the kind of news he was waiting for."

Earl then laughed, kinda nervous-like, and said that Jack's wife, Fannie, had been by to see him. Maybe I've let my imagination work a little overtime here, but by the way he winked I got the impression it had been a friendly visit, maybe a little too friendly.

Twisting around in her chair Edith's gaze for the longest time seemed fixed on some distant horizon. "Hester, before you go on any further, would you mind telling me where and how you got a hold of this?" She said, referring to the Bible.

Hester looked tired. "Here, put this thing out for me, I can't reach the ashtray." Such a tiny remnant of tobacco passed between them that both handlers felt its fire. "Okay, you can help me get back into this old harness so I can breathe."

Moments later, with the oxygen flowing again she had her voice back.

"Honey, I swear I'll tell you about that, too, directly, but first let me first say this, and then you'll understand things a lot better."

"Leaving there, I went straight to the bus stop knowing I wouldn't have to wait more than a few minutes. They'd just started running on the half hour and the next one was due at any time. While waiting I got to feeling guilty about leaving him like I did. Not knowing about the raid, I thought maybe I should call the law, but Earl had warned me against ever doing that. He said it could jeopardize the whole thing, but remember I was scared. When the bus pulled up, I got on and rode back to Gastonia, trying to figure if I had done the right thing or not. By the time we made it to Franklin Avenue I decided if I was going to go back, I had to do it right then.

"Later, I told the law that since it was a drizzling the rain I suddenly realized I'd left my umbrella. Anyhow, when I got back to Dallas, the hour it took to make the roundtrip gave me plenty of time to think. I decided if Earl seemed okay, I'd just forget about it and go on home. Otherwise, I'd call the law whether he liked it or not, and either way I'd have done all I could.

"With the out-door lights all turned off, the tent looked dark and deserted. Of course, that made me feel better since I thought maybe everybody was gone, but then my heart just sank when I saw that two cars were still there. Both were parked up close to and back behind the tent. One was Lance Boyle's old Ford and the other was a Buick, belonging to Earl. Stepping into the auditorium, even though it was awfully dim, I could tell that it was empty. As I moved up toward the front, though, I could begin to hear voices in the back. Now, all this so far is exactly the way it happened and it's what I told in court, too. It's also true what I said about overhearing them working on a sign. After all, remember they were getting ready to start a new series of meetings. I just stood there listening for a while; really, I didn't know what else to do.

"Edith, what I'm fixing to tell you now is where the court records differ from the facts. I lied when I said I left there the second time without speaking to anybody. It didn't happen like that at all, but one of the reasons I told it that way was to establish an alibi. Later, when asked to verify our time, Claude and I claimed the same thing and it was ironclad. Since it also provided a time frame for the whereabouts of Lance and Guy, they became the scapegoats."

"According to their story, which no doubt was true, they left there around 10:45. But once they got home, Lance realized his knife was missing, so they headed straight back to get it. Now, the prosecution questioned that, saying it was just a way for them to get around explaining their true whereabouts. Now isn't it ironic how they accepted my story about an umbrella, yet wouldn't theirs for a knife?"

"Hester, I've always known some of your account wouldn't hold water, but I never let on."

"Well, that's because you're smart! But not everybody is... Anyhow, Lance never wavered, claimed he couldn't take a chance on it being stole, since not everybody who went to church was a saint. That got him a few laughs, but not much else. He went on to say they were greatly shocked at finding Earl dead, especially since it looked like his knife was the murder weapon. Said he knew right then this would make him the prime suspect, so in desperation he threw it as far as he could out into the weed patch. Claimed he begged Guy not to take Earl's wristwatch, but that he was beyond reasoning with. Guy's argument, he said, was that if he didn't take it, somebody else would. Together they decided to make it look like a robbery and without a weapon; the law couldn't tie them to it. You could tell the jury didn't like the way he said things, and that really hurt their case. Another thing they denied was turning the main lights back on; they claimed they were off when they left. Problem was nobody saw much relevance to it.

"The prosecution claimed they killed Earl a little after eleven and then tried to cover it up. Jack, as you know, later turned state's evidence and testified that he saw Lance throw something out into the weeds, said it was sometime around eleven-fifteen. Now, I have to tell you it all sounded pretty convincing, the watch, Jack's testimony, the knife, and them being there at the right time; it all came together to really cook their goose.

"You'll remember the coroner estimated the time of Earl's death to be around eleven o'clock and that was based mostly on witness testimony. Something that bothered a lot of us was Jack *just happening* to be there at the exact time Lance threw his knife away. That and knowing those two didn't have much legal help caused a lot of public skepticism. I think folks sensed that the prosecution was out to get a conviction, come hell or high water. There was lots of evidence not fully questioned, for instance, this Bible here. Lance and Guy both insisted Earl had it with him when they left but found it missing later, when they got back. Obviously, this suggested that somebody else besides them had been there. The state just dismissed that out of hand, saying they merely destroyed the Bible in an effort to create an alibi. Unfortunately, since there was no way to prove their claim, their lawyer just let it slide.

"During cross-examination Jack was asked why he didn't let them know of his presence, since supposedly he wasn't aware that anything had happened. His answer was that when he got there and saw the place lit up like a Christmas tree, it made him nervous. Said he'd got word earlier that Earl was the informer and that a big raid may have been in the works. Not knowing what they had on him, he claimed he wanted to be around just to see what happened, but to do it from a distance. All that had a ring of truth to it, but everything else he said sounded like a pack of lies."

Suddenly tiredness became a giant sponge to soak up her strength, and create the need for a few minutes of rest.

Gripping both arms of her chair Edith showed remarkable self-control in not trying to help with a situation, which was well beyond her ability. Finally, Hester nodded and smiled, it was her way of saying that while she was not yet able to talk, she was receptive to listening. Edith seemed a little unsure if this was a good time to bring up what was on her mind, but Hester sensed her indecision and nodded again. This was Edith's sign to begin.

"When Bruce passed away I was satisfied, and I think most us were, that he pretty well had things figured out. I believe, too, the shock of that run-in with Claude Conway was more than his old heart could take. From what Gutch Reece told, and he overheard a lot, was that Claude tried to accuse you and Earl of messing around. But the Mayor refused to listen to it, and let me say right here, I wouldn't have either; not with Earl."

With effort, Hester gave her response. "Edith, I appreciate your wisdom and normally such talk would infuriate me, but I know the truth and before this day is over you will, too. I guess you're aware of what's happened to Claude, aren't you?" She paused again, but this time to cough; a deep, nonproductive effort that brought tears to both women's eyes and left the one in bed unable to speak again for several disquieting minutes. Edith took the time to smooth her pillows, straighten up the bed and brush cigarette ashes mixed with cracker crumbs onto an old coffee-stained "Redbook." It all then went into the wastebasket.

"Other than him moving back to Gastonia, I ain't heard much out of that sorry thing in years, what finally did become of him, anyway?"

"Well, when I figured out I wasn't going to make it, I sat down and wrote Fannie. I decided it was time to find out what she knew. It surprised me to get an answer right back and this is the letter; I want you to read it." Hester's hand trembled enough that she left it for Edith to pull the folded pages from the envelope. It had been there all the while, yet not obvious since several letters and get-well cards had kept it partially obscured. Bold feminine script on the pages matched that found in the address, Edith read aloud:

Dear Hester,

I had not thought of you in years and was very surprised to get your letter. I was sorry to hear of your illness and hope that you are some better. I am in tolerable good health and I guess you know that my Jack passed away four years ago this coming July the 10th. The children are all pretty well scattered with the closest one living in Stecoah. I don't hear much from any of them except when they need something. It gets awful lonesome here on Pin Hook since most of the people I used to know have either moved away or died.

You asked me what I might know about the Reverend Earl Aker's murder. Well, first let me say not that much. I only saw him the one time and that was when I went down there where Jack was working. I didn't know anything about their bootlegging and moonshining until I got there and then it liked to have killed me. Then after I learned that Earl might turn Sonny in, I got scared. So I went and tried to talk to him about it, but he was so unreasonable and rude that he wouldn't listen to a word I said. He kept throwing it up to me how he was a preacher of the gospel so I just finally gave up and went back to the apartment. But I did go back on the night he was murdered to hear the preaching; I never spoke to him though. And when the services were over the Reverend Conway was kind enough to take me home. That's all I know about Reverend Akers except what they said about him in the paper.

A lot of people thought Jack did it and some even said I had something to do with it too, but Jack told the truth when he was on the stand. He didn't go to the meetings that night because he wasn't there. I found out later he'd gone to Lincolnton and hid out his stuff, so he couldn't have got back there until after Earl was dead. He had witnesses to back him up, too.

Me and Claude stopped for a milkshake and got to talking, so I didn't realize how late it was until I got home. The best I can recall, and this is what I told them under oath, the clock in the hall said it was about twenty past ten. Jack told the court that he got to the tent around eleven-fifteen. So that means it was about an hour after I got home and right at the time when them two awful men were coming out. The one named Lance was full of wrath when he throwed the knife out into that weed patch, but of course at the time Jack didn't know what it was. Naturally, after they found it, he had to tell what he saw and he couldn't help it if the jury found them two guilty. Until my dying day I'll always believe they were the ones who did it. That's all I can tell you, but I'm glad you wrote because it finally gives me a chance to set the record straight.

As far as what happened to Reverend Conway; well the last I heard, which was some months ago, he had been placed in a nursing home. After he left Robbinsville, back around 1954 or '55, he moved to Gastonia again. I kept up with him off and on by the grapevine, and learned that he later got married. Along about the same time he started a small church down there. But from what the word was they churched him for messing around with the head-deacon's wife. Anyway, he's got the old-timer's disease now and they say he don't know his own name most of the time, but still talks constantly about Earl and Sonny. It's awful strange and he's pitiful. I feel sorry for Claude and wish there was some way I could take care of him, but that wouldn't do, not when neighbors like to talk about you the way mine do. Well, I'll close for now. Write me back if you're still living.

Fannie Woodcock

Before she could utter a word, Edith succumbed to sniggering. The condition must have been contagious for Hester caught it, too, leaving them both speechless. Finally, after multiple false starts, Hester was able to blurt out; "See why I figure she'd been real friendly to Earl? And it's no wonder she thought he was rude, by throwing it up to her how he was a minister and all."

"Now let me think for a minute," Edith said, with a gaze that pierced the heavens. "You must have got back to the tent around ten twenty, but was gone say by ten thirty-five, or so. The only others there besides Earl was Lance and Guy, and they both claimed to have left a few minutes after you did. Then according to what Jack told, he showed up sometime between eleven, and eleven thirty, coming in from Lincolnton and just in time to see Lance throw his knife away. So... if Fannie got home like she wrote, then everybody is accounted for. That leaves something less than forty-five minutes for Earl to be alone and for the murder to occur."

"Yes," Hester agreed, "you've got the time-line right, but I've not told the real story yet and when I do, it will answer a lot of your questions."

Edith tenderly beheld a face, once beautiful, but now reflected battles that long since had been lost to congestive heart failure. Puffed and swollen, large baggy lids did not detract from the burning glow that still shined in her eyes. They were as attractive as ever and full of admiration. However, reaching across the two feet separating them took all the effort that Edith could muster. Uncomfortably, she blurted out; "This is not easy for me to say, even though I've come to love you more than I ever thought possible. It's not always been that way, though, there was a time when I literally despised the ground you walked on. But over the past few years I've come to see what a truly good woman you are. When it comes to religion, Hester, you put me to shame, and I really do believe you're a good Christian woman. So, I guess what I'm trying to say is that I need to have you forgive me."

"Why, Edith, my goodness, I couldn't be a Christian and not have forgiveness in my heart. But I feel it's the other way around; I just hope when I'm finished with this you'll understand and be willing to forgive me, too."

Reaching out the two joined hands while their teardrops mingled on the pillowcase; "You've been brave up to this point, but you've got to go on and tell the rest. It's been on your heart long enough now and I know you don't want to carry it to the grave. I've listened so far with my mind, but now I'm ready to listen with my heart. From what's been said, though, there are a couple of things yet I have to ask you."

"What I said about you being smart, Edith, is true, and I guess that's another reason I wanted to talk to you; I figured you'd be the only one who could get the whole thing out of me. But it's going to be hard, the hardest thing I've ever done. Ask whatever you want to and I promise not to keep any secrets. Knowing you, though, that probably wouldn't be possible anyway, would it?" she laughed

Edith sat back down; an understanding smile confirmed Hester's question. "Well, like I said, that excuse you gave about going back to get the umbrella just didn't set right with me, never did. Think about it, a man might forget an umbrella, but a woman never would, not if it was rainy weather like you claimed. A woman just wouldn't take a chance on getting her hair messed up."

Hester's nod silently sent an acknowledgment of her observations. "You're probably right," she smiled, "but the Sheriff's department bought it hook, line, and sinker. Maybe if they had a woman on their force, they might be able to solve a case now and then. It's hard to believe, but they were satisfied with Claude's story, too; I guess being a preacher just automatically puts you beyond question."

"You may be right there, especially if he happens to be in league with the devil. The other thing, though, and it's the one that stands out the most; the question I asked earlier about the Bible."

"Oh, yes, that?" Hester looked perplexed. "I did promise we'd talk about it, but I meant later. I kinda see how you picked up on the umbrella, but not this though; you'll have to explain it to me."

"Why that's the easy part; remember I just read from Earl's Bible where he'd underlined that passage? But before we go any further, let me ask you; you did leave there like you said, didn't you?"

"Why, of course I did; everything I told up to that point was absolutely true. I was the first one to leave."

"Well," Edith paused, and even though it was only momentary, it still allowed her time enough to seal and unseal to her lips. "If you never saw Earl alive after that, then how did his Bible get into your possession? It's easy to prove that he still had it after you left, because following his last sermon a photographer was there taking pictures. They were for the upcoming meetings. Kathleen still has one and it shows Earl holding the same Bible you've got right there. She showed it to me not too long ago. So, there's no doubt that it's the same one, but the question is; when did you get it? It had to have been after you went back and I believe it's key to solving this mystery."

Soft weeping echoed the sorrow of a million tears; meanwhile Edith stroked the long gray curls of her sister-in-law's still beautiful hair. No effort was made to staunch the flow; they just fell until she could talk again. "I'll hush in a minute, Edith, just wait on me. I want to finish this before Claude Earl gets back; he's supposed to be here give me a shot at four."

CHAPTER 44

"Earl was just a lamb led to its slaughter, and that's what hurts so much. And you're right about the Bible too, but I never dreamed it would show up in a picture like that. I swear, Edith, you're just amazing..

"Everything I have to tell you from here on is exactly the way it happened. Like I said, there were voices in the back of the tent and I quickly figured out who it was, but I never let on I was there. At first they were working on the sign, however, things suddenly turned nasty. Obviously, they knew about Earl's undercover work and this caught him by surprise. Guy was talking loud and threatening him, said it wouldn't be the first time he'd killed. Up until then I'm not certain they knew just how serious the charges were, but when Earl mentioned that people may have died from the whiskey, that's what did it. Clearly, you could tell they were furious. Then the scuffling began; it sounded like they were pushing Earl around and roughing him up. There was a lot of loud laughing, weird-like, with both making fun of him. Lance sneered he'd take care of him just like he did the two in King's Mountain. To even hear that mentioned was chilling; see, a year before a woman and her daughter over there got their throats cut.

"I crept to a corner of the tent and squatted down, trying to hide. I'd never been so scared in all my life. From what I could tell, Guy grabbed Earl and started screaming for Lance to help him. I reckon Earl was able to break free, at least for a moment. He told them that since they didn't make the whiskey all they faced were charges of bootlegging, which were minor compared to murder, and they needed to think about that. Also, he said that very shortly the law would be there and they'd know exactly who to go after if anything happened to him."

"They just ridiculed that and said they knew all about the raid; then they began to argue over the best way to get rid of him. Meanwhile, my mind was racing a mile a minute, trying to figure out what to do. I knew if I exposed myself, they'd kill me, too, so I looked around in desperation. That's when I saw the main power switch and my first impulse was to flip it off; that way Earl might be able to escape. Then I realized that could make matters even worse, so I decided to do just the opposite and flood the place with light. That would be easy since the levers were all in one place. I hoped they'd think that some of the Feds had got there early and make a run for it. Well, that must have been what happened because the moment the place lit up they were gone! By just hearing their car race away, I nearly peed on myself.

"Quickly, I went in to where Earl was and he was completely overwhelmed. Seeing me really surprised him. At first, you could tell he was pleased, yet he, too, had thought it was the law and since it wasn't, he seemed frustrated. Turning on me, he said; 'I've asked you to stay out of this, so leave here and go on home. You're in grave danger right now, and if they come back they'll kill you, too.'"

"I told him that was exactly why we *both* needed to get out of there. He smiled that silly little grin of his and said not to worry about him. 'Claude will be here any minute now, and I'll get him to stay with me until the law comes. This little fracas is about over and I plan to see it through.' Suddenly we heard a car drive up and Earl asked me to step outside, 'I'll bet that's old Claude now,' he said, 'but we won't take any chances.' For some reason I noticed a knife lying on the floor and just to see it made me shudder. I figured Lance had dropped it when he got scared.

"You can't believe how much it tickled me to see that it, indeed, was Claude and to hear him carrying on just like always, but before I could reveal myself he turned serious. 'Earl,' he said, 'I need to ask you something; there's a rumor going around about you working for the revenuers.' He didn't wait for an answer, but just kept talking. 'Son, I hope not, because if so, you're playing a dangerous game here, one that could get you hurt. What I say is let Caesar handle his own business. Why, Earl, as a minister of the gospel you don't need to be messed up with something as rotten as this. So, I beg of you my good friend, stay out of it. But if you are, then please just walk away from it right now!'

"Hearing him sound so concerned I felt like it was safe to go back in, but you know the minute I did he turned on Earl. Wanted to know what in the devil I was doing there, anyway.

"Holding up the umbrella, I lied about coming back to get it and tried to make the story sound reasonable. You could tell though, he didn't believe a word

I said. His face was as red as fire… why, I'd never seen anybody act so rude. He started accusing Earl of whoring around after me; that he'd noticed us together all the time. I swear it looked like he was crying when he said it. Then he claimed I was just a slut and had gone out and got myself pregnant. 'They ain't no telling who it belongs to,' he nearly screamed. 'She's just a little vixen and for all I know, it could be yours, the way you keep following her around! And you still call yourself a preacher, do you?' He then took a folded piece of paper out of his shirt pocket and waved it in front of Earl saying, 'You're in love with her, ain't you, buddy?' He acted like somebody who was insanely jealous.

"Edith, let me set this straight right now, Claude Earl does not belong to Earl Akers, and certainly not to Claude Conway, either. I swear to you, I never once had anything like that to do with either man, never! I'm going to confess something else to you though, something that has to be told about Claude Earl. But that'll have to wait for a few more minutes."

"Here, take a little sip of water," Edith offered. "Your mouth's all dried out and it'll make you feel better."

"Yes, thank you, Sweetie, I believe it would help and, if you don't mind, get me a pill out of that little brown bottle over there." Quietness brought a welcome interlude and although brief, it seemed to heighten Edith's interest.

"I couldn't believe what I was hearing," Hester continued. "Here was a man I'd put so much faith in, telling one lie after another. I'm still not exactly sure what his motive was except that maybe he was jealous of me and Earl. But he knew better than that, why it was just plain ridiculous. Then suddenly he changed the subject back to the bootlegging. He said, 'So I guess it's true then, you have been sticking your nose into stuff that ain't none of your business!'

"Earl didn't back away, not one iota, even though I wish he had. Calmly he asked, and I'm certain it hurt him to do it, but he asked, 'Claude, are you in on this, too? Is that the reason we've been getting all these good offerings lately? If so, then I'm the one who's been betrayed here, but even more, so has Christ!'

"Well, that's when the fat hit the fire and it was awful. Claude got right up in his face and started screaming; sounded just as bad as Lance and Guy had. I heard him spout things I'd never heard come out of anybody's mouth before. Earl tried to cool him down, did the best he could, but it didn't faze Claude; if anything he got worse. Next, he threatened Earl, saying if he planned on turning him in, he'd kill him on the spot. 'You hypocrite,' he said, 'you ain't got nothing on me because I'm innocent, but if you go ahead with this, it'll ruin my ministry. And it'll hurt a lot of other people, too, good innocent people. Do you think folks will come back after word gets out? I promise you, though,' he said, looking as wild as a buck. 'You ain't going through with this, because I aim to stop you!' Then he asked Earl straight out, 'So what's it going to be, Buddy, will you listen to me, or do you plan on playing the fool?' Well, I knew right then things could only get worse; Earl would never back down in the face of evil and Claude had just put himself on the wrong side by threatening him. But even then I really believe if he'd only backed away, Earl would have dropped it.

"Earl begged Claude to sit down and reason with him, but he wouldn't. 'You've already answered my question,' Claude hollered, and then he slapped Earl just as hard as he could. Earl turned around and started picking up his things; yes, including that Bible there. You could see the tears in his eyes when he spoke, 'This is my shield and buckler, and yea though ye slay me, I will trust in God.'

"Claude lost his mind then, I guess seeing the Bible lifted up against him like that made him go crazy. He hit it just as hard as he could, and since it fell right at my feet I just automatically picked it up. I guess if nothing else had, this must have convinced Earl that there now was no reasoning with him, so he turned to leave. But Claude struck him again, this time from behind and nearly knocked him to his knees. Somehow, he staggered over to one of the main supporting posts of the tent and tried to hold on, but like a tiger, Claude went for his throat and started choking him. Oh, it was awful!

"Now, keep in mind this happened so fast it had my head spinning like a top and made it all seem like a bad dream. He had Earl pushed up against the post and kept banging his head against it. I could see the life just draining out of him; he looked pale as death. I knew I'd better do something, and do it fast. I was already screaming, and when I hit Claude with my fist, it never fazed him. Grabbing his hair, I started pulling, but that didn't work either so I was getting desperate. Earl had ceased struggling and it looked like he either was dead or had passed out.

"Suddenly, I remembered the knife and there it was. My only thought was to cut Claude's hands loose from Earl's neck. Yet, just as I lunged forward, they whirled around and I slashed Earl instead. The blade made a gash from right above his Adam's apple to just up under his jawbone. About all I can remember is seeing blood on Claude's hands. Then I fainted, but before that, I recall Claude standing over Earl and staring down at him. He looked so pitiful laying there with his head party covered in blood and sawdust. Claude half dragged, half shoved me into his car; yet for the whole time I was in a daze, just coming and going.

"I must have been out for several minutes and even after getting mostly back I still was awful groggy. It took awhile for my head to clear, but somehow I knew we were in Claude's car and he was driving like a maniac. I don't know how it happened, but through it all I wound up with both Earl's Bible and the umbrella in my lap. I believe Claude must have put them there, for certainly it was to his benefit that they were.

"The minute he saw I was awake he lit into me, 'You've really fixed it now,' he said. 'Earl's dead and you killed him.' He didn't speak again for a few minutes, but when he did he sounded a lot more reasonable. Said he knew it was an accident, but there was no way to prove it, and if I went to the law, they'd claim that we both were in on it, maybe having an affair. That the best we could ever hope for would be a life sentence, but more than likely it'd be the gas chamber. 'The only thing to do,' he said, 'is to keep our mouths shut and act like we know nothing about it. With all the witnesses that'll come forward just say you left there early, but had to go back to get your umbrella. Then tell how I came along and picked you up at the bus stop. That way it gives us both an alibi and if you stick to your story, nobody will ever be the wiser!'"

"Oh my goodness, this is awful," moaned Edith. "But, no wonder you clung to that ridiculous story about the umbrella; well, at least, now I know why."

"Yes, that and also because the bus driver remembered me going back there that night. See, I'd become quite familiar to him, having ridden the bus so often."

"Uh-huh… him and any of the others who saw you leave early, they could've caused you a problem," Edith agreed.

Hester nodded, and then picked up where she'd left off. "He grabbed the Bible and shoved it into my face, 'and you'd better keep this thing out of sight,' he cursed. 'Bringing it along wasn't very bright; there's no way you can ever explain having it. But we can't take a chance on going back, either, so you better just hang on to it and keep quiet. It could be destroyed, but I doubt you'd ever do that. I'd let it be a reminder to me that this thing was just an accident, anyway. The umbrella, though; now that's different. Don't ever, not even for a minute, let it get lost because, like I say, it's our alibi.' He kept repeating, over and over, there was nothing we could do, now or ever, to bring Earl back. 'And besides you didn't do it on purpose… did you?' He asked."

"At that, I suddenly threw up all over the floorboard, just spewed stuff until my stomach was empty. Fortunately, none of it got on the Bible or the umbrella, but it did set off another round of cursing.

"I finally stopped retching long enough to realize that what he was saying made a lot of sense. It was true, why I wouldn't have hurt Earl for anything; in fact I was trying to save his life. God knows it truly was an accident. I've lived this thing over and over in my mind every day since then, praying it would just somehow turn out to be a bad dream, and that I could wake up to find Earl alive.

"But here I was pregnant and knowing if this got out, I'd probably never get a chance to even hold my little baby. Edith, can you imagine what kind of torment that would be like for a woman like me? One who'd been barren all those years and now having to face a life sentence without the hope of holding her child? Why, it'd be a fate far worse than death and I'd take the gas chamber over it anytime."

Edith leaned over with a washcloth to sponge away the tears as they surged down her face. "Go ahead, Darling and cry; you need this to ease your soul. I don't know how in this world you've stood up under it, anyway."

"I'm sorry," she sobbed. "Every time I think about it, my heart just breaks and, you know, until today I've not been able to talk to anybody about it, but there's more, a lot more yet to tell."

CHAPTER 45

"I was so thankful that Willard was still at the plant, when Claude got me home. Remember, he was working the graveyard shift at the time. Claude, though, wasn't done with me yet, and I could tell his mood had changed again when he grabbed me by the back of my head. I'll swear if he didn't look just like Satan. 'Keep your mouth shut,' he said. 'Even if it was an accident, it's still your fault. You just had to be the little vixen, didn't you; just had to throw yourself at every man you saw. But look at what it got you. If you ever tell I went back to that tent after leaving, I'll swear that I saw you kill him. And they'll believe me, too. Now, I don't know if Earl knocked you up or not, but if you breathe my name in this, I'll claim he denied it was his and that you killed him in a mad fit. So, if you know what's good for you, you'll go in there and act like nothing's happened. And, oh yeah, one more thing, too, keep that sorry husband of your's of my sight.'

"Of course, you understand. I was so glad to get away from him I would have promised anything."

"With so much guilt and heartache to bear I can't see how you kept from losing Claude Earl or your mind either, as far as that's concerned. You must've been awfully depressed when Willard saw you. What did he say about the way you acted?"

"Actually, I didn't have to worry that much, since he was so worried over Keith. Remember, that was right at the time his fever was running the highest and none of us knew whether he'd make it or not. Of course, with me having been so fond of the preachers it was only natural that I'd be grieving deeply. I did start spotting, though, and it looked like I might lose the baby and that's another reason why I call him a miracle. I'm satisfied now, that without a lot of prayer he wouldn't be here today."

For the first time in several minutes Hester's face suddenly reflected sunshine. "Edith, if you'll help me I'd like to sit up for awhile; this old bed's just about got me wore out."

With the patient comfortable in her chair Edith stripped the bed and refreshed it with new linen. "Knowing the kind of person Claude was, how could you have ever named a child after him?"

"I figured you'd ask about that and I'm not sure I have an answer you'll accept, but all I can do is tell you the truth. That's all I've got now and yet it's like Jesus said, 'ye shall know the truth and the truth shall set ye free.'

"Up until that night I'd upheld both men to the very highest. After all, Claude was the one who led me to Christ. Earl helped, too, but Claude was the lead evangelist for that set of meetings. I guess I thought both men walked on water. When I was raised, we didn't go to church, not unless it was to a funeral or something special. Daddy didn't trust Christians. I did get to go to Sunday school a few times though. It was the summer I spent with my aunt up in Asheville, and it left a hunger in my heart that just wouldn't go away. At the time Daddy made it clear he didn't want me going to church, so I tried hard just to ignore my feelings. I could forget about it for a while, but it kept coming back and I'd get this longing to go.

"Then after me and Willard got married we talked a lot about church, but never got around to going. You know he's ten years older than me, not that it ever mattered between us, it's just that I wanted a baby and he did, too, but not as much as me. I guess it might have been my constant harping on it that made him grow distant; and then things just kinda stayed that way for several years. We both were lonely and I don't know exactly why, but I started going to the tent meetings. I think maybe it had something to do with a neighbor; she'd been a few times herself. I remember how from the start, it seemed like I just couldn't stop going because I wanted to hear more and more of the preaching. All day I'd think about getting back that night to the singing, and fellowship; I just couldn't stay away.

"After I got pregnant, even considering what happened, I was still praying it belonged to Willard. I had all my hopes and dreams wrapped up in that little unborn child. God had entrusted me to bring it into the world and I could be a real woman at last. I just knew that I was part of a miracle, especially since it didn't happen until I surrendered my life to Christ.

"Now, I'll admit I gave a lot of the credit to the preachers. Why I even picked out names before I knew what it would be. If it had been a girl, it would have been

Earla Claudine; that's what I told everybody. Well, of course, after what happened I wanted to just use Earl's name. But I knew it wouldn't look right if I didn't include Claude's, too, so I just left it like it was.

"Edith, would you to light me another cigarette? And Honey, I need a little help here to get out from under this old oxygen again, but, meanwhile, why don't you go in there and fix yourself a bowl of soup or something? There's plenty to eat; Willard always acts like we're going to starve every time he goes to the store. I don't want anything myself, since I ain't got much of an appetite anymore."

"I ain't hungry, neither, but I do think you need a little break; this has got to be awful hard on you. And yes, I do understand now why you named him Claude Earl. It just seemed strange until you explained it."

"Please don't take me wrong, Edith, but I wonder; would you be this understanding if I weren't dying?" Again, flirtatious eyes signaled that the question really did not beg an answer. "Don't worry, I wouldn't put you on the spot like that, the only reason I asked is because of what's coming up later. That, I'm afraid, will take all the understanding you can muster. Before we go on, though, I need you to tell me about Kathleen. I'd like to know how you come to find out where she was and how she's been doing. I've thought about her so many times over the years, but totally lost track of her a long time ago."

"Getting back to your question, Hester; trying to be fair with you, at one time I couldn't have. But like I said earlier, I've come to see just how badly I'd misjudged you. So from what you've just said, I doubt I would have done things any different than you did." Then looking through a swirling layer of blue smoke, Edith told of her trip to Dr. Smithfield's office. Starting with how she met Kathleen there, the story ended with Michael's mysterious appearance and subsequent departure.

"Why, Edith, that takes my breath away. Can't you see God's hand in all of this? My goodness, you, and your family have been in the palm of His hand all this time. Who knows, I may run into Michael myself before long and if I do, I'll be sure to say hi for you." Laughing brought more deep, dry coughs and with them the need to get back in bed. Comfortable again, she lay quietly for a few minutes. Edith seemed surprised when Hester abruptly resumed her account of events.

"One thing I hoped wouldn't happen was for them to put Lance and Guy on trial for murder. I had prayed and prayed they wouldn't, but when they did I nearly died. Claude, though, from the start acted unconcerned. Said he didn't think they'd be convicted, but even if they did, they'd get exactly what they deserved. Now, to me this sounded awfully hollow, coming from a man who'd tried his best to choke Earl to death. He kept saying they were guilty of other murders and that the world would be a lot better off without 'em, but oh, my Lord, what a nightmare! The only way I've been able to live with it was by remembering the way they threatened Earl; they really did intend to kill him."

Nodding, Edith was quick to concur; "Honestly, Hester, I think they got just exactly what they deserved and I hope right now they're both burning in hell. With Claude Conway, though, I doubt even old Satan would dirty his hands on him. He may be an old fox who's spoiled a lot of vines, but the sun won't always shine on that mangy tail of his."

Hester stared hard at the back of her left hand while clasping it tight by the other for what proved to be a long minute before continuing. "Edith, what I'm fixing to tell you now is in many ways, even worse than what you've just heard. But before that let me remind you of how I feel about Willard. I've always loved him and that love has grown over the years, even despite the fact I lost him a long time ago. Actually, I lost him the night I conceived Claude Earl, and he gave up on me that night of the fight with Claude. Oh, I wish you could have seen him, he was magnificent, my knight in shining armor. I watched him fight the forces of evil in defense of my honor, and even against three of them, he still won. I believe he would have killed Claude right there on the spot, if I hadn't stopped him. Unfortunately, Willard never understood why I screamed for him not to do it, and saying that little Claude Earl needed his daddy. He thought I meant Claude Conway, but that was not it at all. What I meant, as God is my witness, was that if he killed Claude, he'd go to prison or be executed and then little Claude Earl would never know what a kind, good daddy he had. I'm satisfied Willard still don't believe me, because deep down he knows Claude Earl is not his, but he's always treated him just like he was.

"I'd like to tell you something else, though, something you may already be aware of, but I'll tell it, anyway. Willard does have a boy, one that's about two years younger than Claude Earl; he and my sister Marilyn had a fling right after her divorce, and she even named him Willard. If you've ever seen him you can tell that he looks just like his daddy. Marilyn never denied it and I have to tell you it broke my heart, but I never stopped loving him because of it. Next to Willard and Claude Earl, I love that nephew more than I love anybody in this world. One thing though, and you'll find this funny, his hair is exactly the same color as Claude Earl's. So, I guess you can say there is a redheaded Rose after all.

"Edith, what I'm fixing to tell you now will be the hardest thing I've ever done and I warn you, there's nothing pretty about it."

CHAPTER 46

Taking a long breath Hester sighed deeply and prepared to bare a soul that had long suffered torment by the vilest imps of hell.

"Long after I got saved I still felt that everybody there at church was a saint, and I guess most were. They all treated me like I'd never been treated before, but as I found out later there were wolves among the sheep, too. Sometimes we have to learn the hard way that just because we give our life to Christ, it don't mean everything will be perfect. No, in fact, I think that's the time when the old devil really gets interested in you; he figures that if you're not with him then you must be his enemy, so he declares war. It's my belief that after a person makes their profession of faith, they're going to be tested, and that's exactly what happened to me.

"I need to back up here for a minute, though. See, ever since I was a little girl I liked the attention I got from boys and, of course, later on from men. I developed a habit of flirting and it was fun, but really, I didn't mean anything by it. You may never have even noticed it, but I used to flirt with Wade. He liked it and I did, too."

"That ain't news to me," Edith shot back. "Wade's shin bone still carries scars from what I noticed. But I think he's learned his lesson with flirty women; he's like Jesse was about electricity. One time, when we went to see Aunt Josie's in Bryson City, Jesse was intrigued over how her radio could play without a battery. When she said, it works on electricity, that didn't make a lick of sense to him, so he decided to find out for himself. By following a wire from the set to the outside, he found where it hooked on. Remember, they wired houses back then different than they do now. Well anyway, he reached out and grabbed a hold, but just as soon as he did, he got the shock of his life. A bone-shaking force surged through him strong enough to make his ears hum, but he couldn't turn it loose! Jesse knew he had to, though, or else he'd die. Yet he just couldn't do it. Fortunately, there's a Power greater than the one that held him, and it jarred him loose. I hope both Wade and Jesse have learned their lessons; flirting is a lot like electricity; it may look harmless, but it can get you killed."

"Unfortunately, flirting got to be such a habit that most of the time I didn't realize I was doing it. Probably, that's one reason things happened the way they did. Most nights I'd get to the meetings early because I enjoyed talking to the different members and just feeling a part of the congregation. Occasionally, this fellow, who was about Willard's age, would come over and sit with me. He didn't come every night and, as a matter of fact, there were times when I wouldn't see him for weeks on end. Then he'd be back for a few meeting. I didn't think much about it, but after a while I noticed that he seemed to be getting a little too friendly. Still I didn't worry, because after all we *were* in church and who'd try anything there?

"That fall it had been unusually warm, actually pretty hot with temperatures during the day rising to over ninety. One night it come up an awful storm, the lightning was about as bad as I'd ever seen it and the thunder just shook the tent. Finally, it got so loud they had to stop preaching for a while. You couldn't half hear what was being said, anyhow. Ultimately, Earl announced they were going to dismiss early, saying this was tornado weather and that we'd all be a lot safer at home. Well, of course, this caused a problem since the bus wouldn't be due for another fifty minutes or so. They were still on the hourly schedules at that time.

"I guess Earl didn't realize this, but I mentioned it to the fellow I was telling you about. Well, immediately he stood up and announced that he had a pick-up truck and could take some of us home, if anybody needed a ride. There was this older couple sitting right in front of us who turned around and took him up on it. Then a woman, maybe a year or two younger than me asked if he had room for her, too. But he said no, that I was next in line. Now I have to admit that made me feel a little queasy since I hadn't asked him. Still, it seemed reasonable enough, considering I was the one to bring up the problem in the first place.

"The man's wife sat in his lap and I had to squeeze in next to the driver. The cab was small and very uncomfortable. The thing that bothered me the most, though, was when he changed gears, he'd let his hand rest right up against my leg. We had to drive a good ways to get the couple home and thinking about it later, it would have made a lot more sense to drop me off first. At the time, however, not really knowing where we were headed, I didn't protest. But once we got there I realized where we were and pretty well knew the quickest way back. So when he started off in the wrong direction I asked him where he thought he was going. 'Oh, I'm about to run out of gas,' he said, 'and there's a service station just down the road. It's a lot better to be safe than sorry.'

"We stopped at the station and while they were filling up the truck, he went inside to use the bathroom. Coming back out he seemed upset, 'Never can get them things to work when you need to,' he complained. I didn't know then what he was talking about, but later I figured it out; he went in there to buy rubbers."

"Why, Hester," Edith gasped, looking embarrassed.

Hester looked uncomfortable, too, but not enough to slow her down.

"He threw gravel everywhere taking off, and in just a minute we were going at break-neck speed. I knew we were still headed in the wrong direction, but by the way he was driving, I didn't know whether to say anything or not. Then he whipped into a side road and that's when I spoke up, asking him what he thought he was doing. Mad as fire, I told him to turn right back around and take me home.

"He just laughed and said, 'Me and you've got a little business to take care of first, Honey, so just sit back and enjoy the ride.' We didn't ride much further, though, because he pulled into this little dirt path; you know one of those farm roads made for sleds and wagons. Suddenly, he put the brakes on so hard that I bounced up against the dashboard. Then, before I knew what was happening, he put his arms around me and started trying to feel of me. His old cold-slobbery lips were on my throat, and he tried to kiss me. He held me so tight I could hardly breathe, and it took a minute or two to collect my wits. When I did, I elbowed him as hard as I could, right in the ribs. That surprised him enough that I got free for a second or two, but it also made him mad as fire. He reached over and dragged my head down across the steering wheel, forcing my face up toward his. Then he tried to kiss me again, but this time when he bent down, I bit his chin. I really sunk my teeth in and he screamed like he'd been shot, it was bad enough that he carried a scar there for the rest of his life.

"That got me loose again and even though it was dark I could see he was bleeding. Not waiting around to apologize I jerked the door open and started running, running as hard as I could down that little lane. I didn't get very far, though, before running into a fence; not barbwire, but one of those checked-wire kinds. By now, most of the clouds had cleared and since the moon was about three-quarters full it was just bright enough to see that I'd really run into a makeshift gate.

While still doing my best to get it unhooked, he caught up with me and suddenly I was on the ground. Sitting a straddle of me, he somehow undid the fence; I believe he was very familiar with the place. Then he was all over me, jerking at my blouse to strip it off, but he didn't try to kiss me anymore. I remember being thankful for that since his breath smelled like a wet dog. Meanwhile, I was struggling just as hard as I could and screaming at the top of my lungs. I guess that caused him to put his hand over my face, cutting my air off, and I thought, oh, my Lord, this may be it I could be killed here.

"It took a couple of minutes before I blacked out, but in coming to I realized he was carrying me toward this old house, where he shoved me onto the porch. I knew I'd be raped if I didn't stop him and that thought alone seemed to renew my strength. So, I began fighting with everything I had, slapping and scratching his face. Praying, too, but I didn't scream any more because even in the heat of battle I knew if he started smothering me again, it might be fatal this time. We fought for what felt like an hour. Of course, it wasn't that long, but it sure seemed that way. He was all over me, trying to spread my legs apart, then when he'd get on top I'd spin over to get away from him, but he kept on and on until he'd torn off almost all my clothes. I was called every name in the book and told that I'd led him on. He kept saying he was going to get it if he had to kill me.

"With him on top most of the time I couldn't get loose, and every once in a while he'd hit me right in the stomach. When he did, it weakened me even more and finally I couldn't fight any longer. I'd fought as hard as I could and didn't have any fight left in me. I was exhausted and he must have known it for he seemed to get stronger.

"At that moment I didn't really care what happened, actually all I wanted to do was die, and I never really got over that. Even today, I don't fear death because, in many ways that night I died. Yes, I went on existing, but the person who God created as me was dead. My life has been a lie ever since then, right up until now. Well, anyway, he raped me, but thanks be unto God for one thing; I guess all that fighting did something to him; he didn't last but a few seconds. Yet it was long enough to kill something inside of me. Like I said, not only did it destroy me as a person, but I gave up Willard at that moment, too.

"He ranted and raved, then cursed and called me every name in the book. He slapped me so hard my nose bled, but I didn't care. He bragged that he'd slept with hundreds of women and that I was the sorriest of them all. Then he said he'd do it again, just to prove he could. I don't know whether God intervened or not, but he couldn't do a thing. I'd prayed that the Lord would protect me and I still don't understand why He didn't stop him in the first place. The only thing I can think of is that God usually doesn't step in to prevent evil from happening. But He can and does keep it from getting worse and according to what St. Paul says He'll bring good out of the bad. You remember what's written in Romans 8: 28 don't you. 'And we know that all things work together for good to them that love God.' Well, there's a whole lot more to it than that, but I won't quote it here. That part, however, I've held onto all through the years and, without it, I could never have survived. Believe it or not, those very words came to me while laying there on that porch hoping to die. When Claude knocked the Bible out of Earl's hands, something remarkable happened. Here, let me show you something."

Hester reached again for Earl's beautiful tome and after lifting the scarlet ribbon, it opened to the New Testament book of Romans. Her hand tenderly caressed the leaves until she reached chapter eight. The rip in the page ran from the top down, pointing like an arrow to verse twenty-eight.

"I didn't find this until several days after Earl died. Since it already was my verse, I knew right then that God had never turned loose of my hand, even while it was taking the life of Earl Akers. Earlier you asked how I was able to hold up under all this; well you're looking at it right there, that's the reason. Only by the grace of God and through the power of His unfailing word, have I done it. Remember now, this happened to the Bible several months after I'd been raped. So that's why this verse is so special to me."

"Oh, my Lord, Hester," Edith's face betrayed her desire for a calm demeanor. "You've asked me to be understanding, well let me tell you something; you didn't need to do that. While I may not be able to detect every lie that's told, I do know the truth when I hear it, and I believe every word you've just said. I noticed one thing, though, when you talked about Earl you couldn't keep from crying, yet you didn't shed a single tear over this."

"Like I said, Earl was a lamb led to its slaughter and looking back now; it's obvious, he was a marked man. Being so good and wanting to do God's work, the devil meant to destroy him and I'll cry over that as long as the Lord gives me breath to. This other thing, though, after he finally quit trying I just lay there on the porch. I was nearly in a, what do you call it, a catatonic state. I could hear him cursing me and calling me every vile name he could think of, but I couldn't move a muscle. I can still see him sitting there on the edge of that porch with his legs crossed, smoking a cigarette. After a while, he just hushed and stayed quiet for several minutes, like he was thinking. I guess, because I was hardly breathing, he reached over and slapped me hard on the hip. 'Hey, wake up!' he laughed. 'I didn't satisfy you that good, did I? A hot little number like you ought to be able to take it all night.'

"Next he got down right in my face and shouted, 'You need not be thinking about hollering rape. Everybody knows what kind of a slut you are and they ain't going to believe it! At the meeting, all those people know how you've been all over me. And I'll tell you what about church folks; they don't have much sympathy for whores. Now, you put that little butt of yours in the truck if you want to go home!'

"I still couldn't move; tormented as I was I couldn't move a muscle. He waited a minute or two then reached down and jerked me to my feet. Since I just stood there, with what few clothes that hadn't been torn off, he must have got frustrated for he slapped me again. It wasn't as hard as before, but it snapped me out of it. I started crying, just bawling, and that made him even madder. So to get me moving, he twisted my arm up under the shoulder blade and walked me that way back to the truck. Did the best I could to cover myself up using the few rags that were still hanging on me. But like a maniac he laughed and said I didn't have a thing he hadn't already seen up close. I didn't say a word. In fact, after he raped me I never spoke to that man again as long as he lived.

"I have no idea how long it took to get home. Probably not as long as it seemed, but he complained all the way about his chin; he said, 'they ain't no telling how bad this is, and it hurts like heck. I'll bet anything it looks so bad I won't be able to go to church Sunday. God, you ought to be ashamed of yourself!' But, anyway, we finally got there and then all at once he wanted to know if my husband would be waiting. Of course, Willard was working the graveyard shift and did for over a year until they made him supervisor, but I wasn't about to tell him. He got mad because I wouldn't talk, so he literally screamed for me to get out of his truck. Well, I can tell you right now he didn't need to do that, because I was ready to jump the minute he slowed down. Before he'd let me go, however, he grabbed my arm to warn me; saying, 'If you go in there and tell a bunch of crap, I'll just admit it to your husband and say that yes we've been going together. Then you just watch it break up your marriage, I've seen it happen before. Like I said, they ain't nobody in their right mind who'd believe a slut like you, so if you want to save your marriage, you'd better keep that mouth shut!'

"Going into the house I felt so dirty that I didn't even want to sit on the sofa.

I knew I'd never feel clean again. After about an hour, I ran a tub of the hottest water I could stand and sat in it until daylight. In fact, I was still there when Willard came in. There were cut marks and bruises all over me and I wanted to keep him from seeing that, so I put a housecoat on and wrapped the towel around my head. Brushing by him, I went to the guest room where I usually slept to keep from bothering his sleep. But for some reason he was curious and wanted to know what was wrong. Well, I lied and told him that I'd been up most of the night sick. That seemed to satisfy him so he went on to bed.

"I managed to pretty well avoid Willard for the next week and by that time I probably looked like somebody who'd suffered through a bad case of the flu. Oh, I cried for weeks on end, hardly able to sleep and didn't eat enough to keep a cat alive. I sometimes wonder now how I ever survived. Mostly I kept the window shades down and walked around the house like a zombie. Willard got concerned enough that he wanted me to see a doctor, but I couldn't face anybody like I was. Then I believe the Lord spoke to me again. That verse in Romans kept running through my mind like a stuck record. He began talking to me, saying to rise up and hold my head high, that I was the victim here and, though I wasn't perfect, I had done nothing to deserve this. He said something else, too, said there would be a day of judgment and that vengeance belonged to Him. But the thing that meant the most to me was His promise to bring something good out of the bad.

"I knew what it was because I'd already missed my period. I'd always been regular as clockwork and when it was late my first thought was, it was because of the trauma. Then I started worrying about it and thought back, well, yes, me and Willard had had relations about a week before the rape, so that kinda put my mind at ease. Then when God gave me His promise, I experienced that 'peace which passes all understanding.' I know you've read it in the book of Philippians.

"Now, to your question about me not crying over this; Edith, I did that years ago and now have no tears left to shed over it. I mourned my passing then and that's one reason I'm not sad about dying. Oh, I hate to leave Claude Earl and Willard, but I'm not sad for me. The Lord showed me that when I was born again the old self died at that time. I just hadn't got around to living the new life yet. So coming to that truth gave me another perspective. I saw for the first time that I wasn't living for me anymore, but for Christ who lives within me. It turned my thinking around; while I couldn't be myself anymore I could live and do for others. So I've spent a lifetime living and growing in Christ. Why, I was still very self-centered, even when we made that trip to Sweetwater right after Claude Earl was born. Do you remember?"

"Oh I'll never forget that, but when are you going to tell me who raped you?"

"I've worried about that for some time now and decided not to… Here's why. The minute Claude Earl was born I knew he wasn't Willard's. He looked just like the rapist and I had to fight to keep from hating that precious little baby. As innocent and pure as he was, all I could see was that awful man's face. Then, suddenly, a miracle happened, a true miracle; he changed right before my eyes and never, even to this day, has he ever favored him again. Looks exactly like my mother's people, and even acts like them too. After I picked him up the first time, well that was it! He grabbed my heart and never turned it loose. If I were to tell you who it was, I'm afraid you'd feel differently about Claude Earl, and I don't want that. He believes you're his aunt and loves you very, very much."

"I don't know whether I'd feel different or not," Edith sighed. "But, honestly, I don't think so because I've known for a long time he didn't belong to Willard. You ought to know by now that I take a person for who they are, and not on somebody else's account."

"Excuse me, Edith, but did I hear a car drive up? Claude Earl is supposed to be here at four to give me a shot, but it's not quite that late is it?"

"No, according to your clock radio it's just a little past three. It may be Wade and Max, you know they went to the racetrack over in Charlotte. Wade was hoping to see Banjo Mathews and his crew. Let me look out the window for a minute. ...Yeah, yeah it is, it's them, and I see Wade coming to the door right now. He'll want to be leaving pretty soon; you know how him and Max are. We're planning on spending the night in Marion before driving on home in the morning."

Squirming to find a position higher on the pillows, Hester pressed Earl's Bible tightly against her breast; "Edith, I want you to take this to Kathleen. It really belongs to her anyway, but it's just so hard to give up. After all these years and everything that's happened, I feel like it's a part of me. Still though, it's not right to keep it any longer."

Once harpooned, love's line to the heart holds fast.

The new arrivals effectively put an end to a conversation that had brought both participants to near exhaustion. "I'll bet you two ain't done a thing but set here and talk about your good-looking men!" Wade laughed. "

Edith shot a look at Hester. "Oh, my Lord!" she gasped. "He's found out about my boyfriend!"

A broad smile underscored Wade's unconcern; he and Max had spent a good day together. They remained standing, hoping to send a signal that it was time to go. "We need to be on the road pretty soon," Max said. "I'd like to get back to Arnold's before dark." By then, however, Edith was on her feet and gathering up the few things, she had brought.

Looking down at Hester their eyes exchanged feelings that mere words could never express. Finally, Edith spoke; "I know exactly who it was and you needn't worry about me and Claude Earl. After all, he is my nephew. One thing you ought to know, though, but for the Grace of God it could've been me."

On the way out, they ran into Claude Earl in the driveway, he'd returned home a little early hoping to catch them before they left. After passing a few pleasantries, Edith extracted a promise that he would call the minute Hester got into trouble. "If at all possible, I want to be with her at the end." As their car slowly backed out into the street, Edith looked at Claude Earl and saw something quite revealing. It was then; perhaps in a moment of subliminal memory, he lifted his brow to blare his eyes. "Yes," Edith murmured. "But for the Grace of God and a .38 special it could have been me."

Three days later, at exactly seven minutes past eight on Tuesday morning, a call from Claude Earl brought the news. "Edith? ...Mother passed away." Soft words, arrow tipped with sorrow, went straight for the heart to send quiet sobbing sounds through the receivers of both telephones. "She went peacefully and Daddy found her about an hour ago. He would have called himself, but he's in too bad a shape. I guess I never really knew how much he loved her until now. They always seemed a little distant toward one another, but you can tell his heart is just broken. There's another thing I need to mention while I've got you on the line, and maybe you can make some sense out of it. Mother slept nearly all day yesterday, she was so weak, yet when I saw her last night it seemed like she'd rallied and was acting more like her old self again. She made me promise to call you today and let you know that Michael had come by for a few minutes, just to get acquainted; said she really fell for him. She also wanted me to be sure and say that he had a message for you; said he'd take good care of her and actually that would be a snap after serving you Gernons' all those years. He went on to tell how you folks had just about run the hound out of him. Now, Edith, I don't have the foggiest idea where all that came from. I was home all day and nobody else was here; if they were, I certainly would have known it. I guess maybe she was just dreaming; either that or was delusional. But I did promise to do it and somehow I'm glad I did."

"I'm glad, too," Edith agreed and soon they hung up. "That Michael," Edith smiled through tears. "So he's left the Gernons for good has he; well, if he thinks anybody cares he's barking up the wrong tree, that's all I can say!"

CHAPTER 47

The time at hand was at once both exciting and challenging, for it offered an opportunity to begin again. After four years without a paycheck and now with two daughters in college and another starting high school Jesse was itchy to get going. Thus, when after his first week's work they were able to deposit over nine hundred dollars in the bank, he felt it was an event worth celebrating. Never mind that the receipts were not nearly enough to meet expenses, money was finally coming in, and that was the bottom line. Maggie, practical as ever, eyed his exuberance with concern. "This has been a long time in coming, Jesse, but we're not out of the woods yet, so let's not go overboard," she cautioned.

Although it looked antiquated, his used office equipment was in fine condition. A retired optometrist had made him an excellent deal, and after a little cleaning and polishing it presented well at "open house." Considering the large turnout, Jesse had good reason to believe they were off to a good start. Adding to his optimism were all the kind words said about his staff. Maggie had agreed to work the front desk for a while. Nancy, an LPN, was very enthusiastic about her new job, and proved to be a quick and eager learner in optometry. Carolyn, another LPN, would join them a few months later.

Fannie Woodcock appeared nervous while scraping mud from her shoes onto the front porch steps. Her taxi, a brand new Impala, sat with its motor humming powerfully by the roadside. Obviously, she had cut straight across the yard, now sodden by recent rains. "Should have used the walk," she mumbled " Oh! Edith, I'm sorry, I didn't see you standing there. Tell me something, though: Is that boy of yours the new eye dentist over at Andrews?"

"Fannie, don't just stand there with your mouth hanging open, come on in…

Or if you'd rather we can sit out here on the porch?" Edith sounded friendly, yet guarded.

"We'll stay out here if you don't mind; I can't stay but a minute, anyhow."

By the time Edith finally got around to the question, her answer seemed oddly out of place. "Well, yes, he is, Fannie; Jesse's the new ostomestrist over there. I never can say that word," she apologized. "Anyhow, he is, but why do you ask?"

"Soon as I get my new Medicaid card, I need to make an appointment. It's got so I can't read a lick for nothing." Her voice suddenly took on a happier note. "But my eyes ain't so bad I can't see what a good looking man Verlin Bradshaw is. Ain't he the prettiest feller you ever saw?" With that, she beamed a broad smile directly at her driver. "Verlin's taking me to Stecoah to stay a few days with my daughter Anne. She ain't doing no good, been down with her back now for several months. It's all because of that sorry man of hers. He left her and them little young'ins to take-up with some old rip. What I've stopped here for, though, ain't got a thing to do with that, and like I say, I can't stay but for a minute. Anyhow, I reckon you know I've been keeping Claude Conway at my house; he came about two months ago. You'd heard about it, hadn't you?"

With the wisp of a smile teasing Edith's lips, she otherwise looked noncommittal. "I've heard some talk Fannie, but I didn't pay no attention to it. Actually, I thought they had him in Broughton and that his mind was eat up with some kind of disease."

"Well, I figured you had, the way people love to talk. But I'll swear to God all I ever wanted to do was help the man out a little bit. Lord knows he ain't in any shape to do nothing." She now sounded a little sad. "It was quare the way that happened. He tells me it come on him all of a sudden-like. First, he got to feeling poorly and just couldn't seem to get over it, so finally he went to a doctor there in Gastonia. It was pretty soon after that when this other thing hit. I reckon they put him on some drugs, tranquilizers and the like, and then he really started going downhill in a hurry. The next thing you know they had him in a nursing home and he stayed there for about a year before going to Broughton.

"There they treated him like a crazy person, said most of the time he hardly knew who he was. They kept him there until a little over three months ago when a new doctor took a good look at him and then run a few tests. Do you know what? In just a few days, the old feller had his mind back. They said it was from a bad thyroid and that he had been taking the wrong kind of medicine all that time. Why, them old tranquilizers were eating him alive, so when they started doctoring him right, he snapped right out of it. Well, nearly, he got his mind back, but still he seems awful blue and talks all the time about Earl Akers and Sonny. You know Sonny is what Jack's folks always called him.

"I've got to be leaving in just a minute, Edith, but the main reason I stopped was on account of Claude. He wanted me to ask if you'd come and see him. If you would, then you'd better do it pretty soon because he's liable to be gone. There's something bearing on his mind, but only the Good Lord knows what. He mumbles all the time and I can't get him to hush up, even while he's eating. So, if you will, I'd sure appreciate it and I know he will, too."

Gazing through the glassed-in panel Edith looked past the creek, and toward where Grandma's old house used to stand. Now, however, a line of new-growth walnut trees obscured her view. Noticeably, the leaves were just beginning to turn; their color had gone from green to yellowish-brown in less than a week. The cooler air served as a reminder that seasonal changes were taking place. "Yes, tell him I'll come, but as you know Hester died a few weeks ago and I need to make a trip to Gastonia first. I'd like to go see about Willard before it gets too cold. Tell Claude, though, I'll be up there to see him just as soon as I get back… and that'll probably be in a week or two," she added thoughtfully.

Two loud honks on the car horn told them that Verlin was getting impatient.

"I've got to go, Edith, but I'll tell him what you said, and I know he'll be glad." Fannie's glee was evident; she was a girl again and rearing to go. "Verlin's tired of wanting," she giggled. "My goodness, what do you reckon that boy's got on his mind?"

Hardly had the car pulled away before Edith reached for the telephone, but never had the chance to dial before Wade walked in.

"Who was that…another one of my old girlfriends?"

"You'd better be careful, Romeo, or you're liable to be right for a change!" Knowing the look, Wade wisely chose not to pursue the matter.

"That Rose bunch," he grumbled. "They ain't a lick of humor in none of 'em!" Resigned as he was, he still was in no mood to banter.

As always, however, Edith stood ready to defend her family. "Why, Wade, that ain't so: every Rose I know of has a big belly-laugh every time they hear your name."

"Well," he snorted. "I'm going over to Max's for a while, he's still working on that house of his'n and I might be able to offer him a hand. If I ain't back by supper, just holler when it's ready."

Edith quickly turned her attention back to the telephone, and to calling Ollie Grindstaff.

"Hello, is that you Ollie? This is Edith, yes, Edith here on the head of Sweetwater. Are you doing okay?

"No, we're all just fine on this end, but I needed to speak to you for a minute. You remember sometime back when you'as up here and we talked about the Earl Akers case?

"Well, we did and it was right after you got elected to be Clerk of Court. But, anyhow, you said then that you had a good friend who worked in the Gaston County courthouse.

"Yeah, Melanie, I believe that's her name.

"You remember now?

"Well, okay. See, since then I've come up with something, and what I need to do is dig a little deeper. Do you reckon you could get Melanie to let me see the trial records? If she would, I'd just need to look at a thing or two, and it wouldn't hurt nothing.

"Huh?

"Yeah, what I need to do is get the facts on something that might finally put an end to all this speculating. And, too, Claude Conway just sent word this morning that he wants to talk to me. It's vital that I get to see them files first though, otherwise I can't hold his feet to the fire. But from what I hear he's in pretty bad shape and could die at anytime. So, if we're ever going to get to the bottom of this, it's got to be pretty soon!

"Do what? Oh yes, do whatever it takes; I need to make another trip back down there, anyhow. Can you believe it was a month ago today that Hester died? You ought to go with me, maybe take some time off.

"They, Lord, no, he's got plenty of room, and would be pleased to death to have you. You know how people are there in Gastonia, all of 'em. They just love for us folks here on Sweetwater to come down. I reckon they're lonesome. Yes, call just as soon as you know."

Hanging up, Sweetwater's queen of sleuth began cooking supper, and within an hour had it on the table just when Wade walked in.

"Edith, all I wanted was some fried chicken and a little gravy; you know I can't stand them old Arish potaters, they ain't fit for a dog to eat."

"Set your hind-end down here and eat, or I'll kick it for you. And I don't want to hear nothing more about potatoes, neither; I'll bet you a five dollar bill they won't be a bite left when you finish."

Edith would have taken the pot had they bet. "Well, I'll swear if these ain't about the best'uns I ever tasted," he averred while wiping his plate clean. A huge pile of chicken bones lay to the side of it.

"Get the phone, Wade," she demanded at its first ring.

"Yeah, she's here, Ollie, but what do you want to talk to her for when you've got me? Edith, it's Ollie wanting to say something." A look of chagrin accompanied his displeasure at handing over the instrument.

"Hello?" Edith sounded almost surprised.

"No, no, Ollie, I'm glad you called. I was just thinking about that.

"Why, Wade and Max, I reckon; they can take me.

"Oh, you could, well that would be a lot better. And that'll give you a chance to see Melanie, too, won't it? She must be a fine person.

"No, I think that'd be wonderful, if she could. Will Ralphie go, too?

"Stay with his daddy, oh, I see, well let's just plan on that then. We can leave here Friday morning and if nothing happens, be back Sunday.

"Yes, I'll call and talk to him, but I know Willard's going to be pleased to death to hear it.

"No, I'm sure of it, we'll leave here about seven, and that'll get us to the courthouse before one.

"Huh?

"You say they don't close 'til four? Well, that'll give us plenty of time then, and I'm just tickled to death that Laura wants to go, too, but how's she going to get off from school?

Why, yes, I hadn't thought about that, she'll get a substitute.

"Okay, that's good.

"No, I've got to tell him, but he's setting here now puffed up like a big frog. He'll get over it though, just wanted you to talk to him, I reckon. Wade ain't near the bear dog he wants me to think he is, and, besides, I just cooked him one of the best fried chicken suppers you ever saw. If he ever wants another'n, he'll straighten up.

"Why, yes, he could if he wanted to, but you know how Wade is. Anyhow, I appreciate you calling and we'll just plan on that, then. I'll be in touch with you in the morning, maybe sometime around ten.

"Okay, well, 'bye."

"By Ned, I'm putting my big foot down this time! You'uns ain't got one bit of business taking off to Gastonia like this. Three women out on the road by their self... why, no sir! That wouldn't look right a-tall and, besides, they ain't one bit of need in it."

"Now, you listen here, Wade Gernon, this just happens to be the twentieth-century; women get out and do things these days. Besides, this has to do with Keith and his secret, so, if you don't like 'er then Buster you can lump it, because we're going and that's final!"

They left Sweetwater on time and according to plan. Laura drove her car, but the two magpies she took along nearly drove her batty with their incessant chatter. They made excellent time by stopping only twice, arriving in Gastonia just a few minutes before noon. Although a tee-totaler, Laura felt like heading for a bar.

CHAPTER 48

Melanie, a trim brunette about Ollie's age, welcomed them into her office. The fact that this southern belle looked much younger than her age took nothing from her professional abilities. The presence of certain files seen resting on her desk spoke volumes about her influence; a word to the Gaston County archives custodian had been sufficient. "Now, you all just make yourselves right at home," she said. "I've got to run out for a few minutes, but I'll be back directly, then we'll just sit here and have us a good old-time visit, you hear?" With that and a nod toward the desk, she was gone.

Edith wasted no time, "Ollie, if you will, start looking in the medical examiners and coroner's reports that describes how Earl died. I'll be going through the court records. Laura was amazed at how quickly they rifled through the huge quantity of material; it took only a matter of minutes.

"Here's something!" Ollie said sounding pleased at being first to strike pay dirt.

"Yeah, well lay it to the side for a minute; I'd like to see what this says first." Edith was onto something too, and continued to skim through the files for another five minutes. "Yes, yes this is it," she smiled. "Ollie, could I get you to write this for me; this paragraph right here, everything it says, now let me see what you've got."

"All these years," she exulted in triumph, "and I've wondered if Jim Gernon was right. You remember, don't you, Ollie? It was that Christmas a few years after the war." Suddenly her countenance darkened. "Poor Hester," she lamented. "Everybody was so wrong about her, but what's even worse she was wrong about herself. I just hope she can be at peace now."

"Edith, I've known all along part of what Jim said was true, but I couldn't see what it had to do with anything. Remember, even though he was quoting Mayor Sluder, he still came up with some cock-eyed conclusion that made no sense at all."

"My Lord, Ollie, what else would you expect from Jim? With this, though, and now that Hester's gone it's vital I talk with Claude just as soon as I can. He's the only hope we've got to ever get to the bottom of this. But if, and it's a big IF, he'll just level with me, I believe we can!"

"Or, *if* he don't die first," Ollie conjectured, sounding concerned..

Moment's later a breathless Melanie rushed back into the room. "Oh, now look at that," she panted, "I've gone out and left all those files on my desk. They're classified and, of course, y'all realize they're confidential. But," she brightened, "I'm willing to swear I didn't see you touch a thing, so why don't we just leave it at that. My motto is, see no evil, hear no evil, and say no evil. Do I hear an Amen from anybody?"

Seemingly, out of control, the spinning clock hands barely allowed time enough for Laura and Melanie to renew their friendship before it was time to say goodbye. Willard, worn out from waiting, was obviously peeved when finally they pulled into his driveway. "I figured you folks would come rolling in here around one," he grimaced.

"No Willard, I explained that to you, we had go by the courthouse first! Ollie here wanted to see her friend, Melanie." Then, in an obvious attempt to change the subject, she gestured toward Laura, "It's been a long time since you saw this young lady, ain't it? I'll bet she was just a teenager back then. Why, no," Edith corrected herself, "you saw her at the fish-fry that time! I swear, I don't know where my mind is lately." Glancing around she found the place to be spick and span, yet it still looked somewhat in disarray. *Needs a woman's touch,* she mused.

"Well, find yourself a seat and let's talk awhile before supper," he offered. Resigned, though he was, Willard now was back to his old self again, easygoing, friendly, and quiet. The visitors soon learned that Claude Earl was working another double shift and probably would be away all night. The conversation slowly began to drift and in time, Willard excused himself in order to feed his pet beagles. Once out of earshot Ollie plied Edith with reasons why they should leave for home early the next morning. Laura's voice of protest, however, came across as a whining challenge. "Well, why do you want to do that for?" she pouted. "Tomorrow I'd like to do a little shopping and maybe go over to Charlotte." Ollie's feet were set in concrete, however, and refused to budge.

"Now hush, Laura, it's just too lonesome here, and that's reason enough."

Willard enjoyed his company, almost as much as he did the food they prepared; cubed steak and gravy with biscuits. It was refreshing for Edith to serve Irish potatoes without hearing complaints. "Best supper I've had since Hester died," he said. Then his shoulders began to shake as the tears rolled copiously down both cheeks. Shed for the woman he loved, it was apparent that the hurt was just as acute now as it was the moment she died.

They all retired early, Laura and her mother to an upstairs bedroom while Edith napped on the couch. Willard slept in his room on the first floor. Left unsaid, however, was what to do with Claude Earl since no one knew when or even if he would come in. Edith, therefore, resolved that should it happen during the night she'd fix him something to eat before sending him on to bed. These plans, however, never materialized.

Not sleeping well, Laura decided to arise early and by six forty-five, had both showered and dressed. Quietly making her way to the kitchen she soon located the coffee and had a pot going when an almost inaudible click sounded at the side door. Her heart skipped a beat at the sight of him. Claude Earl, with his day-old beard looked a little wild and seemed genuinely surprised by her presence. They stood just staring at one another for over ten seconds, an interval that easily could have filled a ten-minute time slot.

He was first to break the silence with a muttered, "Hi," she responded in kind, but was unable to contain a smile that ignited an otherwise somber moment.

While searching for something else to say she offered him a cup of coffee. "Yeah, thanks, I'm really beat this morning." He seemed politely appreciative while stirring in enormous quantities of sugar and cream. "Like a little coffee in my cream and sugar," he joked lightly. "Daddy said you and your mother were coming with Edith, but I didn't think you would."

"Why? Why did you think that?"

"Well ..." he paused. "Anybody who couldn't take the time to answer a measly letter certainly couldn't be expected to make a trip like this."

"I *ANSWERED* your letter!" Unfortunately, the words sounded harsher than she really meant them to. "But you didn't bother to answer mine, did you? So, case closed!"

"No, not case closed, not just yet. You say you answered my letter, well, why then didn't I get it? ...You don't reckon it's still in the mail do you? Skepticism now flowed thick enough to choke off any further discussion, yet Laura felt a response was imperative.

"Same mail that never brought your answer to me I guess. You think it's easy to make a fool of yourself, just to get embarrassed. I waited around for months. But finally I figured it out; you don't appreciate honesty, do you?"

"If I ever saw it in anybody outside of my own family, I might; so until I do, don't hold your breath. I'd have thought a lot more of you if at least you'd have shown the courtesy to answer back, and just say that you didn't care for me. Now to my mind that would've been honest."

"So, is that what you wanted… for me to reject you? Well, I guess I missed the point! But, if it'll make you feel any better I can do that right now. Is that what you want?"

"Sure, go ahead and do it, may as well make it official, I've already accepted it, anyway. But before you do let's just get one thing straight; you did get my letter didn't you?"

"Of course, I did and I wrote you right back, too, but I suppose that don't really matter now does it?"

"Suppose not, by golly!"

Suddenly they were back to square one, back to just staring at each other in disbelief. This time, however, a third party broke the spell. "I thought I heard somebody out here. My Lord, Claude Earl you look awful, you're plumb worn out, ain't you, Son?" Edith appeared larger than life in her pink housecoat and frazzled hair that had the color of what Wade often described as "piss-burnt brown."

"Oh! Hi, Aunt Edith! I hope we didn't wake you up. I was just getting ready to go on to bed myself, but Laura's been telling me how slow the mail is there on Sweetwater. That's the first I'd heard of it."

"It can be," Edith agreed. "You know since Ed Jennings lost his job and they give it to a new mail-boy, it ain't been the same. But I was hoping that you two could get together, it's obvious you're crazy over each other. I guess I just plain don't understand some people, and I'll swear if you both don't act plumb quare at times."

"I don't deal well with people who can't be trusted," Laura glared. "Or, for that matter, ones who like to play games with your feelings. I've already been down that road once and can speak from experience; it just isn't worth it." With that, she turned and was gone. Edith and Claude Earl sat sipping their coffee, a quiet rain had settled in and the only audible sound was that of a dripping roof. Before ten o'clock Laura had already driven them nearly fifty miles westward, and by early afternoon they were back on Sweetwater. All the way home she had been so preoccupied with her thoughts that even the endless prattle seemed to be of little bother. From Edith and Ollie's perspective, however, the time proved valuable. It allowed them, starting with Keith's illness and Earl's death, to reconstruct all the major events that had occurred. Meticulously, they discussed, in chronological order, each fact before moving on to the next one. By so doing, the outline of a picture began to emerge. "It's like a jig-saw puzzle, Ollie, and I say Claude Conway now holds all the missing pieces. Oh, by the way, I'm really onto something that seems unbelievable, but it's going to take us making a few telephone calls. My first clue came from what Gutch Reece overheard between Bruce and Claude. I think I know now what they meant and if I'm right, it'll blow this thing wide open."

"My goodness, Edith, I wasn't expecting you back until tomorrow. I was making 'er just fine, and getting to like the quiet for a change."

"What's that awful odor in the kitchen? Oh, for crying out-loud, you've ruined the best pot I have trying to cook pinto beans. Well, they're burnt up and I'll probably never get this smell out!"

Laura, after dropping off her mother at home, was unable to contain herself any further and began to fall apart the moment she was alone. Now finally able to do what she'd wanted to all day long, began bawling her eyes out. Sheer guts alone had sustained her through other crisis and because of that, she'd grown strong. Strong enough, she hoped, to help her make it through this one, too, but this time it was different. Unexplained and certainly without reason she'd dared to dream that someday, somehow, she and Claude Earl would be together. Sure, there had been other men to choose from; yet for some reason her heart pined for him. Even in marriage, she couldn't forget him, although heaven knows she had tried, really tried. Yet his face was the one that haunted her dreams, and had from the start. Right from the moment, she first laid eyes on him; her soul knew it had found its mate.

Really now, isn't this being rather juvenile and even ridiculous? I think it's finally time to grow up and get over this summertime crush, she reasoned. Yet, if all of this was true, then why was her heart breaking? She cried until an old nemesis began to manifest. Seeing halos always meant another migraine was on its way. The flickering prodrome convinced her it was now time to give up the fight... it was all futile, anyway. I have to accept the fact that I'm hopelessly in love, but I also know the whole thing is just a big mess, and that's a real fact. Perhaps the headache will go away if I can get a little fresh air, she reasoned. However, that is when the doorbell rang. Oh, my Lord, I don't need some nosey old neighbor dropping by and telling me about their rhubarb patch. I'll just ignore it and maybe they'll leave. Later on, I can say that probably I was in the shower.

Whoever it was did not intend to leave, as evidenced by the sound of an iron fist pounding away at the door. Finally fed up she stormed out; "I'll put a stop to this right now!" Indignant, she reached for the knob, ready to put them on their way.

"What do you want?" She demanded as the door swung open. "Oh, my goodness, how dare you!" Suddenly she was staring into the face of Claude Earl Rose. "I've got nothing more to say to you and I thought I'd made that perfectly clear this morning."

"Well, I've got something to say to you! And considering that I drove up here without a wink of sleep for over forty-eight hours, don't you think I deserve at least a word or two? Just give me one minute, please. I love you, Laura; I always have, and always will! There has never been anybody but you, and nobody in this world makes me feel the way you do. I started thinking right after you left that maybe you did write me back; otherwise, why would you've even bothered to acknowledge it? And since you did then you must've felt the same way I did, or else it wouldn't have mattered. Now, I have no idea of what might have happened to your letter. But my heart tells me that you love me, too... Am I right?"

"If you'd asked me that this morning I might have said yes. Why do you think I went down there anyway? Certainly not just to hear two old women run their mouths for four hundred miles. But now I don't know what I feel, except maybe a little numb; that and this migraine I've got."

"Well, let me tell you this; I've got a fire burning inside that won't let me be until I know how you really feel. I'm going up to my Uncle Arnold's place on Sweetwater. He calls it his sugar shack, you know where it is, that little hut above Wade and Edith's. I'm going to sack out there for a while; you can see I'm totally exhausted. So if you find that you love me and want to give it a try then be there by this time tomorrow. Otherwise, I'll be gone and you'll never see me again. But, oh how I pray you'll come, Darling. I love you, Laura, with all my heart."

If only he had turned back around while walking away, he would not have missed seeing something quite remarkable. Eyes, only seconds before that had looked hard as steel, now suddenly became blue pools of endless love gazing at a form they adored.

Trance-like he moved to open the door and moments later, after stepping into the shadows, sleep took over. Just how long he slept became knowledge that mattered not.

She stood there in the pale morning moonlight looking more beautiful than any reverie he ever had of her. And there had been plenty. Words, if uttered at all, went unheard for their arms held each other so tightly they suddenly became as a person. No separate thought, no separate spirit, no separate heartbeat, for, yes, they became flesh and blood made as one. Love, true love is eternal, and when it finds a way, the most physical act of flesh becomes spiritual and thereby partakes of the divine. For it is in this expression, love of human for human, that the endless cycle of God's highest physical creation can continue. And it is blessed, for it was pre-ordained by Him to be thus until the fullness of time is come, soul unto soul, mind unto mind, body unto body, becoming one spirit that responds to a single harmonizing chord. Then the words, the music, and the lilt combine in an aria worthy of celestial glory, a love song, a sweet song that will never grow old.

The blending of our spirits
Is it the ending of our lonely nights and days?
The melding of our hearts
So long, they've been apart
But now love, true love, has found a way.

All that is past they forgot, and the future became but an elusive dream too far away to reach, so for over two days and two nights they dwelt in the blessed now. Once, during that time, Claude Earl woke up to see Laura sitting on the floor, cross-legged and just staring at him. At first, she seemed to be a little embarrassed, but then after tracing his body beneath her hand she spoke. "You look so perfect lying there. I could go on and on and be happy here with you forever. We're Adam and Eve all over again in this, our own little world. Say to me and mean it; say that this will never end."

He reached out to touch her lips, "So beautiful, Angel Face, you're so incredibly beautiful." His finger lifted a coil of blond hair, once silky, but now dried and sticking to her forehead. They laughed together as he pulled her back into bed. Later they discussed food and decided to try a restaurant in Bryson City.

On the way back, Claude Earl asked her to marry him.

"Silly, do you really think you need to ask? The question really ought to be when."

"Well, I do have to work a two-week notice you know, so that's when. I want us to live up here; this is more home to me than Gastonia could ever be. It's lonely down there since Mother died and I believe Daddy would sell out in a minute and move, too, if I left."

That settled it. They tried for a while then to discuss the future, but found it borrowed too much from their present joy, so they gave up the effort. Both cried when they parted, she going back home and to work and he leaving for Gastonia. Faithfully, they promised, and meant it, that they would never be apart for this long again. Oh, pity the poor helmsman who thinks to steer his own ship of destiny. Nevertheless, let us take comfort from knowing that the Great Captain has power to guide us all safely into the harbor and home at last.

CHAPTER 49

"CLAUDE! HEY CLAUDE!... WAKE UP! EDITH'S HERE!" Fannie, wasting no kindness on her companion, roused him from a deep sleep. He had been snoring loudly since a little before noon and now it was just past two.

"Huh? What... do what? Oh yeah, wait a minute. Yeah, let me see her. I need to talk to Edith."

While Wade was willing to drive her to Pin-Hook, not once did he even entertain the idea of going inside. Actually, it seemed that he could not get away from there fast enough. "I'll be back in about an hour and toot the horn when I do," he said. But you can come on out when you're ready." Wade's eyes stayed focused straight ahead, as he spoke.

All the way there, Edith's thoughts clung to the importance of this talk. Her expectations were high, buoyed up by the mere fact that Claude was still alive. Perhaps Providence was guiding matters after all, especially when considering all that had transpired since her "chance" meeting with Kathleen. Following that, of course, had been Hester's confession; reversing the two events would have caused much of what they now knew to be lost. In addition, it was encouraging that Claude had asked for her and not the other way around.

Edith was shocked at his appearance. Here was a man in his early sixties, yet he looked to be well past the age of eighty. Her worries about getting to him in time had certainly been well placed. *Time may have just run out*, she grimaced. "Preacher Conway, why I ain't seen you in years; how have you been?"

"Not good Mrs. Gernon, they liked to have killed me down there in Morganton, and may have, anyway. Most days it takes all I can do to crawl out of the bed. I needed to talk to you, but not in front of her. FANNIE, YOU KNOW WHAT I SAID, NOW GET ON OUT OF HERE!"

Startled, Fannie obeyed immediately by pulling the door shut behind her, however, when she did the room suddenly felt cold and dark. Edith looked around at the grayness; only one window and it let precious little light in, yet even so it still helped to soften the otherwise dismal surroundings There was no paper, paint, or pictures to grace the walls, a tiny rusting wood heater, an old sofa, and a cheap, metal poster-bed completed the furnishings. Worn-out linoleum covered the floor. *She could've at least put sheets on that mattress and it's no wonder he's dying, he ain't got nothing to live for*.

"Why did you need to see me, Claude?"

"Mrs. Gernon, there's something on my heart that's got to be said. You know about me losing my mind then getting it back again, don't you?" He waited for a nod before proceeding. "Since I'd been sick for such a long time it took a good while before I got to where I could remember things, probably about two months, and when I did it liked to have killed me. I remembered stuff that nobody ought to have to face. I kept telling myself that it was all just a bad dream, but deep inside I knew better. Then about a month ago, I finally realized I had to own up to it; everything I remembered was the truth. I guess before getting sick I had a seared conscience, just like the Bible talks about. Well, let me tell you, it ain't that way now. There's times when mine tortures me so bad I can't stand it. I've asked the Lord to forgive me, so that I might be delivered from this torment. Sometimes I believe He has, but, Sister, I can't forgive myself." Claude unexpectedly stopped talking and drooped over in his chair. Edith feared that he might pitch to the floor, but after straightening back up she saw that his face was awash with tears.

"Do you need me to get you anything?" There was genuine compassion in her voice.

"No, Mrs. Gernon, but I thank you, anyway… Now, I'm not fixing to preach you a sermon here: God knows I ain't fit to do that, but remember this: only He can both forgive *and* forget. I believe humans can and must forgive one another, but it's impossible to forget. It all goes back to the original sin, partaking of the tree of the knowledge of good and evil, this inability to forget. It's a blessing when it keeps us from repeating the same old mistakes over and over again. Yet at the same time, it's a curse when we finally realize what our sins have done. Only in heaven will we be able to finally forget, so let's be grateful for that! I've asked Him to tell me what I can do to try and make things right, before I have to face Him. And I think He has."

Thinking she now knew the purpose for the trip, Edith was perplexed at herself for feeling such sympathy for him. In measured tones she asked the obvious; "What has God instructed you to do, Claude?" Immediately, however, she realized the question was a loaded gun with it pointed straight at her.

"God told me to talk to you. But He also let it me know that with all the harm I've done, a lot can never be undone. Yet, He made it plain that the truth must finally be told; if I'm to have any peace."

An incredulous Edith dared to venture another question, "If you don't mind my asking, how did He go about telling you this?"

"See, that's the strange thing. He first laid it on my heart, and then about three weeks ago this feller came by here. I was on my knees praying to have this burden lifted, when I looked up to see a great big feller setting right where you are now. He spoke in such a good clear voice that I figured he must be a preacher. His first words were that God had forgiven me, and that He would never reject a person who sincerely repented of their sins. Then he mentioned you by name and said to tell you everything. There was something about him though, that scared me; I guess maybe it was his eyes. Anyhow, I glanced off for a second, but when I looked back again, he was gone. Now, don't that beat all?"

"Was he a great-big red-headed feller with pretty teeth?"

"I didn't notice his teeth," Claude smiled. "But, yeah he was a big feller all right, red-headed and just like you say. Why, do you know him?"

"Our paths have crossed a time or two, but this is the first I'd heard of him being back around here. Yes, I believe God did send you a message, Claude, and I'll do everything I can to help. Now, though, we've got a lot of serious talking to do, and I counting on you to set everything straight. Unless you do, you'll never find that peace you need. I hate to have to ask you this, but you murdered Earl Akers, didn't you?" She watched the blood drain from his face.

"They, my Lord, so you already know?"

"You also know that Hester Rose passed away, don't you?" His affirmation came amid anguished sounds of labored breathing. She waited patiently before pushing on. "Well, Hester died just a few days after telling me everything. She went to her grave believing she did it. One of the things to convince me that it was you, though, was Earl's Bible. Remember, Hester left the meeting early that night, just as soon as he quit preaching. There's evidence to show he still had his Bible after that, making it impossible for her to have it, unless she came back later."

Claude was quick to jump in. "That's at the very heart of what I've got to say."

Edith's first response was a hard look that quickly softened. "Well, like I said, she confessed to everything. Told me about you and Earl fighting that night and then how she accidentally cut his throat. She could only remember a little of what happened after that until she ended up in the car. It surprised her to find the Bible and umbrella in her lap. We both figured you planted them there to serve your purposes. The Bible was a perfect way to tie her to the murder and the umbrella provided an alibi for you both. But I'm getting ahead of the story here, and besides it's you who ought to be telling it, not me. One other thing though, then we'll come back to this later."

Claude looked anxious. "Yes," he agreed. "We've got to do that. "

Edith continued. "I learned a lot by reading what the medical examiner wrote in his report. It plainly showed that while Earl indeed did die from bleeding, it wasn't from the knife wound. There's a bone in the neck called the hyoid, and when Earl's fractured, its sharp-edge cut through an artery. So, yes he bled to death all right, but it was internal, and not from the knife wound. The doctor's note stated that he wanted to tell all this to the jury. But the state insisted that he keep it simple by just describing the knife wound, and then tell how Earl died from massive blood loss. Their point was that since whoever cut him had done so with the intent to kill, so why confuse the jury with facts. Interestingly, the defense lawyer never questioned a thing, but I reckon if you don't look, you don't know, do you?"

"Hester remembered seeing blood on your hands, but if she'd cut an artery and him still alive, it would've spurted all over the place. Why, even the coroner said there was less than half a pint of blood on the ground, besides his neck wound was not deep enough to be fatal. What I still can't quite figure out, though, is why were you so angry at Earl? Obviously, you had nothing to do with the bootlegging."

Claude paused to process what he'd just heard. When at last he replied, Edith detected relief in his voice. "You're right about the bootlegging; I never was a part of that, and you've got just about all the rest right, too; it's just like you were there. I knew right away Hester hadn't done it, because what blood there was come out of his mouth, so he was probably already dead when she cut him. No doubt, when I struck him from behind or slammed his head up against the tent post, that bone in his neck snapped. I've learned since then, if it happens, knife-edged bone fragments can slice right through an artery, causing a person to die almost instantly. Oh, I've looked it up many, many times. But yes, and may God forgive me for it, I killed him and you know when I realized what had happened, I panicked. But that lasted only for a second or two, because I knew right then if I got caught, I'd be the gas chamber.

"My first impulse was to run, but then I thought no I've got to look around for something that might help get me out of this, and that's when I spotted her umbrella. It took a second, but I figured it out; me and Hester could be each other's alibi and the umbrella would be our way to prove it. The big thing that bothered me, though, was how to keep Hester in line and then I thought of the Bible. Since I knew there were people who would remember seeing it in Earl's possession after she left, and there was no way she should have it; not without returning later. So, while she was still out I put her in the car, threw it and the umbrella onto her lap, and then got us out of there in a flash. She was groggy for another five minutes or so, coming and going, but when she finally woke up enough, I started blaming her both for Earl's death and for bringing the Bible along. I kept linking the two together, saying that she'd better keep it hidden, since there was absolutely no way to explain having it without incriminating herself. Keep in mind Hester was totally convinced that she'd killed Earl, so my words had a powerful effect on her. I knew she was just too plain stupid to destroy it, so I felt safe. Meantime, I explained to her our alibi, and told her that her excuse for coming back to the tent sounded pretty flimsy, but it was all that we had. I kept drilling it into her to say that I picked her up at the bus stop around ten thirty, and that way the law couldn't touch us. She was scared of going to prison, more than to the gas chamber I think. Knowing now that she died with this on her conscience hurts so bad I can hardly stand it. She was a good woman and deserved a lot better than that."

"Yes, she did!" Edith agreed. "So, why didn't you send her word? It would have made all the difference."

Great quantities of air suddenly rushed through his wet nostrils to emit sounds not unlike those of a snorting elephant. Casting then a furtive look toward heaven, he silently begged for mercy and strength. "You don't know how much I wish I could have, but by the time I came to a full acceptance of the facts, it was too late." A moment of silence suddenly ensued that ultimately brought them back to the story.

"Oh, I pled with Earl to stay out of it, 'Let the law take care of it,' I begged and I think he knew I wasn't directly involved; not with the bootlegging, anyway. Now, I'll be the first to say I didn't mind seeing all those good offerings find their way into the collection plate, and Earl didn't, either. I still don't know exactly how far his investigation got, but he just wouldn't listen. Why, there were things not associated with the whiskey that if they got out would have ruined my ministry.

"It seems that just as soon as Guy Fowler and Lance Boyle suspected that Earl was the one, they set out to get him. They thought Keith might be involved, too, and did so for sometime after that. Actually, they worked a lot more for Sonny than they ever did for us, but at the time, we didn't know that. I'll tell you what, though; before this thing was over with, they had me scared. Somewhere along the line they and Sonny decided that our evangelistic meetings would provide the perfect cover for their operation. From what was later told, it had been going on for quite a while, yet me and Earl didn't know a thing. In my opinion, if the Revenue Department hadn't tipped Earl off, then neither one of us would have ever been the wiser."

"Yes, I know about those two," Edith shuddered. Her look of benevolence suddenly turned cold, "but it sounds to me like you're still trying to defend what you did, and avoid having to say why you got mad enough at Earl to kill him."

"Oh, I ain't trying to get out of this, Edith; in fact, much of what's yet to be told deals with that very thing. You'll just have to believe me on this; there are reasons that I still don't understand myself. But try to be patient and I'll tell you everything."

"All right, Claude, but let me ask you this, Jack Woodcock was your half-brother, wasn't he?"

Claude looked stunned. "Why, you could count on one hand all the people who know that and you're getting awful close to something here. Earl found it out, too, not very long before he died. I learned later that he'd looked at Jack's birth certificate and evidently traced it back that way. See, me and Jack had the same mother, but his daddy took him along with the other two and left us. It was then up to Mama to raise me by herself there on Painter Creek, all because she'd had me by another man. Conway was her maiden name, so I went by that. I never knew much about Sonny until I ran up with him a few years ago. Sonny is what Mama always called him, especially when she was crying. We agreed to keep this just between the two us for everybody's sake, especially Mama's."

"Well, after thinking about it awhile, it just come to me that he was, besides, it's the only way to make any sense out of all this. So, I guess you know that makes Claude Earl your nephew, don't you?"

"Actually, I'm not too sure about that, but if you don't mind let me finish this other first. No, I wouldn't have hurt Earl for anything if he'd just left it alone.

And I don't want this to sound like I'm not sorry for what I did, because I am. It was, by far, the worst thing I ever did and it may yet cost me my immortal soul. I guess what I'm really trying to do is answer your question as to why I was so angry. Well, when we got into it that night, it seemed like everything had reached the point where it was going to be either him or me, and I could tell he was past reasoning with. Knowing my brother would go to jail was bad enough, but I wasn't about to let him ruin my good name in the process. Then there's the jealousy part and I have to tell you about that or else you won't understand. I hate to say it, but Hester came between us. Oh, I loved that boy at one time probably more than even my own life, but then he fell in love with her. Now, I don't know exactly when or how it happened, except maybe after she started acting so depressed and all. I noticed them spending an awful lot of time together. Supposedly, he was counseling her, but it looked to me more like babying and petting. Then she told us about being pregnant."

"What you just said there bothers me, Claude, and we've got to talk about it!"

"Forgive me, Mrs. Gernon, but I'm only telling it the way it happened, so just bear with me and you'll see the truth. I've got a note here I want you to read in just a minute, yet no matter what it says, I'm still not sure whether Earl was the baby's daddy or not. Not with him fawning over her all the time, and it made me go crazy just thinking he might be. Now, rumors were everywhere with some claiming me as the one. No doubt you heard that, too, and Willard may even still think so. Others said Sonny went out bragging how he'd knocked her up, but Lance and Guy both claimed he'd raped her. Now, I couldn't believe a word of that, no sir! The reason I couldn't, and this may shock you, Mrs. Gernon, but I knew Sonny to be quite a ladies' man. Why he didn't need to rape anybody." Leaning forward he whispered, "I wouldn't want Fannie to hear this, but he had him a string of women out there in Gastonia. Just don't say anything, though; they ain't a bit of mileage in hurting the innocent here."

"The innocent, oh my Lord," she laughed sarcastically. "But let's put something to rest right here and now, Claude Conway; your brother did indeed rape Hester! There's no ifs ands or buts about it and hell will never be hot enough to suit me for that feller! And just for your information, Willard knows exactly what happened to Hester. So, put your mind at rest there, because I told him."

"They, Lord have mercy, Mrs. Gernon; I wouldn't argue the point with you for nothing. All I wanted to do was bring out that after Earl fell in love with her, it changed everything. Up until then we'd always been just like David and Jonathan. I loved him with my whole heart, and it was a brotherly love, too, so you may as well quit looking at me like that. I still don't know myself just how I felt except to say I loved him and that we had a wonderful ministry together. I never loved another human being like I did Earl, but then that little vixen had to show up and ruin everything.

"Actually, it was your brother, Keith, who found out about it first, and when he did it really tore him up. He started out being suspicious of Hester and me because nobody, and certainly not him, could bring themselves to think that Earl might ever have a carnal thought. In his poking around, however, Keith soon discovered the truth by the way they acted toward one another. What he ultimately learned was that Hester didn't feel the same toward Earl that he did about her, and that she'd even tried to discourage the relationship. Here, though, read it for yourself in the note that Keith had on him there in the alley when those two beat him up. I guess at the time they thought it might be something else. Later, when I heard them laughing and making jokes over it, saying what a fool Earl was, I stepped in. After shaming them for speaking ill of the dead they threw it at me, and it's stayed in that old trunk over there ever since. I guess Earl gave it to Keith, trying to prove her innocence. You know Earl had a weird sense of honor about women, and I figure he did it after Keith had confronted him. Well, anyhow, here it is."

A yellowed note, ready to fall apart, held words barely legible, yet written in a hand she recognized immediately to be that of her sister-in-law.

Dearest Earl,

Your declaration of love flatters me, and to tell you less would not be honest. But I must be honest in all things, and I must be faithful; faithful to you, faithful to my husband, and faithful to myself, but above all, faithful to God.

You have been my friend, my comfort, and in a way my lover. Yes the lover of my soul, but never my lover in the ways of the world. I see you more as a brother, close and caring, bigger than life, and a strong pillar to lean on. Just think for a moment, Earl, if we were to do what you suggest, then you would be denying your Savior and your calling. And we both know you couldn't do that. Oh, maybe for a little while, but it would eat you alive and neither one of us would survive that. I feel you are infatuated with me, your loving kindness, your good caring nature, and the sympathy you've shown has led you into this. It's a temptation from the devil and we must pray that it soon passes. Believe me, it will. Yes, I'll be a little sad when it does, but we both must be strong.

With fondest thoughts,

Your friend, Hester

Edith's emotions swirled through a myriad of feelings; it was now her time to cry. *"So, that's what it was! For all these years I've wondered, and now I know. Oh Lord, how I wish I'd been a lot better to Hester back when all this was happening. Keith was concerned about Earl, not her, and that makes a lot of sense too. It could have ruined his hopes for marrying Kathleen. Still, I can't help but feel a little disappointed; somehow I guess I expected more.*

Tears filled Edith's words when at last she spoke. "I reckon I was like everybody else and thought Earl was just too good to be human."

Claude was kind enough to allow her a few moments more before continuing. "So, you see I was disgusted with her, but jealous of Earl and knowing how he felt ate away at me until I hated the very sight of him. Then when I learned he was willing to sacrifice everything, my anger just overflowed. There were other things, too, so when we got into it I guess I just went crazy. As soon as it happened, though, I knew I'd made a bad mistake and now I can't forgive myself. What makes it even worse is that I allowed two men to die for my crime and let Hester carry all that guilt around until she took it to the grave. I don't know, Edith; I really don't know if God can forgive me or not. I'm told He can, but there's one thing I'll never be able to do and that's forgive myself."

Edith was brooding on something. "Claude, there's one other matter we need to discuss and I'd hoped you might bring it up yourself. I realize it's very personal, and yet it has to be told if the whole truth is to be known. It goes along with what Earl found out, but there's a lot more to it than Jack being your brother, isn't there?"

"Why, Mrs. Gernon," he looked mystified while sounding defensive. "I don't know what you're talking about. As I said, I don't want to keep back a thing. Nothing that's relevant, anyway."

"Well, how about telling me who your daddy is then? It's something that has everything to do with this!"

Slowly Claude's head rolled back and forth conveying a look of utter disbelief. "I just don't see how that could possibly serve anything good here. Hurting innocent people certainly is not the way of the Lord."

"Reverend Conway, we've come so far today, yet now you're holding back on me, trying to hide behind some false sense of honor. I already know who it is and, believe you me; it'll never go any further than right here. But, yes, you do need to tell it, and you need to do it right now! If you don't, then how's the truth ever supposed to set you free?"

Opening his mouth, at first the words wouldn't come, but when they did the floodgates were opened. "Mama raised me by herself and it was just the two of us. Oh, occasionally he'd send us a few dollars, and you know I was nearly grown before I learned for certain that Bruce Sluder was my daddy. She didn't tell me, though; I just figured it out myself. Fact is, I never heard her once mention his name.

"From early on I knew she'd been married before and had three other young'ins that lived down near Gastonia. Oh, how she grieved over them. I can still hear her crying and calling each one by name. On and on she'd do it. The biggest reason I didn't want to mention this was because I honor her memory. Mama was a good Christian woman who lived in shame; she never married again and stayed to herself. Lord, I was scared that if Earl brought this out it would disgrace her even more, and I just couldn't stand by and let him do that Remember, she was still alive at the time. The way he asked me about Jack I knew he'd figured it out, and I vowed right then that it would never go any further!"

"See, when Bruce went to the Akers' family reunion at Winston-Salem that Sunday before everything happened, I believe Earl must have confronted him about it. Of course, Bruce had always kept everything a secret and I doubt even Ida knew. All those years it had been kept hidden and now suddenly he was about to be exposed. But, before I go on any further, I'd like to know how you found out."

"Probably the same way Earl did, I asked Ollie Grindstaff to check with vital statistics there at the courthouse and see if they had your birth certificate on file. There had been things said that made me suspicious, especially after I learned about you and Jack being half-brothers. Anyhow, she found your mother's name on it, but the word 'unknown' was in the space designated for the father. Well, right then I had Ollie look up Jack's too and of course, it had your mother's name listed, but alongside of hers was the name of a John Woodcock. After that, I just picked up the phone, called Melanie down in Gaston County, and asked her to check on divorce records for me. I suggested she look for proceedings that took place somewhere between one and three years after the date of your birth. But guess what? She learned John Woodcock divorced your mother on grounds of adultery, and it took place within a day or two of your second birthday. It turned out to be an uncontested hearing, but here's the clincher: Bruce Sluder was named as co-respondent in the case. Being the mayor, I doubt anybody noticed a thing when the official looking documents arrived, needing his signature."

"What got me to wondering, though, was what Gutch Reece overheard between you and Bruce. He told how Bruce got onto you about the whiskey, saying you ought to quit it, and then implied that he had. He also referred to your brother, pointing out that it ran in the family, and then acted so defensive when you mentioned about being raised like an orphan. Another big clue, though, was what he said about it taking an old fox to outfox a little'un; this, especially in light of his dying words."

"Yeah, he quoted from the Song of Solomon and just about everybody figured that referred to Earl and his ministry. And I guess to a point it did, but not the way they thought. Bruce actually was making Earl out to be a little fox who was trampling on his hidden fruit and by so doing was about to ruin an awful lot of people. He called it 'tender-grapes,' which to him meant his little secrets. That's the way I saw it, too, and there's no doubt about it, Bruce was the one who tipped off the local authorities on how to lay a trap for Earl. With all his connections that was easy to do. From what Sonny told me, following the family reunion Bruce made a telephone call to a certain deputy sheriff and filled him in. They were to make sure Earl would overhear that a load was due in on a given date and time. This, obviously, was just what the Fed's had been waiting for, so when Earl reported it they immediately prepared to make a raid. In order to do that, however, they needed help from the sheriff's office. Therefore, when word got back to the deputy sheriff the circle was complete, it told them that Earl was the one. Bruce told them how to lay the trap and by so doing signed Earl's death warrant. Of course, as you know, they did make a raid that night, but finding Earl dead was the last thing they expected; at least for the Feds."

Nodding, Edith looked askance while reconnecting to the past. "That deputy you mentioned is probably the main reason I began to suspect Bruce. See, a few days before his death he told Jim Gernon about the deputy and since this wasn't brought out in the trial, how could he have known about it without being involved himself."

"Speaking of Gutch Reece and the run-in I had with Bruce, the main reason I wanted to talk to him was to get a permit to hold street services. But since I knew he'd recently testified in a closed-door session of the appeals board, I also wanted to know about that. Remember: Boyle and Fowler's execution was scheduled to take place in just a few days, but always before, they'd got a last-minute reprieve. So, I wanted to know if he thought it would happen again. Bruce had been going around telling everybody how he was working on their behalf, but nothing could have been further from the truth."

Edith held up a forefinger to halt the monologue. "Let me say something right here, Claude; I know about that because the court records had a file dealing with appeals. Not the actual briefs, mind you, but just a list of those who had testified either for or against them. Well, when I saw where the name of Bruce Sluder headed the roster of those in opposition, it floored me. But I guess it took that to show me just who the real Bruce Sluder was. Up until then I couldn't make myself believe that a man I'd admired all my life could be so hypocritical. I'm sorry for butting in here, so let's get on with what you were saying."

"Well, obviously, it was to both our benefits to see them executed, for as long as they still lived there was always that outside chance for something to go wrong. Up until then Bruce had no idea I was in any way involved with Earl's death, so when he asked me why I let Earl learn the truth about all this, that's when I told him everything. You could just see the wind go out of his sails, and I hate to admit it, but I guess that's what destroyed him."

"Claude, do you realize what you're saying? You may have killed your own daddy."

"Edith, in my heart of hearts I believe he did it to himself. Ask yourself, when a lie meets the truth, can the two stand together? But I beg of you in the name of all that's Holy, keep this to yourself. The biggest mistake Mama ever made was having me. She's gone now, so please let her memory and that of Bruce's, too, just rest in peace."

"I agree, Claude, none of this need go any further than right here; so let your mind be at rest. Did you have anything else you wanted to say before I left? Wade just tooted the car horn, so I know he's waiting."

For the first time she saw his face soften. "Mrs. Gernon, you'll never know how much I dreaded this, yet I knew it had to be done. In many ways, it helps to set the record straight. All my life I dodged even thinking about a daddy. I guess I was trying to protect Mama… and myself, too, no doubt. Thing is, however, by sorting through all this her name now has been cleared. She was a victim.

"What scares me most is to think that me and Sonny both might have committed the unpardonable sin. Dave Gernon reminded me one time that when a feller knowingly works for the devil and does it in the name of the Lord, he then is in danger of doing it. Edith, we may have done it, we may have spent our lives living for Satan and if Mama knew that, it would break her heart."

"Claude, you're a lot smarter about these things than I am, but I don't think you have. I'm not going to comment on Jack, though, he's already gone, and I'm not his judge. But let me tell you why I don't think you have. First, you're worried about it and about him, too. Personally, I believe when you've gone too far and grieved away the Holy Spirit, your conscience won't bother you anymore. Just the fact you felt such a need to get the truth out is even more evidence that you've not. And here's another thing, too; you know just as well as I do that the man who showed up here was a messenger from God, now don't you? Then just ask yourself this, why would He have even bothered to do that, if you'as already lost? Besides, remember he told you then you'd been forgiven, so I say take God at his word."

"Ah-h, yeah! But that reminds me of something else. He quoted a poem that went something like this; 'When you go into the valley and walk in a glen, in the darkness there's a light therein.' Well no, that's not exactly right, but its pretty close," he smiled.

Without a word, Edith reached for her pocketbook and seconds later produced the note that Michael had given her in Asheville. "Is this it?" she asked before reading the poem in its entirety.

"That's it, yes sir, that's it exactly!" He beamed. "Where'd you get it?"

She laughed. "Remember, I know him, too." Edith then briefly told him her story. "For a long time I thought it was a warning just for Keith to get his house in order. But, now and especially after reading Hester's note I see things a little differently. Michael told Keith at the time to keep quiet about things and now, of course, we can see why." *Obviously, Keith was worried that he might lose Kathleen over this. But after learning the full story it set his mind at ease.* Edith chuckled aloud as she spoke; "Well, at least it did his."

But as is true with most inner reflections, a pause was needed so that feelings had time to catch up with the words. The brief interlude proved to be a worthwhile endeavor for another reason, too; a new insight emerged. "And, oh yeah," she explained. "While the first verse was obviously meant for Keith, the second one, I think, belongs to you! Listen to this. It says here that when you entered the dark glen you wouldn't have to stay. Remember, although you were blind going in, your eyes would soon open. 'Quickened by the dark... To the Light seeking thee.' No, Claude, you've been a mighty sorry man in your day, and no doubt come awful close to the edge, but I don't think you've committed the unpardonable sin." Although unknown to the other, and yet heard by both, a chorus from the ages suddenly broke through, bringing confirmation, "*Yea, though I walk through the valley of the shadow of death, I will fear no evil... for thou* art *with me!*

Two days later, just past ten-thirty in the morning Edith received a phone call from Fannie. "I hate to have to tell you this, Edith, but Claude died in his sleep last night. He must have gone easy because I didn't hear a thing. There's something else I need to tell you too; right after you left the other day he seemed better settled and to be at peace with himself. Maybe the old feller's gone to glory, I don't know, but I sure hope he has."

CHAPTER 50

Always mysterious, always majestic, High Top now stood veiled in fog and robed with all the colors of autumn. Crowned with sunlight, its peak glowed like a beacon in the afternoon sky. Jesse felt drawn to a spot on the mountainside where he used to visit often. *Why this trip, and why do it now?* He wondered. While bereft of ready answers to the questions, he understood perfectly the need to pull away and return. Deep inside he yearned to believe again, with a desire so strong, he felt overwhelmed. Mystery and myth had often lured him here as a youngster, and that was understandable considering its enigmatic past. This time, however, circumstances were entirely different; today he was responding to a higher calling.

Interestingly, all he could expect to find here was just a small stone staircase carved from a single piece of granite. Nevertheless, legend said they were but the first few steps of a stairway that led to up heaven, and a place where wise men of the Cherokee, when directed by the Great Spirit, sought oracular enlightenment. However, such pilgrimages had ceased immediately prior to the white man's advent. The great sages of time, it seems, grew weary of seeing utter destruction descend upon all they knew and loved.

This present quest was definitely of the heart, one guided solely by the need to assuage grief. Funerals always affected him profoundly for he had never been able to come to terms with death. At times, he could almost wax philosophical about its inevitability and speak bravely that such was merely a part of the natural order of things. Yet, if he allowed himself to dwell on it, he inevitably ended up depressed. It was hard to comprehend a world without being a part of it.

Climbing slowly he avoided the steeper slopes while remaining steadfast toward his goal. To the best of his memory, it was about two-thirds of the way up and off to the left in the Mountain Field. Actually, the place was an open pasture on High Top's west face, carved there by his great-grandfather, Will Gernon. Right after moving to Sweetwater him and his four sons, Tom, Dave, Charlie, and Grady, had cleared the fifty acres for planting corn. With pioneer zeal, they cut and burned an entire virgin forest of huge chestnut, oak, tulip-poplar and walnut trees. It took only a few years to realize their mistake, for that which they thought of as weeds, later would have fetched them a fortune. However, with a family and livestock to feed, such second-guessing was not to be entertained. Primarily a farmer, and with the price of timber being what it was, Will Gernon chose to believe that tilling the soil was his way to make a living. Abundantly and faithfully, the ground yielded its harvest, year after year, until finally spent. Following that, the Mountain Field became grazing range for their horses and cattle.

Jesse pressed on, passing a spring on the way up that brought back memories of the time when he, Frank and Jean were picnicking there, and received the terrible news that Oliver was in serious condition. They later learned that he, on a battlefield in France, had come under the withering fire of a German machine gunner, receiving injuries so severe that they nearly killed him. The myriad of feelings Jesse experienced that day in August 1944, later became a kaleidoscope of indelible memories.

Further along he came to a place called the Dark Hollow. It lay just off to his left where he could still see the outline of a natural structure called the witch's house. Constructed of wild grapevines and storm damaged timber, it still looked sinister. Frank once had him fully convinced that an old warty-nosed hag lived there, and even yet, he shivered at the thought of being there after dark.

Jesse probably would deny it, but his pace quickened enough getting away, that he suddenly found himself at the steps. Seeing them again immediately renewed the awe he had always felt in their presence. Indeed, this was holy ground and even nature itself seemed intent on creating an atmosphere of illusion. Phantasm-like, wily wisps of fog drifted slowly through shifting rays of sunlight, to appear as tall specters against the skeleton face of stacked boulders. Jesse sat down on the steps and cried, great heart rendering sobs that wracked his whole being. Four days earlier he had received the news and yet, until now, he had been unable to cry; that, despite a broken heart. When word came, it nearly devastated him, still as much as he wanted to, he just could not do it. His heart had ached so much he thought it might explode, yet the tears just would not flow. Now, however, the floodgates were finally open, washing away some of the hurt from his soul. The saddest thing we can ever feel is the loss of someone.

Jesse just could not quite come to terms with it and doubted now that he ever would. Death had struck again and this time it seemed so unfair. To die so young and to do it while being obedient to a calling somehow made it obscene. Hester had been right all along; he was a person of destiny. Those brave acts of goodness and sacrifice would live on in the annals of North Carolina history. He was a true hero in every sense of the word and deserved recognition as such. From what Jesse had learned, Claude Earl was on his way home from work after pulling another double shift and, no doubt, was tired. He had three days to go before heading for Sweetwater and to the altar.

Within a mile of home, he came upon an overturned church van and it was the most natural thing in the world for this trained EMT to go into action. The driver, already out, stood beside the wreck along with several of his pre-teen passengers. All were acting groggy and the adult seemed incapable of doing anything, but point at the back seat where a little boy was strapped in and trapped. He appeared to be unconscious. Although the smell of gasoline was intense, it did not deter Claude Earl for a second. His first act was to clear the area of all except the driver before climbing into the vehicle. Once he reached the entrapped youngster, it took enormous effort to thrust him through the window and into the waiting hands of the driver. Then, even as he screamed for them to run, the explosion occurred. The blast contained hurricane force winds, strong enough to move those outside the van beyond the flames deadly reach. However, Claude Earl did not make it. Not only did the inferno burn him badly, it also took his breath. He uttered his last words in the ambulance, saying, "Tell Laura, tell my darling Laura… that we'll meet again, someday."

Laura collapsed when word arrived and it rendered her incapable of speaking for days. To attend the services was for her out of the question and many, including Ollie, worried that she might not survive. The Spirit of Love, however, has power to bring peace; a peace that passes all understanding, and Laura, in time, came to be grateful for that.

Just how long Jesse remained there brooding he, in truth, could never say. Nor could he, satisfactorily, explain the subsequent events that soon came about. As to whether he was in the spirit or in the flesh when it all transpired; even that is impossible to know.

Suddenly, a tremendous rushing sound, not unlike the one he had heard at the grotto that time, caused him to look toward the swirling mist above where he sat. Then she stepped forward, materializing out of the fog with her shoulder-length flaxen hair hanging in long curls. While her form was exquisite, the glow of her face was what got his attention. Jumping to his feet, he felt uncertain whether to kneel or run. O*h my gosh! Is this real or am I dreaming?* Obviously stunned, the question was still searching for an answer when she spoke. Her words seemed to convey the impression that she not only had read his mind, but also was feeling his sorrow.

"Be still, Jesse, that you may learn," she whispered. Tied about the waist of her snow-white gown was a golden sash. "I know thy spirit is troubled, but remember; while there is no night as dark as death, joy cometh in the morning."

She then indicated that they sit together on the steps. Silence moved as a cloud to surround them, muffling all things but his wonder. When he attempted to speak, she forthrightly told him to hold his peace. Questions drawn from their previous encounters began to flood his mind. Somehow, she looked different now without her tiara; that, and she just seemed happier. Yes, he definitely had questions to ask, but *when* suddenly became the issue. Remarkably, the next time he tried, she allowed it. " I know it was you I saw in my visions, but are you also the one who spoke to me about going to school?"

"I've been by your side all the way, Jesse, and yes together we've shared many a mile. Some of those were not easy for you, but that was because you chose not to believe."

"You're not crying now, but in that beautiful valley and also by the seashore, you looked so unhappy… Why?"

"There is a time for sadness and a time for joy. The time for sadness soon will pass. And the time for rejoicing is drawing nigh, but all things in their season."

Jesse looked pensive. "I really liked that cabin of Michael's; do you reckon someday I might have one like it?"

"Oh, I'm certain you will; in fact, Michael's already picked out a spot for you. It's on the ridge just across that little inlet from his, and I think it's perfect. But come with me, please, and I will show you what has been, what is now and some of that which will shortly come to pass." She then reached for his hand.

Jesse hesitated. "Before we go, Michael said you'd tell me what your name is."

"That, dear Jesse, will have to wait, now come on!" She sounded impatient.

Immediately, Jesse found himself at the center of a gigantic cyclorama walled all around with moving pictures. He was amazed at how life-like they looked and he could see at a glance all of his life's history. Every detail, the good and bad, was open for review and he fell to his knees, weakened, even humbled at the sight. He saw scenes from Hoot Owl Hollow with his mother and daddy young again. They were deeply in love, yet either unable or unwilling to express the fullness of their feelings to each other. He cringed in horror when two men of evil intent sought to harm them while they lived in the house beside of the road. Suddenly, the beneath the imagery, a bright line of words streamed the following message: *"Heavenly agencies placed a hedge of protection around you that no power on earth or under the earth could have prevailed against."*

Next, he saw his family become complete, when Max joined them. Then, he was in the first grade, discouraged and ready to quit. The picture changed again and this time he almost shouted at the sight of seeing himself in the baptismal water. Then he saw Dave's funeral, followed by Grandma Gernon's; and even though she died a centenarian, he wept again as before. Quickly then, his life skipped ahead several years to where he was on the road, running back and forth to Indiana. The sight of celestial guardians displaying their displeasure over such a lack of faith made him uncomfortable. Yet the angels rejoiced mightily when he graduated. That and seeing his old Vega parked in the winner's circle of victory lane helped to mitigate any traces of shame still evident.

Jesse would have been content just to stay there and watch his life go parading by, though, in truth, it all could have been taken in at a glance. His guide, however, had other plans. By merely lifting her left arm, they, in a twinkle, found themselves atop an exceedingly high mountain. From there he could see wondrously, as if all things were at hand. Again, the beautiful valley with its meandering stream, clear as crystal, lay before him. This time, however, the view was from the opposite side of the valley. "This," her voice was lyrical with music, "is the way that was prepared for you; just think how pleasant your journey could have been!

"If you look closely, you will see a path winding beside the steam, and it's called the road less traveled. Seen only by faith, the great pity is that while you struggled mightily getting across, it was there all the time. Faith makes all things are possible, yet you repeatedly refused to believe. Even from the beginning you were reluctant to start this pilgrimage and just so shall you one day resist leaving again. Leave you must, however, for that choice is not yours to make. Can you not see that all are pilgrims on a wondrous quest that ultimately leads to the Father in Paradise? Does not the spirit within you yearn for home, especially after that visit with Michael. So, just consider how far superior this journey has been to the former one. Thus, shall it be that the next will even far more exceed this present one, both in scope and glory. But let not your heart be anxious, learn to trust. Such time is still in the gloaming and you must tarry here yet a little longer."

"Does everyone have such a beautiful sojourn?" Jess asked.

"All children are unique; therefore, each has a different road to travel, yet they are all potentially equal in their splendor. I will say this, however; personally, I like those designed for poets and certainly yours reflects that."

"You promised that I would see some of that which will shortly come to pass." Jesse said, seeming impatient to move on.

Her face wrinkled into a smile. "My, this is just like always; you are the impetuous one aren't you? All right, come with me then." Suddenly they were back at the steps, but now the fog had lifted to reveal a nearly circular opening through the trees. Passing north, a sylvan tunnel led deeper into the woods where enticingly beautiful music bid they enter. Jesse immediately recognized that he was listening to the near sacred sounds of the lilting A*sh Grove,* its haunting melody, as always, tugged at his heartstrings. Once inside, however, he found it dim, for they were in the sheltered embrace of several enormous evergreens. His eyes would need a few moments to adjust to the sun-starved shade. She touched his arm, indicating that he was to look to the right where a miniature stage, complete with actors, was positioned. Remarkably, many of the tiny lifelike figures looked very familiar.

"Of course, you recognize this to be your family and those you can't quite identify are your grandchildren that are soon to come. That's Adam, your first and isn't he handsome? He will far surpass all your highest hopes for him and be everything he's capable of being. However, like you, he, too, will struggle so unnecessarily before finding his way.

"Terri's search for contentment will lead her to many places, yet home is where it's finally found.

"Lisa above all needs the healing balm and it is there for her, if she will but be patient and wait for it to come.

"And now I will show you an excellent thing; behold your grandson David! Greatly beloved of both men and angels, a purer heart than his would be hard to find. Keep in mind those with Down syndrome have but a condition and not a disease. They are located in the brightest part on that spectrum called humanity. When the Father in His great wisdom chooses to place a soul amongst men, some have personalities so brilliant their fleshly wear must be a little more subdued, lest they far exceed their brethren and become prideful. Remember, God's objective, always, is to *save* His children!

"Do not despair, for I see you again growing anxious. Yes, you will have a granddaughter and her name will be Bekah. She is David's sister. Born a ballerina with symphony in her every move, she also shall succeed with her mind, but it will take much study and hard work.

"Becky, trusting and altruistic, is destined to become disillusioned. Yet ultimately she will become a paradigm of love admixed with the strength of steel.

"Your help-mate, Maggie, has been steadfast beside you all these years and only in eternity will you finally realize the fullness of God's wisdom in His gift of her to you. Be exceedingly thankful!

"Of all men you know, Jesse, you're the one most privileged by being allowed to see these things. You will remember little of this, yet your heart will experience a deep feeling of contentment when you leave here. Nevertheless, rejoice and thank the Father, for remember it is by His good will that you experience life to its fullness. Do not just live in anticipation of the next event that might happen, accept the *eternal now,* as little children do. Be like them and let our Father surprise you, for His gifts are always good and are bound to please."

"Would you mind answering me a couple of questions?" Jesse asked, sounding impudent, yet not wanting to. "You never really answered me about why you were so sad before… and where's your crown?"

"Sometimes we grow weary of waiting for those of mortal being to see just how much they are loved and cared for. It is our fondest hope they might trust enough to enjoy their journey, and learn to be thankful for all things. That which now seems to be such a burden can and will ultimately become a blessing, if you will only but believe. To answer your question more directly, however, requires that I be brutally frank with you. You Jesse, you were the cause of my tears! I knew just by your nature that you would bring needless pain upon yourself and I love you so very, very much… No, no, now do not look so downcast, but rather take comfort in what I say! Be glad that someone cares this much for you.

"As far as the crown is concerned, it's a symbol of eternal life designating neither status nor rank. Such are never to be worn when in contact with mortals, lest they die, for nothing of sin can exist in the presence of that which is from the Father. Now, was there something else?"

"Yes," Jesse smiled; "Your name! What's the big secret there, anyway?"

"I'd hoped you wouldn't ask me again," she demurred. Jesse could have sworn he saw her blush when she looked down. "I'll tell you what: someday you may doubt what I've just shown you actually happened. If so, I'll reveal it to you then. One thing more, she added. "Should that occur, you must then search very carefully the words of scripture." With that, she disappeared.

CHAPTER 51

By November, Jesse had an established routine of going to Sweetwater every Saturday and spending some of the afternoon there with his parents. Perhaps the loss of Hester and then Claude Earl made him realize just how tenuous life can be, and that he should take nothing for granted. In any event, the Saturday before Thanksgiving found him and Edith seated outside on the porch talking. It being glassed-in made the sunshine feel warm, despite a thermometer reading that hovered near the freezing point. Wade, having taken a neighbor to get their groceries, was not back from town yet.

"Did Fannie Woodcock ever make an appointment?" Edith asked in a voice so flat it betrayed her lack of interest.

"Yeah, I saw her last week and, boy, was she hard to work with. It was her first exam and it reminded me of Miss Frazier's. You remember me telling you about her, don't you?"

"Yes," Edith chuckled, but the only reason I wondered was that she'd asked about you. Fannie's such a put-on I doubted she'd make it."

"Why, I can still recall what good friends you and Daddy were with them at one time," Jesse teased.

Not taking the remark as being very funny, she was quick to tell him so. Poised then to give him a good scolding, she held her fire at the sight of a strange automobile pulling into the parking area. "Reckon who that is?" she wondered aloud.

"I don't know, but they're driving a Mercedes and it's one of their most expensive models. I don't know of anybody around here with a car like that, do you?"

"Well, they're fixing to come in and look at me here in these old clothes. Maybe they're lost, so why don't you go out there and try to head 'em off."

By this time, however, an attractive and well-dressed woman, obviously in her mid- to late-thirties, was walking toward the house. A young man, black headed and about 12 years old, was by her side.

"I've seen her before," Edith murmured as they neared the porch.

"Mrs. Gernon?" she asked in a knowing voice. "You may not remember me, but I met you at Keith's funeral."

"Why, yes I think I do. Come on in, and I hope you'll excuse me, and the way this old house looks. I never expected any company today, except for Jesse here. He's my oldest boy and I don't think you've met him."

"No, I don't believe so. How do you do, Jesse; my name is Luella Donald and this is my son, Liam."

"Beautiful day, isn't it? Just a little too chilly," Jesse offered.

"It was down to eighteen this morning before we left Marion," Luella smiled as she spoke. Soon everyone had seats.

"Now, I remember you!" Edith nearly exploded. "You're Kathleen's daughter. You know at the time I felt so bad about losing Keith that I'm afraid my mind wasn't working too good. Not that it ever does."

"Oh, that was quite understandable under the circumstances. Actually, Keith is the reason I made this trip. Mother and I had a long talk the other day and although she's still in relatively good health, she felt the need to level with me. See, Hobert was my stepfather and, of course, he's been gone now for years, but when I was little he adopted me. I loved him dearly, yet all my life I wondered who my real daddy was. Mother always refused to talk about it, saying that he was dead and that I was not to pursue the matter. Finally, after all these years, she changed her mind and told me everything. She explained how that when she got pregnant with me, she was not married and in those days, such a thing was very shameful. In order to escape the ridicule she went to live with relatives in Wilmington and that's where I was born. We lived there for a while after I came along and by that time, she'd met Hobert. He accepted her story and I guess their love was strong enough for them to get married. Hobert's first wife had died a few years earlier and since they had no children, he was very receptive to me. He and Mother were never able to have any children, so that kinda worked out for everybody. Later, they moved to Belmont and as far as I know, no one there was ever the wiser about me."

"Are you getting ready to tell me something here?" Edith asked with a catch in her voice.

"I think you know," Luella said, then began to cry.

"You've got his eyes!" Edith sobbed. "Oh, my Lord, I never expected this. So *you, you're* the secret, and here I thought I had it all figured out."

"Mother told me that she felt so bad she couldn't tell you. Try to understand that even though so many years had passed, she still felt the shame of it all. According to her, and I believe it, they were so much in love that they just the one time went too far. Keith wanted to go ahead and get married the minute he learned she'd missed a period. But since she'd always been a little irregular Mother insisted they wait another month. Of course, during that time he came up here to visit you and obviously the rest is history."

"So, you didn't know anything about this at the funeral, did you?"

"No, and you'll never know how much I wish I had. Remember, he was in my nursing home at Oak Forrest and we'd become friends… What a coincidence!

"I'm not so sure it was a coincidence," Edith injected.

"Oh I agree, things like this make you realize just how much God is in control. There was a special something between us and I just loved to sit and talk with him. He liked it, too. Oh, by the way, Mother told me how I got to be called Luella. Lucinda was her mother's name and, of course, you know where Ella comes from."

"Keith would have been so proud of you, and there's just no doubt about it, you're a dead–out Rose."

"And a rose by any other name is still a rose," Jesse cracked.

"Listen here, little Wade, another remark like that and I'll let your cousin here know what kind of a blossom the Gernons are."

***

Four years to the day, less one week from the time of Claude Earl's death, Edith and Mae went out looking for yard sales. They left the house excited; it was fall, a Saturday and the weather was unbelievable. Sweetwater was in her full glory. Driving past several displays, they were tempted to stop, but Mae insisted they continue on to Laura's place. She had heard that when Ollie cleaned out her garage and attic, several good items had surfaced. On the way in, they spoke to Arvil, Ollie's older brother. He stood stoically by the walk; rake in hand and burning leaves. A trace of autumn melancholy accompanied the smoke. "They's been a bunch of 'em before you," he offered as they passed by

Unfortunately, what he said was true and now very little remained to choose from; the only item that looked worthwhile was an old leather handbag. Mae saw it as junk, but not Edith. "How much?" she asked Laura.

"Oh, I guess about a dollar."

"I'll give you quarter."

"Suits me just fine; to tell you what, Edith, I'm glad to see the thing go. Mother kept it around forever. Why, I must have been just a teenager when she got it; oh, would you all mind waiting here for just a minute? I need to go check on that young'in and get her back to where I can keep an eye on her. I'll bet you anything she's off playing with that dog again."

Edith looked at the bag; it really was not too bad, just needed wiping off and a good cleaning. With it being leather, she could make it look new again. Although the latch was stiff, it opened with a little effort then she began scouring around for coins among the dried tubes of lipstick and sundry other items of make-up. Nothing of value, however, turned up. Persistent in the search, she poked further and located a secret compartment and that is when she discovered an old letter. Turning it over, repeatedly, she read long enough to see that it was from Laura to Claude Earl while he was still in Viet Nam; yet had never been post-marked. After only a moments deliberation she decided to keep the envelope. Her thoughts were running deep as she left the carport and headed for the fire. Arvil looked up surprised, "What was that?" he asked in a grumpy voice. She had just tossed something into the blaze.

"Oh, just some old stuff that ought to have been burned years ago!" she responded, returning his rancor. Arvil, being the wise man he was, chose just to keep his peace and watch the burning pages slowly mix in with a million other bits of charred cellulose. "Well, that got rid of 'er," he commented dryly, his rake sending a shower of sparks swirling toward the heavens.

"Mother," Mae called from the yard. "Come and look at Hester, ain't she the prettiest thing you've ever seen?"

Indeed she was; not only had Hester inherited her grandmother's name but also the bundles of coal-black hair that hung in curls about her face. The three-year-old was a messy little angel after her best friend, a big yellow-red dog with an immense tail, had tumbled her all over the yard. "Where did you get him?" Edith asked when the big-toothed canine smiled at her.

Laura looked pleased. "You know, he just took up here about a year ago and he's the best old thing you've ever seen, I'd sure hate to have anything happen to him," she added.

"Oh, you needn't worry about that," Edith grinned knowingly. "He'll stay with you just as long as he wants to, but don't expect a lot of loyalty out of him." Mae was certain she spotted a flicker of amusement burning in his amber eyes as he moved to take his place next to Hester.

On the way home, Edith told Mae about the letter and the fact that she had burned it. They agreed that under the circumstances she had acted appropriately, however, Edith felt perplexed over what she had found written on the envelope. "Listen to this," she said, reading aloud.

To: Jesse Gernon
My Dear Beloved,

That which I prayed against has now come to be, leaving much doubt to fill your mind. I must, therefore, keep my promise, but be not overcome with mirth, for remember I am watching you. Now and forever I will remain:

Your friend,

Mataqmayim

"Smells fishy, don't you think?"

Mae looked baffled. "I really don't know what to say, Mother; but since it's Saturday, Jesse will be here directly, so let's just wait and ask him then. I feel certain, though, it's all on the up and up."

"What kind of a name is this *Mata-q*-something-or-other anyway? It sounds furrin to me… or it could be Indian. He'd better not be up to something here," Edith added dryly.

Mae glanced over at the note and saw a very delicate hand written in blue ink, the feminine characteristics were obvious. "Now Mother, you know Jesse better than that; so let's try to show a little faith here," she admonished.

Later, when he got there one look at the message and Jesse let out a yell; "she did it! She did it!" He exulted. "I never thought she would, but I still don't know what it means." Then suddenly he recalled something from right before she left. *"You must then search very carefully the words of scripture."*

"Mother, I need to use the phone," he said.

Edith wasn't pleased. "I don't know about that," she protested. "Who're you calling, anyhow?"

"Mae... Why?"

"Well, go ahead then, I thought maybe it was somebody else," she responded without enthusiasm.

"Mae? ... Yeah, it's me and I'm here at Mother's. Do you still have that concordance we used to use, trying to prove Thomas H. Livermore wrong?

"Well, would you bring it down here? I think you'll want to be in on this.

"Directly? Good! I'll see you then... okay, well bye."

"Humph-h, you meant Thomas H. *Money*more, didn't you? I never could stand that thing. Well, okay, Mister Smarty Britches, it's time now to come clean; what's going on here?"

"You'll know the minute I do, Mother; just hold on until Mae gets here, then maybe we can figure it out. I'm still not exactly sure, myself." He sounded a little breathless.

Moments later Mae entered the room wearing a big question mark on her face.

"Is this it?" she asked, handing over the huge volume.

Both women were getting antsy by the time Jesse stopped making notes. Yet he kept them waiting a moment longer as he continued to inspect the translation he had just written down "It was right after Claude Earl died when I asked her for this," he said, still focused on the envelope. "Now this word here, this name, is actually taken from two separate Hebrew terms, and you pronounce it *Maw-tok mah-yim.*" Handing it to Mae, he took a deep breath and held it, waiting to exhale.

Her first look was one of fascination, and then she glanced again at a signature penned so fine, it seemed to be almost non-existent. Mae's comment to Edith came soft and reverently, one that could easily have been mistaken for a benediction. Yet, even as she spoke, her understanding continued to expand. "Mother," she whispered in awe, "it's about *her* and her *name.* You remember that vision Jesse had up there on the mountain, don't you? Well, he told us about her then... Remember? Oh," she chuckled in delight, "her name is so beautiful... and it means *Sweetwater*!"

The End

EPILOGUE

The dreaded words, when they came, struck like lightening. CODE BLUE, CODE BLUE IN UNIT 3 CODE BLUE! Yet, for those gathered just outside the ICU, they were expected. Peering at the monitor, Maggie saw the dramatic changes first, a racing, irregular pulse followed by erratic EKG tracings and then the straight line.

"Is Pawpaw gone?" Bekah asked nervously.

Becky's answer was a tearful nod. She could not bring herself to say it. Meanwhile, Terri and Lisa held each other sobbing. Adam and David stood on either side of Maggie, their arms overlapped about her waist.

"He lived a good life," Lisa said, speaking to no one in particular.

"Yes, but we're never quite ready to give them up, are we?" responded Terri's husband, Merv, sounding philosophical.

Josh remained silent; however, a tiny tear eked out to spill over and run down his cheek. Secret feelings had just betrayed a cherished macho persona.

Quickly, they were ushered from the area and taken to another quarter to make room for the crash-cart and an onslaught of personnel. In the end, however, word reached them to return. On the way back, they passed several nurses who, over the past two days, had become quite familiar to them all. It had started early Wednesday morning when Maggie was unable to arouse him from his sleep. Soon after she called 911, the ambulance arrived to take him to the ER, and then following that was the helicopter flight to Asheville.

From the start, it looked bad and once the verdict was in, they knew it was hopeless. "He's had a massive heart attack, probably just moments before you found him and I see no way he can recover." Dr. Alden spoke while squatted down before the family that had seated themselves in front of him. As a cardiologist, this was something he had repeated many times, yet it never became routine.

"Naturally, we'll do everything possible, but the damage done is so extensive that outside of providing him with a transplant the situation is hopeless. With his blood type, it would be a miracle to find a donor heart in time. Too, we have to consider his age and the fact that there's kidney disease."

"Just keep him comfortable; I know he doesn't want heroic measures," Maggie said. "Any idea how long it might be?"

"It's now been about ten to twelve hours, so I'd say another day or two at most, but you can never really tell."

Hence began the vigil. At first the whole family remained close to the unit; however, it soon became obvious they needed to create shifts of eight hours each. Becky, her husband Josh and Bekah took the first. Starting at eleven p.m. they remained at their post until relieved at six-thirty a.m. by Maggie, Lisa, and David. Thus, it went for the next forty-six hours.

Meanwhile, quite unknown to them and in a parallel universe two others were also watching developments.

"Oh, it's going to be beautiful," she sighed with admiration. "He'll be absolutely swept away!"

"He likes log cabins," the big man nodded in agreement. "At least he did mine, and this is almost identical to it except for a few personalized changes I made."

"Shines like gold," she said.

"That's because it's gold-clad; gold can be used for structural material as well as for paving."

"Well, the view up here is truly marvelous, looking out over the inlet yet high on a ridge top. All it needs now is a big old hound dog sleeping on the porch."

"That'll come, I just happen to know where to get one," he offered.

"I bet you do!" she giggled. "I think for a little while, though, it would be nice not to have anybody but close family here to celebrate with him. There will be plenty of opportunity later on for the neighbors and friends to come in. You know they'll all want to have a big celebration." A sudden gust of wind, warm and pleasantly scented, gently lifted her flaxen-colored hair, tossing the satin-like tresses over onto one shoulder.

He stooped to pick up a thin wafer of a seashell, studied it carefully before handing it to her. "What I look forward to is seeing his response when he hikes up to the top and looks down on the other side. From there the Holy City looks like a huge diamond glistening in the distance. Of course, with a residence there, too, he'll soon feel right at home in both places."

"He'll be even more surprised to learn who I *really* am," she grinned. "I get goose-bumps just thinking about it."

"One of the great mysteries of God finally revealed," he chuckled. "But it's only the beginning in an eternity that is a long, long never-ending now."

"That's a part of the joy!" she said.

"A small, yet important part," he agreed. "Time as they know it has no relevancy here. Just think how shocked many of them will be to learn how long they've actually been asleep."

"Oh, I know," she nodded. "And it's so seamless, too; one moment you close your eyes and the next you awaken, whether it be an instant or a thousand years, it all seems the same. That way everybody awakens together."

" O My Lo-r-rd, what a morning! What a morning that will be!" Shouting, he sang to the sky. "Hey, where are you going?"

"I'm on duty tonight, so I'd better get moving; what about you though, any idea where your next assignment might be?"

"Not a clue, it's still all a big secret, but I'll keep you posted."

"You'd better! Well, bye, and be blessed!"

"You too; take care now!"

Maggie, helped by Adam, began collecting the few personal items still in his room. "Here, let me help!" Bekah offered, needing something to do until the nurse returned. She had promised to be right back.

"I'm sorry to have kept you waiting, but I wanted to talk with the doctor first. There are so many legal matters we have to attend to and nobody wants a lawsuit."

"You have nothing to worry about there," Maggie said. "You folks truly went the extra mile and I'll never forget it." For the first time she realized just how beautiful the young nurse was. Her flaxen hair, shoulder length, was radiant.

"Before you leave I wanted to give you this; it was in his hand when he passed." With that, she turned and left the room.

"Now how do you reckon he got ahold of this?" Maggie wondered aloud.

"Here, let me see!" Adam whispered. "Hey! Would you look at that, it's a sand dollar! I haven't seen one in years."

Bekah was confused. "There's nothing unusual here; Pawpaw used to treasure his sand dollar before it got lost. My question, though, is when did nurses start wearing those long white dresses again? And did you notice that pukey looking little cap stuck on her head? Had it perched up there like a starched tiara?"

"I think it's fine," Maggie defended. "In my mind that's the way a nurse should look. We're not being a little jealous here, are we?"

"Ginghy!" Bekah protested. "Let's at least wait until we get home to fight. Besides I've got two kids of my own to fuss with, so I don't need this."

"Well, I'm not the one who started it. And having two young'ins don't give you the right to sass me!"

"Now listen here, Ginghy!...."

LETTERS FROM SWEETWATER

Published by Revival Nation Publishing | www.revivalnationpublishing.com

ISBN 978-1-926625-31-7

Printed in the United States of America

Breinigsville, PA USA
24 September 2009

224711BV00001B/2/P

9 781926 625317